I0764494

BEYOND THE SON

P. D. GILSON

GAEA UNIVERSE CREATED BY
DAVID LAGETTIE

Gaea: Beyond the Son

A Helios Publishing Book

Helios Publishing Pty Ltd
262 Gan Gan Rd, Anna Bay, NSW 2316
Australia

ISBN: 978 0 9803910 0 8

CIP catalogue information for this title available from the publisher upon request.

Cover by Tomas Kuklik

www.heliospublishing.com

ACKNOWLEDGMENTS

David Lagettie for his vision, constant guidance, and getting the ball rolling. Peter Morrison for running with it. Adam Williams for astute suggestions and enduring friendship. Tomas Kuklik for visual interpretation and inspiration, and Troels Folmann for the same musically.

"The atomic bomb was the turn of the screw. It made the prospect of future war unendurable. It has led us up those last few steps to the mountain pass; and beyond, there is a different country."

J. Robert Oppenheimer
Los Alamos, 1946

PROLOGUE, 2050

The hardtop jeep crashed through a rotted barricade, headlights dancing across splintered debris. Dr. Emil Gage swerved, switched gears, and accelerated up a steep incline. Although he hadn't returned to Apache Point since his observatory closed, he knew this dirt road like the back of his wrinkled hand.

Emil's heart skipped a beat when the Geiger counter bouncing on his dashboard spiked. This wasn't supposed to be a hot spot. He let his foot off the gas as he watched the needle tick down … Merely a trace reading. He gunned the engine.

A roaming heli-drone swooped, twin search beams scanning the withered aspen.

Dr. Gage skidded, raising a dust cloud. He switched off his headlamps and veered onto a rocky hiking track, hoping the stolen, rusty jeep—and its equally rusty driver—would be up to the task.

On the passenger seat, his precious, cowering cargo coughed beneath a sleeping bag.

"Stay down. We're almost at the summit." Dr. Gage would transmit the message. *And then what?* he wondered.

CT317E//2E4: *handwritten note dated 9/9/2049, discovered in belongings of wanted insurgent, Dr. Emil Gage. Evidence secured by APA officers during search of* Gaea-02 *pilot Doyle Gage's last known terran residence.*

Dad,

Remember your old Sixty-Six-Year theory? You'd drummed into me that true advancements in flight exploration were spaced sixty-six years apart by social necessity. A span of three generations to accept, adapt to, and attempt the next giant leap.

At first I bought it. My own aviation heroes, the Wright Brothers, sustained flight back in 1903, but it took until 1969 to touch the Moon. And sixty-six years later, almost to the day, Gaea-01 became the first manned spacecraft to reach another planet.

But then I said to myself, "I'm not waiting until I'm so old I need a walking stick to visit another solar system." Well, guess what? While I was packing today, it struck me that it's been only fourteen years since Gaea-01's inaugural flight to Mars. I'm sure the irony hasn't escaped you.

So much for your theory, Dad. ;)

– Doyle

P.S. Thanks again (again) for taking care of Lon while I'm gone. Last time, I swear. Just don't fill his head with too many crazy stories.

P.P.S. Hope you don't mind the parting jibe, you smart ol' coot. I'll buy you a bottle of Black Mesa Merlot when I get home.

EV20510214//CT317V//FF6

CHAPTER 1
THE TURN, 2049

Doyle couldn't identify the distracting sound. Faint though somehow familiar, high-pitched, almost hypnotic. He squinted at the suburban sprawl outside his son's bedroom window.

The southwestern horizon, phosphate-choked by Bone Valley's fractured industry spewing skyward, wore the yellow-brown fringe common to blustery autumn mornings. Stale air blowing from the southeast carried a briny bite from the oversaturated desalination plant at Palm Bay.

No hint to the sound's origin on the dreary Florida skyline… but that could wait. This was the last hour he'd have with Lon, and Doyle Gage wasn't about to waste another second daydreaming.

Brrrrroooooommmm—little Lon motor-hummed deep in his throat as he flew his *Gaea-02* model toy in an orbit around his father. A close approach behind Doyle's back and the die-cast metal scuffed against his well-worn UEC flight jacket. Doyle grinned. *I'll have to teach him about flight vectors soon.*

Lon landed his ship on the carpet. He pouted. "Why can't I go too?"

"Can only take a small crew, kiddo. Everyone has an important job to do." Doyle rubbed his chin. "Are you an astrophysicist?"

"No."

"Can you fix an antimatter engine?"

"Nuh-uh."

"So what can you do?"

"I made a picture." Lon retrieved his prized paper from a low desk and proudly handed the crude drawing to Doyle. His résumé for the United Earth Coalition's space corps: a cheerful sun shining on a purple-winged spacecraft, above the blue-brown planet Earth. Two stick figures in the bubble-cockpit, labeled Lon and Dad, sailed into a pastel cosmos. *If only it could be, son.*

"This is great, Lon. Keep at it and maybe they'll fit you on the next mission." Doyle chuckled, but not Lon. The disappointment on his four-year-old face quickly wiped the mirth from Doyle's own. Lon was a tough kid. He'd been through plenty already in his brief life, but Doyle had promised he'd never leave him. He wasn't breaking that promise, Doyle kept telling himself, just bending it. He was brought up a patriot, a world citizen—and the UEC needed Doyle to finish training his replacement pilot for the second Gaea mission. If it wasn't so critical…

Damn, but he hated seeing that sad little face. How much he'd miss it though.

The sound outside intensified.

"Six months, Lonnie, that's all. You and Grandpa will have a blast."

The words had barely left Doyle's mouth when a flash polarized the front yard. A white sheet of eerie silence fell, leaving stark shadows where time seemed to stop, frozen in chiaroscuro.

Cracked plaster flaked onto Doyle's head. The walls convulsed.

Noiselessly, since Doyle's eardrums had burst. Blood flowed from both sides of his face.

An avalanche of liquid fire broke through the stillness outside and cascaded toward the house.

"Lon—" Doyle screamed, unable to hear himself.

The heat arrived first. It stripped Lon's skin, peeling him like a ripe grape. His raw flesh oozed, bubbled away, exposing white bone charred to black soot in an instant.

Doyle gulped air like a surfacing diver.

His dreamflow hadn't snowballed from his control like that for a long while. Lesson two of orbital training was to use your sleeping moments wisely. Recalling happy scenes from Earth can fool the mind into believing part of your life is still spent on terra firma. Most starships kept a simulated day-night cycle for that reason; the human circadian rhythm is a bitch to subdue.

Night terrors had once plagued Doyle, as they did many cadets new to space. Fond memories twisted into horror. But that was over a decade ago, before he'd learned a few simple tricks to control his dreaming, as easy as replaying home movies on a vid-screen. Since then he'd never once slipped back into old habits. So why now?

He was sorely out of practice, Doyle realized. Out of touch.

Ninety days into this six-month shakedown run and a gnawing sense of unease had crept up on him. He couldn't rationalize it; neither could he shake it off. Like his nightmare's familiar, hypnotic sound—awake, he recognized it as a missile delivery rotor—something nagged at the back of his mind.

Doyle rolled off the foam-resin bed. No sheets were necessary, as the ship was laid out in unwavering temperature zones, from the chill of medical to the balmy agriculture lab. Sometimes moving between modules felt like stepping through the seasons.

He slid into the UEC flight jacket that had once been his second skin. He'd tumbled out of more experimental plane crashes in this jacket than his body cared to remember. More than a lucky charm, it was a tan leather shield to fend off the Grim Reaper's swinging scythe. His smooth scalp was another holdover from those test pilot days on Earth, a misguided habit to appear as aerodynamic as the craft he then flew.

Doyle swung open his locker. A daily ritual, he glanced at the two pictures adhered inside while he pulled on his cargo pants. There was Lon's colorful spaceship drawing he'd given Doyle the day he left, and the other was a photo of baby Lon, cradled between himself and his wife. Raven-haired Juni, a descendent of the Navajo nation. Why wasn't she in his dreams? He knew the answer: if his control was slipping, he'd surely see her as she was during those last months, losing the fight against her illness.

Doyle needed to remember her *this* way—a smile full of life, strength, and joy.

He quickly shut the locker door, his reflection blurred on the shiny metal. Doyle's clear eyes sagged from hundreds of hours of *g*-force and had the telltale crow's feet of long periods spent in low-gravity environments. He looked older than he felt. No, that wasn't true. He looked—and felt—older than he was.

The skin-tight communications band behind his earlobe vibrated and piped Dr. Riana Ruschen's voice directly to his inner ear. "Mr. Gage. Your turn now."

"There in a sec," Doyle replied.

Her terse words reminded him that the Turn was only a few days away.

As the needle slid into a subcutaneous catheter implanted in Doyle's arm, he noticed the familiar scent of citrus. Riana squeezed the trigger and his blood filled the syringe. She withdrew, leaving Doyle to hold a gauze pad against the seeping puncture—or bleed to death, as much as he thought she cared. He imagined he could see all eighty-two such recent pinpricks along his pincushion forearm. He'd been subjected to batteries of tests in his time, but this protracted vampirism was bordering on sadistic.

Riana's ash-blonde hair fell around her diamond face as she

slid an agar plate streaked with Doyle's blood under the bio-scanner. She didn't see patients; she studied the biochemical building blocks of life. He'd first met Riana three years ago when Baden—sorry, *Commander* Ruschen—married her. Or was it earlier? Who could tell. The UEC's space corps was a sizable group. *One big, happy family.*

Dr. Avi Farrad, the small crew's traditional surgeon, shone a light in Doyle's eyes and waved it back and forth for him to follow. He liked Doc. The man had patched him up many times before they'd joined the Gaea mission. The oldest of them all, but still spry in his pale green scrubs, Farrad had a salt-and-pepper beard and an aura of trench wisdom that contrasted sharply with the youthful brashness of some of the science prodigies on board.

"Noticed any problems, Doyle?" Riana asked without taking her eyes from her microscopic world.

"Only my freezing, bare ass." The backless smock she made him wear wasn't a great selection for the medlab's stainless steel slab. "Look, I'm the same as yesterday, same as the day before, same as every damn day for the last three months."

"We need daily data to track effects of deep space travel on—"

"Yeah, yeah." Doyle had heard the spiel before. "We're guinea pigs."

"Don't flatter yourself. You're not nearly as cute."

Doyle turned to Dr. Farrad. "You hear that, Doc? You gonna let her keep torturing us?"

Dr. Farrad held his palms up. "Leave me out of it, Doyle. I'm just the sawbones."

Doyle pushed himself off the slab, bare feet slapping on the floor. Riana didn't look up, so he coughed loud enough to get her attention, "Done? I got a ship to fly."

The designers of *Gaea-02* clearly favored utility over aesthetics. To Doyle, the ship looked like a junkyard contraption with a pretty face. A sleek, detachable crew module—with black reentry heat shielding along a curved underbelly—stuck like the head of a cattail reed to an elongated scaffold of antiproton stores, running down to the vast umbrella of its primary antimatter engine. She was light-years away from the dignified megashuttle design of *Gaea-01*. All Doyle really cared about was that it got him home; then he'd be happy to kiss the hunk of metal goodbye.

He reached the bridge—*Gaea-02*'s vibrant brain—where he felt most comfortable on the ship. Colby Xaviera, his young Aussie protégé, had his legs up on the flight console, boots tapping to some catchy rhythm fed from his comms band. Doyle knocked Colby's legs off the console, startling him.

Colby ran his finger along the control band beneath the rim of his knit beanie cap, cutting the tunes. He sat upright for a dressing-down. Doyle wasn't the commander anymore—everyone knew he was there under duress as a civilian—but he held the kind of authority you don't get from a uniform.

"Sorry," Colby started, "Indigo hacked my comms band and—"

"—linked it to the music database she snuck into the ship's system. Right?"

"She told you?"

"Whatever keeps a mind sane on these long runs is fine by me. But don't let Commander Ruschen catch you." Doyle nodded at the flight console. "Smooth sailing?"

"All copacetic, boss. On course for the Turn in one-oh-nine point six hours."

The navigational mainframe handled most flight duties on this behemoth, but Doyle thought he could teach Colby how to handle those rare moments of crisis that circumvented its programming. He should have known better. They'd already simulated a dozen emergency scenarios together, and Colby breezed through them all without blinking. Like the kid was playing a video game and racking up a high score to boot.

What Doyle found he could impart, more than technique, was respect. Respect for the situation, for the machine humming beneath your feet, for the crew whose lives are in your hands. He suspected that's what the brass had in mind all along.

Doyle wagged his thumb toward medlab. "She wants you next."

"Ooh-la-la."

Colby sashayed his hips on his way out, but the clowning backfired. His lanky legs tripped on the threshold and he had to fling out his elongated arms to grip the arch. A gangly spider clinging precariously to his web. Awkward at the best of times, Colby regained his balance and shuffled out.

"Should've been born with wings, kid," Doyle said. He settled into the primary flight chair, thronged by colorful touchscreens, keys, and manual flight controls.

Doyle cycled the bank of *Gaea-02*'s internal monitors. In the engine core, the Jiménez brothers, Sabin and Pach, traded poker chips. Being so alike, Doyle wondered how they could possibly bluff each other.

The medlab camera showed Dr. Farrad distracting Colby while Riana drew his blood.

In the mess hall, four of the scientific faction vied in doubles table tennis on a virtual table. They ran a fiercely competitive league, with an esoteric scoring system that awarded points to individual players instead of pairs. If Doyle were still in command, he would have scrapped the solo rankings and paired up those who most needed to develop a close working relationship. But it wasn't his place to say, and he knew Commander Ruschen wouldn't recognize the benefit anyway.

On the surface, the thirteen-strong *Gaea-02* test crew was a seemingly random mix of personalities and nationalities, which the UEC somehow calculated would work.

Babysitting the ship's downtime, Doyle could largely forget his nightmare and the anxiety it stirred. The moment he had his butt in that chair and the ship under his guidance, he felt at ease.

"We're slowing too quickly," Commander Baden Ruschen interrupted Doyle's reverie, his always crisp jumpsuit fastened snugly around his matchstick neck.

"Good morning to you too."

"Spare the attitude, Doyle."

He knew it was just Ruschen's way—saving the world was more important than making friends. They were never best buddies, but they *were* friendly, or at least they had been before Doyle prematurely retired. They were the first two UEC spacers flagged for the second Gaea mission. Now he wondered if it had ever stuck in Ruschen's craw that Doyle was initially chosen as leader, even though he was ten years Ruschen's junior.

"I rechecked our calcs with the new data," Commander Ruschen said. "Decrease our dec rate by four percent."

"Now hold on a minute. I worked all of that out myself."

"And you were wrong. The stress on *Gaea-02* and my crew is too great."

Nonsense. Doyle knew what a ship this size could take, and he'd personally stared more *g*s in the face. He would've just flipped *Gaea-02* head-over-tail to point it in the opposite direction and let the thrusters rip. Ruschen, ever the astrophysicist, wanted to test a method used in unmanned flights, which would take longer but put less drain on their antimatter cells by harnessing the gravitational pull of a nearby gas giant: thus the Turn.

Doyle projected a holographic three-dimensional nav map from the console and lit a series of points with his sweeping finger. "Look at the plot. Inclination and ascension in accord with all Keplerian elements, a high apogee curving into a tight coasting arc—"

"*Too* tight," Ruschen interjected, "and too fast."

"You'll add six days onto the Turn. Six more days I don't see my kid."

Ruschen glared at Doyle, "Family reunions don't factor into my calculations."

Was this a test? A challenge? A line drawn in the sand?

"Adjust it. Now." It was Ruschen's call and they both knew it.

Doyle finally relented. He punched in Ruschen's alternate flight plan. "The human body can take a lot more than you give it credit for." Doyle added as an afterthought, "Sir."

Commander Ruschen smoothed a nonexistent wrinkle in his sleeve, as though it were his old Navy uniform. "That's what we're hoping to discover."

Doyle wandered *Gaea-02*'s infrastructure. Its function-over-form philosophy was evident in every drab bulkhead and protruding frame. Conduits coiled around bare struts, and the angular walls had an uneven gunmetal finish. Doyle thought back to billboards he'd seen of the Gaea mission, awash in beckoning cerulean blue and verdant foliage. He chuckled at the contrast between this reality and those glossy roadside promises.

For Doyle, the unwritten message had been clear to anyone passing those signs: *Hold on. Things will change. Just give us time. Put up with the crippling water rations for a little longer. We won't let you down.*

He'd even appeared on a poster himself. The face of Gaea. *Trust in this brave pioneer. He will make things right.*

Ultimately, the most effective image had been the simplest. M38. The far-flung planet itself was Earth's valiant savior. Fuzzy as it was, coming from a superluminal probe launched twenty-two years earlier, that single photograph gave the whole world hope. *Look at all that water.* If the probes were correct, it flowed clean, unsalinated, and in an atmosphere analogous to ours. "Like someone had placed it there precisely for us to find," Doyle's father had remarked.

Put simply, Earth was dying of thirst. Through an urgent combination of stringent emissions protocols and alternative energy directives, global warming had plateaued two decades ago, but it had left Earth teetering on the precipice of environmental meltdown. The most pressing problem was a critically low worldwide supply of drinkable water. For that at least, there was a flawed solution: D-salt. One speck could hydrate an entire village, using only wastewater or a bilge full of toxic ocean.

Unfortunately, manufacturing the chemical purifier required too many scarce elements—and a quantity of *untreated* water as a catalyst—to be plausible long-term on Earth. Extreme as it sounded, the UEC coveted an entire, virgin planet as their D-salt production plant.

Mars was a dead-end struggle. Ditto Titan, Europa, and Ganymede. Sure, publicly everyone hailed the first Gaea mission as a success, but Doyle knew the truth. The theories were wrong, the expectations too high. They couldn't easily extract all the essential resources—and of those they could, most were tainted. It would have taken too many generations to reap significant results. The people of Earth craved an answer *now*. Any later would be too late.

So the UEC looked elsewhere.

M38 was their grail. It possessed everything needed for mass production of D-salt and was ripe for habitation. Whether they'd be colonizing a new planet or raping it depended on which side of the ethical fence you sat.

The speed of progress in antimatter drive technology meant that travel had become less and less of a barrier. M38 was in reach. Ten years, hurtling at seventy-one percent the speed of light. Engineers claimed the next generation of starships would complete the journey in eight. With a large enough fleet, Doyle envisioned a regular shipping line to bring home everything Earth lacked for survival. And in time, who knows? Whole populations could transplant for a shot at a better life. Colonies settle, put down roots, and grow into societies. He hoped he could visit M38 some day with Lon by his side.

As he neared the ship's mess hall, Doyle heard raised voices.

Vigorous scientific debate lubricated the wheels of discovery, but it usually just gave him a headache. Rolling his eyes, Doyle was tempted to turn back before anyone saw him. He was hungry though, and a wise man always listens to his stomach.

On his way in, Doyle bumped headfirst into Django's chest.

"Sorry," Doyle had to peer upward to address the North African's face. "You're the terraformer, right?"

Django nodded in reply. He was a colossal man—jet black and hairless—but meeker than a meerkat.

"Barely seen you on the ship," Doyle said. He wasn't sure why a terraformer was sent on their test flight, but Doyle's curiosity was piqued. "Guess your work's saved for planetside, huh? Not much for you to do on a sardine run?"

Django shrugged and courteously stepped around Doyle to leave without uttering a word.

"Nice *talking* to you." Doyle realized he couldn't remember Django ever speaking, even on the UEC Orbital Station before they left. He wasn't even sure Django *could* talk.

If Django was a silent enigma, it was easy for Doyle to develop a mental snapshot of each noisy crew member arguing around the mess hall table.

"—are wrong. My studies show M38's atmosphere will not have anywhere near that level of hydrogen—" The Slavic-tinged accent belonged to Alexei Chechenkov, an astronomer of wide repute. Short, wiry, with deep-set eyes, he was always, always working.

"—irrelevant, since we can extract all we need from the water—" Usef Skouris, the swarthy Greek chemist with dark, wavy hair and a paunchy middle, was a cut-rate Casanova in Doyle's opinion. He'd requisitioned a double-sized bedfoam, though so far none of the women on board were gullible or desperate enough to join Usef in it.

"—there's the rub. Your electrolytic techniques are underdeveloped—" Doyle recalled reading an article about the trim-bearded Brit, Eckerd Woodton. Apparently some childhood brush with cryogenics led him to develop his own liquid hibernation technology. Despite wearing a full-sleeved uniform at all times, Eckerd had an inviting manner and seemed particularly fond of the young woman seated beside him, Indigo Carlyle.

Indigo watched the verbal jousting in rapt amusement. She was more than another science prodigy. Indigo helped develop the interstellar transmission protocols they were field testing, but instead of confining herself to research, she requested to be part of the core flight crew: their on-deck comms officer.

A slender, one-quarter Filipino with a trademark blue streak flowing through her long hair, Indigo added a splash of color and pizzazz to life on *Gaea-02*. She looked up and noticed Doyle staring, so he quickly nodded hello. Violet-painted fingernails caught the light when she gestured for him to come sit with them.

Doyle grabbed a vacuum-sealed ration from a tray on the table and let the macho posturing and technobabble recede into background noise. Leaning near Indigo's ear, he mumbled, "Remember when guys used to talk about sports?" She stifled a laugh.

Doyle ripped open his food pack, took a sizable bite, and instantly regretted it. He held back the urge to spit out the mouthful, instead swallowing with a grimace. Rumor was, now and then you'd find an edible ration amongst the rest. Doyle never had.

A mechanical whirr from across the room drew Doyle's attention to the prototype engineering robot, M.I.T.Z. Man-height in its semi-crouched position, M.I.T.Z. bared its control board for the robotics engineer, Michi Ozaku.

Lithe and athletic—a gymnast, to better understand the science of movement—Michi's ebony bangs hung over her prominent eyes. A cute and upbeat neo-Dr. Frankenstein, she mollycoddled her creation as if it were a pseudo kid.

M.I.T.Z. was bipedal, smooth-shelled with two large, sky-blue rings masquerading as eyes. Down the front of its torso ran a luminescent indicator stripe, which currently shone a vivid teal. Its vocalization routines were offline until Michi could perfect them, but the robot listened well, its petite engineer issuing most commands by voice.

Michi was the first to remind the crew that M.I.T.Z. was far from alive, not even truly sentient—or was she really reminding herself? Cutting-edge artificial intelligence allowed it to perform menial tasks while the crew was in hibernation, but Doyle didn't totally trust the robot for caretaker duties. He knew the real reason M.I.T.Z. was on board was to operate the Mass Prototype Engine, a machine capable of reconstructing anything for which they had detailed plans. Replacement ship parts, primarily. And for that, Doyle would gladly endure its whirring presence.

"Hey, Michi, why don't you program that thing to replicate some bacon and eggs?" he said while chewing another distasteful bite of ration.

"Inorganic matter only, Doyle."

"Then it might want to whip us up a stack of barf bags." He pushed the rest of his meal aside.

A siren's insistent whoop shocked everyone into red alert.

I knew it, was Doyle's immediate thought as he joined the flurry of activity: something *was* wrong. Reacting as much to the emergency siren as to the gut feeling he'd been unable to shake completely, he raced into the main gangway.

Commander Ruschen rushed down the crew module's spine, shouting to Doyle above the din, "It's the engine core!"

Together they dashed toward engineering, at the base of the ship's central column. Doyle saw the open hatchway to the engine core, a heavily shielded dome separating the accessible parts of *Gaea-02* and the guts of the scaffold. Automated safety precautions kicked in; a bulkhead slammed shut before Doyle could reach it.

Ruschen scanned a readout beside the hermetically sealed hatch. "Radiation inside is nominal. Temp twenty-five C."

"Let's hope that's accurate." Doyle punched in the override code to open the bulkhead. The hairs along his arms raised on goose bumps. He tasted the raw power contained beyond, a sharp pang of tin on his tongue. As he and Commander Ruschen jogged inside, the alarm stopped.

They found Sabin and Pach Jiménez by a dismantled console. The brothers didn't seem fazed. "False alarm," Sabin shrugged apologetically.

"Had to remove a cooling panel to get to the regulator. Must've triggered it," Pach said as he crawled under the console with a well-used toolkit.

"Forgot to disable the safeties before we started."

"Sorry, guys," Pach echoed from inside the machinery.

Commander Ruschen bristled. "You incompetent—"

Doyle stepped in before he went too far. "No harm done, Commander. None of us are used to this ship yet. There's a million new protocols to learn."

That was enough logic to mollify Ruschen. Pointing a stern finger, he said, "I want those safety regs back online the moment you're done," then left engineering.

"Let me guess," Doyle said to Sabin. "This is all to accommodate his new course?"

"*Comandante* thinks it's easy as flipping a switch."

Pach poked his head out. "These eggheads just don't get it—"

"—machines aren't factory specs and serial numbers—" Sabin continued his brother's rant in tandem, Doyle's head ping-ponging between them.

"—each one's different—"

"—each one's got a soul—"

"—you gotta know 'em inside out—"

"—treat 'em like you'd treat a fine woman." Pach caressed the machinery. "Give her your respect, your love…" He was about to kiss the alloy coating.

Doyle opened his mouth to speak up, but thought twice and closed it again. Sabin tapped his wrench loudly to draw Pach out of his *romantica mechanicus.*

Pach winked at Doyle: *only kidding.*

"Get that d-line calibrated, bro," Sabin steered his brother's mind back to the job at hand.

The Jiménez brothers rarely stopped their tinkering. Sabin and Pach were mechanical savants, fixing 50cc engines before they were six years old. They weren't twins—Pach was a year younger, with scraggly facial hair, while Sabin was smooth-skinned under his sweat-caked grime—but Doyle sometimes swore they were one person in two bodies. He marveled at their near-telepathic prescience of the other's needs as they passed tools without prompting.

From the engineers' hostile reactions, Doyle doubted

Commander Ruschen had bothered to explain the sudden change in plan personally. Probably an impersonal buzz on the comms system, with the new data transmitted directly to the engine core. Doyle had long ago learned an important lesson: never piss off the mechanics. One day you may need them to bail you out.

Gaea-02's Candlemass artificial gravity system used a superconductive gyroscope—the Candle—beneath the crew module to help generate a localized gravitomagnetic field. For the past eight days, this Candle had been extinguished and retracted into the ship's internal structure while *Gaea-02* decelerated.

When they entered periapsis, the sharpest point of their parabolic trajectory around the nearby gaseous planet, Doyle had Colby switch to manual fly-by-wire for valuable hands-on experience. Space flight was more than raw numbers and computation. Doyle believed a well-trained, intuitive pilot could outperform the nav computer any day of the week.

Doyle floated above Colby's shoulder harness. "Bring the velocity back... line her up, and... lock it in."

The ship was pivoted in reverse and the geometry was mind-bending, but Colby followed Doyle's lead flawlessly. Now that they were fully in the Turn, gravity would draw the ship's arc until it faced the way they came: home, sweet home.

The final step was to reignite the Candlemass. As weight returned, Colby unhooked his grav supports. He leaned back, cupped his hands behind his head, and cracked his long fingers.

"Don't get too cocky. This is the easy part." Doyle landed gently. "When you guys get to M38 for real, you'll—"

Colby cut Doyle off with an awestruck gasp and pointed to a telescopic viewport. He quickly relayed the visual feed to the larger main screen.

Millions of light years beyond their course lay a dazzling gas cloud of unearthly hues, spiraling symmetrically to form a butterfly's wings.

Alexei had detected its existence earlier in the trip and dubbed it the Hades Nebula, but this was the first time they had actually been able to see the cosmic phenomenon.

It was breathtaking.

Doyle opened a comms channel to all areas of the ship, "Ladies and gentlemen, we are now officially in the Turn."

His voice echoed throughout *Gaea-02.*

"If you stick your head out an aft window and suck in some void, you can be the first human to see Alexei's Hades Nebula with the naked eye."

Doyle closed the comms channel, continuing his last comment only to himself, "And it may just be worth it…"

In each room, crew members turned on a viewscreen to witness the majestic sight. All thirteen souls inside the ship, united at that moment.

Doyle almost forgot his resolve to return home. Why not carry onward, strike out into the unknown like the pioneers of old, give in to the thrill of exploration he felt tugging at his heels…? Then Lon's smile invaded the vista of his mind, and the answer was clear.

"Mr. Tour Guide?" Indigo's voice chimed over the comms system. "I have something else here you might get a kick out of."

Indigo whirled her chair around to face Doyle. "I started picking these up when we first slowed for the trip home." An Earth television channel blared from her squat comms station.

"What is it?"

"History," Indigo said, adjusting her console to clean up the signal. "These are the exact television signals Earth was watching sixteen years ago. They've just reached this distance."

Their great society's first contribution to the spaceways, Doyle thought wryly: a cornucopia of inane blather.

Indigo flicked through chat shows, music videos, and melodramas before settling on a real oxymoron: an old news report.

"—formation of the United Earth Coalition to take our planet forward as a unified whole," the smiling newscaster read from her teleprompter.

Doyle remembered watching the original announcements with his father, Dr. Emil Gage. A brilliant new dawn, his father had called it, one that he'd worked tirelessly to see rise. The UEC combined international groups like the United Nations and NATO under one banner, along with NASA, ESA, and other outmoded space agencies. Central control, along with multilateral support from member nations for a global military, meant humanity could focus all its efforts on space colonization.

Still, the new assembly wasn't perfect.

"—resistance to the proposal continues to come from the Chinese-led Asian Pacific Alliance, who refuses to sign the Neutral Arms Treaty," the newscaster continued.

Doyle couldn't really blame the APA. Part of the deal was that all armed forces would be absorbed into the UEC corps and disseminated across member nations, so that each country's homeland security consisted of soldiers from dozens of nationalities. An extraordinary ideology which eliminated corruption, crusades, and coup d'états—*in theory*. For an insular, distrustful regime like the APA, however, it must have seemed that the Satan of the West was heating up the pitchforks to brand their Asian hides.

The utopian "unified whole" was rendered a joke. A third of the global population, wanting no part of the UEC, gave an impolite gesture and withdrew further into the collective shell of their Asian Pacific Alliance.

The United Earth Coalition, misnomer intact, pressed on, whether out of hubris or sheer necessity. Nevertheless, Doyle had signed up immediately. He'd believed strongly in the UEC's cause.

He still did.

Indigo switched the television feed to a cartoon as an animated mule in a pink sombrero kicked a dancing cactus. She giggled when its spiny thorns flew into the air.

Preparations for *Gaea-02*'s return trip were almost complete. Eckerd brought online a dozen Subcooled Liquid Hibernation chambers: oval tubes with molded scoop interiors. Three regulated hoses snaked into each sleep tank for oxygen, nutrients, and byproduct filtration.

A hall of artificial wombs.

Gaea-02's agriculture lab was a work in progress, divided into comparison plots for hydroponics and soil. Doyle liked to slip in when no one was around. The crops reminded him of the New Mexico farmland where he grew up. Though in his youth, of course, he couldn't wait to be anywhere else.

Doyle snapped a stalk off a fledgling tomato plant. That simplest of acts conjured memories of his mother, fresh soil under her nails on spring afternoons. But most of all, this tiny oasis of living, growing things reminded him of Juni. Memories that could reopen wounds if he wasn't careful.

"Green thumb?" Riana asked, entering the lab. She had taken over most of the ag-duties on this trial run, until the full mission's much larger crew would allow for a designated biologist.

Doyle dropped the stalk into the composter. "My wife tried to teach me the finer points of pruning."

Similar to his mother in that respect, Juni was an Earth spirit, his own personal Gaea. A devoted groundskeeper for the Florida UEC base where Doyle was stationed, Juni kept a secret tomato crop and shared her harvest bounties with selected officers. Those juicy tomatoes had tasted almost as delicious as Juni's lips.

Don't go there, Doyle, he silently warned himself.

"My husband couldn't care less... about plants." Riana checked the hydroponic gauges. "I wouldn't have expected it from a maverick test pilot either."

"My old life. I'm flying solo as a dear ol' dad these days."

"I'd heard about your wife," Riana said softly. "I'm so sorry."

"Yeah." *Me too.* "I'll leave all the hotshot stuff to Colby now. He swears 'the chicks dig it.' I'm only here to train him."

"About chicks?"

Doyle laughed, and it surprised him when Riana did too. He had only seen her work face before, but here was her softer side.

Nurturing, caring. He smelled the slight waft of Riana's citrus perfume and watched as she tended the plants, wondering who else aboard *Gaea-02* he had misjudged.

"At least you'll have some real food on the long haul," Doyle said.

Riana studied his face for a second. "You wish you were coming, don't you?"

"Of course he does," Commander Ruschen said as he moved in from the shadows, startling his wife. How long had he been there? Why didn't he announce his arrival sooner? He looked Doyle in the eye and continued, "You don't spend ten years preparing to be a colonist and then quit without any regrets."

Ruschen was baiting him. Doyle had seen it before. So had Riana, judging from a subtle change in her expression. The man had an aggravating need to prove himself, and outright confrontation was often the most expedient way. This wasn't a battle that needed to be fought; Ruschen's point was moot. Doyle had made his decision and was content with it. *Completely*, he reminded himself.

He limited his response to a noncommittal shrug.

Ruschen scoffed. "Eckerd is ready for our sleep. I trust you won't need a lullaby, Doyle." He escorted Riana out, leaving Doyle alone with the sprouting plants and his ghosts.

"This test flight has been an unqualified success." Commander Ruschen addressed *Gaea-02*'s assembled crew in the SLH hall. "One hundred and eighty-seven experiments without serious incident. We should have all the necessary data to launch a full-scale Gaea mission to M38 this time next year."

They congratulated one another while Doyle looked on politely, feeling every bit an outsider.

"Mars was a small step, but we'll be going farther than anyone believed possible. Planet M38 can be humanity's salvation … or a new home. The world's future depends on us." Ruschen finished his speech to hearty applause.

His words were full of self-import, but Doyle knew it wasn't hyperbole. These people would be recorded in history as heroes.

The group broke up as crew members headed for their individual hibernation chambers, despite Usef's salacious offer to share his with Michi.

Riana stripped down and eased into her tube beside Commander Ruschen's without a hint of expectation in her eyes; no kiss nor hug, not even a handshake passed between husband and wife. Ruschen wasn't one for public displays—Doyle was surprised he even wore the simple platinum wedding band that matched Riana's.

Without realizing, Doyle spun his own gold band around his ring finger with his thumb. Never could bring himself to remove it, not even for a shower.

He continued to fidget as he approached his tube. The week-long hibernation on the trip out had been bad enough. Doyle wasn't elated about being an icicle again. "I should be monitoring the bridge, not taking a three month nap," he grumbled to Colby as both men disrobed.

"Eckerd can wake us if we're needed." Colby peeled off his beanie. "Just lie back and cruise, mate."

"You're right to worry," Usef said to Doyle. "Anything could happen in Eckerd's whatsits. Might never wake up, or worse, wake up like him."

"What do you mean?"

"Ignore Usef," Eckerd said as he positioned Doyle inside his tube. "These chambers are perfectly safe." Doyle couldn't tell if Eckerd was joking when he added, "Theoretically."

Before he could reply, Eckerd lowered an oxygen mask over Doyle's face, and it instantly sealed skin-tight. He attached an intravenous nutrient feeder. "See you in ninety days," Eckerd said as he closed the clear cylinder.

Subcooled liquid rushed around Doyle's ankles. The waterline quickly rose above his knees, his stomach, his chest. Doyle shivered and shook until each part of his body became numb, like a slow-motion plunge into a winter lake.

The icy solution reached Doyle's eyes, which shut on reflex.

He couldn't help but grow sleepy. Everything was black, switched off.

Doyle tried to surface. That feeling of unrest haunted him again and he wanted to warn Eckerd to keep his eyes open—*stay alert*—but Doyle couldn't move his mouth. He wasn't sure if he even had lips anymore, or a face.

A face. Little Lon's face…

Doyle's body functions slowed. He no longer felt the cold. The rhythm of his heart relaxed from emphatic jungle drums to an occasional lazy thud.

Doyle finally slipped into unconsciousness, comforted by the knowledge that when he awoke, it would be only two more days until he was reunited with his son.

CHAPTER 2
FOUNDATIONS

Subcooled liquid rippled across Dr. Riana Ruschen's creased brow.

Like the ocean rolling away from the shore to leave hordes of tiny sand crabs scrambling, the mind plays tricks. Granules of memory erode with the tides until sometimes it's difficult to be sure what truly happened and what might have been only a dream.

How young was she then? Riana's glacial mind wondered. Not older than four or five—no, she had just passed her sixth birthday, and she was a lonely little leper, if truth be told. She stuck out like the sore thumb she was: a military brat. They lived on a naval base because that's where her father was an instructor and where her bullied mother crept through life far from her beloved sovereign nation of Quebec, Riana's birthplace.

Why was her subconscious dredging up her ancient history

now? Where was the button to switch the REM projector off? Dream state in a hibernation tube was frightening, but she was always told people could orchestrate their own dreams as if directing a movie. Riana had never mastered that art. She was powerless to change the reel.

The boy's face flickered for a moment as her long-suppressed memories unspooled.

Up until that point, meeting him was the most daring thing she'd ever done. He was two or three years older than herself, she'd guessed. They didn't talk much. She couldn't even say why she followed him. Something—maybe his confident swagger—told Riana that he knew a great secret.

The Foundation Day had gathered many families important to the establishment of a United Earth Coalition, laying the groundwork for a global military and its joint space projects. Riana didn't understand that then, but she knew it was a *big deal.* Young and bored, she found it easy to slip away unnoticed while her father was preoccupied by the day's events. It gave her a giggling rush of adrenaline.

The boy turned his head once he realized she was tagging along behind him. His eyes narrowed. "You following me?"

"No!" she answered too loudly.

"Shhhh," he hushed her and ducked behind a copse of bushes overlooking an aircraft hangar. The way he peeked surreptitiously between the leaves, that hangar was obviously the boy's goal. Riana parted the hedge and frowned. Cadet Baden Ruschen—only in his late teens, but her father's pet student—was patrolling outside the hangar. *Figures* he'd *be on guard.*

"Will you help me?" the boy asked over Riana's shoulder, sending a thrill through her body.

Riana calmed her racing heart. "To do what?"

"I need to get in there," he quietly told her, "and I don't want that guy to stop me."

Even though her excitement was building, Riana reminded herself to whisper, "What's inside the hangar?" She was proud that she knew the correct word, although the boy seemed unimpressed.

"You'll see."

He hardly looked at her while he explained his plan, but Riana was shy too so she didn't mind.

Their scheme went off mostly without a hitch. Riana was the Admiral's little girl, so Cadet Ruschen could hardly refuse her request to use a restroom inside the hangar. The second he unlocked the door, something under the hedge made a noise like caps going off. Dirtbombs exploded, which lured teenage Baden away.

Riana held the door ajar as her accomplice rushed from his hiding spot. "What's your name?" he asked as they scurried inside.

"Deniece," Riana lied.

"Thanks, Deniece," the boy mumbled as he darted among equipment sheathed by white dust covers.

Little Riana felt a chill in the air. She had never been inside such a vast enclosure, the arching frame holding it together like a person's rib cage. She lightly palmed one of the many columns on either side of the central expanse. She shivered. The metal was cold to the touch.

Why would any kid want to sneak into this place? Riana couldn't figure it out, so she asked her companion again. "What's in here, really?"

"I dunno," the boy admitted, "but Dad said it was worth more than all the water in the world."

Ice, more like … Riana felt as though she were inside a walk-in refrigerator.

The boy saw Riana rub her bare arms to keep warm. He pulled a drop cloth off a big piece of machinery and draped it across her shoulders like an oversized cape. His eyes nearly popped from his face when he saw what he had uncovered beneath the cloth.

A scale model of a beautiful spaceship.

A prototype, the boy called it, running his hands over the

polished surface in awe. Riana too appreciated its grandeur. She clutched the drop cover closer around her arms, enthralled to be part of the discovery.

On one side of the spaceship, bold letters were painted: "UEC//GAEA-01," Riana read aloud. She scrunched up her face. "What does that mean?"

"What are you kids doing in here? It's restricted!" a grizzled naval officer roared as he barged into the hangar, clutching at the kids' collars.

He snagged Riana by the cape, but the boy squirmed away and ran out the open door. The officer held tighter to his one captive. Riana turned her face from his hot breath. Other base personnel rushed in to see what the commotion was about.

Riana's memory shattered into a kaleidoscopic blur of irate, adult faces. They demanded to know who the elusive boy was. One of the men recognized him as Dr. Emil Gage's son, Don or Dale or something. She swore she didn't know him, but they wouldn't believe her.

Riana was on the verge of bawling when Baden stepped in to rescue her. He extricated her from the older man's grasp, explaining that she was Admiral Stone's daughter and had permission to be inside. Eventually pacified, they left her with Baden.

"Please don't tell Daddy," Riana sobbed.

Baden must have been angry at the trick she had played, but he said softly, "I won't."

Somehow, her father found out anyway, and never fully trusted his only daughter again. Baden assumed the role of Riana's constant chaperone, then her teacher, always there for her as she grew up. Marriage seemed a natural progression; in a way, she felt she didn't have a choice.

The boy... Riana had recognized Doyle immediately when they met again in later life as part of the Gaea mission, although he clearly didn't recall "Deniece." Why would he? The *Gaea-01* prototype eclipsed his experience. So Riana never let on. Baden likely realized too, but he never once mentioned the incident.

Their discussion in the agriculture lab must have triggered her unquiet slumber, Riana rationalized. She was in such total control over her emotions during daylight hours that when she slept, her freedom-hungry subconscious paid her back threefold.

Or so she thought when she awoke.

CHAPTER 3
A DIFFERENT COUNTRY

Doyle nestled comfortably in the wide porch swing as it swayed with the breeze.

While he was growing up, the farmhouse seemed older than he could possibly fathom. Its familiar, creaking wood and weather-stained shingles were oddly reassuring: they had withstood the test of time.

Doyle glanced to his right, where his wife, Juni, returned his smile with a resplendent one of her own. As the wind picked up, her light blue summer dress rippled. Juni looked like she belonged here, the span of New Mexican landscape sweeping behind her softly fluttering hair.

Maize in the fields swished a lulling symphony. Higher up stood the mountain range where his father spent so much of his life—at the Apache Point Observatory. Some nights, while tossing and turning, waiting for childhood slumber to arrive, Doyle had wondered whether his dad ever lowered the telescope lens to watch over him as he slept.

Doyle hadn't visited this place for many years, not since his mother finally left his stargazing father to disappear into a maze of communes. His father seemed to take it in his stride, and Doyle realized she simply didn't want to be found. He hoped she was happy, but more than that, he wanted to tell her she was a grandmother.

Doyle cocked his head to the left, where little Lon whirled, flying his toy spaceship over the aged, wooden porch as he played out special Gaea missions.

Lazily stretching, Doyle leaned back with a grin and gazed across the swaying maize. Everything seemed fine in his world.

All was as it should be.

He watched the verdant green hills on the far horizon gradually turn a dull brown.

That was odd. Doyle couldn't pinpoint any reason for the changing hue. The sun was high in the sky and no cloudbanks were visible to overshadow the land. Perhaps a farmer tilling his barren grain field was kicking up a dust cloud.

Suddenly, the aberration sped up, thundering across the plains like apocalyptic horsemen.

The hills had lost their lush color because they were dying.

Everything was.

Doyle gawked at the landscape as trees were stripped bare, sucked dry and lifeless before his eyes, left like white, bony claws writhing out from the earth.

Row upon row of crops blackened. The wave of decay tumbled toward Doyle like teetering dominoes. A fetid stench filled his nostrils. Across the sky, rolling smog hung thick and heavy with pollution.

Doyle faced his wife, but Juni was lying in a blue hospital smock, attached to an intravenous drip. Her once exquisite features were strained—sunken and ashen—skin clinging to her bones like sackcloth.

Doyle wrenched away. He couldn't see her like this, not again. He pivoted to find his son, but Lon was out of sight. His abandoned toy twisted and trembled as each new gust hit the creaking porch.

"Lon!" Doyle screamed out.

Shielding his face from swirling dust torrents, Doyle frantically hunted for his boy. Every step he took, the old porch crumbled under his feet, as though the wood was being eaten away from the inside.

"Lonnie!"

The dust storm closed in on Doyle, stinging his eyes, blinding him.

In the dark, a harrowing thought forced its way into Doyle's mind: *he would never see his son again.*

The liquid in Doyle's hibernation chamber quickly drained and his tank opened. The pull of artificial gravity felt unusually strong after floating in solution for so long.

"Give it a moment," Eckerd's voice echoed. His blurry, bearded face filled Doyle's vision.

After three months without use, Doyle's speech was slurred. "Not the face I'd want to wake up to… No offense."

"Lean on me, handsome." Eckerd helped Doyle down from his tube and threw a thermal blanket around his shoulders. He handed Doyle a heated vacuum packet, the spacefarer's sludgy equivalent of coffee, then assisted the others from their hibernation.

Doyle had found that readjustment after prolonged weightlessness was easier if you were off your feet, so he slumped onto a bench to wait it out. He tore the corner strip off his java-mud and slowly sipped the steaming, viscous liquid.

While he couldn't recall any specifics, Doyle felt sure he'd been dreaming. The memory surrounded him like dawn mist, teasing with muted shapes and tricks of light. He didn't remember having nightmares during their first hibernation, but perhaps he had. As Eckerd walked past, Doyle's hand darted out to grab him.

"You supposed to dream?" Doyle's voice croaked.

"Pardon?"

Doyle swallowed carefully. "In the tubes. Are we supposed to dream?"

"What are dreams, really?" Eckerd waffled, "A random firing of synapses? A mechanism for sorting memory fragments into—"

"Didn't ask for a thesis. Just tell me if it's normal."

Eckerd stared at Doyle for a moment. He clearly hadn't asked the question on a whim. "Everyone's experience is different, but your mind has to do something to keep active over three months. If it didn't, you'd come out a vegetable."

Shirking eye contact, Doyle's attention seemed to wander.

"Doyle? Are you okay?"

"Yeah. Fine." Doyle gazed around at the waking crew. The morning after a slumber party from hell. Already Usef had begun arguing with Alexei, who had caught him leering at Michi's bare, sleeping body in her clear tube. "Looks like we all made it through."

"Never any doubt," Eckerd said, tapping the nearest hibernation chamber like a proud parent.

Farther along, Commander Ruschen helped Riana down from her chamber. She threw her arms around him in a spontaneous embrace. Ruschen glanced about for witnesses before giving her an almost fatherly peck on the forehead.

Crumpling his empty drink packet into a ball, Doyle wondered if they'd dreamt of shared, happy memories, and he couldn't help feeling a deep pang of loss.

No, it was more than loss.

Fear. He had an acute sense of fear, and that was way out of the ordinary for Doyle.

Colby checked the flight instruments again. "Status quo. Antimatter engines disengaged, cruising at chem assist velocity, just a few hours out from the Wheel."

"You're sure?"

"Absolutely. What's this all about?"

Doyle took a while to answer. "Nothing. Just missing Lon, I guess. I can't explain it." He'd tried to in his mind, but the fleeting wisp of premonition made little sense. "Keep an eye on the readouts for me?"

Colby nodded. Doyle knew Colby would do what was asked, even if he didn't fully understood why. That made two of them.

Doyle was far from superstitious. He might have seemed reckless to outsiders, especially in his younger days, but there was a rigid logic deep at his core. By the time he reached the communications lab, he'd concluded that his out-of-kilter intuition was nothing more than homecoming jitters. Pathetic for a sojourner of the stars, but it reaffirmed his decision to call it quits when he did.

Indigo was busy at her station when Doyle entered. She held up her hand. "Before you ask, yes, I sent the Wheel a strata beacon when we woke up to let 'em know, hey, we're six days late."

"Good," Doyle said. "Any transmissions from Earth?"

"Only a few old messages that caught up with us on the way back."

"Anything from my son or father?"

"No, sorry."

Doyle turned to leave, but he lingered in the doorway with his brow furrowed. "Are you saying there was *nothing* that originated while we slept?"

Indigo shrugged, "It's not so unusual. They knew we'd be out of touch for a while."

No. There he went again, but that just didn't sit right. Any flight Doyle had ever been on, a steady stream of daily communications was always backlogged. His father would regularly send inconsequential missives, and Juni's encrypted sweet nothings reminded Doyle she was thinking of him—once upon a time. Doyle understood this crew was specifically chosen in part for their minimal outside attachments, but surely they all had some correspondents: mentors, academic rivals, and crass as it sounded, even groupies. Where was the fan mail?

Doyle stepped closer to Indigo's console. "You're picking up terrestrial feed?"

Indigo opened a channel, quickly located the stream of signals, and piped them through to her upper viewscreen.

"Broadcasts haven't changed much," Indigo mumbled as a parade of banal situation comedies flickered across the screen.

"These are old," Doyle said without taking his eyes from the screen.

"This far away, probably from a month or two back."

"No." Doyle took control of the console and rapidly flicked through dozens of channels, all transmitting sitcoms. "Every one of these is at least two years old."

"A connoisseur?" Indigo wasn't taking him seriously. The viewscreen glitched for a moment, but neither she nor Doyle noticed.

"I spent a lot of time in the hospital when my wife was sick. I must have seen every single sitcom twice, and these were *all* playing two years ago." Doyle was hyperaware during those few, long months. Anything that could take Juni's mind off her pain was welcome. It hurt to talk—for both of them—so the idiot box was good for something.

"Guess they're in a rerun slump," Indigo said, unconcerned.

"On every network?" Doyle cycled broadcasts. "Where are the news channels? Not one report? What about Global Net?"

"These receivers are experimental, you know that. We haven't ironed out all the bugs."

"But…" Doyle stopped himself. It dawned on him that he must look crazy to her. He *felt* crazy.

"Look, let me run diagnostics and I'll try to get you some solid answers before we dock. Plus the latest baseball results, 'kay?" Indigo tried to lighten his sullen mood with a little wink.

Doyle exhaled. He gave her a conciliatory grin.

Beside them, the screen glitched oddly again. This time Doyle caught a glimpse from the corner of his eye. "What was that?"

Indigo glanced at the screen. A sitcom was playing.

Doyle was sure he'd seen something else for a split second. "Pause the feed," he demanded, and she complied. "This is cached?"

Indigo nodded.

"Roll it back."

Indigo's lips pursed, but Doyle gestured adamantly, so she rewound the footage.

"Stop. Advance the cache frame by frame."

They viewed the recording one frame at a time until Doyle shouted, "There."

Indigo stopped the forward roll and stared, dumbfounded.

Onscreen was a single frame inserted in the midst of an otherwise innocuous program. A subliminal image of a crouched Chinese soldier packing dirt around a freshly planted tree.

Doyle peered closer at the screen. "What the hell . . . ?"

He'd seen similar pictures before. Hidden persuaders. Twelve years ago he crash-landed in Asian Pacific Alliance territory, left to find his way covertly from the Malay Peninsula to Singapore. While the UEC and APA weren't openly hostile, an experimental pilot veering off course would not be deemed an accident. Doyle had found photos of smiling eco-soldiers pasted to windows and walls along the back streets of Kuantan. They were shams, of course. Staged APA propaganda: the prima facie counterpart of the UEC's own Gaea posters, although lacking a comparable policy behind the utopian facade.

But why would . . . ?

A buzz over the ship's comms system interrupted Doyle's train of thought. Alexei's stilted Kazakh accent was unmistakable. "Commander Ruschen, please come to my lab. This could be important."

Indigo was surprised to see Doyle leaving. He said over his shoulder, "Run those diagnostics. I'll get back to you."

Doyle jogged toward Alexei's lab, remembering to duck under the low door rim at the last moment. If Alexei had found some clue, Doyle wanted to be involved.

He barged into the lab, disrupting Alexei and Commander Ruschen, who were already immersed in weighty discussion.

"Do you mind?" Ruschen motioned for Doyle to leave at once.

Doyle didn't budge. He spoke deliberately to hide his growing anxiety. "Why would UEC television channels be laced with the APA's subliminal propaganda?"

Ruschen and Alexei exchanged a concerned glance.

Alexei broke their silence. "Perhaps he should hear this too, sir."

Ruschen glared at Doyle for a moment before relenting. "Close the door." He nodded at Alexei to continue.

"As I was telling the Commander…" Alexei tapped a key and a three-dimensional holographic globe of Earth sprung from the tabletop. It rotated as he continued, "While I was running some side experiments on the cosmic microwave background, I discovered unusual artifacts in the local radiation field. Very slight, but I traced their origin back to Earth."

Alexei shifted the hologlobe to a spectrum mapping radiation density. Dozens of deep red zones pockmarked Earth's surface.

Doyle knew the answer before he asked: "What are they?"

"Nuclear detonations," Commander Ruschen said without emotion.

"That is the most likely explanation," Alexei agreed. "I estimate up to forty-seven medium yield warheads sometime within the last three months, primarily across Europe and North America."

Doyle couldn't speak, could barely think. Acting on instinct, he rushed for the door, but Commander Ruschen grabbed him. "Where are you going?"

"I need to contact my father. He's taking care of Lon."

"You might alert them that we know."

"Alert who?"

"Whoever is responsible. Most likely the Asian Pacific Alliance." Ruschen loosened his grip on Doyle and pointed to the hologlobe. "None of China's allies were hit, not even former APA nations—Australia, Singapore, the Philippines. It's war—"

"And we lost," Alexei interjected. "If it is true their propaganda is flooding UEC broadcasts, the war must already be over."

Doyle tried to conceptualize what they were saying, but it was just too horrific. Nuclear war hadn't been on anyone's mind for decades.

Alexei pressed a button and the hologlobe dissipated. "What I do not understand is why the UEC did not launch in response?"

Doyle sighed. "The UEC's nukes are pure bluff." It was the coalition's best-kept secret, with only a handful of people privy to the fact. Doyle's father, one of their highest-ranking science advisors, was among them. But wet lips are loose lips, so in one of their father-son bonding moments—over a casket of Merlot—the confidence had passed to Doyle. No sense keeping the cat in the bag now though. "The foundation leaders determined there was no scenario—not even the one staring us in the face—that could justify retaliating in a nuclear conflict."

Alexei was aghast. "They would have us roll over like kittens?"

"A wise decision," Commander Ruschen remained staunchly analytical. "Simulations I've seen predict escalation ultimately results in a ninety percent probability of the human race's demise within twenty years. Pride isn't worth that risk."

"Right, so the UEC purposely allowed their delivery systems to deteriorate," Doyle said. "Better they be obsolete than have some madman hit the launch button one day."

"Trust humans not to put their trust in human nature," Alexei said sourly.

It chilled Doyle to realize that either the APA knew about the UEC's cunning fail-safe—somehow—or they just didn't care. Could the situation on Earth have become so desperate while their eyes were on the stars? Were there hints before Doyle left, hints that his subconscious mind translated into his runaway dreams?

"How long until we have direct comms with the Orbital Station?" Ruschen asked.

Numb, Doyle mustered an answer. "Twenty minutes or so."

"There's a chance the station's been isolated from whatever happened on Earth."

"A safe haven?" Alexei said.

"Let's find out." Commander Ruschen strode from the lab.

Doyle held Alexei back a moment. He had to know. "What kind of effect would . . . ?"

"Total annihilation at ground zero. But radiation above three hundred rems should be confined to a hundred-ninety kilometer radius at each site. Your son?"

Doyle made the mental calculations. "If your map of the blasts is accurate, he should be safe." *But if Dad took him North for a trip, or back to New Mexico . . .* No, he couldn't allow himself to imagine anything but Lon being alive.

Alive, but then what? Stuck in a chaotic, post-nuclear world with only an elderly grandfather, however capable, to watch over him? Struggling daily for survival in an enemy-occupied, radioactive wasteland? Just how bad was it down there?

His son needed him, and that promise he thought he was merely bending now looped like a knotted rope around Doyle's heart.

Alexei followed Commander Ruschen's trail toward Indigo's comms station.

Doyle lingered behind. Something about the timing of this Armageddon—while *Gaea-02* was in another solar system—itched beneath his skull.

His instincts screamed that it was no coincidence, and the placement of nuclear detonations was equally suspicious. Many major cities were certainly destroyed, but each impact zone was slightly off-target. Not aimed at the heart of cities, but the outskirts.

Something familiar about the pattern . . .

He brought Alexei's hologlobe back to life, complete with his radiation markers. Doyle programmed the map to highlight all United Earth Coalition bases across Europe and the USA.

Bingo.

With surgical precision, at each ground zero was a UEC military base.

Oddly though, most of the UEC tech, space, or engineering installations were spared. They had bypassed the UEC's primary launch center at Cape Canaveral entirely. Doyle was thankful for that at least, due to Lon's proximity in Central Florida. But *why?*

The choice of outdated nuclear weaponry was puzzling too. The APA didn't officially possess antimatter technology, but Doyle had heard the whispers. If they had even rudimentary capabilities to generate antiprotons, it wouldn't take much to cobble together enough death in a bottle to wipe whole continents clean. Here was the dark side of progress: the shadow over Oppenheimer's "different country."

That was it, Doyle realized. The APA didn't want to destroy the UEC at all. This was no heat of the moment scuffle.

Once a nation of great innovators, China had scrapped their space program after the Qing-Chen coup, and it was never reinstated by the APA. Without it, they were facing an environmental dead-end.

They needed our technology, and everything that came with it. D-salt. The instruments of colonization. The Gaea mission, *including this crew.*

Now the timing made sense.

They were stealing the future.

Doyle, Alexei, and Commander Ruschen flanked Indigo at her console. They hadn't told her anything more than to try hailing the UEC Orbital Station, affectionately known as the Wheel.

"Why the audience?" Indigo asked over her shoulder.

"Proceed as normal," Ruschen said flatly.

Doyle could see suspicion clouding Indigo's eyes, and he knew Ruschen's curt dismissal wouldn't be enough. "We're just making sure it all goes smoothly," Doyle tried to remain nonchalant. "Momentous occasion and all."

Indigo frowned but accepted Doyle's intention—his unspoken *trust me*—if not fully believing his words. She opened a comms channel. "This is *Gaea-02* on approach to UEC Orbital Station, over."

The transmission would take a minute each way. The quartet waited for a response. None came.

"United Earth Coalition Station from *Gaea-02*, please respond."

Nothing.

"Keep trying," Commander Ruschen said.

Indigo continued sending hails as Doyle and Ruschen spoke quietly behind her back.

"They could have evacuated," Doyle said hopefully.

"Or the station has been compromised."

"They would have seen the blasts with their naked eyes from orbit," Alexei added.

Eavesdropping, Indigo's ears perked. "What blasts?" she demanded. "What's going on?"

Commander Ruschen fingered his temples. Doyle could see the first signs of stress tainting Ruschen's thought process.

Doyle placed a steadying hand on Ruschen's shoulder. "Baden, you have to tell the crew."

Extract from The Consequence of Thirst, *H. Transik, Bridgehead Publishing, 2044, p63:*

The Asian Pacific Alliance's festering mistrust of the United Earth Coalition can be traced back to a single, pivotal event: the cataclysmic earthquake spawned by China's Three Gorges Dam. Contrary to initial, agenda-driven reports, the dam's sheer mass undoubtedly and dramatically caused this tectonic disaster. In fact, UEC scholars later dubbed it the Three Gorges Quake.

Western corporate greed led to the dam's ill-advised construction. Fitting, then, that the erosion of the multinationals' foothold in Chinese society was directly tied to the same thirty-nine billion cubic meters of rushing water that swept away millions of corpses [for death toll estimates from varying sources, see *Appendix B2*].

In the aftermath, it was as though the Great Wall of China was metaphorically built anew. A severe backlash against encroaching foreign-controlled capitalism gave General Qing-Chen the leverage to seize power. His strict isolationist policies garnered favor from China's impoverished majority.

Forming the Asian Pacific Alliance, however, was little more than a thinly veiled ploy to expand China's political borders through economic bribery, coercion, or outright occupation.

Qing-Chen's regime was hugely successful, despite leaving the region's ecology in tatters. For people inside APA dominated realms, the outside world ceased to exist.

20440322//GLOBALNET//HIS866U5

CHAPTER 4
THE WHEEL

Gaea-02's crew took the news worse than Doyle had expected. He kept out of their discussion, letting Commander Ruschen assert his authority. This was no time for a pissing match; they needed clear leadership—one dominant voice—and that should be the Commander's.

As soon as the crew's initial shock wore off, their questions came fast and furious, but Ruschen didn't have all the answers.

That made them angry.

Commander Ruschen did his best to calm the crew. "There's no need to panic—"

"No need to panic!" Michi was incredulous.

Doyle recognized they were all doing their best not to freak out. Indigo quietly twirled a lock of blue hair out of nervous habit. Colby boyishly squeezed her hand, an action that seemed to stoke jealousy in the much older Eckerd.

"Commander, are you certain it was the APA?" Dr. Farrad asked.

"It's more than a guess. What other group has both the capability and the motive?"

"What *is* their motive?" Riana turned to her husband. "What do they want?"

"Us," Commander Ruschen said, hushing them.

Michi was dubious. "They'd blow up half the planet for *Gaea-02*?"

"For the entire Gaea mission. China and her allies desperately need planet M38's resources, yes? Perhaps they—no, make that definitely—they want to arrive there first. Claim it as their territory. We know they don't trust the UEC to share; they've always regarded us as the enemy."

Catching his eye, Doyle nodded in agreement. So, Ruschen had reached the same conclusion. The UEC had been foolish to turn a blind eye all these years. Doyle couldn't have cared less about the politics right now. Let them usurp control. Let them plant their flag on M38. *His* world was a four-year-old boy waiting for Doyle to save him.

The mess hall descended into chaos as people started chattering all at once.

Eckerd piped up, "They're fighting over a planet no one has even set foot on?"

"Look at it from their perspective: the APA's existence, their people's lives, are at stake," Dr. Farrad said.

Alexei was incensed, slipping into Kazakh dialect, "These *svolochs* wish to dominate Earth's future, with everyone under their heels."

"This is all bull, you don't know—"

"I know the type, Usef," Alexei seethed. "I grew up during the Neo-Tzarist Occupation."

Usef shook his head. "These blasts could be anything. Underground tests for asteroid mining—"

"In and around cities?" Michi pointed out.

"They might all be—"

"—dead down there," the brothers Jiménez spoke in tandem.

"Everyone, please." Commander Ruschen appealed for quiet, but the crew ignored him and continued squabbling. Riana gripped his hand as a show of support. He shunned her gesture. Instead, in a feeble attempt to regain the crew's attention, he knocked on the table. The noise went unnoticed among the intensifying quarrel.

Ruschen fell silent and backed away. To Doyle, it seemed that he had given up. Gun-shy. For all his bluster, when the opportunity arose to prove his worth as a commanding officer, Ruschen froze.

Doyle finally understood Ruschen's antagonism toward him and his retirement. He must have resented Doyle for the responsibility foisted upon him, the weight of the world—two worlds—dumped on his shoulders. Doyle even felt a little sorry for Ruschen, but sympathy wasn't going to get him back to Lon.

Doyle waded into the verbal melee and shouted, "Shut the hell up! All of you." He gave each of them a shaming glance. "*This* is Earth's best and brightest? We'll dock with the Wheel in under thirty minutes. We don't need debate. We need solutions. Fast."

Since no one had any, they avoided his gaze.

"How much food do we have on board?" Doyle asked Dr. Farrad.

"A month's worth. A little more."

"Fuel?"

Sabin replied, "Antimatter cells are almost dry."

"First thing we need to do is resupply," Doyle said. "Then at least we can stay in orbit until we figure out the next step. Agreed?"

The crew nodded their affirmation.

Doyle already knew what they had to do—separate the crew module and land *Gaea-02* on Earth—but not before gathering more intelligence. Where was it safest to land? What could they expect when they popped the hatch? Was there a pocket of resistance fighters who could help them? *Was there anyone left alive?*

No sense kick-starting more discourse now, though. They had a job to do.

Commander Ruschen found his voice. "Chances are this is a trap. The APA are likely waiting inside the station for us to dock."

"Leave that to me," Doyle said. Ignoring Ruschen's indignant look, he addressed the crew at large. "I don't know some of you too well, don't know all your skills. Is anyone able to patch into the Orbital Station's subnet?"

"You mean remotely?" Indigo asked. Doyle nodded.

She hesitated to volunteer, so Eckerd stepped forward in her place. "My SLH host streams data directly to their system, avoids all the firewalls. I could piggyback a turnkey."

"Good. Show me." Doyle clasped Eckerd's elbow to pull him along.

Ruschen tried to block their path. "Run it by me first. There's still a chain of command."

"No time," Doyle said as he sidestepped Commander Ruschen and hurried out of the mess hall with Eckerd.

Ruschen followed them into the corridor. He grabbed Doyle's shoulder. "I'm in charge here, Doyle."

So much for avoiding a pissing contest. Doyle spun and pinned Ruschen against the wall while he made the message resoundingly clear. "Right now, action trumps hierarchy. If you want to be in charge, act the part. Work out where and how to get whatever supplies we need from the station." Doyle let Ruschen go. "Meanwhile, I'll try to buy us some time over there… *Commander.*"

Doyle and Eckerd left a stunned Ruschen in their wake. Summoning his resolve, the Commander inhaled and returned to the mess hall to organize the crew.

His crew.

Eckerd modified the data transmission module on his Subcooled Liquid Hibernation mainframe. "Access port is open. Now I…" Eckerd balked. "What will this do, exactly?"

"Trigger a safety drill on the Orbital Station," Doyle said.

"I'd heard you were a resourceful chap."

Doyle shrugged it off. "Nah. Spent so much time in charge aboard the Wheel, I know her drill codes by heart."

Eckerd snapped the final circuit board into place. "Done."

Doyle punched in the code, hoping it hadn't been changed since he'd left the UEC. "The moment our airlock seals, this should lock down the entire station. Only way any doors can be opened is from your console here. Got it?"

Eckerd nodded. Doyle patted his shoulder. "Good man."

Doyle hurried down the crew module's spine. He stopped at a vidscreen to gauge the look on Colby's face when he asked, "You okay to handle the dock alone?"

"Piece of piss," Colby said over the screen.

With any other pilot, his cheeky grin and glinting eyes would have warned Doyle that he was overconfident—but this was Colby. That expression meant he could do it blindfolded.

Satisfied, Doyle rushed along a side corridor and into Indigo's communications lab. "I need a favor."

Indigo turned from her station. "I've been trying to contact Earth, anyone, but no luck."

Doyle expected that; he had another idea. "When I first joined the UEC, my father and I would bounce ciphers off the old *Sagan-E* satellite."

Indigo smirked. "That ancient piece of space junk?"

"Our little joke, using billion dollar gear to transmit chess moves and baseball scores," Doyle grinned, but quickly remembered the gravity of the situation. "Maybe Dad left me a 'message in a bottle' on *Sagan-E*. Look for SHA-6 encryption."

"SHA-6? I heard about it in comms history class, but…"

"You'll work it out." Doyle typed in the encryption key he shared with his father.

Gaea-02 approached the UEC Orbital Station, the proverbial wheel in the sky. Spokes crisscrossed between a series of concentric rings, the outermost torus being the thickest. A barren Earth hung behind the station like a painted stage backdrop.

Nothing seemed amiss from the outside. *Gaea-02* began its intricate docking maneuvers—a dragonfly landing on a swirling flower.

Riana barreled into Doyle on his way from Indigo's lab.

"Doyle." She caught her breath. "What should I be doing?"

"Whatever your commander says."

Her lips tightened. "He told me to stay out of trouble."

"For once, we're in full agreement."

"Don't pretend we won't need all hands on deck," Riana said. "My husband doled out tasks to everyone but me. I'm not useless and don't want to be treated that way."

Doyle hadn't expected such vehemence from Riana. This was the second time she'd surprised him on this journey. As much as he appreciated her enthusiasm, there was nothing he could think of for a biochemist to do, without his taking the time to instruct her how to do it. Time they simply didn't have.

"Sorry. Not now." He didn't explain why. That was a mistake.

"I do know how to handle myself. I grew up on a naval base—"

Damn it, I don't need this, Doyle thought.

"—my father was a four-star admiral, you know—"

Yeah, he was an acquaintance of Dad's, but so what?

"—just because I'm female—"

That's got nothing to do with it.

"—and wear a lab coat—"

No time for this.

"—doesn't mean I crawl into a shell whenever—"

Doyle gripped Riana's wrist and forced her to keep in step with him. Barely two minutes remained until the dock was complete, and no way he could foresee ending this argument soon enough. *Fine. Have it your way.*

Doyle roughly escorted Riana to the bridge and sat her in

front of a monitor bank. "Once we're docked, you'll be patched into the station's security monitors. Watch 'em like a hawk."

"Right. Okay." She seemed more at ease with a job to do. Doyle felt stupid for not thinking of the task immediately. Maybe the pressure was affecting him too. This was new territory for all of them.

He addressed Colby at the flight controls. "Be ready to leave at any moment, kid."

"Roger that."

Doyle sprinted to the airlock, squeezing inside just as the bulkhead sealed shut behind him. He couldn't tell whether Commander Ruschen was glad he'd made it in time.

Members of the crew's hastily assembled strike force adjusted the communication bands behind their ears. They were a motley group of scientists and engineers, but most had received basic military training from the UEC. Sabin and Pach Jiménez, Usef, Alexei, huge Django, and petite Michi. Considering they were all unarmed, and no one knew what to expect on the other side of the airlock, Doyle could excuse their shaky hands and nervous glances.

Colby's voice issued from a speaker. "Candlemass deactivating in three . . . two . . . one."

The crew clung to handrails as the artificial gravity abated. Doyle always found these short freefall stints calming. He let himself drift, anchored by the rail so he didn't break his legs when the gravity returned.

"Doyle, you'll head the group to retrieve antimatter cells. Take Usef and the engineers," Ruschen ordered.

Doyle wondered if Ruschen even knew the Jiménez brothers' names, but Pach didn't take umbrage. "We're the fuel pumps," he said perkily to Doyle.

"The rest of us are on food and general supplies," Commander Ruschen finished.

Doyle got the crew's attention. "Travel one door at a time. Eckerd will open each one remotely, then close it right behind us. If anyone's lying in wait over there, we can avoid them."

Ruschen couldn't resist a dig. "If your plan works."

The ship shuddered into position as it docked with the Orbital Station's storage sector. A siren pierced Doyle's ears. The lights dimmed red, pulsing to darkness and back.

A computerized voice filtered through from the station. "Hull Puncture Drill in progress. Please follow standard procedure. Lockdown will end in thirty minutes."

Perfect. Doyle couldn't hide a relieved grin. Half an hour wasn't long, but it should be enough time to get in, grab what they needed, and get out.

"Wait..." Eckerd's voice came over their comms units. "There's atmosphere inside the station, but the artificial gravity must have been disabled. The torus should have started spinning automatically when we docked."

Commander Ruschen touched his control band to reply. "Can't you restore it manually?"

"Normally, no. But with this backdoor, I might be able to rig it." They listened as Eckerd tapped a sequence of keys on his modified mainframe.

The wide, outer torus of the Orbital Station began to revolve. As it picked up speed, the centrifugal force simulated gravity. Floating crates inside the station's docking bay touched down on the grating.

Clasped like a limpet on the huge torus shell, *Gaea-02* revolved in sync with the Wheel. As the gravity increased, the crew's booted feet eased onto the airlock floor.

Ruschen hesitated at the exit, watching his anxious crew for a long moment. Doyle nodded, eager to get on with it. Ruschen pressed the airlock release pad.

Grinding slowly, the giant bulkhead opened.

Gaea-02's crew members stepped cautiously into the station. Red, syncopated lights cast misshapen shadows, offering plenty of places for enemies to hide.

Doyle doubted anyone was in the docking bay, especially while the gravity had been nixed, but he didn't want any of his companions walking into the butt of an APA soldier's gun. He took point, scouting out the immediate area.

The Jiménez brothers spread out on Doyle's flanks to aid his search. The duo used cover effectively and kept tabs on each other's backs. *Good,* Doyle thought, *at least those two know how to handle themselves. That'll help.*

The station was old, built early in the century from the ashes of the International Space Station after its Near Earth Object collision. It had a grimy feel, with grated catchments and ceiling conduits running every which way. Constantly being added to over the years had given an unfinished texture to the patchwork modules. Hardware trinkets from each era lined a thieving magpie's nest. Doyle used to appreciate its quirky charm, but now it felt chaotic and cramped.

Finding the station's gravity deactivated still troubled him. On the one hand, it added weight to his initial theory that the support crew, worried about their families on Earth, had evacuated and braved unassisted reentry. He could empathize with that. Then why was there still atmosphere present? The air tasted slightly stale, but during extended unoccupied periods it was protocol to cease oxygen cycling completely. Did they simply forget in their panic? Sure, it's possible.

Unless that's what somebody wants us to think.

Doyle wasn't taking any chances. He completed his reconnaissance, linking up with Sabin and Pach. He whispered on Commander Ruschen's comms channel, "Clear," then wondered why he had instinctively lowered his voice. Was his subconscious trying to tell him something? He added to his communication, "Go slow."

Ruschen motioned for Alexei to check a junction door on the left. Alexei raised on the balls of his feet to peer through the clear porthole. He gestured that it seemed vacant and tapped his comms band. "Eckerd, open junction A2."

The door slid up. Ruschen led Michi and Django toward it.

From the other side of the docking bay, Doyle noticed Django's uneasy, stilted gait. The Coriolis force produced by torus rotation could cause dizziness and nausea. The rest of *Gaea-02*'s crew seemed unaffected but the biggest of them, Django, clearly felt the odd, veering pull on his body. Being so large shouldn't have made a difference. It finally dawned on Doyle: the reason Django was on their test run at all was that he urgently needed the physical experience in these environments. Had the terraformer never been in space before?

Doyle opened a private channel to Django. "Keep your head still when you move. Just focus on where you want to go. Your body will do the rest. You'll be fine, the queasiness will pass." Django nodded slightly, then stiffened his neck and continued walking.

Commander Ruschen's party passed into the A2 junction and Eckerd sealed the door behind them.

Doyle led his group to a starboard junction. "Open A3." The door whisked up, then down once the quartet had entered.

They skulked along a passageway lit only by the maddening, red security beacons. No sound, apart from the constant background hum of automated air scrubbers.

Doyle knew his way around the station by rote, even in this nightmarish, abandoned state. There were no signs of conflict, no laser-scarring or bullet impacts. Everything appeared to be in place, minus the people.

Pach and Sabin trailed Doyle, with Usef dawdling at the rear. Usef didn't seem interested; he obstinately maintained that this was all a conspiracy theory. Doyle couldn't decide if he was being genuine or was simply too scared to admit the truth.

The dim, crimson crossways bordered on labyrinthine. Slowly moving from bulkhead to sealed bulkhead, Doyle's group passed through countless cloistered rooms and corridors before reaching their destination.

Doyle established a comms channel to Eckerd on *Gaea-02*. "We're at the engineering bay." He was whispering again.

They hadn't seen any evidence of enemy occupation along their route, yet a foreboding aura lingered. *Maybe it's the mood lighting*, Doyle thought, trying to embarrass himself out of the idea that something sinister was afoot.

The door to the engineering bay slid open. Doyle eyed his men. Sabin and Pach nodded their readiness, while Usef remained aloof. Doyle led them inside and made a cursory check of the area. "Riana, you read me?"

"I'm here." Her voice came through Doyle's comms band with a hint of static interference.

"Can you see *anyone* on your monitors? Dead or alive?"

"No. No one, and nothing to indicate any disturbance. It's like an orbital *Mary Celeste*."

"Exactly what I was thinking." Doyle flipped over a blank repair manifest on a discarded clipboard. "A ghost ship ..."

"I don't have full coverage, though. Some rooms are pitch black and a handful of cameras aren't functional."

"Keep watching." Doyle closed the channel.

Pach whistled loudly from an antechamber. "Over here!"

Doyle and Sabin followed him into a storeroom, where the air felt almost voltaic. Pach grinned and wagged his thumb toward his discovery. "We hit the mother lode, amigos."

Two wide racks were stocked high with cylindrical antimatter cells.

Two thrumming mag carts hovered above electromagnetic rails embedded in the torus floor. Commander Ruschen coordinated Django, Alexei, and Michi as they loaded food satchels, medical supplies, and packets of D-salt to recharge *Gaea-02*'s fluid recycling system.

A sharp, metal clang from elsewhere in the station startled the group. Tense, they strained to listen ... but the sound didn't repeat.

Michi knew space stations were like old houses—unexplained noises were common—but her grandfather's tales of *oni* demons and spectral *yūrei* slithered into her consciousness. Ojiisan's shadow play ogres came to life in the pulsing, red light, their unsheathed claws groping across the room …

Django saw Michi's vacant stare and quivering lip. He placed his massive hand gently on her shoulder. Michi glanced up at his concerned face and felt silly. She grinned to assure Django she was okay.

Michi silently vowed that for the rest of this mission, wherever it took her, she'd remain strong. Not swayed by trivial emotions. Like M.I.T.Z., left behind to watch over *Gaea-02*'s engines, they could always depend on her.

She moved a case of rations onto a mag cart. "It doesn't make sense. The station crew knew we were returning. Surely they would have left an envoy behind. And if the APA really are here, wouldn't they have tried to stop us by now? Why haven't we seen anyone from either side?"

"Maybe there is no one to see," Alexei said.

Michi left her immediate thought unsaid: *Or maybe they don't want to be seen.*

Riana skimmed through the station monitors, jumping camera views every second for maximum coverage.

One of the first things she'd done when *Gaea-02* docked was, with Indigo's aid, access the Orbital Station's data banks. No log entries had been made for three months, although it was unclear whether more recent data had been erased.

Riana could tell that particular detail had made Baden uneasy when she relayed an update. She hoped her husband could cope.

She hoped he was safe.

Riana kept sequencing the monitors. If other people were on the station, she was going to find them.

Doyle and the Jiménez brothers packed a mag cart with antimatter stocks. Doyle strained to lift a heavy power cell.

"Careful," Sabin said. "One of those—"

"—could blow the whole station," Pach finished his brother's warning.

With due care, Doyle laid his antimatter cell on the cart. He was impressed by how coolly the brothers were reacting, as if this were just another routine supply run.

An announcement buzzed over the station speakers. "Drill lockdown will end in fifteen minutes."

Doyle quickly counted the stacked cells. They were ahead of schedule. "Riana, Eckerd," Doyle tried raising them on *Gaea-02*'s comms system, "we're almost done here." Severe static clogged the line. "Riana? Anyone there?"

"Save your breath," Sabin said.

"These raw power cells block transmissions like nuthin' else," Pach added.

Doyle wiped his brow. It was okay, they'd be out of there in a few more minutes. He squinted into the bleak light. "Where's Usef?"

Usef wandered around the far end of the engineering bay. He mumbled to himself repeatedly, "Big deal about nothing … this is ridiculous … paranoid shits."

His older brothers used to pull these sorts of tricks on him as a child, whenever they returned to the vineyard on shore leave. Some concocted story about a rampaging Minotaur would lead gullible little Usef on a fearful hide-and-seek chase through the grapevine maze. One time, he was so convinced the legendary hairy beast was lurking around a corner, he'd wet himself. His brothers almost died laughing. Usef wanted to dig a hole big enough for one, crawl in, and never see the light of day again.

He wasn't about to be that scared little boy now. No, just like then, there was really nothing to be scared *of.*

He leaned against a bulkhead that partitioned off an adjacent module and rested his head beside the circular window.

A palm suddenly slapped against the clear pane.

Usef recoiled, scrambling away from the bulkhead when he

saw four slender fingers sliding down the other side of the plastiglass. He gathered his wits, regulated his breathing. *There is no Minotaur.*

Usef sidled up to the window to peek inside. A terrified female stared back at him from behind the blockade.

"Help me." The woman's voice was muffled by thick plastiglass. "I'm trapped."

Usef could make out the collar of her UEC uniform in the scant light that spilled from the engineering bay. He thought he'd seen this woman on the station before they left, but he couldn't be positive.

"What happened here?" Usef asked through the bulkhead.

"We were in the middle of a shift changeover when this lockdown hit. Most of the others left this morning. The new crew is due soon."

"That's why the gravity was off?"

"Two-ton machinery is easier to unload when it's weightless."

"You're saying it's business as usual?"

"It was until a few minutes ago." The woman stepped closer to the window, trying to peer into the engineering bay. "What's going on? Is there really a hull breach?"

"No. No, nothing like that," Usef said with a chuckle. His fears were allayed. "It's okay, there's no danger. What's your name?"

"Katy McLelland. Can't you let me out?"

Usef considered it. He knew he should inform Commander Ruschen first, but Ruschen was such a hardass he'd probably let the girl stew while they ran a billion quarantine protocols.

"I'd feel better out there with you," Katy said. Was she flirting with him? Usef hovered on the edge of being convinced. As he told the woman, there was no real danger. More to the point, she *was* kind of attractive. It had been a long time between drinks, and Usef sure was thirsty. They could get to know one another better while the others crept around in the dark afraid of their own shadows.

Usef checked the direction Doyle and the Jiménez brothers had gone. No sign of them. And no good reason not to help out a fellow UEC officer—no, make that a damsel in distress.

"Eckerd?" Usef moistened his lips. "Please open door E6."

Riana overheard Usef's transmission. She switched over to the engineering bay's monitor. Usef's head bobbed and his mouth moved, but the cameras didn't pick up sound. She muttered to herself, "Who are you talking to . . . ?"

Riana changed her view to the module beyond bulkhead E6. In a small pool of light filtering into the otherwise dark room, she saw the stranger. Why didn't he report finding someone? *What the hell are you playing at, Usef?*

There was movement on the monitor. Three figures emerged from the darkness. One of them held a knife to the woman's back.

Riana's eyes widened. She opened an intraship comms channel. "Eckerd, belay Usef's request! Do not open that door!"

"Too late, the command has been transmitted. What's wrong?"

"They're not alone."

Eckerd's voice wavered. "I can't close the bulkhead again until its open cycle is complete. There's nothing I can do from here."

Riana opened a channel to Doyle. "Usef's springing a trap at E6. Get your people there now." No response. "Doyle? Did you hear me?"

She checked the station map. Commander Ruschen's boarding party was on the other side of the torus. She was the closest to Doyle's group. She was the only one who could do anything.

Riana hesitated for the briefest moment before racing out of the bridge. She sprinted along the crew module's spine toward the airlock.

Riana's voice was broadcast over the comms bands of Commander Ruschen's entire team, though the message was clearly intended for him alone. "Baden, we have company on the station. At least three wearing… it looked like they were in APA uniforms. Soldiers."

"Understood," Ruschen replied.

"They're gaining access near Doyle's group, but he's not responding. Baden—"

"Maintain proper comms protocol, Doctor. Critical transmissions direct to personal bands only."

The next message came only to Commander Ruschen's ears, and the ire in Riana's voice was evident, "I'm on my way to warn him."

"Negative. Remain on the ship." Ruschen cut communications.

Michi, Django, and Alexei put down the supplies they were loading and looked expectantly at Commander Ruschen. He could tell what they were thinking, but he wasn't about to let them run off half-cocked and jeopardize the entire operation. Logical thought was required. He had lapsed briefly on *Gaea-02*—an anomaly, nothing more—but he was confident of his role now. "You have your orders. Continue loading supplies."

Michi spoke up. "What about Doyle and the rest? They'll need our help."

Regardless of the betrayal Ruschen felt when Doyle forsook the Gaea mission, he still had complete faith in the man's UEC training. The best of the best was a fact, not a slogan. "Doyle was a soldier himself. If any of us can handle the situation, he can."

The others clearly weren't pleased with Commander Ruschen's decision but he knew it was correct. They were too far away to assist, and attempting to would only put more of his people in danger. Besides, they needed these supplies. There was no difference in the grand scheme of things between being shot today and starving to death in a month.

Yes, Ruschen assured himself, *my way, the majority of my crew has a chance of survival.*

The Gaea mission will continue.

It must.

¤ ¤ ¤

The E6 bulkhead's mechanisms whirred. Usef glanced around the engineering bay once more. Good. All alone.

The door slowly rose. Usef's grin widened as more of Katy's long legs were revealed.

His face fell when six heavy boots stepped beside hers.

Riana rushed into the Orbital Station from *Gaea-02*'s airlock. The decision to ignore her husband's command wasn't made lightly, but it was justified. She felt like she'd been following orders from men—her father, Baden—all her life, even when she didn't agree with them. But there had never been lives at stake before.

She'd asked Doyle to give her something worthwhile to do and here it was. She could prevent a third of their crew from being captured, or worse.

She used her comms band. "Eckerd, clear me a path straight to Doyle's team—and leave it open."

Riana jogged along the same route Doyle had taken earlier. Eckerd made each bulkhead slide open in advance of her arrival, to keep a brisk, unhindered pace.

She was almost out of breath when she judged Doyle's group was close enough to hear her shout. "Doyle! Soldiers on board!"

Riana filled her lungs with oxygen and she shouted louder.

Doyle heard her. At least, he thought he heard someone. He carefully set down the antimatter cell he carried and hushed Sabin and Pach. *Yes, there it was.* "Sounds like Riana," he said. "What's she doing on board?"

Pach scrunched up his face, straining to hear. "Something about . . . *soldiers*?"

All three men dashed out. They reached the main segment of the engineering bay at the same time that Riana burst in from the opposite direction.

Between them, an Asian Pacific Alliance soldier held Usef hostage with a dragon-hilted blade pressed against his flabby throat. The titanium metal drew blood. Usef murmured with bubbling noises, afraid to form words.

Two more black-uniformed APA soldiers—one female and a second male—circled the room, assault rifles raised and supported at their shoulders. Their legs were oddly unsteady as they scuttled across the floor, herding the Gaea personnel into one group.

"Wobbly," Sabin observed quietly.

Doyle whispered back, "Haven't got their sea legs yet." They must have been waiting in freefall as a ruse for longer than they expected and weren't used to the rotational gravity. Ruschen's six-day delay on the Turn may have been a blessing in disguise.

Katy, Usef's alluring siren, cowered in the corner. No longer useful, she seemed forgotten by the others. Occasionally, her muted sob broke the silent tension.

Doyle noted that the soldiers were gradually moving toward the passageway Riana had used: a direct route to *Gaea-02*. He wished he could let them enter the corridor, then drop the bulkheads and trap them—but not while they held a hostage. Even a sleaze like Usef's life was worth no less than the rest of the crew's. There had to be another way.

Doyle ran through the possible scenarios. None were pretty.

Usef's captor shouted in Mandarin. Doyle knew a handful of words in the language, but none of what was spoken. He looked to Sabin and Pach to see if they understood, but the brothers were equally clueless.

"He said to open all the doors on the station," Riana calmly translated. "They want the ship."

The soldier holding Usef at knifepoint kept backing toward the junction. Usef shuffled along to keep his throat from being slashed as they moved. The other two soldiers remained stationary and leveled their assault rifles at Doyle and Riana.

Fearless, Sabin and Pach leaned forward as though they were about to spring an attack. Doyle held them back. He looked at the brothers sternly, his message clear: *not yet.*

Riana whispered to Doyle, "Why don't we just do as he asked? The way to *Gaea-02* is already open."

"They know that."

"Then why does he need . . . ?"

"Because there are more soldiers hiding on the station. He wants to let them loose."

Doyle saw Riana's face alter as her realization sank in: if Doyle hadn't put the station in lockdown, they might all be dead by now. She clearly wasn't used to thinking this way. Like a soldier. Doyle was a bit rusty himself but quickly getting up to speed. Although his own little posse was defenseless, he reasoned they must hold some bargaining power. The APA wouldn't have taken Usef hostage otherwise. That slim advantage wouldn't last long. The doors would all open automatically in another twelve minutes.

However questionable the APA's dictators were, Doyle knew their foot soldiers upheld a strict code of honor. Even when they'd invaded Taiwan, their rules of engagement had been clear and precise. If *Gaea-02*'s crew posed a threat, they would be eliminated on the spot. But if they were cooperative, they would certainly be taken as diplomatic prisoners. Ironically, that was their safest passage to Earth, and once on land, escape—or liberation—became a realistic option.

He'd be one step closer to Lon.

Doyle turned to Riana. "Tell him the APA can have *Gaea-02* without our interference—if they guarantee our safety."

Doyle didn't count on Riana's reaction.

"No," she said firmly.

Doyle stared at her. "Do it."

"I can't make that decision, Doyle."

"Yes, you can."

"No. And neither can you."

Damn it, the choice to surrender went against everything in his nature, but at least it gave them a fighting chance. *Gaea-02* was their only leverage.

Usef's captor shouted again in Mandarin as he backed into

the junction archway. He butted up against something solid. He looked over his shoulder, where a dark-skinned face glared down at him.

Django.

The man-mountain had disobeyed Commander Ruschen's orders. Without a word, he rammed the soldier's face square into the wall, introducing him to oblivion. The dagger clattered on the floor. Relieved, Usef clasped his blood-slick neck.

In unison, the Jiménez brothers rushed at the other two soldiers while they were distracted. Sabin pinned the female to the wall, pressing her own gun across her chest.

Pach seized the male's arm, wrestling for his assault rifle. The soldier released his gun and drew a dagger in the same movement. Pach pressed his advantage with a straight thrust of his fist. The soldier parried, made a sharp riposte, and sank his blade deep into Pach's neck.

Twisting the handle, he ripped Pach's throat asunder. Blood gushed, black under the red security lights.

Spatters of blood sprayed across Katy's face while she huddled in the corner. She screamed and stumbled away. Sabin turned, an image of pure horror forever etched on his psyche: his brother's torn-apart trachea gurgling as air escaped.

"Pach!" Sabin released the female soldier and rushed to Pach's aid. Recovering rapidly, the soldier aimed her assault rifle at Sabin's back. Doyle lunged and punched her across the jaw, knocking her unconscious. This was no time to be a gentleman.

Pach slumped to the floor like a marionette with severed strings.

The remaining soldier stepped between Sabin and his brother, brandishing the blood-drenched knife. Sabin leaped at the enemy, barreled him across the room. The knife went flying. The men caromed off a wall and fell into a fierce grapple on the floor.

Doyle opened a comms channel to Dr. Farrad on *Gaea-02*. Static was loud, but he was far enough from the antimatter cells to get through. "Doc, we got a man down. Get your butt over here."

Riana knelt beside Pach's immobile torso. His neck was mincemeat, eyes glazed. An ocean of blood pooled under his head. She shook her head grimly at Doyle. Pach was already dead.

Doyle nudged his comms band, "Cancel that, Doc. Stay where you are."

Sabin rolled his brother's killer onto his back, viced his head between both hands, and slammed it into an electromagnetic rail. The soldier's eyes rolled into their sockets but Sabin didn't stop. He lifted the man's head and rammed it down, over and over, until the skull cracked and blood jetted from his mouth. Doyle didn't realize what was happening until too late.

Sabin wiped the soldier's blood from his own mouth. He crawled over to Pach's lifeless body and cradled it. "I got your back now, little bro. Everything's all right…"

Doyle glared at Usef. That module didn't open by itself. This was his doing.

Colby pushed his chair back. He'd done all he could; nothing left except to wait.

He took stock of the bridge. Dr. Ruschen had run out of there with her panties in a knot. Colby barely noticed her departure, so focused was he on initiating parts of the launch sequence in advance so they could make a clean getaway.

Sometimes, when he was behind the joystick, he'd enter a kind of fugue state. When Colby had been a nipper in Oz, his Dad had thought Colby was borderline autistic. He *became* the craft. He forged his identity in the air. That's what the bloody therapist reckoned, anyway. All Colby knew was, the world was a gray haze before he had learned to fly, but afterward, he soared in vibrant color.

About to tee up a music playlist on his comms band to ease his nerves, Colby thought he'd better check Riana's vacated monitors first, to see how the teams were getting on.

He saw plenty of activity, but not from *Gaea-02*'s crew.

"Holy…" Colby blinked, not sure if he was hallucinating. He cycled camera views. Nope, it was real.

Asian Pacific Alliance soldiers swarmed several rooms. They'd ditched their hiding spots and ripped computer panels from doors, hacking into the circuitry.

Colby opened a comms channel to all crew. "Guys, we got soldiers *everywhere*. They're comin' out of the woodwork."

Commander Ruschen responded person-to-person. "Copy that. Can you see Doyle's group?"

Colby switched to the engineering bay camera. "Yeah. A couple of blokes down, but looks like most of ours are sweet, I think."

"Is Ri—Dr. Ruschen with them?"

"Yeah, she's okay."

A slight pause before Commander Ruschen said, "We're heading back now. Make sure the airlock is clear."

Doyle's comms band buzzed. Commander Ruschen's voice was fed into his ear. "Doyle, did you copy Colby's update?"

The floor was covered in blood. Doyle cleared his sandpaper throat. "Yes."

"Get your team back to *Gaea-02* ASAP."

"Wilco. Gladly."

Doyle motioned Django, Riana, and Usef toward the antimatter storeroom. "Finish stacking the last few cells and let's go." Riana was busy examining Usef's neck wound. "Leave it," Doyle growled. "He won't bleed to death. Get moving."

Sabin rocked back and forth with Pach's body in his arms. He rambled on to his dead brother, "Remember when you were seven an' we fixed up *Tío* Jorge's old Cessna? *Tía* Marta cooked us *sopaipillas* as a reward. Taste 'em now, Pach?"

Although Doyle wasn't technically in command, Pach's demise weighed on his conscience. He'd never lost a man before, not even a co-pilot. Who was he kidding? He'd barely ever been in real combat, not since the early days of the UEC. Doyle hated himself for not being able to prevent the death. Maybe if he hadn't been so willing to surrender, if his personal desires hadn't clouded his judgment.

Doyle knelt by Sabin's side and squeezed his shoulder. Sabin didn't seem to notice.

A transmission from Eckerd crackled over Doyle's comms band. "They're trying to override our lockdown. I can't block them from here."

"Do what you can." Doyle said softly in Sabin's ear, "Sabin. We gotta go. *Now.*"

Riana and Usef returned, guiding the full mag cart along the station's electromagnetic rail. They took care to bypass the track where the soldier's shattered skull still lay. With his immense strength, Django hauled a surplus antimatter cell on one broad shoulder.

Doyle attempted to help Sabin stand but, in traumatic shock, Sabin refused to budge. Losing Pach must have been like losing a limb. Doyle signaled to Django. "Give me a hand?"

Django lifted Sabin by the collar with his free hand, set him on his feet, and prodded him. Sabin walked in a trance, sometimes stopping and needing another gentle jab to remind his legs to trundle forward again.

Doyle hurried his team along. No time to worry about Pach's corpse or finding the woman Usef released. Deep inside this hornet's nest, they could be besieged at any moment.

Speeding around a corner, the cart veered from the rail and dipped sideways. An antimatter power cell tumbled off—Riana gasped.

Doyle caught the volatile cell an inch before it hit the floor. He gingerly replaced it on the cart. "Take the corners slower. No sense blowing everyone up."

As they traversed the winding corridors, he had to continually usher Sabin onward, balancing pace against compassion. All the while, Doyle kept expecting a door they'd just passed to open and gunfire to ring out. Those strobing, red lights were never more disconcerting.

They reached the docking bay and met up with Commander Ruschen's group at the airlock. Greetings were perfunctory as the combined crew worked double time loading supplies and power cells onto *Gaea-02*.

Doyle pulled Ruschen aside. "Baden…we lost Pach Jimen—"

"I know. Carry on." Ruschen betrayed no emotion whatsoever. *Just a grease monkey, right?* That infuriated Doyle, but he had to admit such composure befitted a commander. If only he could shrug it off as easily himself. Vexed, Doyle glanced away. He didn't see Sabin in the airlock.

Doyle stepped into the station's docking bay, but there was no sign of him there either. "Sabin's gone," he said loudly. "Anyone see where…?" His question trailed off, since he already knew the answer. Sabin had returned to Pach.

The station's mechanical voice reverberated around the docking bay. "Drill lockdown will cease in five minutes."

Doyle raced for the A3 junction. His mind knew it was wrong but his body kept going.

Commander Ruschen shouted after him, "Doyle, get back here! We can't wait for you!"

Doyle heard, but didn't slow down. He knew Ruschen wasn't being melodramatic. *Gaea-02* would leave without him. He wanted to let the crew know that was okay; they should do whatever they had to do. He opened a comms channel to the bridge, but allowed the entire crew to hear his message. "Colby, get ready to disengage… whether I'm on board or not."

Doyle sprinted through the Orbital Station, backtracking along Riana's open route. When he reached the engineering bay, Sabin was struggling to lift his brother's body. "Sabin…"

"Can't leave him here."

"Listen to me—"

"Can't leave him here," Sabin repeated, monotone.

Arguing would be useless. Doyle grabbed hold of Pach's feet, while Sabin cradled the corpse's shoulders. They hoisted the body between them. If Doyle had to drag one of the two brothers, he figured it might as well be Pach. They still had a couple of minutes of lockdown, enough to reach *Gaea-02* if they were lucky.

They weren't.

Doors and bulkheads started grinding open all around. Doyle angrily opened a comms channel. "Eckerd, what're you—"

"It's not me, Doyle," Eckerd's transmission crackled. "They're in."

The sound of stampeding boots on metal approached fast. Doyle locked eyes with Sabin and issued a single command:

"Run."

They hauled Pach's body out of there.

Doyle and Sabin bustled through narrow passageways, slowed by lugging the corpse. Doyle could hear the soldiers' bootsteps gaining. Only the relatively short junctions kept them out of shooting range. Mandarin shouts echoed off the walls. They'd surely seen the mess Sabin made of their comrade. Surrender was out of the question.

Doyle glanced over his shoulder. A squad of APA soldiers rounded the corner and opened fire immediately. Bullets lodged in the wall beside Doyle's head. He and Sabin careened around a junction, out of sight.

Doyle huffed as he ran. "We gotta drop the body."

"No."

"*We're* still breathing," Doyle said.

Sabin shook his head, dazed. "I gotta ... gotta fix Pach."

Doyle realized no amount of logic would open Sabin's eyes. So he lied. "We'll come back for your brother later. I promise."

Doyle's insincere words tasted foul on his parched tongue, but they did the trick. Sabin gently sat Pach's corpse against the wall.

Doyle grasped Sabin's arm and forced him into a loping run. They rounded another corner and sped for a T-junction. They nearly made it.

A voice behind them yelled a sole demand in Mandarin. It was one of the few words Doyle understood: "Stop!"

A warning shot blasted into a side wall. Doyle and Sabin froze at the sobering sound and slowly turned with their palms raised high. Four APA soldiers stood at the end of the corridor with their guns trained.

Junction markers riveted to panels on the T-intersection indicated that the wall behind Doyle was also the edge of the torus hull. He knew one stray bullet near Sabin and himself could breach the hull for real, not just a drill.

The soldiers edged forward, barking orders outside of Doyle's limited Mandarin vocabulary. They must have recognized the warning panels; otherwise they'd have already gunned Sabin and him down.

A gear shifted, clanging as it lowered an emergency bulkhead from the ceiling to block the intersection in front of Doyle. The APA soldiers had no chance of reaching it in time.

Doyle was stunned. Eckerd's voice thundered from his comms band. "Move! That won't hold them for long."

Doyle forced Sabin down a side corridor and raced along behind. He heard the bulkhead rise and the soldiers continue their pursuit, but Eckerd's diversion had created enough of a head start to elude them, always staying one junction ahead.

The torus curvature made Doyle feel as if he were running up an endless hill. He heard more bootsteps from another direction. They were too far off to be a threat, provided *Gaea-02* was still docked and waiting. Everything hinged on that.

Doyle and Sabin surged into the docking bay, almost colliding with strewn cargo in the faint, red light.

Gaea-02's airlock was wide open, Commander Ruschen standing ready by the controls. Doyle had never been so ecstatic to see his stern eyes and gaunt, locked jaw.

Urging Sabin forward, Doyle sprinted the final few yards toward *Gaea-02*. Ruschen hit a panel to lower the airlock bulkhead. Doyle shoved Sabin inside the ship and dived in after him.

Propped on his elbows, Doyle nodded breathless thanks to Ruschen.

Gunfire cracked across the docking bay. Bullets sparked off

the descending airlock door. One shot grazed Doyle's upper arm, ripping through his flight jacket sleeve. Ignoring the sting, he bear-hugged Sabin and rolled them both out of the line of fire.

The nearest APA soldier rushed for the closing airlock. He slid like a baseball player going for home plate—until the bulkhead dropped its final inches, crushing his outstretched leg. The limb was severed cleanly; his agony resounded outside.

"Fly, Colby!" Doyle shouted hoarsely into his comms band.

Gaea-02 snapped free of the station's coupling. Without braking the rotating torus, Colby pushed off the station and let momentum boost the ship until their chem assist engines kicked in. It made for a rocky ride, but they were free and clear into the void.

Freefall lifted the burden of gravity from Doyle's weary limbs. He found himself floating alone with Sabin and Ruschen in the airlock. He hoped Colby would delay reactivating the Candlemass.

Drifting, Doyle let the adrenaline drain from his system.

Blood spilled from his flesh wound and danced around him in tiny, perfectly formed orbs. He closed his eyes, ignoring Commander Ruschen's attempts to debrief and chastise him for irresponsible actions. Doyle wasn't even fazed by the soldier's amputated leg suspended in midair beside them like a grotesque trophy. No, nothing at that moment could displace one simple, primal feeling:

We survived.

The fact that his son was still four hundred kilometers below, on a war-torn planet, was just one more obstacle to overcome—and he would, or die trying.

UEC//Gaea Subcommittee Report on Ecological Challenges, 2034// Section 6f "Water"//summary, p.283:

PROPOSAL: D-salt.

BRIEF: Synthesized ionic compound. Meticulously absorbs all elements from a liquid except hydrogen and oxygen, leaving 100% pure water.

ADVANTAGES

- Treatment of both effluent and seawater.
- Unlike desalination, D-salt's compact, solid by-product is easily disposed of via burial or solar furnace.
- Tactical restriction of highly portable supply; possible to exert control over belligerent UEC member nations.

DISADVANTAGES

- 1 kilogram of D-salt necessitates 5 years of refinement and relative cost of Û1 billion.
- Production requires quantity of untreated freshwater. Catch 22.
- Projections from current stockpile and production capacity predict worldwide demand will exhaust supply within 60 years.

RECOMMENDATION: Implement D-salt distribution as stopgap measure until *Gaea-01* Mars project yields results [*ref. sec. 7b*; newly discovered M38 as possible alternative].

UG021234//S6F//P683

CHAPTER 5
LOS CABOS

Floating in *Gaea-02*'s airlock, Sabin squeezed his eyes tightly shut so he could pretend that everything was normal.

No. This isn't real. It isn't happening.

Sabin knew he was fooling himself, and he was no fool. Pach wouldn't ever be back. This time, he couldn't save his little brother.

Cinnamon and orange peel, melted butter. The humble kitchen always smelled so good. Fried bread soaked in honey, nothing better in the universe.

Tía Marta and *Tío* Jorge were the only parents Sabin and Pach Jiménez ever knew. The four worked side by side on the dusty airstrip they called home.

"*Ocho tazas de agua,*" Marta recited as she carefully measured out eight cups of water, their family's daily allowance.

Mimicking a *luchador*, Pach carelessly elbowed a full cup and its contents soaked into the floorboards. His uncle Jorge slapped the back of his head and Pach ran outside sobbing.

Twelve-year-old Sabin brazenly raised his fists to defend his younger brother, but Jorge clutched his collar and dragged him onto the veranda. He sat both boys down, and they were surprised to see he wasn't angry. Jorge sighed and dusted off the legs of his overalls. "Do you know where that water comes from?"

Sabin braved an answer. "San Jose del Cabo." He'd seen the signs plastered on the truck that delivered their monthly ration.

His uncle nodded. "And where did *they* get it from?"

Pach sniffled and shrugged. The boys saw rain only once a year, each time lasting for a week. The liquid that fell from the sky tasted so different—pure and sweet—that it couldn't have come from the same source.

"The ocean," *Tío* Jorge said, sparing them the knowledge that a growing percentage was poorly treated waste. "But every time we take and clean that water, we put back more salt. What do you think happens when there's too much salt in the ocean?"

"The fish taste better?" Sabin proposed.

Jorge chuckled. "The fish die, *sobrino*. And the weather, she changes. El Niño. So 'less you want me whipped up in a hurricane next time I fly over Costa Azul, *don't spill the water*, eh?"

Their uncle was teasing them, of course, but the boys understood that water was precious. The Mexican landscape was so arid apart from that one wet week per year. Every few days they would hear of someone in Cabo San Lucas dying because they had nothing to drink. The wells were dry, and everyone was waiting for a miracle.

"The cargo is loaded, Jorge," Señor Reynald called from the hangar. Hombres like Reynald didn't pray for rain; they sold it. Sabin knew nothing of hydropolitics, but he'd heard *Tía* Marta refer to Señor Reynald as *agüero*, the local term for water smugglers. What had been the tourist strip of Los Cabos had become a black market bazaar.

Once per month, Reynald and his men would load an unmarked crate into Jorge's Cessna and have him deliver it to an equally remote southern airstrip, avoiding the customs checkpoints. Whenever Sabin asked what the cargo was, Jorge's answer was the same. "I don't ask, don't touch, don't need to know. I just fly the plane, *comprende?*" Sabin figured it was usually bottled water for the rich people who wanted more than their fair quota.

This month was different.

Señor Reynald handed Jorge an envelope with money, as expected, but the *agüero* seemed more nervous than normal. When Reynald saw Sabin looking curiously at him, he snapped, "*Que chingados quieres!*"

Jorge calmed Reynald and urged his nephews toward the hangar, "Go get the plane ready for tonight."

Sabin and Pach whipped through their maintenance routine. The boys had been the airstrip's sole mechanics for the past two years. It wasn't just a way to save money. They were the most skillful grease monkeys in Los Cabos and everyone knew it. It didn't matter that they were only eleven and twelve years old.

Stowing a toolkit in the Cessna's cargo hold, Sabin saw the package Señor Reynald wanted delivered. This one was much smaller than usual, a box of only ten square inches, loosely wrapped in tarpaulin.

Sabin had to know what was inside. Pach begged him to stop, but he lifted the tarp. Sabin saw an official UEC stamp and a partially torn label that meant nothing to him:

D-SALT.

Tío Jorge flew the *aguacorridos* without navigation lights, under cover of night when the moon was full. Gray duct tape obscured the plane's registration number.

Since he never knew when the old Cessna would refuse to make the return trip, Jorge always took his nephews along for repairs. The boys would sleep on the way down, to arrive at sunrise.

The Cessna was flying low, assisted by a zippy tailwind, when a much larger twin-engine surveillance plane filled Jorge's rear window. "*Los Federales,*" he muttered.

Sabin and Pach woke sharply at the jolt of *Tío* Jorge slamming his Cessna's throttle forward. The two aircraft engines howled as their cat-and-mouse chase sped above desolate mesas and dry riverbeds.

Jorge had no hope of outflying the authorities. He aimed for a dirt road behind a sugarcane field. As soon as the Cessna landed, its doors popped open and *Tío* Jorge, Sabin, and Pach bolted for the sugar fields.

They heard the larger plane land and the Federal Agents shouting in pursuit.

Scrambling wildly in the dark, Sabin and Pach lost sight of their uncle among the canes. Jorge risked capture by yelling his nephews' names. The boys sprinted in the direction of his voice, but in his haste Pach tripped and sprained his ankle.

Sabin clutched his brother close, dragging him under a swad of broken cane. They remained hidden as the agents ran past, hollering threats. Sabin dared a peek through the cane. The unkempt men's uniforms seemed threadbare, and their weapons were a crude assortment of rifles and machetes. He doubted they were real agents, but criminal rivals of Señor Reynald out to hijack the contraband that had made the *agüero* so edgy at the airstrip. *What made this D-salt stuff worth fighting over?*

Gunshots reverberated. Sabin cupped his hand over Pach's mouth to muffle his cry. "Everything'll be okay, just stay quiet and trust me, bro," Sabin whispered. "I'll protect you."

Pach clung to his older brother, huddled beneath their camouflage, until the taunting *agua-toads* gave up their search.

An explosion shook the ground. The blaze from Jorge's torched Cessna kissed the black sky. Sabin was certain his uncle was dead. He cradled his distraught brother and whispered, "I'll never leave your side, Pach. Never."

Every beat of his heart painfully reminded Sabin he was still alive.

His eyes opened for a moment to glance around the airlock. Doyle and Commander Ruschen were drifting in freefall beside him. *Where was that* cabrón *who let the soldiers out? Usef's gonna pay, little bro. Don't know when and don't know how, but Usef's gonna pay with his own useless life.*

Sabin wanted to sleep. Part of him—the part ripped from his soul by that APA soldier's blade—hoped never to wake up. Pach was with *Tío* Jorge and *Tía* Marta now, and Sabin didn't know how the hell he was supposed to continue living without him.

CHAPTER 6
CUCULIDAE

Gravity tugged hard at Doyle's dangling heels. His feet touched down and he reached out at once to stabilize Sabin, who looked as if he were about to collapse in a heap under his own weight.

By the time they reached *Gaea-02*'s supply bay, Sabin's grasp on reality had seeped back. He sneered at Doyle with an angry realization. "We're never goin' back for Pach. You lied to me."

"Yeah," Doyle replied, "but you're alive."

As though that made the lie okay. Clearly, Sabin didn't think so. He swiped Doyle's arm away and wandered off.

The crew members who had boarded the Wheel were busy stowing the supplies they'd salvaged. Dr. Farrad was also on hand. He cleansed the blood from Usef's neck and wrapped gauze around his skin-deep wound.

Doyle wondered how Usef could have been so ratbrained. If it was up to him, he'd have the chemist court-martialed for dereliction of duty. But with such a small crew, they'd need everyone available in the coming months. Besides, Usef would live with the guilt of Pach's death forever on his conscience. To Doyle, that was punishment far worse than anything the UEC could dish out.

Usef caught Doyle's reproachful gaze. He mumbled while Doc dressed his lesion, "Sorry... so sorry..."

"Try not to speak," Dr. Farrad said before moving on to his next patient. He removed Doyle's lucky flight jacket, revealing a deep gash in Doyle's forearm.

Doyle nodded sideways to Sabin, who brooded on a catwalk. "Check him out first, Doc."

"He's in shock," Dr. Farrad said. "Not much I can do for the poor boy right now."

"Drugs?"

Dr. Farrad shook his head. "Time."

Doyle held out his injured arm. Dr. Farrad ran a hand laser along the bullet graze to cauterize the wound. The odor of his own burning flesh stung Doyle's nostrils, but he never flinched. When Farrad was done, Doyle flexed his arm and felt only a dull throb. "Good job, Doc."

Doyle appraised the rip in his flight jacket's sleeve. Not too bad; the ol' boy scraped through another one. Mending could wait until he was home. *Home.* Doyle shoved that thought aside for now. He threw the jacket over his shoulders.

Riana paused in Doyle's path. She started to apologize—for refusing to translate his terms of surrender, he assumed—but Doyle saved her the trouble by saying, "You did fine."

Commander Ruschen overheard. "*Fine?* Your father would have been furious, Riana."

Riana's mouth tightened into a half-smile, a tactic Doyle had witnessed his own mother use to avoid arguments. He couldn't let Ruschen's comment slide. "She showed real guts to give us a heads-up. Probably saved our lives."

"Don't mistake impudence for bravery," Commander Ruschen

said sharply. Turning to Riana, he spoke more gently. "You could have been killed." He seemed uncomfortable showing a softer side in front of Doyle, so Ruschen said to his wife, "We'll talk about this later."

Doyle read the undercurrent of the Commander's spousal concern. It was amusing to picture the hard-as-tacks bastard fretting over her like a jumpy househusband. He made a grudging concession. "Baden? You did fine too."

Maybe he wasn't such a bad choice to lead the Gaea mission after all. Not that it mattered now, since their mission was DOA.

Colby guided *Gaea-02* into a wider orbit around Earth. They hadn't traveled far from the Orbital Station yet, but he doubted they'd be returning there.

His gaze drifted to an external viewscreen. Below their ship was the isolated jigsaw piece he knew intimately as the Australian continent. He switched off the screen. The only one he ever truly cared for down there in the dust was his dad, and—selfishly, he admitted—that was mainly because he'd let Colby fly his medical plane. But a Flying Doctor's life was way too dull, treating saddle sores, heatstroke, and taipan bites.

No, up here was where Colby Xaviera belonged. He knew that for bloody sure now, and he wasn't looking forward to going back down.

The flight console beeped. Colby checked the reading.

"Bugger me."

Colby's excited voice echoed from a speaker in the supply bay. "Don't drop your panties yet. I'm picking up two contacts headed straight for us."

Commander Ruschen went pale. "Atmospheric Defense Missiles."

"Comet busters?" Doyle was amazed by the APA's gall. ADMs were designed for Earth's protection, not assault. They could lock onto a Near Earth Object, drill into the core, then blow it to smithereens. Fission nets cleared up any stray debris heading planetside.

Alexei snorted cynically, "If the APA cannot have *Gaea-02*, they make sure no one will."

Commander Ruschen paced. "This is insanity. We pose no threat."

"They don't know what we'll do," Doyle said, "and that makes us dangerous."

For the first time since Doyle knew the kid, Colby's voice sounded worried. "Four minutes to impact. I can't get enough speed to outrun the bloody things without squashing us all like meat pies."

Doyle and Ruschen huddled. Problem solving had once come so naturally together, and an old spark of that collaboration was reignited.

"We could generate a burst of EMP, fry their guidance systems," Doyle proposed.

"We'd risk shorting half our ship."

"Orient the chem engines and burn up both bogeys before they hit us?"

"Neither hot nor fast enough, I'm afraid." Commander Ruschen rubbed his chin. "We need to jettison stage four."

"The hell we do."

"Outside *Gaea-02*'s electromagnetic sheath, the active antimatter will rupture. Timed right, we'd destroy those missiles entirely."

Alexei interrupted them. "You want to eject part of our *engine*?"

"Stage four is only necessary during liftoff."

"And reentry," Doyle added, wondering why Ruschen omitted that fact.

"We could land without it."

"If we're lucky. There's gotta be a better option," Doyle said.

"There isn't."

Doyle had to bow to the Commander's judgment on

astrophysical matters. Ruschen's way, they ran the risk of being marooned in space, but time to find another solution was rapidly running out. Doyle nodded.

"Xaviera, did you catch that?" Commander Ruschen said into his comms band.

"Yeah, but—"

"There's absolutely no margin for error." Ruschen moved to a telemetry console. "We'll need to come to a full stop for this to work."

"*Sir?*"

"No arguments. Do it."

Doyle felt the ship tremble under his feet, and he knew Colby had obeyed Ruschen's order.

Commander Ruschen's fingers tapdanced across the console, frenetically calculating speed and trajectories of dual incoming threats. Hundreds of digits cascaded down his screen. He spun the view in three dimensions, verifying his plot from every angle.

On *Gaea-02*'s bridge, Colby put Commander Ruschen's plan into motion. Stage four was primed and decoupled. The safety override codes had been input.

Ruschen tapped his comms band, "On my command…" His steely eyes monitored each screen refresh as the missiles approached.

"*Now.*"

The moment Commander Ruschen's order hit Colby's ears, he pulled the jettison lever. A section of *Gaea-02*'s massive antimatter engine detached from the ship, propelled by a burst of escaping coolant.

Doyle shouted over Colby's comms band, "Get us out of here fast!"

Colby punched the chemical burners to push *Gaea-02* deeper into the void. He urged the sluggish ship on with muttered pleas. "C'mon, girl, don't be coy…"

Two Atmospheric Defense Missiles rapidly bore down on them.

The jettisoned engine section drifted between *Gaea-02* and the missiles. Ripples of energy laced its surface as active antiprotons collided inside. Stage four achieved critical mass in less than a second, and it ruptured in a gigantic, soundless explosion.

Both missiles were caught in the blast, causing them to detonate prematurely and add greater fury to the expanding eruption.

Gaea-02 couldn't escape fast enough. Debris hurtled into the ship's hull.

A small chunk of one missile's diamond-tipped shell casing ripped through *Gaea-02*'s supply bay wall and whizzed past Doyle's head.

A whirlwind engulfed the room as atmosphere was pushed out through the puncture, into the ravenous vacuum outside. Crew members clung to anything secure to avoid being pulled into the maelstrom.

Systems failed shipwide. Warning lights flashed in a hyperactive rhythm.

"Hull breach in the supply bay!" Colby's voice screeched from a speaker.

"We know," Doyle shouted into his comms band as he held fast to a sturdy shelf. His mind raced. Gravity was zilched. The Candlemass must have been fried in the blast. Who knows what other parts of the ship were hit? Although, if it was something critical, they would have been vaporized already. Cold comfort.

He saw Riana gripping a workbench alongside Commander Ruschen. A toolbox rattled behind the couple. Doyle yelled a warning. Riana turned as a roller-wrench jerked out of the box and flew at her. She had to let go of her mainstay to dodge the tool as it zipped by her head. Riana flailed in midair. Commander Ruschen clutched her wrist, pulling her close.

The wrench collided with the hull puncture, suspended for a surreal, still moment against the wall… until the tool's metal twisted in on itself. The vacuum's immense power crushed the wrench until its mangled form squeezed through the tiny gap and was hurled into space.

Escaping atmosphere whipped around Doyle. He focused his thoughts. *Remember the procedures.* He located the emergency repair cabinet on the wall near Michi. Doyle gesticulated wildly to direct her attention. Michi understood and flung open the cabinet latch. She unstrapped a puncture press, which flew across the supply bay.

Doyle pushed away from his anchor to catch the puncture press en route. His fingertips hooked the edge of its plastic cover.

The whirlwind pulled Doyle in, whisking him toward the hull at terrific speed. He knew there wasn't time to do what he had to *and* orient himself for a safe landing. Chances were he'd break his neck on impact, or worse, be pushed into the breach and have his bones crushed to jelly in an excruciating instant.

Doyle put the crew's lives first. He ripped the airtight seal off the puncture press, half a second before he slammed into a strut jutting from the hull wall. He felt a rib—maybe two—crack, but the impact saved him from being thrust into the void. Ignoring his pain, Doyle jammed the conical press over the hull puncture. It sealed around the jagged hole, flooding the cone with a ceramic goo that hardened on contact.

The compound held. The whirlwind subsided.

Doyle fell to the floor as Colby restored their artificial gravity. With his ribs busted like that, he would have preferred freefall.

He tried to take a deep breath but gagged. It wasn't his ribs. *There wasn't enough air.* Too much oxygen had been lost in the breach. Everyone in the supply bay gasped minibreaths, anxious to squeeze oxygen from the thin atmosphere.

Doyle tapped the comms band behind his earlobe. "Colby ... pressurize ... ox ... gen ... fast ..."

Colby's voice sounded extra loud in his ears. "Workin' on it, boss." The kid would need to reboot the system, open the valves and pump in a huge amount of the life-giving gas. Doyle tried to calculate mentally whether there'd be enough time before they suffocated, but the numbers kept slithering away like snakes through the undergrowth of his oxygen-starved brain.

Feeble, Doyle could only watch as the crew slowly succumbed. Some were already unconscious; death would go easier for them. His heavy eyelids drooped.

Riana shook her husband's listless shoulders to keep him awake. Her arms finally gave out. She was dying. They all were.

Doyle let his eyes close for what he thought was the final time. The dark was comforting. Whispered lullabies he'd sung little Lon to sleep with lazily swam through his head.

The rasp of a breath being drawn broke Doyle from his lethargy. He hazily realized it was his own husky breath he was hearing. His eyes fluttered open as he sucked in the most delicious oxygen he'd ever tasted.

All around, *Gaea-02*'s crew recovered. Doc Farrad and Riana aided those most affected by anoxia. Doyle weakly tapped his comms band. "Thanks, kid."

Django reached down to Doyle, offering his hand to help him to his feet. Doyle winced as his broken ribs crunched together. Silent Django nodded his head, his eyes expressing more gratitude than his voice ever could.

Gaea-02 had taken a pummeling, but there was nothing they couldn't eventually fix. They had M.I.T.Z. and the Mass Prototype Engine to fashion replacement parts. Sabin—if he were up to it—could go EVA with Doyle to make structural repairs and patch up the hull. At least the explosion bought them enough time to move out of missile range before the APA figured out they weren't dead.

The crew's morale was high, their bigger problems—such as being blockaded in orbit above a hazardous planet—forgotten for the moment. They crowded into the mess hall for their first meal since escaping from the Wheel. Everyone, that is, except for Usef, who Doyle assumed had slunk off to wallow in his shame. He made a mental note to smooth things over with Usef after dinner. People make mistakes; maybe he shouldn't have been so hard on him.

Dr. Farrad had set Doyle's ribs and numbed the pain, so sitting at the mess table was almost bearable. Sabin sat alone, morose, but the others were especially upbeat as they ate and drank. They'd snuck by that skinny guy with the dark hood and scythe, and that made for a big appetite. Some of the new rations they'd salvaged didn't even taste half bad.

Colby paraded around, hobnobbing from under his Akubra hat that he pulled out on special occasions. His collision with Django's huge shoulder—"Sorry, mate!"—made the big man spill his food. Django shrugged and scooped up the mess in one wide palm.

Doyle nodded toward Django. "May not say much, big guy, but I'm sure glad you pack a wallop. I bet that soldier's still in Shangri-la."

Indigo and Eckerd chuckled. Django couldn't hold back a broad grin that showed off his gleaming white teeth. Commander Ruschen leaned across the table to address Django directly. "I may even forget that you disobeyed a direct order. Big guy." His deadpan delivery unintentionally set off another round of laughter.

Sabin seemed to take each guffaw personally. Red-faced, he grunted a sardonic, "Ha. Ha. Ha."

Doyle chided himself for a lack of sensitivity and motioned for the others to tone down their glee. Trawling for a change of subject, he recalled his earlier request. "Indigo, any luck with *Sagan-E*?"

Her mouth full, she nodded excitedly. Indigo inched closer to Doyle and tapped a tabletop viewsquare to activate it. While she swallowed, her fingers navigated the touchscreen. "Two packets, minus some junk data. The SHA-6 was a cinch, and if I'm right . . . well, see for yourself."

The unencrypted message flashed on the tabletop: L SAFE. EARTH NOT. USE CUCULIDAE.

"'L.'" Doyle could barely contain his joy. "Lon's okay."

Colby slapped Doyle's shoulder. Riana smiled. "I'm sure you'll see him soon, Doyle." He breathed an audible sigh of relief.

"Earth not . . . safe," Alexei read out, dampening the mood.

"Not safe specifically for *us*, or for all humanity?" Dr. Farrad asked. "We don't know the full extent of the UEC's damage."

"However bad, the APA is obviously in control of the ashes," Eckerd said.

"My father had to reach *somewhere* secure to transmit his message," Doyle pointed out.

Michi forced some optimism. "Maybe all isn't lost. The acronym in charge has been switched but maybe life goes on sort of normal down there?"

"Normal?" Alexei almost laughed. "Millions undoubtedly dead, ten times that number with radiation sickness. At each ground zero, the sand would be turned to *glass*. This is not normal."

Indigo pondered a second before turning to Doyle. "What does 'use cuculidae' mean?"

"That's Latin for cuckoo, an extinct bird," Doyle said. "Dad told stories of how the mother Cuculidae would find another species' nest and secretly lay her eggs inside it. When the baby hatched, it'd throw the other bird's eggs out."

Indigo frowned. "Charming critter."

"Are you sure you translated it right?" Doyle asked her. "How's it relate to us?"

It was strange how silent Commander Ruschen had remained while the crew discussed Earth. Yet he needed only one word to capture their full attention: "M38."

Doyle was mystified. "Say again?"

"Planet M38 is the nest. And we are the proverbial Cuculidae."

Eckerd shook his head. "It's barren. There's nothing on M38's surface but water, rock, and ice."

"Not now," Commander Ruschen admitted, standing, "but there will be." He paced in a circle around the baffled group. "China will build her own starships using UEC technology. They'll colonize M38 as we were meant to. There's no other option for them."

"How does that help us?" Riana asked.

"It could ... if we took the long way there."

"I don't follow," Doyle said, although he was afraid he did.

"We hibernate. Travel slow enough that it takes us thirty years to reach M38. By then, an APA colony will already be established, with everything we'd need to survive."

"Big assumption," Doyle said.

Commander Ruschen ticked off his fingers: "Ten years for them to create a fleet, ten to reach M38, ten to build the infrastructure. We'd arrive at the perfect time, when the current conflict would be resigned to history. The Gaea mission could be reborn in a brave, new world."

The passion in Ruschen's voice convinced Doyle he'd been plotting this long before Indigo retrieved the *Sagan-E* message. Did he ever intend to return to Earth? Worse still, Doyle saw the crew's faces light up at the bold suggestion. If he let it seize their imaginations, he might never see Lon again.

"That's ridiculous," Doyle scoffed. "I mean ... it's impossible."

"No, it could work," Alexei said with growing excitement. These were scientists. Telling them something was impossible was like dancing before a raging bull in a bright, red Flamenco dress.

Eckerd sounded elated. "I can modify the SLH tubes for an extended period, anywhere up to four decades. I've been testing gene extracts from Arctic frogs to prevent cell degeneration. We'd only age a few days per year."

"And I could program M.I.T.Z. to maintain the ship's systems while we sleep," Michi added. "It can replace drained antimatter cells, tend to—"

"Hold on," Doyle interrupted, rising. "M.I.T.Z. is a prototype. This is all experimental stuff you're talking about."

"What's the alternative?" Commander Ruschen stood face to face with Doyle. "Right now, we're only equipped for a test flight, not to sustain a new colony on our own. And if we try to land on Earth, you know as well as I do that the APA will intercept us."

"But what you're proposing ... No one else thinks this is nuts?"

Doyle looked around for support, but none was forthcoming. Even Colby shuffled uncomfortably. What had gotten into them? He felt as though he was alone in a crowd of strangers, and the only one missing the punch line. "You'd all so easily abandon our home?"

"Doyle," Michi said softly, "we already planned to make M38 our home. Everyone here . . . except you."

Her words hit Doyle like a meteorite. *Of course.* They'd made their peace, bought their tickets—this was merely a slight revision to their schedule. But Doyle wanted off the runaway train.

"My son is waiting for me. On Earth." He looked each crew member in the eye. "You all have people who care for you. Friends, relatives, they're all there, aren't they? You're just going to forget about them?"

Their indifference deflated him. Doyle knew he was clutching at straws. They wouldn't be on this ship if they had unbreakable ties. He was the anomaly.

"Our mission is clear," Commander Ruschen said.

"What about the APA already on M38?" Doyle carped. "We'll just boot them out of the nest?"

"Diplomacy is a powerful tool. We can trade our scientific expertise for food, materials . . . In time, we could build a fertile UEC outpost—"

"Swiss Family Ruschen?"

"Don't be obtuse. The universe is big enough for both of Earth's factions."

"Earth's *factions*? What happens to everyone back home in the meantime? No, I won't accept this crap." Doyle felt his world sliding through his fingers. He had to fight for his boy. Desperate, he flung out his arms. "Majority vote. A majority vote decides what we do."

"This isn't a democracy," Commander Ruschen said firmly. His temper had the others stepping into the background, leaving Doyle and him to duke it out.

"The UEC's probably in tatters. Rank means nothing." Doyle

jabbed his finger into the UEC logo on the Commander's uniform. "All bets are off."

Ruschen butted up against Doyle. "I'm still in command of this ship. This crew is my responsibility."

"And you're happy condemning them to drift in space for thirty years? Another of your little experiments?"

"It's your own father's idea."

"We don't know that for sure! He could have meant anything."

"It's my decision to make!" Commander Ruschen thundered back.

Doyle lowered his voice. "Not in a mutiny."

Ruschen snatched at Doyle's collar. Doyle clutched Ruschen's.

"I'll have you up for treason, Doyle."

"In what court, *Baden*?"

Doyle heard the sneering tone of his own voice and knew at once that he'd fallen into Ruschen's trap. He'd been baited into acting irrationally. If there was ever any chance of using reason to convince the others to land *Gaea-02* on Earth, it was now lost.

Alexei stood and said, "I vote…"

Each pair of eyes in the room turned to stare at Alexei. He cleared his throat, "I vote for M38." He raised one arm to indicate a ballot.

Doyle snatched his flimsy opportunity. "Who else? Who else wants to kiss Earth goodbye?" Had he somehow swayed them, even a little? Doyle made himself sound less panicky than he felt. "Raise your hand if you choose to leave everything you've ever known behind—forever."

For several agonizing seconds, no one moved… until Sabin kicked his chair away and thrust his arm above his head. "Might as well go to M38. I got nuthin' left down there."

The floodwaters broke. Eckerd lifted his hand. "M38 for me."

Dr. Farrad's palm rose with a respectful nod. "We'll be killed if we go back now. Why not finish what we started?"

Michi raised her hand but she wouldn't look Doyle in the eye.

Django silently voted for M38. His motives, as usual, were unfathomable.

Indigo shrugged and lifted her hand with a measured nonchalance. Doyle supposed she was trying to spare his feelings.

No such sympathy from Commander Ruschen, who humored Doyle by voting with a stern jab of his arm.

Riana gripped her husband's hand and stretched her other arm up to vote for M38.

With Usef absent, only Colby remained to make his decision. He reluctantly extended his arm. "Sorry, Doyle."

Apart from himself, it was unanimous; they all held their palms aloft. Doyle slumped into a chair.

Michi lowered her hand. "What about the lifeboat?"

"She's right. You could ride back to Earth alone in the emergency pod," Eckerd said. "There's no need for you to come with us. The pod's untested, so it's quite a risk, but—"

"Hell, I'll take it." *Risk? It was more like suicide.* "Anything to get to my son." Doyle locked eyes with Commander Ruschen. "Unless you've got some objection?"

"None whatsoever."

"Great. I'll drop you a postcard." Doyle pushed through the group on his way out.

Colby dogged him. "No hard feelings? I just…"

"Don't sweat it, kid."

Doyle placed his family photograph and Lon's spaceship drawing in a duffel bag along with a spare uniform. They weren't allowed to bring much onto *Gaea-02*, so packing to leave was easy. No sense spending more time on this floating hulk. He wanted to reach Lon as soon as possible. Doyle knew where his duty lay: he'd promised.

Still, Doyle fumed a little over the crew's decision. Assuming the pod made it to Earth, splashing down in the middle of an ocean with no one ready to fish him out was a different homecoming altogether from a neat landing in a self-sufficient rig like

Gaea-02. He'd have limited guidance control, for a start. It'd be a fluke to fall close enough to any coastline he could reach via the inflatable dinghy. Of course, the pod might instead slam into bedrock at a leisurely twenty-eight thousand kilometers per hour.

Doyle had already preset the pod's course as best he could; now it was on a wing and a prayer that its reentry heat shields would hold up long enough to even roll those particular dice.

He was suddenly aware of Riana's presence in his doorway. "You'd better not ask for a final blood test."

"I just wanted to tell you ... good luck on Earth. I mean that. I hope your family is safe."

Doyle zipped his duffel bag. "You never said anything during the vote. What did you really want?"

Riana stepped into Doyle's quarters, taking her time to articulate long-suppressed desires. "What I chose *was* what I wanted. Good or bad, M38 is everything I've worked toward for most of my life. I can't give up on that dream now. I don't know how to."

"I would've said the same a few years ago." Doyle slung his bag over one shoulder. "Good luck yourself." He walked past her.

"Doyle?"

He glanced back.

"Thank you," Riana said.

Doyle carried his duffel along *Gaea-02*'s spine. There was no big send-off. He wanted to slip away unheralded to spare both parties any embarrassment or recriminations.

He couldn't hate the crew. In a way, returning to Earth with *Gaea-02* would be just as risky as catapulting into deep space not knowing what they'd find on M38. To people like them—the way he was before his son came into his life—better the devil you *don't* know.

A warning light flashed on the ceiling. A short siren blared before a recorded voice announced, "Lifeboat launch initiated."

Doyle's eyes widened as he sprinted down the corridor, racing for the pod's launch bay. He slipped around a corner in his desperate scramble to find out what the hell was going on.

Indigo was slumped against the wall at the launch bay entrance. Her head was bleeding.

"What happened?" Doyle shouted.

Dazed, Indigo replied, "Usef. Knocked me out. Doyle, he's taking the pod."

Doyle dropped his bag and ran helter-skelter into the bay, stopping only at the sealed launch door where the emergency pod rested in its own airlock. Through a clear pane on the hatch, he could see the outer airlock door grinding open. Stars winked beyond.

Doyle beat on the launch door in futility. "Usef! Don't! Please… don't," he cried as the emergency pod was shunted along magnetic rails into space.

The pod's autopilot—preprogrammed by Doyle—used sharp, silent retrorocket bursts to guide Usef toward planet Earth.

"No…"

Despairing, Doyle stared out into space, the sight of the escaping pod shrinking as it moved further away… until the outer door snapped shut.

CHAPTER 7
FRAGILE

Usef went as far as placing his hand on the mess hall door. He heard the muffled conversations inside and could imagine what the crew was saying about him. How it was his fault one of them had been killed.

They were right.

He couldn't face their incriminating stares. Especially Doyle and Pach's brother, accusing him with venomous eyes. The rest of the trip was poisoned now. Usef was not one of them, if he ever had been.

He came to a decision. He'd stay out of everyone's way and lock himself in his quarters until they were safely back on Earth. Living like a hermit, he'd sneak rations from the supply bay when no one was around. Soon they'd forget he ever existed.

Usef heard shouting from behind the door, a heated argument. He listened closer. "M38," someone said distinctly. "Hibernation." They weren't returning home—that was clear.

He hadn't counted on this. Usef shuffled away from the mess hall.

Later, seated on his double-bedfoam, dismayed face in his soft hands, Usef sobbed like a schoolboy. Try as he might, he was no heroic Theseus. He didn't have the courage to live among fellow travelers who saw through his masks. He'd never be trusted again, even on a distant planet. The crew would spend their days looking over their shoulders. How could any of them live like that?

Usef wanted the Gaea mission to succeed. It was more than a job. He'd have exchanged his own pitiful life for Pach's if he were able, but it was too late for that now. The crew would be better off without him on board.

Usef packed his few belongings in a rigid case.

They'd all been given a crash course in operating the pod, though they never expected to need it. Usef skulked toward the lifeboat launch bay. He made sure no one spotted him. Hearing a noise ahead, he waited and watched from the shadows.

Usef saw Indigo lingering outside the launch bay. How could anyone have known his plan? No one would care enough to say goodbye, least of all her. Did they intend to stop him? Why? He was doing them a favor.

Usef snuck closer. Indigo seemed preoccupied, but there might have been others waiting to ambush him. Usef swung his trunk with all his brawn. Indigo's head was thrown from the impact. Her temple bounced off a metal strut. He hit her with such force one end of his luggage handle broke off. Blood ran down her pretty face.

Usef clambered through the emergency pod's hatch and sealed it shut. He stowed his case in a compartment, nestled into a snug crash-chair and, strapped himself in. Flicking switches, Usef noted that the autopilot had been preprogrammed. Excellent. Someone had foresight. Usef grinned in spite of himself when he activated the launch procedure, just as he'd been shown. A siren sounded outside the pod and Usef's grin disappeared.

A teeth-chattering rumble. Airlock doors, he guessed. There

were no windows; he was completely shut off. Usef felt his chest stretched tight across his rib cage. He thought he heard a pounding noise, but he couldn't tell if it was outside the hatch or just the panic of his racing heart. There was a sudden sense of motion, then the awareness that only the belted straps were keeping his body from floating away.

Time passed. How much time, Usef couldn't be sure. Indicators flashed whenever the retrorockets adjusted the pod's trajectory. He drifted in and out of sleep.

After a while though, Usef felt heavy again.

And then hot.

In his mind's eye, he could see the flames of reentry consume his fragile pod.

Reported by Xinhua News Agency, March 14th, 2050:

Yesterday, the terrorist crew of rogue UEC starship, *Gaea-02*, assaulted the Asian Pacific Alliance Freedom Station, killing two unarmed engineers. The UEC insurgents then stole explosive materials and escaped.

A decoupling error caused *Gaea-02*'s engines to detonate, destroying the enemy craft. There were no survivors.

MR95S//XNA0511149D//03EF

CHAPTER 8
LITTLE WORLDS

Doyle found it difficult to maintain focus on the endless void in front of him. The outdated concept of a soldier's thousand-yard stare had evolved into the cosmonaut's billion-light-year gaze. Up here, he wasn't fighting an opposing army. Instead, Doyle's spirit was crushed by infinity and the vast vacuum that divided him from his son.

Commander Ruschen and Alexei were plotting the course *Gaea-02* would take over the next thirty years, while Colby entered their data into the ship's navigation system. At times they would ask for Doyle's input, occasionally coaxing a monosyllabic answer.

Doyle didn't bother to feign interest. They'd have an easier time consulting a man destined for the guillotine on what color bucket he'd like to catch his severed head.

Doyle's mind teased him. *There was room for you in the pod.* Enough for the entire crew, in fact. If Usef had waited, or had

Doyle spoken with him earlier, as he'd planned to … Such thoughts nettled Doyle like grit under an eyelid.

Worried he might lash out, not wanting to do or say something he couldn't later retract, Doyle tried to leave the bridge without attracting anyone's attention.

"Doyle?" someone asked behind his back.

Doyle mumbled, "Need some fresh air."

The sheer irony of his ill-chosen phrase annoyed him further, and it was all he could do not to scream.

Meandering down the crew module's spine, the quiet solitude Doyle sought proved unattainable. *Gaea-02* was abuzz with activity as the crew prepared for their journey. With the details mostly filled in, they all had jobs to complete—everyone except Doyle.

No one was comfortable assigning him tasks. Or maybe they didn't know what reaction to expect. Was Commander Ruschen concerned that Doyle would sabotage a crucial ship component? Doyle had tried to read the look in his eyes and found that idea amusing.

Sure, Doyle knew at least sixteen ways to strand *Gaea-02* in orbit that no one could prevent, detect, or repair. He wasn't perfect but there were some principles he wouldn't forfeit. A simple rule Doyle lived by: if he could never look Lon in the eye afterward, then it wasn't worth doing. Even now, his moral compass held firm, due north.

Doyle wandered into the comms room, where Indigo was busy at her station. Earlier, she'd relayed the scant tidbits of information recovered from Earth via sporadic underground-radio broadcasts. Life was difficult in the Northern Hemisphere, they reported. Yet hopeful voices resonated over the airwaves, fleeting promises from covert pockets of resistance.

The shattered land of his birth was apparently rebuilding—under APA jurisdiction, no doubt—and people were doing what people in untenable circumstances do: trying to adapt.

Doyle reminded himself that his father had powerful friends. Surely they could help him keep Lon alive. Dr. Emil Gage managed to get that transmission to *Sagan-E*, so he must have access to technology. His simple missive, "L SAFE," was all that prevented Doyle from going over the edge. His mantra for sanity: *L-safe... L-safe... L-safe...*

"Indigo? Send a return message to *Sagan-E* for me?"

"SHA-6?"

Doyle nodded.

Indigo queued an encryption algorithm. "Go."

Doyle dictated, "D SAFE. GO M38. LUV 2 L." Forming those few meager words was heart wrenching and made the current situation unbearably real.

Indigo encoded the transcript and was about to press SEND when Doyle came to his senses and stayed her hand. "Wait."

If the APA intercepted his message and traced it from source to receiver, he could be causing a security risk for both his family and *Gaea-02*. A goodbye note wasn't worth putting the hounds on their scent. As much as it tore him up, Doyle hit CANCEL.

To her credit, Indigo didn't question why, although she could have guessed. Doyle gave a curt but sincere, "Thanks anyway."

He trudged past the medlab. Inside, Riana conferred with Dr. Farrad. Doc was the closest thing to a psychiatrist on board, but even he had been unable to penetrate Doyle's depression. Doyle simply didn't feel the need to spill his guts; he'd work through this on his own. Riana saw Doyle outside the lab and smiled reassuringly, but he pretended not to notice.

He roamed near the SLH hall, where Eckerd adjusted their sleep tanks for the crew's extended hibernation. Eckerd detached a small, molded aperture and carried it across to Michi's robotics lab. Doyle had nothing to say to either of them, so he kept walking.

As he strode past, he glimpsed the M.I.T.Z. robot inside, controlling the ship's Mass Prototype Engine. A claw-like molecular laser array swirled and danced over the Anvil as raw elements recombined and new forms were wrought. In a matter of seconds, the machine had forged a perfect clone of Eckerd's SLH part.

An idea suddenly occurred to Doyle and he kicked himself for not thinking clearly enough to see it earlier. The Mass Prototype Engine. It was so obvious. They could recreate the emergency pod's components and assemble a new one in the airlock.

He rushed to Michi's console. "Doyle? Can I help?" she asked, but received no response.

Doyle opened the *Gaea-02* parts database, scrolled through hundreds of entries: machinery, infrastructure, hull sections. No pod. He reached the end of the directory and scrolled back up. Maybe he missed it the first time through?

No. It wasn't there. His jaw quivered. "The emergency pod, where are the plans? Tell me they're buried in here."

Michi took over navigating the database's search engine. Eventually, she exited the program. Her facial expression told him something was wrong. Doyle wet his lips. "What is it?"

"We have all critical schematics, but … we were in the process of analyzing certain ancillary components—"

He closed his sagging eyes. "You don't have it."

"The database wasn't scheduled for completion until after our test flight—"

Doyle didn't need to hear the excuses, so he stormed out. Michi called after him, "The pod design wasn't finalized, we never … I'm sorry, Doyle."

He'd had enough apologies in the past few days to turn his stomach. Doyle raged along *Gaea-02*'s spine, toward the crew's private quarters.

He ran out of steam halfway and realized he was being asinine. It wasn't Michi's fault his hopes were raised. Acting like a jerk wasn't helping anyone.

"Accept it, Doyle," he softly admonished himself. "Deal with it."

An aroma tickled his nostrils. He'd strayed close to the agriculture lab. Inside, the tomato plants were in full bloom. Doyle was struck by how much they'd grown while the crew had slept.

He'd forgotten about these plants, yet here they were: plump, red fruit hanging from tall, healthy limbs. Each juicy tomato was like a miniature planet. Nourishing little worlds.

The tomato crops stirred something inside Doyle. He found renewed purpose in his step and by the time he arrived at his quarters, a resolution had crystallized. Wallowing in self-pity was never his style. He wouldn't—couldn't—just throw in the towel. Not Doyle Gage. Armed with a newfound clarity, his goal was clear: reach M38 safely with the others and *then* find his way home to Lon.

Thirty years traveling in one direction, then ten years or less for his return to Earth. Okay, half his son's lifetime. But during their time apart—like those tomato plants—Lon could flourish while Doyle slept.

He unzipped the duffel bag that still sat by his bed. Doyle hung his family photo inside his locker, pausing to caress Lon's cherubic face with his thumb. Next time they'd meet, his son would be a fully grown man. He'd never get the chance to teach little Lon about those flight vectors, but they *would* be reunited.

Doyle unpacked Lon's brightly colored sketch. Out of habit, he was about to mount it below his old photo, but instead he carefully folded and tucked Lon's drawing into a pocket against his chest.

Modest changes before momentous ones.

Someone was shouting. Doyle's ears were always so attuned to his vessels that he could hear a screw loosen on the other side of a hull. He left his quarters and jogged down the corridor.

The hubbub emanated from engineering. One antagonistic voice clearly belonged to Commander Ruschen. The other was softer but Doyle assumed it was Sabin's. As he got closer, the words became more distinct.

"Sorry, sir—"

"Listen carefully. If you don't make these modifications correctly, we'll be marooned midway."

Doyle waited at the entrance to sum up the situation.

"I can't do it without Pach," Sabin said.

Commander Ruschen provoked him: "Do you need your mommy to hold your hand too?"

"Go to hell."

Damn, Baden, did you even read their files? Mama Jiménez died during Pach's birth. Getting under a man's skin to shame him into action was one thing, but that was a low blow.

"No excuses," Commander Ruschen threatened Sabin. "Get it done or you'll spend the next thirty years in the brig."

On his way out, Commander Ruschen barged past Doyle. *Way to motivate the crew, boss.*

Sabin half-heartedly returned to his task, merely going through the motions. Working without Pach, he seemed profoundly alone. They weren't just brothers; theirs was a team forged in blood and oil over two decades.

Doyle cleared his throat. "I'm probably the last person in the universe you want to talk to now…"

"Got that right," Sabin said.

"You need a hand?" Doyle asked. "I'm no Pach, but I can turn a wrench."

Sabin shunned his olive branch.

"Trust me, my heart's not in this either," Doyle said with a sigh, "but there are nine other people relying on us to get them where they're going."

Sabin's head hung low. "He's such an asshole."

"Commander Ruschen's more stressed than anyone. Everything that happens now rests on his head." Sabin appeared surprised at Doyle's compassion. Doyle held up his hands. "Hey, I want to chuck him out an airlock too, but at least I understand the guy." He ran his finger along a rivet-punched gasket. "I didn't know Pach as well as you, of course, but I get the feeling he'd want you to fix this girl up right. Pretty sure he'd kick your butt if you didn't."

Sabin chuckled. "He'd try to."

He handed Doyle a hex cutter and showed him what alterations they needed to make on the engine restraints. Sabin became more animated as he engaged with the machinery.

"Pach is still here, you know," Doyle said. "He's in every nut and bolt of this ship."

"Yeah." Sabin patted a nearby conduit, a vibrant, humming artery pulsing life throughout *Gaea-02*.

One giant, panoramic viewscreen covered an entire wall of *Gaea-02*'s observation deck.

Doyle leaned against the screen, peering out at the planet he was being forced to relinquish. He was resigned to the fact that this was the last time he'd see Mother Earth for a long while.

"Seems so near, doesn't it?" Commander Ruschen said from the doorway.

"Not in the mood for your gloating, Commander."

Sauntering close to Doyle, Ruschen's neatly pressed uniform gave off a telltale whiff of ozone from the ship's flash-cleaner. "I won't lie, Doyle. I'm not sorry we're going to M38. I honestly believe it's best for our crew. For the human race." Commander Ruschen folded his arms behind his back. "But I genuinely regret you can't be with your boy. I do."

Side by side, the two men gazed at their native planet. Doyle took Ruschen's admission at face value. He didn't sense any game-playing, no contest of wills unfurling, but the Commander seemed… uneasy. If he expected Doyle to say thanks, he'd be waiting forever.

Ruschen kept his eyes on the screen as he spoke. "Years ago, when you were still in command of the Gaea mission, you said something that stuck with me." His voice raised in pitch and timbre as he quoted: "The pioneer's flame burns brightest in the darkest moments."

"Things change," Doyle quietly replied. "Guess I did too." He let his guard down. "When Juni passed, Lon and I—all we had left of her was each other. I promised him I'd come home soon."

Ruschen shuffled awkwardly. "I served under your father briefly at Apache," he said. Doyle wasn't aware of that, though UEC appointments at the Observatory were common. Ruschen was so private about his life; Doyle realized he knew little about him outside of Gaea. Commander Ruschen continued, "Dr. Gage is a brilliant man. Your son couldn't be in better hands."

Doyle trusted his father with all his heart, but that didn't take the sting out of the situation. He tapped on the viewscreen. "I feel like some sort of cosmic hostage, Baden."

"Once we're established on M38, I'll do everything in my power to get you home." Commander Ruschen faced Doyle and extended his hand. "I give you my word."

Only now did Doyle comprehend the true purpose of their conversation. This was Ruschen's way of offering a treaty. Doyle could handle the crew in subtle ways that Ruschen couldn't, yet without Ruschen's resources and authority, he'd find it difficult to gain passage to Earth.

We need each other.

Doyle grasped the Commander's hand firmly. Their bond was sealed.

M.I.T.Z. waited patiently—if a robot can be said to possess such a virtue—while Michi made final adjustments to its caretaker programming. The sleeping crew's lives would be largely in the robot's plasmolded hands.

Doyle judged that a similar level of responsibility rested with several people. If Alexei and Commander Ruschen's astrogation was off by a fraction of a degree, they would overshoot M38 and drift aimlessly for eternity. If Eckerd's fancy tubes malfunctioned, the crew would all drown. If the repairs he and Sabin made didn't hold, *Gaea-02* could lose power and become the most expensive tomb in history.

From the pensive silence in the SLH hall, Doyle presumed his concerns were echoed in everyone else's minds. No one talked about it for fear of triggering thirty years worth of hibernation nightmares.

Commander Ruschen's speech to the assembled crew was brief. Doyle half-listened, catching some cliché about rising from the ashes, before Ruschen finished with a salute. "I'll see you all at our new home."

The group dispersed to their individual sleep tanks. As he stripped off his clothes, Doyle felt an overwhelming wave of apprehension. He blurted to Colby, "What if he's wrong?"

"Who?"

"Ruschen. Even if we make it to M38, the APA could be behind schedule or still consider us hostiles. What's waiting for us?"

"Mate, you worry too much."

Doyle was envious of how easily the kid let it wash off his back. This tabula rasa future the others had prophesied might actually be more perilous than any present threat. It was all speculation, smoke and mirrors.

Eckerd prepared Doyle's chamber. He saw the vacant look on Doyle's face and brought him around by saying, "I suppose Usef couldn't face getting into one of these again."

"And I wouldn't have to if that dagger slid a little deeper into his damn neck." Until he spoke those words, Doyle hadn't realized how bitter he remained about Usef's premature escape. "Ah hell, I didn't mean that," Doyle said as he sealed his lucky jacket in an airtight compartment.

Eckerd shrugged. "I wouldn't blame you if you did."

Riana rolled up Colby's sleeve. She raised a pistol syringe full of gray liquid: Eckerd's amphibian gene cocktail she'd refined and synthesized.

Colby pulled his arm away on reflex. "This frog stuff won't give me webbed feet or a ten-inch tongue, right?"

Indigo leaned over, flirting. "That wouldn't be so bad." She viper-flicked her tongue.

Riana jabbed the shot into Colby's arm, eliciting a boyish, "Ow!" She plucked a new syringe from the tray Dr. Farrad held.

Riana dabbed an alcohol swab on Doyle's skin. As she injected him, their eyes locked. Doyle couldn't read her expression. An unspoken apology, or something more? Without uttering a word, she moved on.

Eckerd helped Doyle into his hibernation chamber. "It's a little different this time."

Doyle sat in the scoop and frowned. "No oxy-mask?"

"Liquid oxygen," Eckerd said. "Hybrid perfluorocarbons, like deep-sea divers gave up trying to use by the '20s. Reduces strain on your lungs in differential pressure."

"Great, I'll be a friggin' fish for the next thirty years."

"Don't worry, we've perfected the application. HPFC delivery is seamless. The process has passed rigorous testing."

"Unlike the rest of this setup," Doyle mumbled.

Eckerd closed Doyle's chamber, which immediately started filling with a frigid, pinkish liquid. Anxiety made Doyle restless. A speaker in the tube amplified Eckerd's voice. "You'll feel some discomfort at first. Just relax."

The pink liquid rose above Doyle's mouth and nose. Extreme cold numbed his face. Soon, he had no choice but to inhale the foreign substance.

Doyle's body convulsed.

His palms slapped against the clear tube. He writhed like a drowning man—which, in essence, he was. As fluid filled his lungs, Doyle's thrashing intensified.

Such an alien sensation. He pictured his lungs as gigantic sponges, soaking in liquid then painfully wringing out every drop. He would have cried for mercy if his vocal cords hadn't been immersed.

Doyle's reluctant body gradually grew accustomed to its new

state. His wrenching subsided. Eventually, his eyes closed and his heart rate slowed…

Eckerd leaned close to the plastiglass shell. "Sweet dreams, Doyle."

CHAPTER 9
SLEEP OF REASON

Indigo was the last of the crew members to be enveloped by Eckerd's subcooled oxygen solution. To Eckerd's delight, she'd remained chipper during the whole process, culminating in a flattering giggle and a wink as he closed her chamber.

Eckerd feared he fancied the girl far more than he should. He tried to quell his arousal as Indigo's supple body writhed in the icy, pink bath like a candy-coated mermaid. His libido almost got the best of him, watching her chest spasm when the liquid filtered into her lungs. Eckerd bit his lip until he drew blood. He couldn't afford to be smitten, not with things the way they were.

Eckerd waited until Indigo's EKG readouts settled at the desired levels.

He wasn't surprised the crew's hibernation states had been executed flawlessly. He'd tested the fluid-breathing systems himself a year ago. Eckerd wouldn't subject anyone to a process he had not personally experienced first; that's how his early fascination with cryoanesthetic dormancy began.

Eckerd was four years old when his parents were given a harrowing ultimatum. The Woodtons could watch their sickly son waste away from a rare hemolytic anemia to die within months, or they could place him into an experimental form of cryogenics with a slim chance of ever waking up. They decided low odds were better than no odds.

It took six years to develop the drug that stimulated sufficient hemoglobin regeneration in Eckerd's pale, little body. Six years existing in an odd limbo.

Once safely thawed, Eckerd Woodton was literally a child out of time—chronologically half a decade older than he seemed—and something of a minor celebrity in his native Manchester. A living anachronism. One injection per year kept him alive, but he wouldn't need any for the duration of *Gaea-02*'s big sleep.

Eckerd removed his uniform, folded it neatly, and placed it in a compartment below his own hibernation chamber.

His skin was horribly scarred from neck to ankle, a side effect of the imperfect cryogenic technique that had saved his life.

As a youth, his scaly appearance prompted taunts from cruel, local kids and whispers from ignorant grownups. He felt the hurt anew whenever he glimpsed his own reptilian flesh.

Finally though, all those barbs seemed worthwhile. He had done something *important*. Eckerd gazed at the row of SLH chambers, *Gaea-02*'s crew slumbering peacefully inside. When they awoke, he would help them forge a new world.

He had no regrets.

Before he settled into his chamber, Eckerd called M.I.T.Z. over and issued a few simple instructions. With a satisfied smile, he observed as the robot set his process in motion. The plastiglass cover swung down and sealed Eckerd in.

As soon as the pink, chilled liquid stung his body, Eckerd sensed something was wrong. Not with the machinery, but within his body. A sudden tightness at his temples. He lost all feeling down his left side.

The hibernation process was beyond his power to halt. His lungs filled with HPFC solution.

Eckerd struggled against his inevitable torpor, tormented by a twisted sense of déjà vu.

The stench of Sobranie cigars tickled Alexei Chechenkov's throat, but he could not cough.

On *Gaea-02*, Alexei's hibernation chamber seemed excessive for his bantam body, like a child's baggy hand-me-downs. His dream state, however, fit like an iron maiden.

His past felt present and tense. Alexei *was* his ten-year-old self as he crawled through the tobacco-stained air vent. Prone, he muffled one palm over his mouth to avoid coughing. He couldn't risk being heard.

Young Alexei craned his neck to check behind and was buoyed by the half-imagined outline of his elder brother peering in from the Astanan winter night. Viktor had lifted Alexei up to the vent and passed him the knife. Being too large to follow, he'd promised to wait for little Alexei in the gloom outside.

Their mission now rested solely on Alexei's lean shoulders.

Ilya Musabayev, the officious scum who owned this opulent residence, sided with the Soviet Neo-Tzarists in their violent reannexation of Kazakhstan. He helped orchestrate the events that turned their nation into a wretched Tartarus and orphaned Alexei and Viktor.

From his astronomer mother, Alexei had learned science. From his father, a revered politician, patriotism. And from the underground, stealth. Alexei's unique combination of training made for an adroit saboteur, and his young age meant he could operate without suspicion.

Tonight, he would become the child assassin.

Alexei followed the vent shaft as it coiled inward. The metal casing was tight around even his diminutive frame. Bent elbows and outstretched toes shuffled his torso along. He reached a grating, right where the memorized blueprints had indicated.

Bending his mobil-skrew to the required angle, Alexei hooked it through the grate and quietly swiveled its handle until the tip pushed into a screw head on the opposite side. The battery-operated tool whirred low, undoing the screws one by one.

The Kazakh Resistance had allies from other proposed UEC nations secretly funneling them weapons and supplies. An obligation driven by culpability, since their UEC foundation talks had sparked the Neo-Tzarist Occupation.

Alexei slid slender fingers through the grating to ease it off its mount. He flipped the grate lengthwise and turned it inside the vent, nestling it under his compact body. Inching forward again, Alexei snaked into the room as far as he could. Precariously balanced, he dangled down to touch his fingertips against a wall-mounted security console.

Alexei had tinkered with his mother's observatory computers since he was a toddler. Musabayev's system was primitive in comparison. Within seconds, Alexei had disabled all infrared, temperature, and pressure monitors.

His tiny, bare feet were in motion as soon as they landed on the plush carpet.

Lamenting strains of a Zauresh mourning march drifted from Musabayev's study. As Alexei approached, his ears were assailed by the depths of infinite grief captured in music. What had the fat pig to be sad about? There he was, the traitor, reclined in a luxurious chair, dozing in his silk smoking jacket, a snifter of imported brandy in one plump hand.

Alexei assembled his knife. The ceramic blade was cleverly sheathed inside a wooden handle ornately carved with two entwined serpents; it appeared to be nothing more than a decorative *objet d'art*. He undid the hidden catch and slid the concealed blade out, flipping it to screw onto the hilt and become complete.

The knife's weight in his palms made his heart jump and his

forehead grow hot. He'd never killed before, but the Resistance had groomed him to slit Musabayev's throat if brother Viktor was unable.

Alexei raised his knife to strike. The handle was so wide he needed both hands to hold it. The sharp tip pointed down at the pig's flabby skin.

The boy's will failed.

His trembling hands halted the blade an inch above his target. Try as he might to conquer his fear, Alexei couldn't go through with the assassination.

How long did he stand there shaking like that? Minutes? Hours? Long enough for his brother to be discovered by a passing guard. A commotion erupted outside the manor.

Musabayev startled awake and raised one bushy brow, but he did not stir. His bloodshot eyes showed no fright, only a sorrow that young Alexei couldn't comprehend. Alexei's blade, suspended like the sword of Damocles, seemed somehow expected, even welcomed by Musabayev.

The shouting spilled inside an adjacent room. Alexei recognized his brother's anguished cry and he instinctively rushed to Viktor's aid.

As Alexei dashed out of Musabayev's study, his head was clamped between two rough hands. A sneering guard twisted the boy's soft neck until he blacked out.

For weeks afterward, young Alexei lay imprisoned in a murky cell while the blood-soaked civil war raged outside. Monotonous days spent choking on air fouled by his own waste. Sleepless nights staring at stars beyond the high bars.

The Neo-Tzarist bastards' laughter provided a raucous soundtrack for his brother's suffering. Viktor's daily torture became more horrific by degrees, until death liberated him.

The Resistance arrived one day too late.

If only he hadn't hesitated. If only he had plunged the shiv into Musabayev's heart and escaped with Viktor when he had the chance.

If only…

The stench of Sobranie cigars tickled Alexei Chechenkov's throat, but he was unable to cough as he crawled through the smoke-stained air vent…

In Alexei's *Gaea-02* hibernation chamber, his adult body flinched and twitched. His mind relived those dire weeks of capture and incarceration over and over like an antique vinyl record stuck in a groove, the stylus skipping for three decades.

If Commander Ruschen had been more conscious, he would have been disgusted at his own ill discipline, the wild meanderings of an unfettered mind.

Milliseconds stretched into days during hibernation. A heart beating just once every ten minutes drip feeds oxygen to a sluggish brain, blooming starbursts of synaptic dissonance. Unbridled snatches of past fears erupt and fade.

A crumpled Québécois birth certificate—Riana Amelia Stone, born 11th April 2018 to Abril Benoit Stone and Admiral Nailor Stone—smoothed out and filed alongside his own at the bleak registry office. No flowers. No ceremony. No honeymoon.

Baden Ruschen's cortex flashed and cartwheeled, each lazy thought taking a full week to transmute.

Riana's wanton, teenage abandon caressing his coarse lips with her own. The fumbling student aching to seduce her UEC instructor. Ruschen hastily repelled Riana's maiden advances. Had he been the naive one? Was she merely trying to provoke her overbearing father?

Ruschen grasped for the reins of his galloping mind but they slid through his clutches.

Their wedding anniversary. It didn't matter which year; there was little difference between them. A union of convenience, rendered sterile through greater conviction and mutual purpose.

Gaea was everything.

Ruschen felt the familiar, cold flagstones of the Naval Air Station in Brunswick under his soles.

No, he realized through the languor; his bare feet were touching the smooth floor of *Gaea-02*.

Staggering outside his hibernation chamber alone, Commander Ruschen's dream was over.

CHAPTER 10
EXIGENT

A rapid stream of distorted screams and nightmare visions pummeled Doyle's waking mind.

His emaciated wife, Juni, wasting away on the end of an intravenous drip. *Stop!* Blood spraying Doyle's face as he—not Sabin—cracked the APA soldier's skull. *No, it wasn't me.* Nuclear fire stripping little Lon's flesh. *That never happened.* Doyle—not the enemy—stabbing Pach in the neck. *It wasn't my fault!* Drifting in the emergency pod, a demonic grin twisted Usef's face. *Enough!*

Doyle realized he was truly falling. His toes squished gunk and he slid, whirling wide-eyed alongside the pinkish liquid gushing from his thrust-open hibernation chamber. He stuck his hands out to soften his collision with the wet floor.

The chaotic screaming from his dreamflow was louder here in the real world. Doubled over, Doyle vomited liquid oxygen residue. It took a few seconds before he could breathe normally.

Colby ran past. "Doc! Where's Doc?"

"He's dead," Sabin bellowed. "We're all dead!"

Doyle wiped the rosy fluid from his mouth. He lifted his waterlogged head. Dr. Farrad's lifeless eyes stared at him from across the floor.

Doc's face was strained, skin split along his cheekbones, his limbs jumbled like a rag doll's at the foot of his hibernation chamber. No blood, but drenched in pink goo. He must have died inside the tube and his corpse tumbled out when the shell opened.

"What the hell went wrong?" Doyle asked nobody in particular. He wanted an answer so he repeated it louder, "What the hell went—" A coughing fit overcame him. When he inhaled, the heavy air felt like a serrated knife scraping exposed nerves.

The pain focused Doyle's senses, allowing him to single out Michi's voice screeching for help.

Michi was still enclosed in her splintered hibernation chamber, her bare thigh impaled on a long shard of plastiglass. Doyle joined Sabin and Colby to lift her out slowly. She cried as they eased her leg from the spike, catching tendons on its jagged edge. Had it punctured her femoral artery, she'd already be dead. Even so, she was a bloody mess.

"Someone grab a medkit," Doyle shouted as they gently placed Michi on the floor.

Although wracked with pain, she tried to explain, "My door jammed and shattered … *kuso itai!*"

Doyle fetched a jumpsuit from the nearest compartment and tied it around Michi's thigh as a tourniquet. M.I.T.Z. stood nearby, passively observing the damage to its keeper. Doyle gestured angrily at the robot. "Why didn't it prevent all this?"

"Fallback AI," Michi groaned, "barely a five-year-old's IQ."

Doyle was stunned. "We put ourselves in the care of a child?"

"No … we programmed situational responses."

"Then it should have woken us when Doc died."

"Commander Ruschen set parameters. Three ... three deaths."

"Three people had to die before it broke our hibernation?"

Michi grimaced, her face and hair dappled by pink ooze. "He calculated ... risk of waking us early was greater."

Typical, Doyle thought. Ruschen would sacrifice half his crew for the mission's success.

Indigo arrived with a first-aid pouch. "Where's Riana?" Doyle asked. With Doc Farrad gone, they'd need her to treat Michi's wound properly. Indigo shook her head and started tending to Michi herself.

Setting off to search for Riana, Doyle's atrophied limbs wobbled like cooked pasta. He seesawed along the row of SLH chambers.

Doyle saw Alexei squatting at the foot of a tank, muttering to himself but apparently unscathed. The crew hadn't visibly aged, so he couldn't estimate how long they'd remained asleep. Ten years? The thirty they intended? A hundred? Django was still in peaceful hibernation. No sense having Eckerd wake him yet in this mess. *Where is Eckerd, anyway?*

Doyle caught a glimpse of Riana, shoulders heaving beside her SLH module. She knelt over Commander Ruschen's desiccated corpse.

Judging by the almost mummified condition of his body, Doyle guessed he'd been deceased for months, perhaps years. A small mercy that Eckerd's gene extracts had retarded putrefaction.

The magnitude of Ruschen's death hit Doyle immediately: *This changes everything.*

In tears, Riana held her husband's cadaverous hand. Doyle moved to comfort her but stopped when he spotted another body, in a pool of pink muck. Eckerd.

"Damn it," Doyle inadvertently said aloud.

Horribly scarred below his neck, Eckerd appeared dead. Doyle was about to concede their third casualty when he realized that would mean M.I.T.Z. *did* wake them up. Unless ...

Doyle squeezed Eckerd's scaly wrist. Doyle's fingertips tingled over what might have been a faint pulse. Placing his ear against Eckerd's chest, the faint *ba-bump… ba-bump…* confirmed it. Doyle leaped to his feet, almost toppling from vertigo in his weakened state, and staggered to Riana.

"Eckerd's barely alive," Doyle said without tact. "He needs help."

Riana replied numbly, "Let Dr. Farrad handle it."

"Doc's gone, Riana. I'm sorry, but it's up to you now."

"No, it isn't," she said in a clipped monotone. "Just leave us alone."

"*Dr.* Ruschen, you're on duty."

"I have to be with Baden. Don't you understand?"

He understood all too well. Doyle forced Riana to look at him. "I know how bad it feels. You want to tell the whole world to go to hell. You want to die along with him. When Juni passed, the only thing that dragged me out of that netherworld was Lon needing me as a father." He let go of her face. "The people on this ship are depending on you. You won't let them down, will you, Doctor?"

"I'm a biochemist, not a surgeon. I can rearrange your genetic code, but I've never fused a bone or removed a spleen. I'm no use to you."

"You're all we've got."

Doyle's urgency overrode decorum. Riana didn't resist as he steered her toward Eckerd. She knelt by him but seemed perplexed at what to do next.

Doyle shouted for Indigo to bring the medkit, at which point Riana finally snapped to. She retrieved a hand scanner from the kit and ran it over Eckerd's patchwork skin. His skeletal structure flickered on the rollscreen.

Doyle asked, "What caused those scars?"

"He's had them since childhood." She seemed flustered. "Quiet, I need to think."

Riana cycled the multiscan to display Eckerd's circulatory

system, then his neural function. She sprang to her feet. "Get him to medlab, fast."

Between them, Doyle, Sabin, and Colby lifted Eckerd onto the operating table. Riana injected him with a stabilizing drug and connected the panoptic life support.

"He must have stroked," Riana said. "Either during hibernation or upon waking. There's still hemorrhaging." She pulled across a buzzing bone drill on a support arm and squeezed the trigger to get a feel for the torque. "I need to relieve the pressure on his brain. Clear the room."

The others left her alone. Riana inhaled and slipped a medical mask over her face. She hadn't performed surgery since choosing biochemistry for her major discipline in the UEC science program. The world seemed more logical through a microscope. Stark contrast to the drill in her hand, which brought a surge of terror up from her gut. No time for second-guessing; she had to trust that her diagnosis was correct and move promptly.

Riana bore the whirring drill into Eckerd's skull, careful not to drive in too deep. Flecks of bone pattered her mask.

A crude procedure, but without the luxury of poring over databanks for a better way, primitive expediency made sense. She just hoped the SLH thawing process had prevented enough clotting inside the cranial cavity, or nothing she did would matter.

As she withdrew the bone drill, to Riana's great relief, blood oozed out of the neat hole she'd made. She quickly attached a suction tube to aspirate the cerebral hematoma.

Riana swung a monitor device over the table and locked it into the control board. A green, fluctuating holographic grid spread around Eckerd's body. It looked impressive, but the graphics were merely a positioning guideline for the more mundane instruments hung above and embedded beneath the operating table.

Riana studied the data closely as each scan was completed.

¤ ¤ ¤

It seemed many hours later when Riana finally left the operating room and removed the mask from over her mouth. She idly stretched the elastic between her hands, testing its limits.

Doyle waited with Michi, whose thigh was heavily bandaged. He watched Riana's body language for a clue. Her face seemed weary, the flame that usually glowed just behind her eyes had dulled to ashes.

"How is he?" Doyle asked.

"Comatose," Riana said. "Indefinitely."

"Couldn't you—"

"I *did* what I could," she snapped. "His vital signs are stable. He's even breathing on his own, but his brain needs time to heal."

Doyle tried to modulate his reaction. "If we have any intention of returning home one day—and I sure as hell do—we'll need Eckerd very much alive."

"That's all you care about? You selfish…" Riana stopped herself before she said too much. She flung her surgical mask in the waste unit and turned her back on Doyle to examine Michi's thigh.

Gaea-02 was disturbingly quiet as Doyle traveled from the storage bay to the bridge. None of the usual discussions, arguments, or experiments taking place in every niche.

He wasn't unaffected emotionally by Commander Ruschen's death. He'd spent twelve hours a day working beside him for seven years. That bond was hard to forget, but they all had to put their grief aside for now and move forward, the way Baden himself would have done.

Doyle was still annoyed that Riana had misunderstood his motives earlier. Yeah, getting back to Lon was his number one priority, but not at the expense of his crew.

His crew? The way that notion slipped into his mind gave Doyle pause. Everyone naturally supposed the ship's command would fall on his capable shoulders once more. No one else had his experience; even Ruschen was offered the assignment only after Doyle withdrew. Although he secretly dreaded the prospect of being in charge again, Doyle was never one to shirk his duties.

Settling at the flight console, he was pleased to see that Colby had already made most of the navigation systems operational.

"2079," Colby read from the screen. "Accounting for relativity, we lasted the full thirty years."

"Some of us did," Doyle said grimly. "Are we on course?"

"Three days out from M38."

"So we got something right."

"Should have contact with those long-range probes soon, if the old buggers still work," Colby said.

"Indigo's on it. I don't want to fly in there blind."

Colby ran further diagnostics. "Ship's already slowed to chem assist velocity. How are our engines?"

"Sabin's down there now checking how far that damn robot let them deteriorate."

"What have you got against M.I.T.Z., anyway?"

"Computers are great. Automation, fine. But Artificial Intelligence? We don't need machines to think for us."

"Maybe what went down on Earth wouldn't have happened if they did," Colby spoke solemnly, a rarity for him.

Doyle viewed Colby through narrowed eyes to see if he was kidding. "You getting political on me, kid?"

"Me? Shit no." Colby laughed it off. "Hey, the big guy's alarm clock go off yet?"

"Yeah, he's fine." Django had come to on his own while the crew was busy elsewhere. Doyle practically jumped out of his skinsuit when Django suddenly tapped him on the shoulder. He wasn't about to tell Colby that part though. "He helped me carry Doc's and Commander Ruschen's bodies to the morgue."

"We have a morgue?"

"Temporarily, in the storage bay. Django started building a couple of coffins from spare materials, so I left him to it."

"He speak to you?"

"Not a single word."

Colby rubbed the light patch of fluff on his chin, "So what killed Doc and the Commander?"

"Age?" Doyle shrugged. "Riana hasn't done an autopsy. Says she doesn't know how to, but I don't think it's a coincidence they were the two oldest crew members."

"S'pose not."

"I'm next in line, huh?" Doyle meant it as a joke, but he came off somber.

"Nah mate, you look pretty good for sixty-five." Colby's quip did nothing to cheer him up.

Silently, the pair watched the feed from an external camera. An exotic solar system, bustling with twelve close-set planets and countless moons. Doyle's sense of awe was tainted by uncertainty and mortality. They were far, far from home.

Colby peered at his mentor. "You okay?"

"Keep me posted," Doyle said as he left the bridge.

Up ahead, Alexei leaned against the doorway of his astronomy lab. Doyle had the notion he was speaking softly to someone.

As Doyle moved closer, it became obvious that Alexei was alone. He was having a full-fledged conversation with himself, and he didn't skip a beat when he turned to grin at Doyle. "A lot to think about, yes?"

It took more than a little eccentricity to ruffle Doyle's feathers. "Have you updated this sector's starmap?"

Alexei motioned to his lab. "My computers are still processing the new data. This is an exhilarating time for an astronomer."

"I'm sure it is," Doyle said. "When you're done, give Indigo a hand tracking down those probes."

Doyle found himself slipping so easily into his former role as a commander. "Sorry," he said to Alexei, "I'm not your boss. You guys know what you're doing."

"You are wrong to apologize. These people need a leader."

Doyle sighed. "I shouldn't even be here."

"But you are, are you not?"

¤ ¤ ¤

Following protocol, Doyle removed Commander Ruschen's stored belongings from beneath the deceased's SLH chamber.

Outside the Commander's private office, Doyle fiddled with Ruschen's special comms unit, which doubled as a key. Not knowing what to expect inside, he swiped the band across a head-high receptor and the door whisked open.

The sparsely furnished room had one wall-length desktop covered by a parade of carefully arranged mementos, science awards, and photographs: Riana with her father, the late Admiral Stone, but none of Riana and Baden together, nor any of Ruschen's own relatives. Doyle saw a scale model of the *Gaea-01* prototype that he recognized from a Foundation Day he'd attended as a kid and an archaic snow globe of planet Earth, its once-twinkling flakes mired at the South Pole.

The cherished treasures on display surprised Doyle, but it was far too late to tell Baden Ruschen he might have seen him in the wrong light all these years. It was especially difficult to believe that this room was where Ruschen wrestled with the notion—and came to the conclusion—that the crew would not return to Earth.

Doyle switched the command console on. He wasn't sure this would work, but they needed to unlock the command codes in order to detach the crew module when they reached M38. He pressed his thumb against the fingerprint reader, hoping his clearance had been reinstated for their test flight. Officially, he was here as a civilian consultant.

The screen flashed and loaded a video log, recorded in the same room where Doyle watched it. Seeing Ruschen's face again was spooky. His video-self seemed relaxed. "Well, Doyle, unless someone has cut off your thumb, I'm speaking to you. It's day six of our *Gaea-02* shakedown, and since the UEC hasn't assigned me an official 2IC for this mission, I'll feel a lot better knowing you can take the reins if something goes wrong—which, since you're viewing this, it obviously has. Maybe you've strangled me for giving you such a hard time?" Ruschen's video-ghost smiled, as did Doyle.

"I'm sorry," Ruschen continued. "It's the only way I can deal with your being on board again. I see it in the others' eyes. Some of them would still consider you their leader if you hadn't told them not to. If you hadn't given up on our dream. I need to assert my authority now, if I expect them to follow my orders on the full mission next year. Then again, if you're watching this video," Baden said with a smirk, "this little soliloquy is moot."

His open demeanor seemed out of keeping with the man that Doyle knew and tussled with on *Gaea-02*. "Damn, Baden, all you had to do was talk to me. I could have helped," Doyle announced to the screen, but he knew how difficult it was to say what you mean in person, especially for Ruschen.

"Anyway, Doyle, on this console you'll find everything you need in an emergency. I'm trusting you to steer this ship right and to do what you can to fulfill the Gaea mission. I know your son takes precedence, but *Gaea-02* was *my* child. She belongs to all of us."

Doyle tilted a framed photograph of himself and Ruschen with the newly constructed *Gaea-02* crew module. The two of them weren't all that different, really.

"One more thing." Commander Ruschen's recording hesitated. "Please watch over Riana for me. I hope that's not too much to ask. She . . ." He seemed to want to say more but struggled with the words. A knock at his door was audible, so Ruschen awkwardly smiled onscreen before he reached forward and the recording ceased.

Riana draped the blue and green United Earth Coalition flag over a clear-topped, makeshift coffin containing Commander Ruschen's body.

Doyle did the same for Dr. Farrad's. Both coffins sat in *Gaea-02*'s airlock, a waiting room for the afterlife.

"Hold up," Sabin said as he jogged in with a small, flag-wrapped box. He placed it beside the two larger caskets. "Can't forget Pach."

The trio stepped in from the airlock, joining Alexei, Michi, Indigo, Django, and Colby.

Doyle sealed the bulkhead. He wasn't sure if he should say anything. Commander Ruschen was agnostic, and he didn't know what, if any, religious denomination Dr. Farrad had been. Doyle decided the most dignified eulogy for cosmic voyagers was silence.

He opened the outer airlock door. The remaining crew watched through a clear panel as the atmosphere inside rushed out, delivering the coffins into the void.

Doyle saluted first. The others followed suit.

Serenely, the three tombs drifted away from *Gaea-02*. If you didn't think too hard about what you what you were seeing, it was beautiful.

You move so fast in space, Doyle mused. It seems as if you're dawdling across the stars, but you're really speeding at thousands of kilometers per hour. Ruschen and Doc would be hurtling like frictionless bullets throughout the galaxies, perhaps forever.

Baden would have liked that.

The ship's tomato crops had withered and died long ago. Doyle wondered whether the hydroponics or soil cultivation bore fruit the longest. Juni had preferred soil, but then, she liked getting her hands dirty.

The state of decay here reminded Doyle of a dream he only half recalled. Lifting an atrophied leaf between his fingers, it crumbled into coarse powder.

His comms unit buzzed with Indigo's voice. "Doyle? We've got a read."

Doyle's heart sank when he saw Indigo's hologlobe of M38. Commander Ruschen's expectations had been grossly inflated.

By triangulating feedback from the early contact probes still in orbit, Indigo plotted any non-atmospheric energy sources. Only a handful of weak, yellow dots speckled the planet's surface.

"Not what I'd call a thriving colony," Doyle said.

"These results may not be accurate." Indigo tried to sound optimistic, rotating her three-dimensional map. "The probes could have some anomalies. Remember, they're over sixty years old."

"I know how they feel." Doyle wished he could ignore his foreboding impression. If only they had something more to go on. As it was, they were crawling through the dark by flickering torchlight. "Can you receive communications from the planet?"

"No-go so far. It was always a gamble. Their technology is decades ahead of ours, so they might be using completely different protocols."

"Meaning we can't transmit to them either?"

"We can talk 'til we're blue in the face, but I doubt they'll hear us."

Doyle stared at the globe. He wasn't even certain if it was still called M38 or had been renamed while the *Gaea-02* crew members were catching some *Zs*. The diplomatic tactics Ruschen had outlined no longer seemed feasible. Apart from the roadblock to communication, a miniscule settlement like this couldn't easily support an extra nine colonists out of the blue. They'd present additional mouths to feed, for starters. Doyle would have to rethink a more workable overture.

"Should I wake the others?" Indigo asked. *Gaea-02* was in night cycle and most of the crew were undoubtedly appreciating the texture of their bed-foams after floating in aquariums for so long.

"No," Doyle said. "Let them sleep. We'll hold a briefing in the morning."

Doyle pondered planet M38 on the observation deck's panoramic view-wall. Dense clouds engulfed most of the sphere. He touched the screen to zoom in closer.

All of the scenarios he could envision for their landing and approach ended with the same themes. Aggression. Hostility. Violence.

Riana entered, hesitated when she saw Doyle, but sat beside him anyway. Together, they stared at the murky planet.

"Not exactly beautiful," Riana finally commented.

Doyle held his tongue. He needed her to lead the conversation. He didn't want to risk offending the grieving widow again. She wasn't talking though, so they sat side by side in silence.

Doyle attempted to decipher M38's topography through narrow, fleeting breaches in the all-encompassing black clouds. Stratospheric lightning flashed at regular intervals. The old superluminal probe photos depicted a far more temperate and cloudless planet. None of the forecasts predicted prolonged storm activity on this scale.

Riana asked suddenly, "Did you mean what you said about returning home?"

"To see my son one more time is worth any hardship."

"He'll be almost as old as you, if he's even ..."

"I can't think of *ifs.*" The harshness of Doyle's reply quieted Riana. Damn, he hadn't meant to do that. He zoomed out the screen to a wide angle. "I'm sorry ... for pushing you so hard after Baden ... He and I had our problems, but ..."

"You were right. I have a job to do." Riana assumed a blank-faced stare. "A military brat like me should betray no emotions, correct?"

"Did he tell you that?"

"I'm not a fool, Doyle. I've heard the scuttlebutt. Whispers that Baden only married me to keep me on track for the Cause."

There she went again, misreading him. "That's not what I ..."

"He did love me. In his own way."

Tears pricked Riana's eyes, but she was stoic and her cheeks remained dry.

It was none of his business, but Doyle had always thought the gossip was only half right. Both Commander Ruschen's video recording and Riana's reactions confirmed as much. It may not have been an earth-shaking romance, but they truly loved each other.

Doyle eased his arm around Riana, comforting her. "You're not in the Academy now. Let it go."

The self-constructed dam keeping her emotions in check finally burst. Riana sobbed uncontrollably on Doyle's shoulder.

He held her as planet M38 slowly rotated below them.

All eight of the active *Gaea-02* crew huddled around a mess hall table. Indigo touched a panel and the shiny tabletop surface faded like melting snow. The underlying viewscreen rendered a map of planet M38 with its paltry energy readings.

"M38 might not be the land of milk and honey some of you were counting on," Doyle said.

Sabin frowned. "That's an understatement."

"Bloody hell, look at the temp," whined Colby. Beneath the map, a display stated the average global surface temperature as four degrees Celsius. "That's spanner weather."

Indigo raised her eyebrows. "Spanner weather?"

"Tightens the nuts," Colby explained for Indigo's amusement.

Michi kept on topic. "Why haven't the APA terraformed? Geosynchronized?"

They all turned to Django who, true to form, only shrugged his non-reply.

"Perhaps it took them longer to arrive than we expected," Alexei offered. "Did we overestimate how quickly they could reverse engineer our tech?"

Doyle took the floor with authority. "Folks, there could be a million reasons. We need to get planetside to figure it all out instead of leaping to false assumptions again."

Taking control of the map, he pinpointed an area containing a few yellow dots. "Far as we can tell, these are resource bases, drilling platforms, mining outposts. Relatively small energy radii at each point, not enough for real settlements. These other two keep moving around but are pretty large, so they're probably boats of some description."

"Boats?" Colby asked.

"The surface is ninety percent water," Alexei said. "A series of archipelagoes."

"Right." Doyle straightened. "I won't pretend this is good news. Whoever is down there will likely be struggling to establish their colony and probably won't welcome intruders with open arms. That's exactly what we'll be, *personae non gratae.*"

"Trespassers." Sabin clearly wasn't fazed by that tag. "So what's the plan?"

"Michi, can your robot make us weapons?"

She responded stiffly, rubbing the fresh bandage on her thigh, "M.I.T.Z. can use the ship's Mass Prototype Engine to recreate anything it has detailed plans for."

Doyle tried to keep from sounding snide. "I'm guessing that means, 'No.'"

"We had no reason to compile weapon schematics."

Riana spoke up for the first time during the briefing. "You're forgetting we're scientists, Doyle, not soldiers."

He remained firm. "We have to adapt to the circumstances. We can't contact the APA aside from knocking on their door."

"And they could answer with a bullet," Alexei finished the thought.

Doyle pointed to an energy signature on the map. "*Gaea-02* was built for sea landings. I say we set down near this base and use the amphibious lander. We go in hard and fast to secure the beachhead. Once we have leverage, we can explain our position without risk of reprisal."

Riana shook her head. "Isn't that extreme? It's not like they'd just kill us on sight."

"Are you positive? Can we jeopardize everything, everyone on this ship? We learned from Mars that the smaller the colony, the greater the chance societal norms will break down. They hushed it up, but with three hundred people in the *Gaea-01* settlement, there were four murders—a rate two hundred times higher than Earth's. My father showed me a classified report on the killings, and one line always stayed with me: 'Even the most noble ethos can and will degrade into brutality in the cold reaches of space.'"

Doyle switched off the map and the table returned to normal, but the crew's faces had changed. He wished Commander Ruschen had been less zealous in his assessment of this endeavor. He'd given them false hope. "The reality is we could be the match in a powder keg on M38. The APA were xenophobic at the best of times." Looking around, he could see the trepidation in their eyes. "If anyone thinks there's a better way, let's hear it now."

No one proposed an alternate plan. Doyle glanced at Riana to check that she was with him. A slight nod of her head was all the reassurance he needed.

"Okay, then. We leave orbit at oh-nine-hundred hours."

CHAPTER 11
DESCENT

A tiny speck against the gray planet, *Gaea-02* drifted toward M38.

Vapor dispersed from the base of the crew module like colorless blood spraying from a slit throat. The lengthy rear platform would remain in orbit while the decapitated module, acting as a self-contained shuttle, cast off to become *Gaea-02* on its own.

"Satellite platform unbound," Colby announced on the bridge. He manned one side of *Gaea-02*'s primary flight console, Doyle the other.

"Leave it on silent running for now," Doyle said. "Let's hide our tracks."

Indigo looked up sharply from her telemetry console. "Why?" She forced a smile. "I mean, what's the point?"

Fair question. She was the comms officer, Doyle reminded

himself; it was understandable that she'd be jittery without their major transmission horsepower. He asked her, "You can handle terrestrial comms with the crew module only, right?"

"Yes. If I have to."

"Then until we know what we're facing, I'd prefer not to publicize the fact that we're here to any APA ships that happen along. We'll switch it back on after we're established planetside, deal?"

"You're the boss." Indigo turned back to her station.

Colby started to initiate reentry, but Doyle stopped him and nudged Indigo's shoulder. "I'm not Commander Ruschen. My word isn't gospel and I've been wrong plenty of times. For the record: if you disagree with something I say, I want you to tell me. Got it?"

Indigo softened. She patted Doyle's hand. "'Preciate that."

Doyle set the crew module in motion. He closed the fore blast shield and a viewscreen activated in its place. Planet M38 loomed ever larger. Doyle tapped his comms band. "Batten down the hatches, folks. With our stage four engine gone, this may bruise."

In a secure landing carapace at the shuttle's heart, the non-flight crew double-checked their reentry seat harnesses. The Candlemass was doused; however, freefall wouldn't last long. The next time they experienced gravity's pull, it would be the real deal.

Gaea-02 entered M38's thermosphere.

The view from the bridge was blocked by dense cloud cover. Due to the planet's uncanny similarity to Earth—M38 being a fraction smaller—Doyle was comfortable the landing would go the same as dozens he'd performed back home. "Engage APLS," he told Colby, "but keep a close eye on your monitors. We won't have a support crew down there if we bungle this."

Under autopilot guidance, *Gaea-02*'s nose climbed, its belly facing down to add drag. An external monitor showed heat trails washing over the craft from fore to aft. Reentry burn-up was a constant threat but kept in check by their advanced Thermal Protection System.

To Doyle, the licks of flame coursing around *Gaea-02* evoked beauty instead of danger. They were glorious Olympian fireballs hurled at the starship for defying the gods. Such a potent rebellion made Doyle feel invincible. Immortal.

Colby watched with amazement as fire-swirls saturated the viewscreen's corners. He glanced at a readout. "Heat's staying within norm."

Doyle regained the sensation of weight. Gravitational force caressed his face. He felt like a kid pedaling his bicycle into the wind.

The ship juddered.

Severe turbulence suddenly took hold, its strength far greater than any Doyle had ever encountered. The flight stick thrashed back and forth, uncontrolled. Doyle tapped a keypad. "Damn. Autopilot is shot."

Indigo clung to her seat. "Thought you guys fixed everything after the ADM blast."

"Apparently not," Doyle mumbled. He gripped the flailing flight stick. "Switching to fly-by-wire."

The shaking intensified. Those in the landing carapace were almost jerked from their reentry seats. Michi caught a glimpse of Alexei smiling. *Smiling.* She was about to ask what was funny when, next to her, Riana detached her safety harness. Was the entire crew going mad?

Michi screamed above the rattling din, "Riana, don't!"

Before anyone could stop her, Riana clambered out of the carapace and into the crew module's spine.

Heat and flames escalated around *Gaea-02*. Sustained tremors knocked loose a sheet of hull shielding, which flipped end over end as it flew off behind them.

Colby reacted to a warning beep. "We lost a chunk of our heat shield!"

Doyle didn't panic. Early in the century, this would have been a disaster, with their ship disintegrating in seconds. The

UEC had learned from those tragedies. Even at sixteen hundred degrees Celsius, *Gaea-02* could last at least a minute with its TPS compromised. But one minute wouldn't be enough. "Indigo, reroute all nonessential systems to cooling."

Indigo shifted to a tertiary console. She cut the power to anything that wasn't keeping them alive.

The lights went off while Riana was stumbling toward her medlab. She palmed the wall to steady herself, allowing a few seconds for her eyes to adjust to the darkness. *There:* her route became visible.

The ship's center of gravity was skewed, so Riana had to lean back to stay vertical. She bent her knees as she walked, letting them absorb the intermittent shocks.

Blinking lights on Eckerd's monitors guided Riana to her comatose patient. She tightened the straps holding him down. With each seismic jolt the belts loosened again. She was waging a losing battle.

The room seesawed violently. Riana tried to stabilize Eckerd's body as best she could.

The descending ship was a cataclysmic phoenix, entirely engulfed in flame. Majestic plumes of superheated plasma crested its arching wingspan, radiating out to a hypersonic tail of fire.

The more spectacular the sight was to behold, the more difficult it became for Doyle to tame the ship's controls. The manual flight stick had a life of its own. Sweat dotted his forehead. He gritted his teeth to stop their chattering. "Come on, girl…"

Doyle forced *Gaea-02* into the wide S-turns necessary to burn off speed. They plunged into M38's upper mesosphere, soot-black clouds diffusing around their hull.

The bridge shook incessantly.

HUD and flight avionics failed one by one.

Doyle shut his eyes. He was flying blind anyway. He sensed which angles to turn by the vibrations under his feet. The ship told Doyle where in the sky it needed to be.

"Heat critical!" Colby shouted.

Gaea-02 was at breaking point. Deafened by the clamor, Doyle refused to let go. He would steer them all to safety.

The clouds thinned.

Black faded to gray and finally white. Flames dispersed. The tossing and buffeting ceased.

Doyle opened his eyes and released a long-held breath. He eased the flight stick forward, pitching the craft's nose down.

Snow pelted the viewscreen. *Snow.* After the hellfire they'd flown through, the incongruity made them giddy. Indigo smiled at Doyle, who chuckled back. Colby punched Doyle's shoulder and yelled expletives of praise in his ear.

Laughing, Doyle pushed Colby aside. "We still on target?"

"Close enough," Colby said, checking his instruments. "Scanners are whacked but judging by our coordinates, we're over the correct expanse of sea—just a few degrees off your splash site."

Better than he'd hoped. Doyle ran through a damage check with Indigo. They were in pretty good shape, considering. A few unimportant modules had melted down and the hull would need shoring up. Doyle's controls were responsive enough though. His radar altimeter was erratic, but he wouldn't need it for an ocean put-down.

He opened the blast shield. Layers of wispy vapor obscured their view.

The whirling snowflakes hardened into jagged ice.

Crew members in the landing carapace relaxed and joked, thinking the worst was over.

Alexei climbed from his reentry seat.

"Where you goin'?" Sabin asked.

"My lab." Alexei sauntered out as though they had already landed.

Ice shards sprayed the ship's hull as it approached planet M38's surface on a slender twenty-degree angle.

Doyle wasn't overly concerned about the storm. He'd landed in worse weather and on a narrow runway instead of an open ocean. This should be a no-brainer.

"Splashdown in thirty seconds," Doyle announced over his comms band. He added to himself, "Wish these damn clouds would…"

As if on command, the cloud cover parted like stage curtains.

Below them was not the rippling body of water that Doyle expected.

Instead, they were confronted by a sea of *solid ice.*

Doyle immediately yanked back on the flight stick. He scowled at Indigo. "This whole area was supposed to be liquid!"

Indigo frantically checked her console for the error. "I told you, the scans might have anomalies."

"This is more than an anomaly," Doyle growled. "It's game over."

The ice rose fast toward them. They could assign blame later. Impact was imminent. *Think, man. Think.*

"Pump everything into the RCS," Doyle told Colby. "I want this ship flat as a flapjack."

Reaction Control System thrusters above and below the ship blasted into action, straightening *Gaea-02* almost parallel to the ice.

Doyle strained with the flight stick to keep the crew module aloft. At their current velocity, he figured their only chance was to hit the surface perfectly level, like a stone skipping across a frozen pond.

The ice field nearly kissed *Gaea-02*'s underbelly.

Doyle's jaw was set and veins bulged at his temples. *Flatter.* He extended one-twenty flaps to wash off excess speed.

"Approaching full critical stall," Colby shouted.

Now or never. Doyle's throat was clenched so tight his voice barely rose above a whisper. "Deploy brake chute."

Riana heard a garbled voice on her comms band: "Brace yourselves!"

She held Eckerd's comatose body tight to protect him from whatever was about to happen.

A brake chute billowed out behind the crew module a split-second before its belly slammed into M38's frozen ocean.

The spaceship skimmed across the ice. Kinetic force saw *Gaea-02* bounce and crash back down again. Its interior rocked as though at the epicenter of an earthquake.

Violent undulations hurled Alexei against a bulkhead, snapping his left ankle on impact.

Medical instruments toppled around Riana. A heavy, metal tray ripped from its mooring and split her brow, knocking her out.

Sparks flew on the bridge. Doyle was flung from the pilot's chair like a firefly being rattled inside a jar.

The brake chute tore off the ship, flapping away in its slipstream.

Gaea-02 twisted as it ricocheted and rebounded in a din of screeching metal. Chunks of debris were spat out in its wake. The ship plowed into a deep ice bank at a sideways slant, losing all momentum.

A metallic howl echoed across the glacier as *Gaea-02* settled into place on a lopsided tilt, the crew module's stub nose buried in a mound of ice.

Steam rose from the singed hull to mingle with snow flurries.

CHAPTER 12
ARRIVAL

Doyle shivered in the dark.

He couldn't remember where he was or whether he was alive or dead. Perhaps he was still in subcooled hibernation, trapped in a feverish dream. He rubbed his arms and felt like he was caressing an icicle.

Sparks spat from bare wires above Doyle's head. Reality check: he was still on *Gaea-02*'s bridge.

Electricity pulsed; dim lights faded on, then winked off in an annoying cycle.

Doyle's perspective was disorienting. The world teetered at a forty-five degree angle. Tilting his head sidewise, he reached for the primary console to pull himself up. Frost mantled every surface. *Temperature regulators must have been zapped.* He wrapped his arms around himself and called out, "Colby?"

"The judge from Australia awards that landing a three out of ten." Colby's upside-down head shook with sarcasm. His lanky limbs hugged what remained of the flight chair.

Doyle flipped him onto his feet. "See if you can get the Candlemass online, straighten us out."

Colby climbed across the wreckage to reach the controls. Doyle searched beneath the telemetry console, which was now at the bottom of the slanted bridge. He found Indigo buried under broken components.

Doyle dug her out. "Are you hurt?"

"I'm … not *un*hurt." Indigo seemed dizzy, squinting. "Why is everything sideways?"

"The ship must be wedged on its wing where we landed."

"Super."

"Don't," Doyle said. "I got enough on my plate without barbs from my crew."

She clutched her skull. "My head's pounding like a drum machine."

Colby reattached a cable and tapped a few keys. "Got it." He stood back proudly. Nothing happened. Colby kicked the console.

They heard a *hummmmmm* as an undercurrent vibrated through the ship.

The Candlemass extended below *Gaea-02*, melting a hole in the ice as it spun. It helped generate just enough localized artificial gravity at the correct point to shunt the room level again—more or less. Doyle could still feel M38's true gravity pulling him on a two-degree slant, but his brain was tricked into seeing everything as flat. The conflicting gravities left him with a weird sensation just short of nausea.

Indigo shook her fuzzy head, leaning over to check a flashing readout. She blinked and her eyes widened. "Fires in the mess and medlab."

Great. Doyle snatched a compact foam extinguisher from its wall compartment and tossed it to Colby. "You two take the mess hall."

He took a second extinguisher for himself and rushed into the ship's spine.

Eyes closed, Riana was slumped across Eckerd's comatose body. Thanks to her diligence, his bonds had held throughout the crash, but she was repaid with a split forehead. In her semiconscious state, blood crept down a cheekbone into her mouth.

A crackling sound agitated Riana.

She had only one memory from Quebec: being cradled by her mother before an open hearth. A scorched log had collapsed and sent embers drifting into her mother's long, black hair.

Riana could hear that long ago flame and feel its heat. "*Trop chaud, Maman,*" she heard herself say. *Too hot, Mom.*

An amber flicker. A coppery taste on her tongue. Riana's eyelids fluttered open and her shock registered.

A ceiling-high inferno raged across the medlab. Jolted into cognizance, Riana scanned the burning room's layout. Her only escape route and the lab's extinguishers were blocked by the fire. She and Eckerd were trapped.

Flames inched closer, fueled by a cocktail of overturned chemicals.

Riana unhooked the straps holding Eckerd in place. She strained to lift him off the table. She stumbled backward and fell, Eckerd's body knocking the wind from her when he landed on top.

Pinned, Riana struggled for breath. She heard a bottle shatter from the heat and smelled burning magnesium.

She mustered strength for one mighty heave and managed to roll Eckerd off. No longer shielded, her face was seared by the nearby flames.

Riana dragged her comatose patient to the far corner of the room. She huddled there with him as fire consumed the table he had occupied moments before. There was nothing else she could do. At least *he* wouldn't feel the agony of being roasted alive.

Blue-tinged smoke spread across the ceiling.

Terror devoured Riana's resolve. If she remembered any prayers, she would have broken down and said them. Baden wouldn't have approved. Composure until the end was his motto. Blood seeped from her head wound and dried instantly on her face, but she was beyond noticing anything except the macabre dance of flames.

Riana clutched Eckerd's limp hand, more for her own comfort than his. *So this is how it feels, Baden.* Tears evaporated before they could roll down her cheeks.

Riana had once thought the sweetest tones in the world came from a Leblanc clarinet—the perfect mix of melancholy and wistful promise. From that moment on, her favorite sound was a nozzle spraying foam. Riana could hear it dousing the wall of fire from the opposite side.

Roaring flames dwindled to ashen, soapy flakes. Doyle stepped through the smoke, a spent extinguisher at his side.

Riana blinked in disbelief as Doyle wiped the blood from the corner of her eye.

Indigo finished bandaging Riana's forehead. Doyle draped blankets over both women's shoulders.

The crew huddled in the chilly mess hall. Although the fire there had been minor, doing no structural damage before it was smothered, the smell of burnt rations tickled their noses.

Alexei sniffed the air, discolored flesh swelling around his fractured ankle. Colby, in turn teasing and sympathizing, recounted accidents of his own clumsy youth in a fruitless attempt to cheer up the Kazakhstani.

Riana took the medical kit from Indigo. Wooziness struck hard as she stood, but Doyle held her steady. "Lie down, you're still concussed."

"I'm fine." Riana knelt by Alexei and let her fingertips gently explore his ankle. Her frustration showed when she turned to Indigo. "I … it's stupid. I've never done this in practice. Do you know how the bones are supposed to sit?"

Indigo shook her head, but Michi raised her hand, "I know." She rolled up her sleeves. "I did extensive anatomical studies while designing M.I.T.Z." She hobbled over, pleased to prove her worth.

Michi firmly manipulated Alexei's ankle, studying his face to make sure her adjustments weren't too painful. Once done, she smiled up at Riana. "There."

"Great. Hold it stable." Riana retrieved a tube from the med-kit to spread a white paste around Alexei's puffy, realigned limb. In seconds, the paste hardened into a solid cast.

Alexei showed no reaction at all during the entire process. Riana was mystified. "That should have hurt a *lot.*"

Deadpan, Alexei assured her, "It did."

Sabin's voice buzzed over Doyle's comms band. "Got the regulators online. Everyone should be warming up in a sec."

Doyle tapped the band to reply, "Fast work, Sabin, I'm impressed." He stepped aside so the others wouldn't hear him say: "How long can we last out here?"

"Enough juice for nearly a week. Solar collectors aren't gathering much joy in this weather."

Doyle rubbed the light stubble on his cheek, before quietly communicating to Sabin, "Finish up there and get a few hours rest."

"We're rolling out?"

"Yeah."

When Doyle turned around, he was surprised to find Colby standing right behind him. "In all seriousness, Doyle, no one else could have landed this bird. Including me."

"Well, neither of us can fly her now. She's down for the count."

"There'll be other ships, mate. Should be a steady traffic of APA colonists by now."

"Should be, sure," Doyle concurred, "or maybe everything here's automated. Maybe they already gave up on this place."

Riana, Michi, and Indigo made plans to take advantage of the calm before the next storm to freshen up: vibro showers and a couple of overdue haircuts to remove the last matted clumps of pink hibernation goo.

"They've got the right idea," Doyle said to Colby as the women left the mess hall in lighter spirits. "We've just gotta do the best we can."

Doyle wished he could have extended the crew's downtime, but they had to move ahead.

He'd sent a shipwide command to meet him in the vehicle bay at the rear of the crew module. Only Django hadn't verbally responded via his comms band. No surprise there, but the silent goliath hadn't shown up on schedule either.

Doyle knocked on Django's private quarters. Hearing no reply, he mashed the pad to slide open the door.

Django was seated on his bedfoam, writing in a thick, leather-bound book.

Although the Commander had been allowed more, each regular crew member was permitted only three personal items, and this must have been one of Django's. Real books had long been considered dead weight, especially since *Gaea-02*'s computers could store complete digital copies of Earth's combined libraries.

Stepping inside, Doyle's boot crunched on scattered remnants of a clay figurine broken during the crash. He bent to pick up an intact Pahouin tribal mask, which had fallen from the wall. *So these were Django's other two personal effects?* On a whim, Doyle turned the mask over and looked through the empty eye sockets at Django, who continued scrawling in his journal. The perspective from those two dark slits made the big man no easier to penetrate.

Doyle spotted Django's comms band, discarded on the bedfoam beside him. With a flash of irritation, Doyle scooped up the comms unit and waved it in front of Django's face. "As long as you're part of this crew, you keep this on at all times. Understand?"

Django peered down at his book but humbly nodded his head twice when Doyle was done scolding him.

Fidgeting with Django's comms band, Doyle sat and gestured at the damaged artifacts. "Must be rough." His voice was suddenly full of empathy. "Separated from your land, your culture, your people. I was shoehorned into this and I'm missing my boy like hell. Why did you volunteer to leave everything behind and come here?"

His big eyes watched Doyle closely, but Django guarded his reasons. He accepted his comms band from Doyle, wrapped it around the back of his wide head, and plugged the two-prong control jack into the holes behind his ear.

Admitting defeat, Doyle stood and simply told him, "Vehicle bay, two minutes."

The sole vehicle on board *Gaea-02* was a chunky, clunky, four-wheeled amphibious truck. It was a token gesture to the engineers testing load weights; *Gaea-02*'s crew was never intended to actually drive the thing. Doyle could see why the first time he'd set eyes on it. The driver's station was too high and recessed, while the rear bracings were too low to the ground. Might be fine in water, but it would steer like a fish on dry land.

Riana handed Doyle a viewtablet with scientific gibberish scrolling down the screen. "Alexei's scans confirm the data from our old probes."

Balanced on a metal crutch cobbled together from busted bits of infrastructure, Alexei pointed out the critical section to Doyle. "Seventy-six percent nitrogen, almost twenty-four percent oxygen."

"Even richer than Earth's air," Doyle mused. Finally, something in their favor. As planned, the crew could breathe unassisted on M38.

Strolling around the amphibious truck, Doyle surveyed its light damage from their crash landing. He asked Sabin, "This rig been tested?"

"Pach and I gave it a spin back home. For the full mission, we were gonna pack this whole bay with the latest gear, right bro?" Sabin saw the look Doyle gave him, so he spread his fingers out on *Gaea-02*'s hull as though he could feel his brother's spirit. "Like you said, man, he's here. He always will be."

Doyle squeezed Sabin's shoulder, then signaled to Michi, whose new haircut was surprisingly short and spiky. She tapped a panel to open the huge bay door, which hinged down to form a gangplank onto the ice.

Outside, the bleak, glacial scenery—which they saw at a forty-five degree slant from the cockeyed ship—was ravaged by relentless storms. Snow flurries whisked in, and Doyle instantly felt the temperature drop well below zero.

He accessed a digital map on the view-tablet and projected it holographically against the wall for the rest of the crew to see. "We're farther from our mark than we'd hoped. What's the truck's range?" he asked Sabin.

"On solid ground, eighty klicks. In snow… thirty-one."

Doyle traced a line on the holomap. "It's thirty-six klicks to the base. We'll need to hike the last five."

Colby smirked. "Anyone bring skis?"

Since joining the UEC, Doyle hadn't tackled any mission without his lucky flight jacket. Juni used to joke that he'd sleep in it if she'd let him. She was right. It was a security blanket and the largest of the three personal items he'd brought aboard *Gaea-02*. Lon's drawing, neatly stuffed in his pocket, and his family photo were the other two, but none would be accompanying Doyle. His jacket wouldn't fit either underneath or over the skin-tight environment suit that Indigo handed him.

The bulky suits were originally supplied as protection if *Gaea-02*'s radiation shields were ever penetrated, but they were also engineered to resist landfall climate extremes. Heavily insulated, each one was laced with circuitry for both heating and cooling. A hood could be pulled over the wearer's head, but Doyle let his hang at the nape of his neck for now.

He flexed his arms. The suit was designed not to restrict physical movement, so the snug fit around his muscles was more pleasant than he'd expected.

Doyle handed his flight jacket to Indigo for safekeeping. "Stay here and jam all communications to or from the APA base beyond a one klick radius. If we have to take it by force, I don't want them calling in reinforcements."

"I'll be honest with you, Doyle, I don't know if I can."

"Try."

Django and Sabin donned their envirosuits. After the Orbital Station clash, Doyle was confident these two could hold their own in combat.

"Colby, suit up," Doyle said.

"Me? Are you kidding? I'd be dead five steps out on the ice."

"We need at least four people for this." Doyle let his annoyance show. "Quit stalling."

"I'll go," Riana blurted.

Doyle pretended not to hear her and tossed an envirosuit to Colby. "Suck it up, kid."

"*I said*, I'll go." Riana snatched the suit from Colby, who was happy to let her have it.

She had the leggings up to her waist before Doyle gripped the suit's collar and ordered, "No. You need to look after Eckerd."

"Medlab's computers will keep him comfortable, and Indigo has emergency training." Riana tugged the suit from Doyle's hand and continued dressing.

The rest of the crew watched their confrontation. Had a bucket of popcorn been handy, Doyle wagered, they'd be snacking. On any planet, that's entertainment.

He was grateful when Riana pulled him aside for a tête-à-tête, although her fresh dab of citrus perfume was mildly distracting. She edged close and spoke softly. "I appreciate you saving me from the fire. I do. I'd never been that scared before, and you show up like some shining knight. I . . ." She looked at the floor. "Baden used to think he was my shining knight, my shield. But sometimes it felt more like shackles. I didn't need his protection then, and I don't need you safeguarding me now." Riana locked eyes with Doyle. "I *do* need to do this, though. You know I'm capable."

She held his gaze. Commander Ruschen had asked him to take care of Riana, but Doyle doubted Baden ever realized how strong she was.

Doyle relented with a wave of his hand.

Riana zipped up her envirosuit. "Besides, you might want a translator again."

"I might," Doyle agreed reluctantly.

Behind them, Michi winced while lifting her injured thigh into an envirosuit.

Doyle rolled his eyes; this was getting ridiculous. "Not a chance, Ozaku. You can barely walk."

Michi didn't stop suiting up. "You'll need M.I.T.Z. if they have any automated security systems."

"Why would they?" Riana asked her. "There was never any indication of indigenous life on M38."

"Ever consider that the *non*-indigenous life might be expecting us?"

Michi's question puzzled Riana, who looked to Doyle for his opinion.

He knew the APA colonists could be armed if this was a military-run operation—which was highly likely—and the prospect of their being actively prepared for *Gaea-02*'s arrival on M38, while less probable, had also occurred to him. In the short time he'd known Michi, Doyle had judged her a little naive, yet she might be saving them a major headache.

"Okay, we'll take the robot to interface with their system. But not you."

Tiny Michi grew big in her defiance. "You need *me* to tell M.I.T.Z. what to do. And don't worry about my thigh." She clambered onto the robot's back like a rodeo cowgirl. "I'll ride piggyback."

¤ ¤ ¤

Doyle revved the amphibious truck's engine. It stuttered for a worrying moment before settling into a low-register purr. The vehicle trundled down the ramp onto planet M38's surface. Reaching the ice, the truck tilted in the genuine gravity until its tires thumped down flat. In the rear section, the others—Riana, Michi, Sabin, and Django—bounced with the taut suspension.

Taking an injured techie and a biochemist—whatever their gender—on a potentially dangerous assignment didn't sit well with Doyle. He wasn't entirely pleased about the damn robot coming along either. They'd had to strap M.I.T.Z. to the truck's roof. Best place for that unreliable machine, Doyle reckoned.

The frozen expanse appeared flat and featureless from afar, but when they actually drove over the ice shelf, it became a myriad jigsaw of tors and craters. White on white parallax turned the middle distance into a shifting optical illusion, inducing headache and eyestrain. Every now and then, Doyle had to turn away and blink for a few moments to recalibrate his vision.

The weather worsened the farther they traveled. Neither of M38's two moons, nor its warming sun, were ever directly visible. Light filtered through clouds, reflected by the ice fields in haphazard halos.

Disoriented, Doyle lost track of how many hours he'd been behind the wheel. On a pleasant Sunday stroll, he could've walked the same distance in half the time. From a rough calculation, he figured they were nearing the limit of their fuel range.

The amphibious truck plowed through a snow bank and mounted a ridge. Doyle heard the axle strain. The front wheel lost traction and the vehicle careened down a precipice. The truck skidded as the slope evened out. Doyle hoped the crew in the back hadn't cracked their skulls.

The truck slowed at the bottom of the slope, lights dimming as the final power cache drained. Doyle squeezed a few more yards out of the engine before it fully conked out.

His passengers eyed the halogen light-rim in their rear compartment as it faded to darkness.

¤ ¤ ¤

Swirling ice stinging his face, Doyle handed out transponder poles to Riana, Sabin, and Django. Michi clung to M.I.T.Z., so he kept the last one for himself.

Riana went to switch on her pole's beacon, but Doyle stopped her. "Leave it off."

"Excuse me? Won't these keep us together?"

"If anyone in the APA base is scanning, transponder signals will flare up like roman candles on their porch."

Sabin pulled his envirosuit's hood over his head. "You don't think they already noticed a big-ass rogue spaceship landing next door?"

"Maybe not," Doyle said. "Indigo thinks this planet's atmosphere fouls up suborbital tracking pretty well. But a beacon on their doorstep? Dead giveaway."

Riana waved her inactive transponder pole. "Then what's the point of this?"

Doyle jammed his pole's base through the deep snow. "Test the powder depth before each step, so you don't wander into a hole. If there's bare ice, give it a sharp tap to make sure it's not brittle. Got it?"

Riana nodded. Doyle sealed the envirosuit over his bald scalp. He didn't want to advertise the other reason for bringing the transponder poles just yet. They weren't much of an arsenal, but they were heavy enough to swing like baseball bats if the need arose.

"So what about keeping track of each other?" Michi asked from atop her robotic mount's shoulders.

Doyle retrieved the waterproof rope they'd used to tether M.I.T.Z. to the truck. He lashed it around the robot's torso, looped out a six-foot length, and tied that to a support buckle on his own waist. He made identical safety lines for each member of the party, ending with Django. Doyle yanked the slack tight after each knot to stiffen its clutch.

"Michi," Doyle had to yell against the howling wind. He tossed her a rucksack of rations. "M.I.T.Z. has the coordinates locked in?"

She slid the sack over her shoulders and gave him a gloved thumbs-up.

"Everyone ready?" Doyle asked, allowing them a moment to appreciate the wonder of walking on a foreign planet without any kind of breathing apparatus. A harsh climate couldn't dull their pioneering spirit.

Doyle signaled for Michi to take the lead aboard M.I.T.Z. The robot's blue ring-eyes glowed brighter, illuminating their path with a ghostly cast.

The guide rope kept them all in a staggered line as they headed away from the abandoned truck, its wheels already buried by snowfall.

M38 was a slightly smaller and less dense planet than Earth, so the pull of gravity was weaker. The crew shed around sixteen pounds just being there, although their lighter strides were more than offset by the blizzard's ferocity.

Progress was torturously slow and visibility virtually zero. Prior to every step, they prodded the snow ahead with their transponder poles like four blind mice, relying on M.I.T.Z. to navigate out in front.

The robot's heavy soles crunched the ice underneath in a monotonous, mechanical dirge.

The group needed another rest. Envirosuits filtered moisture from the air to keep their bodies hydrated, but their limbs ached from the unremitting slog.

The team paused at the tip of a downslope where, for a brief moment, the snowstorm cleared. Riana made the mistake of gazing across the open ice valley. The altitude and lack of any discernible horizon made her woozy.

She swayed on the apex until Doyle pulled her guide rope taut. He assisted her back onto steadier footing.

Michi passed the rucksack to Doyle, who handed out rations to boost their flagging vitality.

Despite his suit's hydration system, Doyle was thirsty as hell. Their journey through the ice was as dry as any desert crossing. They'd lost a lot of bodily fluids just moistening the cold, dry air they were breathing.

They hadn't lugged any additional liquids from *Gaea-02*, and all that clean ice taunting them for as far as the eye could see was far too cold to suck. Doyle laughed. "Water, water everywhere…"

Catching his drift, Michi jabbed her transponder pole against a jutting ice-fin, snapping a frosty chunk off. She commanded M.I.T.Z. to heat the block of ice in its wide, cupped hands and directed the resulting liquid toward Doyle. "Water for the gentleman?"

Eyebrow raised, Doyle cautiously sipped from the robot's thermodynamic 'goblet.' It was the purest, freshest liquid he'd ever tasted, and it rapidly quenched his thirst. When they'd left Earth, quality water like that would have been more expensive than gold bullion. Michi had M.I.T.Z. share the thawed bounty around.

Watching his bedraggled crew drink from the robot's hands, Doyle wondered if they'd be in any shape to fight if they did meet resistance at their destination. What were they walking into?

When they were ready to carry on, the tempest rose again. Doyle had an unnerving sense that the planet was against them and their path would never be easy.

They'd been hiking for more than six hours when they finally encountered solid landmass.

Exhausted but newly motivated, the group approached a ridgeline where the glacial shelf joined an iced-over peninsula. Trudging up the rise toward terra firma, M.I.T.Z. led with Michi on its back. Doyle, directly behind, tapped on the ice with his transponder pole, an action now performed by rote. He lifted his boot to step forward.

The ice cracked.

A faultline zigzagged between M.I.T.Z. and the rest of the crew. The robot's heavyweight crossing had stressed the ice to fracture point. In a split second, the tenuous ridge dropped away completely.

Behind M.I.T.Z., the crew tumbled into the chasm, huge chunks of ice plunging around them. No one could react fast enough. Transponder poles splashed into the sea.

M.I.T.Z. clambered for a foothold on land, its indicator stripe changing from blue to emergency red. As each crew member reached the limit of their guide rope below, the line snapped taut and jolted the robot again. Michi slipped from its shoulders, but she held on with one hand, flailing backward. M.I.T.Z. dug its long fingers into the icy rock, sharply arresting its slide. Michi recoiled, flung against the robot's back with a jarring thud.

Doyle, Riana, and Sabin collided against the ice cliff, each dangling from the rope fastened to M.I.T.Z. above. Django, hung lowest on the guideline, dipped into the frigid water.

Doyle heard the splash and looked down to see Django fully submerged. He screamed, "Django!" but saw no movement.

Michi crawled close to M.I.T.Z.'s head to issue frantic voice commands. "Up. Forward. Go, go, go!"

The robot extended its limbs to haul its body forward, thereby dragging the rope up. Django, limp and lifeless, was hauled from the water.

M.I.T.Z. rose to full height and slogged like a beast of burden, drawing the crew farther from the chasm with each laborious step.

Once Doyle had hold of the cliff edge, he tried to climb onto the slippery land. He failed. The guide rope pulled at his waist with the weight of three people hanging below him.

Doyle inhaled deeply. As icy air stung his burning lungs, he shimmied one leg onto a foothold and squeezed the release latch on his suit's support buckle. The knot binding him unlooped. He pushed with his legs and vaulted over the ledge.

M.I.T.Z. worked faster without Doyle's weight added to its load, but every wasted second counted for Django. Doyle leaned over to help pull the rope up. When Riana was in range, he thrust his hand out for her to clutch.

"Let me take your weight," he yelled, and Riana released the guide rope. He coached her—thankful of the planet's lower gravity—as she pendulum-swung up. Doyle caught and placed her on solid ground. The two assisted Sabin above the ledge, leaving only unconscious Django suspended at the rope's end.

M.I.T.Z. tramped the final steps, hauling Django into Doyle and Sabin's waiting grasp. They each grabbed one shoulder and together motored the giant man down the peninsula's icy ridge, his heels leaving trails in the snow.

They placed Django prone at the bottom of the slope. Riana lifted his eyelids to find his pupils rolled back into their sockets. Her head against his broad chest, she warned the others, "He's breathing, but in severe hypothermic shock. We need to raise his body temp."

Doyle pointed to M.I.T.Z. and shouted at Michi, "Get that thing to dig a hole, fast."

Michi said, "We can do better." She tapped M.I.T.Z.'s cranial shell. "Heat. One meter radius."

The robot extended its arms to the side of the solid ice ridge, its long, flat fingers turned upright. Invisible, highly concentrated microwaves emitted from its palms. The ice heated instantaneously. M.I.T.Z. circled each hand in opposite arcs, melting out a small cavern.

Doyle and Sabin rolled Django into the hollow. The interior was warm—tepid liquid dripped down—but it wouldn't be enough.

Riana retrieved a shiny square from her envirosuit pocket and yelled to Doyle, "Get that suit off him. It's doing more harm than good now."

While Doyle and Sabin stripped the sodden, shorted-out envirosuit from Django's immobile body, Riana unfolded her metallic square into a wide strip of ultrathin thermal insulation. "Here, take one edge," she told Doyle.

Between them, they wrapped the shiny material around every inch of Django, sealing in his body heat. Doyle thought he looked like a Pharaoh mummified in foil. If they couldn't do more soon, he'd be dead as any Pharaoh too.

Doyle undid his hood and loosened the neck seal on his own envirosuit.

The moment Riana realized the sacrifice Doyle was planning to make, she gripped his suit's collar. "Don't. You'll need it."

"It's over a klick to the base, through that." Doyle gestured at the merciless ice storm. "He'll die without a dry suit."

"So will you."

"I'm not the one already in shock."

Riana tried to speak, but Doyle silenced her reproach. "What did Baden like to say? 'No arguments.'" He wrenched his envirosuit off.

Doyle wore only light underclothes. He might as well have been completely naked as the cloth offered no barrier to the murderous cold. Wind blasted his bare skin like an ice dragon's breath.

Staving off hypothermia by pure force of will, Doyle lifted Django's feet and guided them into the envirosuit's legs. The extra layer of insulation foil crinkled loudly as he tugged the suit up Django's body. Doyle's suit was smaller than Django's had been and although the latex hybrid expanded around the big man's torso, it didn't quite fit over his massive shoulders.

Doyle reached under Django's left armpit. "Sabin, on three, lift." After his count, they hoisted Django up, slinging his arms around both their shoulders. Django was so heavy—dead weight—Doyle felt his already dwindling strength sapped after a couple of steps. He knew there was no hope they could make it all the way to the APA base.

His gaze wandered to the guide rope drooping from the robot's waist. The other end was frozen solid to Django's discarded envirosuit. That was it. He yelled to Michi, still mounted on M.I.T.Z., "Sorry, you'll have to walk. We need to borrow your mule." Michi slid down the robot's back and hobbled over the ice on her injured leg.

Sabin and Doyle hauled Django against M.I.T.Z.'s back. Riana understood what they were doing. She snapped the frozen tip off the guide rope like a stalk of celery and fastened the rest around Django's body. Three loops across to bind him securely to M.I.T.Z., tied off with a seaman's knot.

Michi ordered the robot, "Proceed to original target." M.I.T.Z. rose to full height. Its head swiveled as it determined the coordinates, then plodded onward with Django firmly attached.

Sliding his arm around Michi's waist, Doyle lent his support so she could limp along. He could hear the pride in Michi's voice when she asked, "Aren't you glad we brought M.I.T.Z.?"

Doyle's teeth were chattering too much for him to respond. It was impossible to ignore the cold fire that flayed his skin. His frozen body threatened to shut down. For all the time he'd spent in subcooled hibernation, he thought he'd be less susceptible.

Giving up on himself was one thing, but deserting a member of his crew was unacceptable, so he concentrated on helping Michi along. His cone of spatial awareness narrowed to nothing except the robot's deep imprints in the snow. One shivering step at a time.

A familiar crinkling sound brought Doyle back to his surroundings. Sabin had unfolded his insulation wrap, draping it around Doyle like a cape. "You look a little chilly, *gringo*." Michi followed his cue and wound her sheath of insulation around Doyle's torso. It did help a little. He gave a grateful nod.

Sabin lifted Doyle's arm around his own shoulder, bearing the majority of Doyle's weight. Michi shifted to Riana for support. They walked that way, one leaning on another, as the minutes seemed to stretch into hours.

On the peninsula, Doyle faded fast. Without Sabin's buttressing, he would have collapsed. Through the white haze, his mind traced the outline of a huge shape. As they moved toward it, he dared to believe it wasn't a hallucination. He mustered the strength to raise one arm and draw the others' attention.

Half buried beneath a snowbank, the metallic, cylindrical object stood at least eighteen feet tall.

"Supply pod," Sabin said. "Looks like it's been here a while. Dropped from orbit, probably disposable."

"Automated recovery?" Riana asked.

"Can't tell from here. The hatch is shut, but—"

"Unless AI has changed drastically, a robot wouldn't bother to secure a disposable object," Michi said.

"Humans have a pathological instinct to close the door," Riana added.

"So we'll assume the base is manned. And that means..." Michi shielded her eyes and pointed. "There it is."

They focused on a structure in the distance; it was illuminated by a dull light swinging back and forth in the furious wind.

The crew arrived at an industrial base blanketed in snow. Dwarfed by a looming central complex, the uninviting gray spheres of an adjunct refinery offered momentary refuge for *Gaea-02*'s weary wayfarers.

None of the peripheral structures hinted at any sign of life within. M.I.T.Z. confirmed the absence of active security systems. Only the sole lantern hanging above the main building's giant entryway gave any indication that the base was still in use. But even of that, none of them could be sure.

They looked to Doyle for guidance. Riana dusted the frost from his numbed face and said, "What do we do?"

Doyle croaked, "Django?"

"He's holding on. He needs treatment ASAP."

They were clearly in no shape for battle. No time for stealth. Proud of their persistence to reach this far, Doyle felt he was letting them down. Grandiose plans of humanist colonies vanished in the face of simple survival; they had no choice except to throw themselves on the APA's mercy.

Doyle drew the insulation foil closer around his body, feeling more useless than ever before. "Get us inside," he managed to say.

Together, the Gaea squad approached the manufacturing base's ample hangar doors. The dull, gray sky seemed to darken at every step.

Michi commanded M.I.T.Z., "Open sesame."

Django still bound to its back, the robot extended its squashed-ovoid face close to a keypad beside the entrance. The blue rings encircling M.I.T.Z.'s hollow, black eyes shimmered and rotated.

Riana asked Michi, "What's it doing?"

"Computing the most effective way to—"

M.I.T.Z. suddenly drove a fist into the keypad and ripped the whole mechanism out. With its other hand, the robot sent a spark of electricity into the bare wires snaking from the wall.

The wary crew waited as the enormous door ascended, its gears grinding loudly.

They were greeted by the sight of a stunned Asian Pacific Alliance engineer holding a hot drink. Steam wafted outside as the Chinese man, his slack mouth twitching, was utterly stupefied to find a group of unknown humans on his alien planet.

Servos whirring, M.I.T.Z. lurched forward to hulk over the short engineer, who gawked up at the curious robot.

The punch came from nowhere. Before Doyle could stop him, Sabin knocked out the unarmed engineer.

"We come in peace," Sabin said acidly as he stepped over the sprawled body to enter the base.

CHAPTER 13
PRESAGE

Fei Haisheng tasted engine oil on the gag between his lips. He dimly recognized the tall, arching ceiling of the manufacturing base foundry.

The entire series of events was confusing to him. For a start, he had never been punched before. He found the ache in his jaw fascinating.

Of course, everything paled in comparison to the mystery of these interlopers' identities. From what Fei could tell before losing consciousness, they were unarmed and two were in dire need of medical assistance. But who were they? The only non-Asians in the colonies were a Kenyan couple on the M41 survey team.

He was also curious about the M.I.T.Z. unit with them. It was so crude it looked like the schematics he'd seen of the original, long-outdated prototype. How could that be possible? That model was destroyed along with the infamous *Gaea-02* thirty years ago.

Fei heard a noise.

The man who had punched him was searching the base. He seemed quite determined. Would he be relieved or disappointed if he found no one else here?

Fei's life of duty was solitary. His rotation would last a further eight months before he could return home and some other lonely soul would take his place. Until then, he'd keep the machines running for whenever the carrier crews deigned to stop on this forsaken plateau. He supplied them with crucial parts, repairs, and hydrogen fuel; in return they gave him absolutely nothing. No companionship, no invitation to traverse the open waters or visit the other bases. Fei fulfilled his thankless, tedious tasks without complaint.

He was honored to serve.

However, after two years and four months of reliving the same dull day over and over again, this sudden incursion—while a frightening experience—was a welcome change of pace.

Fei was aware that the other APA forces on this planet, although they numbered only a few dozen, would not be so tolerant. They weren't all passive engineers like him. Most would not take the time to inquire why these strangers were here. They would assume this was an enemy invasion and defend themselves accordingly...

The scruffy Hispanic returned, dragged Fei Haisheng to his feet, and said something Fei couldn't understand. Fei wasn't positive, but it sounded like the forbidden language: English.

In *Gaea-02*'s medlab, Indigo supervised Eckerd's diagnostic tests precisely as Riana had specified. The only deviation in his status was a slight dip in blood pressure, yet she couldn't shake her impression that Eckerd was fading away.

Indigo knew he had been attracted to her. She also realized she was the last person to see Eckerd awake, before their hibernation. Perhaps she'd be the last person who would ever see him alive.

As she lightly caressed his forearm, the texture of his scarred skin felt like bamboo thatch beneath her fingertips. "No news is good news, right?" she said aloud to the comatose man, unsure if she was referring to his unchanged condition or to the fact that she hadn't picked up any signals from Doyle's expedition.

On the return trip to her comms station, Indigo noticed the indicator on Alexei's lab door. He'd locked himself inside the moment the others had left and hadn't come out since. She wasn't missing Alexei's company, although she idly wondered what kept him so busy—presumably his vaunted starmap.

Passing by the observation deck, Indigo saw Colby inside, watching as night fell on M38. During the crash, their panoramic viewscreen had suffered a zigzag fissure in its liquid crystal surface, but Colby looked past the flaw. He seemed to shiver as each lightning flash lit the snowscape. Indigo suspected he was regretting not accompanying Doyle. Guilt has a way of catching up with you.

"They'll be fine," she gently assured him from the doorway.

"Yeah," Colby replied without conviction. He couldn't pry his eyes from the relentlessly grim planet.

Doyle's quintet wasn't alone in facing danger. *Gaea-02*'s heating and life-support systems would shut down in six more days. Indigo couldn't risk that happening.

She was determined to develop a transmission protocol to communicate with the APA. It would be difficult and, if she succeeded, the others might never forgive her—but it could save all of their lives.

CHAPTER 14
ZERO SUM

Lon.

Doyle hadn't allowed himself any thoughts of his son since landing on M38. He'd needed to maintain strict concentration on the situation at hand. But now he had no strength left in reserve to fend off sentimental pangs.

In the dim light, lulled by a steady EKG beep, he thought he was dozing beside Juni's hospital bed. Little Lon, curled on his stomach, his tiny lungs breathing in and out three times to Doyle's one.

The syncopated rhythm soothed both father and son.

Michi scrounged in a storage compartment for spare blankets. The synthetic polymer material was so thin she could carry a dozen in one hand. She remarked to Riana, "These are lighter than rice paper."

Riana studied printed labels of countless medical bottles. Most of the text was Chinese—*zhôngwén*—and after a while the teensy, intricate figures slithered and danced before her eyes. She squinted at the cluttered font until she felt a migraine developing. Riana rubbed her eyes.

In her youth, her father had ranted and raved about the APA as some malevolent bogeyman, prompting Riana to secretly explore their culture. Another act of passive rebellion, she admitted to herself and yes, she'd learned the foreign language on a teenage whim. But she was positive—then as now—that her father was dead wrong.

People living in Asian Pacific Alliance strongholds were cloistered and leery of the outside world, yet fundamentally no different from anyone else. Riana had met several scientists who'd fled APA dominion, and their reports were more favorable than one would expect. Without exception, these refugees had left for a sole purpose; to one day use their UEC-funded research to heal their homelands. Sadly, the Qing-Chen regime had cared little for their collapsing environment—until it was too late. The deceived populace only wanted to live in harmony.

Baden had intended for the Gaea mission to benefit all of humanity, both UEC *and* APA. He held out hope that the world could be reunited, even if that meant finding another planet on which to do so. Riana joined the project on that proviso and admired her husband for upholding those ideals.

She could tell his faith in peaceful coexistence was shaken by the APA's nuclear assault, but Riana vowed to make good on his legacy. She sighed at the realization they were breaking into an APA installation and had already assaulted an engineer. Not the best start.

Riana deciphered the label of an adrenaline vial. *Ah, there it is.* She snatched the drug and a hypodermic trigger, sliding the 10cc bottle into its vacant barrel.

Doyle opened his eyes, at once blinking away from the glaring overhead light. Letting his vision adjust, he glanced around the austere medical module.

Nearby, two small, metal cots had been pushed together to accommodate Django's hulking frame. He was hooked to an IV and a portable EKG heart monitor, which looked like an old alarm clock. The big man was out of it but breathing on his own. Riana injected his chest with adrenaline and Django's heart rate spiked. Michi covered him with a clutch of polyblankets.

"How is he?" Doyle rasped.

Riana laid an extra blanket across Doyle, pleased he was awake. "No permanent damage, thanks to your suit. He'll be fine." She tenderly tucked the cover under Doyle's chin. "So will you."

Doyle could feel his face was raw where skin had peeled. He tried to wiggle his feet to make sure they were still there. The movement caught Riana's eye, so she lifted the blanket to reveal his gauze-wrapped legs. "Saved your hands too."

"Knew you'd be good at this doctor stuff."

"Liar. You thought I was a heartless bloodsucker."

Doyle's cracked lips formed a crooked grin. "Changed my mind."

"You're just lucky the medical computers on this base are so complete. Detailed procedures for every emergency I could imagine—and some I couldn't. This certainly isn't a half-baked operation; they've been here a while." Riana chewed her lip. "Doyle, about the APA … I've been thinking …"

"All clear," Sabin shouted as he led in the tied and gagged APA engineer, Fei Haisheng.

Doyle lifted his head from the cot. "No one else? You're sure?"

"Not another soul on the entire base. Just our friend here."

Riana gestured toward their captive. "Then is the gag really necessary?"

Sabin shrugged and removed the cloth from the cowed engineer's mouth. They waited until he quietly stuttered a short phrase in Mandarin. Riana translated his question to Doyle: "Who are you?"

"Explain it to him," Doyle told her. "And ask him why he's been left here alone."

It was no wonder the operations lounge seemed seldom used. An angular chair chafed Doyle's back, the lighting was dimmer than it should be, and the air colder than in other sections of the base.

Doyle pulled a blanket around his shoulders. His rapid recuperation was aided by a steady flow of powerful medication. Even Django was up and walking already—a minor miracle. The APA had made massive strides in pharmaceutics during the previous three decades. Doyle wondered how much of the Gaea mission's pre-shakedown research had been incorporated. Were some of these new drugs Riana's progeny after thirty years of refinement? Were their comms systems based on Indigo's innovations? Did they utilize Eckerd's hibernation technology? In a roundabout way, perhaps *Gaea-02*'s crew had achieved some of what they first set out to do.

Riana controlled a console flooded with Chinese text. From Fei Haisheng's answers and the base's computer records, she could piece together most of what Doyle wanted to know.

"Seems M38 is only the APA's staging area," Riana said as she skimmed through entries. "Resources, mining, manufacturing—that includes a D-salt production facility. The climate isn't stable enough for dwellings; they project the current storm season might last for centuries. Mr. Fei here says their main colony is being established closer to this sector's sun."

Riana smiled at the captured APA engineer, who seemed to enjoy her attention. Fei spoke to her in Mandarin and she elaborated. "They've terraformed M41's third moon, Taurus. Its atmosphere required some minor adjustments, although days there last only four hours."

"Must go through a lot of coffee," Doyle tried to sound upbeat as he chomped into an APA ration pack, which turned out to be tastier than the swill he was used to choking down.

Riana continued, "The colonies are spreading onto the sixth

moon and M41 itself. The way Fei explains, it sounds as if the APA are moving whole populations into this sector a lot sooner than we would have."

Alarmed, Doyle leaned forward, the blanket falling from his shoulders. "They're abandoning Earth?"

Riana had a short conversation with Fei, then turned to Doyle. "No, not completely. He says that when he left Earth ten years ago, the situation there was improving. Global warming was finally in reverse. Since then, their fleet of transit ships has been staggered so that one arrives and departs for Earth every few months."

"That's the scale we always dreamed of." Doyle cast aside the blind optimism he'd been relying on; this was genuine confirmation that he could—*would*—see Lon again. He'd get his crew safely to Taurus, then just hitch a ride home. "When's the next transit due on M38?"

Riana tapped the touchscreen. "In nine days, a fresh colony ship will be retrieving one vessel, a C-class survey carrier, plus crew, for redeployment to M41."

"Planetside retrieval?" Doyle said in disbelief.

"Apparently."

"What are they using? Antigrav landers?"

Riana shrugged. "I can translate the words, not the concepts. Sabin should look through these tech documents with me."

Doyle eyed the flat digital map over her shoulder as he stood. "We've gotta be aboard that boat when they pick it up."

The screen displayed locations of all active APA vehicles and structures on the planet. "There are two carriers," Riana said.

"Which one are they taking?"

"*Red Dragon* is the call sign on the manifest, but the key labels on this map are coded. I can't say with any certainty which of the two blips it is."

"So we have a fifty-fifty chance?"

"Wait, I remember reading…" Riana pulled up the base's maintenance timetable on the screen. "Yes, it says this base is scheduled for carrier maintenance. Doesn't list which one, but it's two days from now. Could be a last-minute tune-up before retrieval."

Doyle motioned to Fei. "Ask him which carrier is due here."

Riana spoke in Mandarin but didn't appear pleased with the response she received. "He says they don't tell him anything. I get the feeling Fei's little more than a caretaker here."

"Well, our odds are even. Either way, let's be ready." Doyle flexed his hand, thinking aloud. "We'll need guns."

"*Guns?*"

"Nothing's going to stop me getting on that colony ship."

"If you're looking for a firefight, that's what you'll find. We were lucky this time, no one but Fei was here. If we approach the carrier peacefully—"

Doyle forced her attention to the console, jabbing his finger at a Chinese character on the screen. "You know what this symbol means, don't you?"

Riana's lips tightened. Doyle answered the question for her, "That carrier is a *military* craft."

"It doesn't mean they're hostile."

Doyle asked the APA engineer, Fei, "If we board that ship, how will they react?" Fei stared wide-eyed at Doyle, so he raised his voice. "Will they attack us?"

Riana repeated Doyle's question softly in Mandarin. Doyle paid attention to the tone of Fei's long, reluctant reply. When he ceased talking, Doyle looked to Riana. "Well?"

"He… he said…"

"Go on."

"Maybe I didn't understand it correctly—"

"Don't lie to me, Dr. Ruschen. I've picked up a smattering of Chinese in my time, and I heard him use the word *kill*. Now tell me everything he said."

Riana took a deep breath. "He claims conflict on Earth has continued unabated. Resistance fighters, sporadic militia. When he was growing up, anyone involved in sustaining the UEC was labeled a traitor and… executed."

"And?" Doyle prodded.

"Some of the carrier crews act the same as they did under Qing-Chen back home. They wear naval uniforms and their holsters are never empty."

Doyle shook his head sadly. "Even out here in uninhabited space, they're just waiting for an enemy to cross swords with."

"Are you any different? Remember your first instinct a few minutes ago?"

"Yeah, to take the carrier by force. But I'm fighting for my *son*."

"Everyone finds a reason to fight."

Doyle clenched his fists. Why was she being so difficult? "I've no desire to rekindle a war begun light years away."

"And yet..."

Doyle tempered his exasperation with a self-derisive laugh. "For a moment there, I let myself think Baden's gambit had worked. Peaceful coexistence with warfare left in the past."

"It *can* work."

"There are no rules out here, Riana. These soldiers have been in space a long time. Trigger fingers get itchy. We need to negotiate directly with the colonists in power. And this is the only way to reach them."

Riana threw down the gauntlet. "When Baden proposed we land here instead of returning to Earth, you called for a vote. It's only fair you allow the same now."

"*Fair?* If life was fair, I wouldn't even be here having this conversation."

Riana glared and Doyle realized their disagreement in orbit had merely been a precursor to this face-off. He needed to weigh losing her hard-won respect against getting his own way.

"Call everyone together," he finally consented, unsure of what he'd do if the crew sided with Riana.

"I'm not advocating a slaughter. No casualties... on either side." Doyle spoke directly to Sabin, Michi, and Django. He wanted to make certain they fully understood his proposal. He and Riana stood poised at opposite ends of the room; two sides of the coin they were flipping.

Sabin backed Doyle immediately. "They murdered my bro. I'm not gonna shake their hands and give 'em footrubs."

"*They* never even met Pach," Riana said. "That was thirty years ago. Some of these people probably weren't even born yet."

Shaky on his feet, Django moved beside Riana to add his support. He offered no explanation and Doyle knew better than to bother asking. Riana nodded gratefully to Django.

That left Michi burdened with the tiebreaker. She glanced between her two options. When Michi stepped next to Doyle, Riana was incredulous. "Why?"

"When Japan broke away from the Asian Pacific Alliance in 2017, China fired a cruise missile into the center of Kyoto," Michi said matter-of-factly. "Not very powerful. Only seven people died. Merely a warning: if you oppose us, we will strike first."

"If you want revenge..."

"Not revenge." Michi wore a Mona Lisa smile. "Game theory. Maximizing outcomes from interaction. It's integral to M.I.T.Z.'s artificial intelligence, but lately I've begun to think about most things in those terms."

"This isn't a game," Riana said.

"Everything is a game." Michi blanked a console and ran her finger across the touch-sensitive screen, leaving a multicolor trail. She drew a two-by-two matrix to indicate the consequences of their decision. "This isn't a zero sum equation; if we go in with open hands, by default we rely on their disposition to determine the result. But if we attack first, we can control the outcome."

"Assuming we win the battle."

"I trust Doyle," Michi said, "and we have surprise on our side. It's the optimal choice, Riana."

"Remember, this is the same group who tried to blast *Gaea-02* out of orbit," Doyle said. He tallied the vote. "Three to two. I can count on you and Django to follow orders?"

Django nodded and, grudgingly, so did Riana.

Doyle instructed Sabin and Michi, "You two check out the manufacturing facilities. Sitrep in one hour." Sabin lent Michi his shoulder to lean on as they left.

"Django, get some more rest. We may need you in action." As Django humbly padded out, Doyle was again struck by how quietly he moved for such a big man. That would be an asset soon.

Alone with Riana, Doyle adopted a more conciliatory tone. He couldn't figure something out, so he asked her, "Back on the Wheel, you wouldn't let me surrender our ship to the APA—I was wrong to try, I accept that—but why your about-face in tactics now?"

"Baden was commander then."

"And I'm in command now."

Riana's terse laugh escaped. "Is that so? And once we're on Taurus, will you faithfully stick by your crew? No, you'll leave us in your moondust and zoom straight back to Earth. I don't blame you for that, but please don't pretend you have everyone's best interests at heart. The rest of us have to remain in this sector and somehow work alongside the APA. You don't."

She strode out. Doyle didn't try to explain his position further. He'd damaged their rocky relationship enough already. He knew he wouldn't betray the crew and Riana was wrong about his motivations.

At least, he hoped she was.

The cavernous foundry housed a single piece of machinery. The circular anvil and chaotic splay of laser-lances belonged to a Mass Prototype Engine six times the size of the one on *Gaea-02*.

"Wow," was all that Doyle could muster as he stared up at the titanic MPE. An ionized vacuum trough ran underground to a bed of raw materials and chemical components, and a flat belt-line carried output to a terminus grid for robotic assembly. The ultimate production line.

"As well as the obvious increase in scale," Michi gushed, "they've improved the internal design. From what I can tell, this can reproduce just about anything."

"Except organic material," Riana said.

"Not yet. But I wouldn't rule it out." Michi led M.I.T.Z. to a console, into which it jacked an articulated cable, coiling like a metal snake from its cranial shell.

Against the wall stood an inactive, newer-model M.I.T.Z. robot, its striking design a manifest evolution from Michi's original prototype. While interacting with the computer, *Gaea-02*'s faithful M.I.T.Z. cocked its head sideways to study its inert descendant.

Doyle was curious. "Can M.I.T.Z. recognize itself?"

Michi blinked. "I honestly don't know. Its behavioral learning unit could conceivably form a sense of self-identity. I haven't had the opportunity to fully examine what effects the last thirty years have had on it."

Sabin smirked at the inquisitive robot. "Sure looks like it sees a family resemblance."

"Does this make me a grandmother?" Michi giggled.

M.I.T.Z. finished hacking into the APA manufacturing system. Michi checked the console readout. She turned to Doyle. "You'll be pleased. Look."

Blueprints for thousands of weapons and vehicles zipped past Doyle's widening eyes.

"Seems like every military schematic from the twenty-first century is in there," Michi said as she disconnected M.I.T.Z.'s interface umbilical.

That wasn't far from the truth. Everything from the Chinese Type 99 Battle Tank to a spherical device whose function Doyle couldn't even guess.

Michi gestured toward the Mass Prototype Engine and asked Sabin, "Want to learn the basics?"

"Sure." He helped her hobble over to the MPE control bay.

Doyle paged through the APA's weapons database. He became

aware of Riana's shadow across the screen. *Watching. Judging.* "Need anything?" he asked.

"Change of clothes," Riana said. "And if I can tear your eyes away from your toys for a moment, you might want one too."

She navigated the console menu to bring up the design of a specially modified APA envirosuit. The material in the photo seemed to shimmer.

"Good thinking. Thanks," Doyle said, but Riana had already left.

The Mass Prototype Engine's speed and accuracy never ceased to amaze Doyle. Taking a completed ESD suppression rifle from the assembly grid, he ran his fingers down the smooth, capacious barrel, over the microgenerator hub. *Flawless.*

Doyle handed the weapon to Sabin. "We used these to quell the Washington Riots. ESDs—ElectroShock Delivery suppression rifles. Fires darts with just enough volts to render your target unconscious."

Sabin lined up the laser-scope. "Won't kill 'em? Pity."

Sabin's attitude reminded Doyle of the bellicose grunts from his first control unit sent in to disperse the violent anti-UEC protestors in D.C. The majority of his multinational team—even his sergeant, a seasoned veteran from Chile—just wanted to wail on some patriotic schmucks.

The Washington Riots had helped Doyle, barely out of his teens, decide to transfer into the UEC's space corps instead. Space had no territories to mark out and defend, no politics or hegemonies. Until now.

Doyle made a mental note to keep a close eye on Sabin. Revenge could be all-consuming if allowed to fester, and Sabin had thirty years of dream state to dwell on Pach's death. Playing soldier for a while might be good therapy… or it could lead him down a darker path.

Doyle passed an ESD rifle to Django. "Sure you're up for this?"

Django nodded. He was a few days away from full recovery but a three-quarters-fit Django was still more than two hands full.

"Ever use a rifle before?"

Django nodded again. Doyle could only wonder where and why. He was a non-com in the UEC and seemed too passive to go looking for trouble.

"ESDs are pretty standard in operation. Slower ROF, but no recoil." Doyle guided Django's hand to a secondary fire module beneath the loading chamber. "This launches a single-shot EMP grenade against hardware, twenty-foot pulse radius—but it could fry your own ESD, so use it only as a last resort. Got all that?"

Django seemed to take it all in his stride. Doyle recalled how jittery the terraformer was in space, yet his demeanor on the ground was rock solid.

Sabin removed a just-fabricated grapple-launcher from the MPE assembly. It looked like a snub bullpup rifle with a fishing reel attached to the rear instead of a magazine. "What's this?"

"Standard issue for test pilots. We'd land in some *inconvenient* places."

Turning the device over, Sabin accidentally hit the release button. A grapple-hook shot past his stunned face. The zipline snagged into the ceiling.

Doyle grabbed the launcher from Sabin like a parent taking a toy away from a mischievous child.

They were ready.

Riana smoothed her blouse. The body-hugging, synthetic slacks were standard APA naval issue circa 2025, but the outfit's simplicity suited her fine and was less cumbersome than an envirosuit.

To her credit, she had cast aside any grievances and proved invaluable, not only with translations and medical preparation, but also through her ingrained knowledge of naval vessels. Riana's insight and analysis of the carrier's schematics put Doyle's to shame.

When the duo had finished going over the plan a final time, he commented, "You know your boats."

"I could say destroyer before I learned to say daddy. Father couldn't have been happier." Riana changed the subject. "Should we contact *Gaea-02*, give them a status report?" She was worried how Indigo, Colby, and Alexei were faring on the stranded crew module. Let alone poor Eckerd in his endless night. They'd all freeze to death without new power cells.

"Not yet," Doyle said. "The APA may not be able to decipher our comms protocol, but an unidentified transmission from this base could tip them off. Or lead them to *Gaea-02*."

Was his second statement an afterthought, Riana wondered, or did he honestly care? *Yes*, she told herself, *he did*. Misguided and prone to rash actions, perhaps, but she'd witnessed his valor.

Michi led the APA engineer, Fei, into the operations lounge at gunpoint. She held her weapon as close as a lover. "Reconsider?" she asked Doyle "My thigh's almost—"

"Sorry, Ozaku, no limping in my boarding party."

She'd practically begged Riana to do whatever it took to heal her injury in time. It disturbed Riana that Michi derived some perverse pleasure from the cold, hard, nonconductive shell of her ESD. Riana had held—and fired—many weapons as a naval cadet and always felt uneasy with them. Michi, on the other hand, looked the part of a confident, spiky-haired manga heroine—so different from when the two first met.

Riana untied Fei's hands. He'd proven agreeable and passive, so she saw no need to keep him trussed like a criminal.

"If you cooperate, you'll be safe," Doyle said.

Riana translated to Mandarin in her own fashion: "Bald Man says to obey."

As Riana seated Fei at the comms station, Doyle told her, "We'll have only one shot at this." He didn't need to remind her.

A Mandarin voice from the incoming carrier was relayed to the engineer's console. Doyle and Michi listened to Riana's translation.

"ETA forty minutes. They'll be sending an engineering squad over for parts while the ship refuels offshore."

"Let's just hope she's the *Red Dragon*," Doyle said.

Riana spoke softly to Fei. He opened a comms channel to the carrier and said in Mandarin, "I will expect you shortly."

Black water rushed beneath the bow of an exploration-class carrier. Lingering night storms highlighted the dark, early morning sky. On this side of the thin peninsula, the swelling sea was dotted with drifting icebergs that the vessel pushed aside like minnows.

Crags stretched between the shore of granulated onyx to a forbidding perch of metallic rock. The carrier's navigation lights ignited a million shiny, jagged edges across the bluff, transforming it into a crazy carnival marquee.

From a secluded niche halfway up the rock bank, Doyle, Django, and Sabin observed the ship's approach. They wore the sleek, new envirosuits from the APA's database. Full-body active camouflage bent light to blend the trio into their surroundings. The mimicry wasn't perfect, but it gave them a slight edge, and muscle support tailored for M38's gravity made movement nearly effortless. Since each suit contoured precisely to the body wearing it, Doyle had an extraordinary feeling of being naked, yet unnaturally strong.

The carrier slowed along the shore, looming above the trio's hiding spot. Two hundred feet long—much smaller than aircraft carriers on Earth—the vessel's streamlined hull curved like a pterosaur's beak at the fore. Two-thirds down the deck, a three-story tower stood cluttered with radar sensors and a dual-mounted plasma launcher for clearing potential mining sites. The aft deck was flat and broad, harboring a vehicle launch bay below the landing zone.

For one magic moment, when the rosy dawn briefly burst through murky clouds, the carrier was polarized, a dramatic silhouette illuminated by a bronze-red aura. Sabin whistled low in appreciation. The vessel's majesty wasn't lost on Doyle either.

His love was aircraft, but he recognized superb engineering, and the way that carrier glided over the waves was sublime. The post-apocalyptic combination of UEC technological expertise with the APA's efficiency and manpower had clearly yielded benefits in more than medicine.

Doyle couldn't afford to indulge in such ruminations for long. Once the carrier bobbed at a standstill, he aimed his grapple-launcher high. *JHOOM*—it shot into the air, arcing over the aft deck, zipline unraveling behind. The sound of the grapple settling on the ship was muffled by a neoprene sheath. The crest expanded into eight spider-legs that dug into the platform with diamond tips.

Doyle steadied himself before firing the launcher's rear cannon to extend a support line into the rocks at his feet. He wound the zipline tight and winked at Sabin and Django. Doyle clenched the grapple-launcher's handle and flicked the recoil switch. He whizzed upward on the zipline, riding all the way to the carrier's lip where he clambered aboard.

Doyle reversed the grapple's switch, sending the launcher back down the taut zipline to his waiting crewmates.

A crash barrier separated Doyle from the main section of the aft deck. He crept to the first gap and peered through.

Across the expanse, three APA crewmen moved a refueling arm into position over the carrier's starboard edge. They began the arduous process of lining it up with a liquid-hydrogen fuel nozzle extended from the manufacturing base. Wind and waves kept knocking their alignment out of whack.

Good, Doyle thought, *that ought to keep them busy*.

Below, Django gripped the grapple-launcher and hit the recoil. It lifted him into the air, rapidly at first, but slowing as the zipline bowed under his considerable weight. Gears grinding, the device struggled to cope.

Sabin kept an eye on the support line attached to the cliffside. Rock flakes whittled and cracked from around the impaled hook.

The grapple held out long enough to deliver Django to the

carrier's rim. Doyle assisted him on board and was about to hold a finger to his lips before he remembered that hushing Django was simply unnecessary. He set the launcher to return.

Sabin observed the grapple making its way down the precarious line to him. Warily, he grabbed the handle and hit recoil. It jerked him upward, almost ripping his arms from their sockets.

Overheated gears slipped. A third of the way along the zipline, smoke billowed from the launcher mechanism.

The grapple jammed. Sabin muttered under his breath, jabbing the recoil switch. The motor whirred but didn't retract any farther. Sabin dangled helplessly in midair, buffeted by rising winds and arctic spindrift.

The carrier's hull suddenly clanged as a large panel started sliding open. A launch ramp extended, angling into the choppy water.

"*Mierda!*" Sabin frantically thumbed the recoil switch back and forth. The launch door was nearly open, right beside him.

The grapple miraculously caught a gear and shot upward—but once more it jammed, leaving Sabin swinging.

The launch door locked into place above Sabin. His camosuit hid his presence well, but he hung like bait on a fishing line before the yawning chasm. An engine roared from inside.

With no time to spare, Sabin swung his legs over his head and gripped the zipline between his crossed ankles. The mechanical beast thundered from its cave: a six-wheeled, amphibious Walrus utility vehicle rolling out of the carrier's launch bay. It was a squat, gunmetal juggernaut with wheels half its height, unstoppable on any terrain and speedy enough to slice through breaking waves. The brute buzzed inches below Sabin's skull before dropping into the sea.

The Walrus propelled to the shore on powerful hydrojets, then easily motored up the rugged slope toward the APA base.

Shaking, Sabin caught his breath. He lowered his legs and gave the grapple mechanism a few anxious jabs. It finally recoiled, herky-jerky.

Doyle clutched Sabin's envirosuit when he came into reach, dragging him onto the carrier deck. Mumbling Spanish curses, Sabin crammed the retracted grapple-launcher into Doyle's hands.

Sabin whispered sharply to Django, "Next time, I go first."

The Walrus drove up an acute incline, six wheels crunching rock until it reached the stark manufacturing base.

Three Chinese engineers and an APA naval officer leaped out of the vehicle. A wraith's breath of frosty air blew through their uniforms. Shivering, they jogged to the foundry entrance, brushing snowflakes off their shoulders once inside.

The quartet stopped in their tracks.

Riana, unarmed, stood under a rail walkway, awaiting them alone.

Going against Doyle's wishes, she'd stashed her gun in a cache on her way there. This was her chance to take the initiative, to prove that Doyle was wrong, just as her father had been.

Holding her palms outward, Riana greeted the APA contingent in formal Mandarin. With a slight bow of her head, she was humble and cordial.

Before Riana had completed her second sentence, the naval officer drew his sidearm and, barging past the stunned engineers, leveled it at her. Rattled by Riana's sudden appearance, he shouted accusations and expletives.

She tried to calm him, to explain who she was, but in her own mounting distress, Riana got tripped up in lingual acrobatics. Mistranslation led to further misunderstanding. She politely asked him to put down his gun, but it came out sounding like a threat.

The officer's trembling finger pressured his trigger.

He let loose a volley of three bullets. Riana's heart almost stopped. The shooter didn't account for M38's gravity or his quivering aim. His shots flew high, skimming over Riana's tied-back hair.

A tiny dart whizzed from the opposite direction, piercing the officer's chest to send a jolt of electricity throughout his body. He slumped, limbs twitching like a swatted cockroach.

Riana reeled around. On the walkway above, Michi was perched at M.I.T.Z.'s bowed shoulder, the barrel of her ESD rifle crackling with live energy.

Doyle had shot three people in his life. Two with a nonlethal ESD in Washington, and one with a decidedly more deadly handgun after his crash in Malaysia. An APA guard, no more than a boy, had discovered Doyle asleep in a gully where he'd hidden during daylight hours, planning his escape. In a blur, Doyle gripped his sidearm and fired, the kickback jolting him awake to face the consequences of his action. Doyle patched up the boy's wound to the best of his meager ability. He also left food and a GPS beacon. Two days later, minutes before he boarded a trade convoy to Singapore, he sent a communiqué to the Kuantan Police stating the boy's coordinates. Whether he was still alive when they found him, Doyle would never know.

All of this explained his hesitancy while training his rifle on an unsuspecting APA engineer aboard the carrier. It was the first time Doyle's finger had been near a trigger since that regrettable incident.

Alongside him, Sabin and Django aimed their ESDs. Three gunmen, three targets. Doyle used sign language to convey his orders. Sabin was well attuned to nonverbal communication with his brother, and Django might as well have invented body language.

Doyle dropped his finger to signal: *Fire.*

Electroshock darts whizzed the short distance across the deck. Two APA crewmen were punctured simultaneously, each barb delivering a current which dropped them like rag dolls. The third shot—Django's—pinged off the refueling regulator with a spark.

Seeing his companions fall, the third crewman froze, afraid to move.

Sabin scuttled out from behind the crash barrier and trained his rifle on the remaining crewman, taunting with a grin, almost inviting him to run and be gunned down as sport. Doyle shot first to release the man from his misery. His body convulsed on the deck.

A spotlight bloomed from the carrier tower, sweeping past a row of idle survey aircraft until it bathed the *Gaea-02* intruders in a bright cone. Doyle shielded his eyes. An emergency siren blared. Amplified Mandarin voices vied with the howling wind.

Sabin swept his gun in a circle. "What now?"

They'd been too slow to capitalize on their blitzkrieg. Doyle saw movement and shot on instinct, but he missed by a wide margin. A fourth APA crewman broke from hiding, ran inside the carrier tower, and budged the massive door until it swung outward.

"The door—quick!" Doyle prompted his team to race across the flight deck. The grapple-launcher hooked on his back rattled with every loping stride. Doyle and Sabin outpaced Django, but the closing door threatened to beat them all.

Doyle leaped at the door, wedging it open with his shoulder mere inches before it could seal shut. Sabin added his strength. The pair met resistance when the APA crewman exerted force from the other side.

The crewman yelled for help inside the tower and it arrived quickly—four officers pushing and making easy work of it. Doyle and Sabin did their best to hold firm, but the door was just… about… closed…

Lumbering across the deck, Django rammed the door wide open with one immense shove, the weight crushing a crewman against the wall.

The remaining three APA officers dashed to a spiral staircase, their boots clanging toward an upper level. Doyle had his first real view of his enemies: two scared, young Asian men and a female First Officer. She was older and barking instructions to her fleeing companions.

Sabin fired twice but neither electrodart tagged a body. Doyle saw the APA trio scatter above, rushing in different directions at the second-level landing. Whether it was in blind panic, or a plan to throw off their pursuers, he couldn't tell.

"Get to the command bridge," Doyle ordered. "Disable communications first, then we can mop up."

He led Sabin and Django to the second level, an open landing before the spiral stairs rose to the uppermost stratum. Doyle spotted the First Officer above, but he saw no sign of her two subordinates.

As Doyle stepped onto the landing, a loud *FWOOM-FWOOM-FWOOM* made him duck. Three searing plasma blades whizzed past, scorching the nape of his bowed neck. The sizzling projectiles thunked into the metal wall, their ultraheated tips burrowing inside.

Doyle rolled forward so the corner section obstructed his assailant's angle of fire. Sabin and Django ran the gauntlet and dove beside Doyle, huddling against the corner wall. The diffused lighting rendered their camouflage technology useless. Doyle winced as skin peeled from his neck onto his glove. "What the hell was that?"

"Old mining tool." Sabin caught his breath. "Sinks a transponder into anything."

Django casually said, "A plasma punch."

"Yeah," Sabin agreed. It took him a moment to realize…

Doyle did a double take, turning to Django. "You *spoke*."

Django shrugged. Doyle was flabbergasted, although now was not the best time to inquire why.

A fiery projectile shot past the corner strut, jolting Doyle back to their predicament. He risked a peek along the platform, hoping he'd still have a face afterward.

Doyle spied the plasma-punch-wielding crewman behind an aluminum crate. The bulky tool made it necessary for him to readjust his grip after each jarring shot. Spotting Doyle, he fired. A plasma blade sank into the wall beside Doyle's head.

Doyle retreated into the alcove to consider his plan. Logically, the command bridge would be at the highest level. That's where he needed to go. The firebrand on this level was just a distraction, although the man would have a clear shot at Doyle on his way to the stairs. An EMP grenade might deactivate the plasma weapon, but at this range it would also short his own gun. That gave Doyle an idea.

He pumped his ESD's secondary barrel and launched his only grenade high at the upper level to zap any comms systems up there. The EMP grenade clattered at the top of the stairwell and emitted its pulse. The lights above the stairs went out immediately, but those on the command bridge were unaffected.

"Must have a Faraday cage around their nav systems," Sabin said. "Protection from the storms—and EMPs."

There was only one thing for it then. "Cover me," Doyle told Sabin, who tilted his ESD rifle to blindly fire a salvo past the corner. Doyle broke away, crossing the gap and propelling himself up the narrow stairs.

By firing a constant burst, Sabin's ESD cartridge was sapped prematurely. His suppressing fire stalled, leaving the plasma punch open to blast at Doyle. Globs of liquefied metal splashed when what felt like a miniature sun collided with the step beneath Doyle's heel.

As though a rug had been pulled from under him, Doyle tumbled to a lower rung. Molten droplets spattered his envirosuit, eating through the fabric like acid.

Doyle felt his flesh bubbling and fusing with the suit. Gritting his teeth, he pulled against the railing with both hands, vaulted over the melted step, and staggered to the upper level.

He heard excited voices from the command bridge. A tower-length window crisscrossed with near-invisible circuitry sprang to life as a heads-up display on Doyle's passing. Resisting the urge to smash it out of frustration, he crab-walked to the side breach, rifle at the ready.

The First Officer and a Chinese Captain in full APA regalia

were hollering into transmitters. Doyle heard them shout the word *Gaea*. He cursed the delays that had prevented him from arriving sooner. He could only hope that Indigo's jamming was effectual.

Doyle ran past the gap, shooting. The First Officer drew her regulation firearm but an ESD barb thunked into her chest and she toppled, limp. Her cap rolled from her head as it smacked against the floor; her inky hair unraveled.

The Captain dodged behind a bank of computers. Doyle saw him fumbling at his belt before he stepped into the open, his eyes squeezed shut and hands curled into fists at his sides. Assuming he was surrendering, Doyle advanced.

Keeping his eyes closed, the Captain opened his fists. One hand was empty. The other held an emergency flare.

He tossed it at Doyle's face.

White-out.

The ringing in Doyle's ears voided all other sound. He felt his mouth move to form questions, but no words were audible.

He stood in a white room that was not a room. An eerie absence of any floor, ceiling, walls. Profoundly … empty.

Space's vacuum had always comforted Doyle. He found solace and reassurance in a vast, ordered cosmos. But this bright, white abyss raised his hackles. He shouted in silence until his lips were rubber and desert-dry.

A speck abruptly appeared on the blank canvas. The tiny shape in the distance whisked nearer as though magnified under a microscope lens, enlarging life traces on a glass slide. The speck grew into a smudge, the smudge became a moving blur, and finally, he recognized a little boy.

Lon.

Scampering away from Doyle, the boy paradoxically seemed to be moving closer. Lon wore his favorite pajamas and was laughing over his shoulder. A game of hide-and-seek.

The ringing in Doyle's ears faded, replaced by a male grunt. Then a loud crack.

In moments, Doyle's pure, alabaster world was drenched crimson.

He wiped blood from his eyes and his vision finally cleared.

A punch shattered Doyle's left cheekbone.

Kneeling on the command bridge, he'd been pummeled repeatedly. Spots of light danced nonstop on his corneas, a lingering remnant of the flare's intensity.

The APA Captain landed another solid blow, rocking Doyle into reality.

The Captain's knuckles were skinned and smeared with a mixture of Doyle's blood and his own. A release of primal aggression built up during years of passive duty.

Doyle's mind was fuzzy, but his reflexes were incisive. When the Captain hurled his bloody fist, Doyle crushed the punch in his palm and struck back, doubling the man over.

Doyle stood and brought a swift knee up to smash the Captain's jaw. Slamming against the computer bank in a spray of blood and sparks, the Captain crumpled beside his fallen First Officer.

The carrier's comms station squawked as an insistent Mandarin voice filled the channel. Doyle switched off the transmitter. *So, the Captain's message got out.*

Disheartened, he knew their only chance now was for Indigo to block any warning transmissions from M38 to the colony ship when it reached orbit. But if she couldn't even jam the APA's terrestrial comms, what hope was there of that?

Woozy, Doyle hunkered down to gather his wits. He blinked without recognition at an inch-long, pink lump on the floor, round on one end and jagged on the other. Pinching the pliant object between his index finger and thumb to pick it up, Doyle realized what it was and where it once belonged.

Here was the tip of the APA Captain's tongue, hewn off by his own sharp teeth when Doyle delivered his knockout blow.

Sabin heard the sizzling noise as a plasma blade melted deep into the thick steel behind his head. Thankfully, it didn't burst through.

The APA crewman kept up his relentless bombardment. His side of the wall looked like the pockmarked surface of Callisto.

Sabin wanted to make these scumbags pay. His ESD hadn't recharged fully, so he reached for Django's weapon. The big guy wasn't such a great shot anyway. When Sabin gripped the barrel, Django yanked the rifle, jerking Sabin forward. At the same moment, a fresh plasma blade hurtled straight through the weakened wall, in the exact spot his head had been.

Sabin combed through the smoking tips of his singed hair with his fingers. Shell-shocked, he murmured to Django, "Thanks."

Battered and bruised, Doyle leaned over the upper level's rail.

M38 really was a miserable planet. The leaden, gray carrier faded against a gray sea, beneath a dull, gray morning sky. An intrusion of color came from the fiery plasma punch below, flashes so razor-sharp they hurt Doyle's still-sensitive eyes.

The APA crewman maintained a steady assault on Sabin and Django's fragile haven. They wouldn't be safe for much longer.

Doyle unhooked the grapple-launcher from his back. He spread its spider-tip and clamped it to the side rail. He guesstimated the distance between the two levels, pulled and looped the required length of zipline, and locked it into place on his handle-grip.

Doyle stepped back and sighed. He couldn't believe he was even considering doing this … Holding his grapple in both hands, he ran forward and hurdled the railing.

As he catapulted into midair, Doyle's breath was swallowed by the sight of the churning sea seventy-five feet below. Nothing lay between him and the icy deep.

He plummeted until his zipline snapped taut, making him a human yo-yo. Doyle's momentum arced him toward the tower's second level. He twisted and raised his legs to control his swing, aiming for the APA crewman below.

Doyle overcompensated. He missed the mark and crashed into a wall. Startled by this new arrival, the crewman swung his steaming plasma punch around.

Doyle rolled onto his haunches and fired the rear cannon of his grapple-launcher at the crewman. Its support line undershot, passing between the crewman's legs with the diamond hook impaled in the wall beyond. The wire slackened along the ground.

The crewman smirked at his lucky escape. He hefted his plasma punch to fire at Doyle.

Doyle punched the grapple recoil. His launcher ripped from his hands as it retracted upward, drawing the support wire tight. The zipline flicked up painfully between the crewman's legs, knocking him into the wall. The plasma punch tumbled from his hands. Its blistering-hot barrel liquefied his boot, along with the flesh and bone inside.

Mercifully, the crewman blacked out, left with half a foot and wedged upright between steel and wire.

Sabin and Django came out of hiding. Sabin's eyes followed Doyle's zipline to the upper level. "You're one *bastardo loco*, Doyle."

Doyle massaged his sore shoulder. His body was only thirty-five, but right now he felt every one of his *sixty*-five chronological years. "Man my age should know better…"

Sabin walked up to the unconscious crewman and slapped his face. "That's for my hair." He curled his hand into a fist. "And this is for—" Doyle and Django both gripped Sabin's arm at the same time, preventing his strike.

Doyle caught something in Django's eyes and a flicker of understanding passed between the two men. Neither wanted to watch Sabin ditch his humanity for spite.

Sabin wriggled from their grasp and adjusted his envirosuit. He seemed chagrined, although far from apologetic.

"Better take this guy to Riana," Doyle said to Django. "Help me get him down." Django levered the zipline away so Doyle could slide the crewman from his trap. Django draped the injured enemy over his burly shoulder.

Doyle froze when he saw what was uncovered on the wall: a bas-relief jade dragon.

Sabin peered over his shoulder. “Dragon don’t look red to me.”

Crestfallen, Doyle said, “It’s the wrong carrier.” In seven days they needed to be aboard the *Red Dragon*, but this vessel, judging by the insignia, was the *Green Dragon*.

“Hey!” Sabin shouted, pointing at the aft deck. An APA officer sprinted across the carrier below. Doyle had completely lost track of the remaining crew in the face of more immediate threats.

Sabin fired his recharged ESD but the gale skewed his aim.

Doyle snatched Django’s rifle and dashed to the staircase, leaping over a puddle of molten sludge. He cannoned down the steps two at a time.

Rushing onto the deck, Doyle couldn’t locate the stray officer. He searched along the landing chicanes, poking his rifle into gaps to ferret out his prey.

An engine hummed behind Doyle.

VTOL jets blasted as a Manta survey aircraft rose from the deck, the force of the vertical liftoff knocking Doyle off his feet.

The APA officer was visible in the pilot’s chair. Two free-moving turbine thrusters flanked the Manta’s cargo hold, while the clear cockpit sat higher and flush to the left, giving the craft an appearance of a one-eyed bug rather than its diamond-shaped aquatic namesake.

Its turbines revolved and the Manta picked up airspeed as it flew over Doyle.

Doyle rolled onto his back, in the same motion launching an EMP grenade from his rifle’s secondary barrel. A pure reflex action, one he regretted instantly.

The grenade struck the Manta and detonated a short-range electromagnetic pulse. The aircraft lost all power. Its engines whirred down and it plunged from the sky.

The Manta crashed onto the carrier’s deck at high velocity and flipped end over end, flinging debris in a manic gyration. Flames erupted. A fiery turbine broke free and cartwheeled past Doyle. He shielded his face from the shower of cinders and ice.

The demolished Manta skidded to a flaming stop at the end of the carrier's flight deck. Doyle rushed to pull the pilot from the wreckage, but stepped back when he drew too close to the scalding heat. No one could possibly have lived through that inferno.

Doyle tossed his weapon aside. He'd boarded the wrong damn carrier, he couldn't prevent the APA from dispatching a warning, and now he'd senselessly killed one of their men.

The mission was nothing but a disaster.

CHAPTER 15
DISTRACTIONS

Only a boy.

Riana stared at the APA naval officer who had opened fire on her. Taking a good look at him, now that he was closer and without a weapon, she was astonished by his youth. He couldn't be more than twenty, although she reminded herself to add another eight to ten years for interstellar hibernation. Even so, he would have been born right around the time of the nuclear catastrophe on Earth.

His birth was almost a demarcation point in human evolution. The first generation since—*what did they call it? The Great Blast? World War III?* Her own lifespan was largely spent before it, while his was wholly afterward.

Riana asked the soldier in his native language what name they gave mankind's defining event of 2049?

"The Liberation," he curtly replied in formal Mandarin. "The magnificent day we threw off the yoke of our oppressors and fulfilled the glorious destiny of the Asian Pacific Alliance."

Oppressors? Is that what we're called? How we were seen back then? Riana's first impulse was to chalk it up to historical revisionism, but she couldn't deny there was an iota of truth there. The UEC hid a dark underbelly. Some in the ranking echelon exploited their technological monopoly by wielding an iron grip on the world-wide water supply. They told themselves such manipulation was for the greater good, but Riana had often questioned whether that had been lip service to appease their collective conscience.

At least the Gaea mission transcended such cynicism.

Michi rapped her rifle's muzzle impatiently on the doorjamb. "We have more prisoners to bring over."

Riana cast her a sour glance but nodded. She left behind a supply of blankets, rations, and water for their four captives before securely locking the barracks. Riana caught up with Michi in the corridor.

"You suspect I'm enjoying this too much," Michi said.

"Are you?"

"Holding a gun is a novel experience for me, exciting, yet not what I'd call pleasurable." Michi opened the foundry doors.

The weather outside had improved slightly, from abominable to bitter. On the crag, the *Green Dragon*'s immense Walrus stood idling. Subzero winds formed beard-like stalactites along its dripping hull.

"You're sure you can drive that *kaijū*?" Michi asked with a shudder.

"It's not a monster; or if it is, I can tame it. My father taught me how to handle amphibious craft before I turned ten." There was no pride in Riana's statement, more wistful regret for her lost childhood. When she clambered into the forward hatch, however, her lessons from decades ago proved beneficial. The Walrus controls felt self-evident to her. In no time, Riana had a deep engine-bass grumbling from the six-wheeled colossus. It gave her a jolt of undesired, but undeniably, intoxicating power.

Careening down the steep slope to the shore, Riana barely felt a bump, with all shocks absorbed by recessed suspension coils as large as a man. She splashed smoothly into the ocean and felt the gears retract as intake valves opened to direct jetstreams of water.

Headlights sparked off the undulating waves, spinning gray to gold in an eye-catching alchemy. Riana sped up the carrier's gangplank into its vehicle bay, where Django was waiting to welcome her.

He helped her down from the high-sitting Walrus with a silent, gallant bow. Taking in the oil slick decor, Riana mused, "Just like my prom night. That was on a carrier too."

Doyle observed from the command bridge balcony as wisps of smoke rose from the Manta wreckage smoldering on the deck. He'd retrieved the pilot's charred body after the cockpit burnt out and was keeping it on ice until Riana could translate the wishes of the APA crew held in the carrier's brig. With no soil on M38, cremation or burial at sea were their only options.

What a way to arrive.

Doyle wished he could contact *Gaea-02*, but his fear of giving away the crashed ship's location had intensified since the bungled takeover. Better to wait until he was near enough to offer his left-behind crew some protection. The captured *Green Dragon* had an icebreaker's bow and a battery of plasma cannons. *Great for us*, Doyle reflected, but it also meant the enemy's *Red Dragon* had equivalent destructive capabilities.

Bottles clinked as Sabin carried a case of wine and empty glasses up the stairs. "Found the Captain's private stash in his quarters."

As he handed a bottle to Doyle, Riana and Django stepped onto the landing. Riana said with a wry grin, "Auspicious timing?"

"We've only done half the job, but I guess you've all earned a brief furlough," Doyle said. "And I mean brief. We'll be on the move soon."

Sabin loaded up with a bottle and two glasses. "Taking a Walrus to the base. Michi could use some company."

Doyle skipped the obligatory lecture about fraternization. Sabin wasn't asking for permission. Besides, maybe Michi could help ease the pain of his losing Pach. Kindness from an attractive woman had soothed many a savage beast. "Be back in three hours and bring some antimatter cells with you. We've got a delivery to make to *Gaea-02*."

Doyle doled out a couple of bottles to Django, who accepted the wine wordlessly. He hadn't spoken again since the attack. Doyle chose to respect his silence instead of forcing a conversation. Django popped a cork, took a large swig, and wandered off.

Riana reached for a bottle from Doyle but stopped short when she saw his swollen cheek. "Your face..." she said as Doyle shied away from her touch. "I'll find a medkit. Wait here."

Colby's head bopped to music fed directly into his inner ear, his feet rat-a-tatting on the bridge flight panel.

Restless, he scanned his control band to find something he hadn't already heard a thousand times during the four days they'd been stranded on *Gaea-02*.

Neither Indigo nor Alexei would hit the ping-pong ball with him, despite his constant badgering for a game. He was bored stupid.

Sequestered in her comms room, Indigo studied wide-band frequencies for any APA transmissions *Gaea-02*'s system could recognize, sending modified bursts in return.

Taking a break from her monotonous work, Indigo spliced into Colby's headset to listen in on his mix of tunes. She sometimes did this, as if he were her personal DJ. The Aussie bloke had funky taste and a knack for aligning music to her moods. He was currently grooving to a deep cello line with pindrop synths and a plucky vibroflute, enough to keep the mind active but also relaxed. *A good choice*, she thought, and couldn't resist humming along.

She wasn't aware of a shadow watching her every move from the doorway.

As Indigo turned to another console, she noticed her voyeur from the corner of her eye. "Alexei!" she squealed.

Alexei continued to stare quietly, his face half-obscured behind the wall.

Indigo caught her breath and tried to make light of his presence. "You scared me. Need something?"

Alexei leaned heavily on his metal crutch, white-knuckling the haft until it made a high-pitched skreak over the floor as he limped away.

Unsettled, Indigo returned to her work. Alexei had become increasingly withdrawn and, well … creepy. She hoped the others would return soon, because she had no idea how to deal with him, and she had enough problems of her own.

Doyle sat alone on the *Green Dragon*'s uppermost command deck, an empty glass in one hand and an unopened bottle in the other. He watched the snow drawn to the window collect in a frosted ooze until it slithered down to leave a glistening snail-trail.

"There you are," Riana said, finally locating Doyle. She laid an APA medkit beside him and used swabs and antiseptic to clean his face. She taped gauze over his worst lacerations, then ran a hand scanner by his swollen cheek. "Not too serious, but you won't win Miss M38."

Doyle's face hurt when he chortled. Riana spread an anesthetic paste across his cheek to deaden the pain. He tested it with an appreciative smile.

The sky outside darkened with nightfall's approach. Packing her kit away, Riana quietly admitted, "You were right."

"About what?"

"Everything. That we'd be greeted with suspicion and hostility. That we shouldn't have taken the risk."

Doyle stretched his legs. "What do I know? I just fly planes and spaceships. I'm the wrong person to lead us into a war."

"Don't say that. Like you told me on *Gaea-02*, you're all we've got."

"A ringing endorsement." Doyle poured wine into a glass and handed it to Riana. "Cheers."

"You're not drinking?"

"Not a drop since the week after Juni died. Decided then to always be sober for Lonnie. Guess it doesn't matter now."

Riana clasped his hand. "Don't lose hope."

"I never will," Doyle said softly. He noticed the plain, platinum wedding band on Riana's slender finger. "Not ready to let go?"

Riana touched the gold band on Doyle's own ring finger. "You're one to talk."

"I'll remove mine if you do."

Riana rubbed her wedding ring like a genie's lamp. Doyle didn't really expect her to agree. Or was he hoping he wouldn't have to go through with his end of the bargain?

Riana took a deep breath and wiggled the skintight band above her knuckle. She let it fall onto the flat of her palm, stared at the metal for a moment, then turned to Doyle.

"Your turn," she dared him.

Doyle clasped his ring between thumb and index finger. He worked up the courage and yanked it off in one swift action.

He felt exactly the same afterward. He loved Juni no less, but he sensed a new lightness in Riana's bearing, a hint of the spark reignited in her eyes.

They said simultaneously, "You seem different…"

Riana slapped her hand over her mouth as the pair burst into laughter.

She twirled her ring between her fingers. "It's always easier to recognize change in others than in yourself, isn't it?"

Doyle slipped his wedding band into a pocket. His tone grew serious. "Riana…" He'd been avoiding this long enough. "I haven't told the others yet, but I think the APA Captain got a message to the other carrier."

"Wasn't Indigo jamming?"

Doyle shrugged. “Someone responded to his Mayday, and I heard him say *Gaea*. We’ve got to assume they now know we’re on M38.” He wheeled a chair over to a data console and gestured for Riana to sit. Doyle inserted an ID cube he’d confiscated from the Captain in the brig. The device granted access to all classified files. “Find the APA’s record of *Gaea-02*’s crew. If they’re not aware how few we are, or that we’re mostly noncombatants, maybe we can bluff them into surrendering.”

Riana scrolled through menus. Mandarin characters swamped the screen with detailed accounts of every facet of the UEC’s past, demonized and propagandized into an almost mythological nemesis.

She paused on a photo of *Gaea-02*. Riana tapped the screen to open up a series of entries and trawled through every section, byte by byte.

Doing her best to absorb the information overload, Riana told Doyle, “The official line is that we’re dead. We’re kind of like the boogeyman . . . but these records contain everything—and I mean *everything*—from before our supposed demise. I don’t know how it’s possible. They even have results of onboard experiments from our test flight.”

“*What?*” Doyle leaned over her shoulder. “We never had time to report those before everything went to hell.”

“Something else that’s odd. They list someone named Mya Lyn as part of our shakedown crew.”

“Who?”

Riana opened Mya Lyn’s record. Her dossier photo contained a face familiar under another name. “Indigo?”

Doyle was perplexed. “Indigo isn’t her real name?”

“Dr. Farrad had her birth record. She was born Indigo Carlyle.” Riana ran her finger down the screen’s edge to scroll farther. Reading the Chinese characters, her face blanched. “No . . . oh, no . . .” She stammered, “Mya Lyn was an informant for the APA. The woman we know as Indigo, whatever her name is, she’s an elaborate fake.”

Doyle shook his head. "No, that can't be right. You mistranslated."

"I wish I had." Riana read from the screen: "'Operative Mya Lyn bravely gave her life aboard *Gaea-02* to further the Asian Pacific Alliance cause.'"

"Then why didn't she tell them we'd survived?"

"Self-preservation? She was aboard *Gaea-02* when they launched their missiles at us. I doubt she wanted them to try again."

Doyle stubbornly refused to believe the evidence. "It's impossible. The UEC screening process was painstaking. Deep background checks, full security canvas..."

"The Philippines were dominated by the APA in the early days. There would have been some who stayed loyal to the regime. An extensive intelligence network to construct Indigo's false past. It's certainly plausible. Doyle, who else could have sent them our final test reports?"

Doyle was silent but his mind was reeling. *A traitor in their midst.* How could he have not seen it? The timing of the APA's attack on Earth, Indigo's 'inability' to jam the *Green Dragon*'s transmissions. He thought back to when Usef stole away in *Gaea-02*'s emergency pod. Indigo had been there as well. Why? At the time, he assumed she was saying goodbye, but what if she'd been planning to escape in the pod herself until Usef bludgeoned her? A rat leaving the marooned ship.

Who better to spy on us than our communications officer? Doyle mulled. She had access to every secret in their databanks and could freely transmit without oversight. What else was she capable of? Was she dangerous? A saboteur? Violent if provoked? It dawned on Doyle: "We left Colby and Alexei alone with her."

He jabbed his comms band to open a long-range channel to *Gaea-02*—whatever the consequences. "Colby, do you read?" Static. "Colby? If you can hear me, you and Alexei must confine Indigo to quarters immediately. Colby, respond. Over."

Hearing the buzz of an incoming message, Colby muted the

music on his control strip. The second he realized it was Doyle's voice—after so long incommunicado—he couldn't contain his excitement and yelled across a shipwide channel, "Hey Indigo, Alexei, it's Doyle! They're okay!"

By the time he restrained himself, Colby only caught the tail end of Doyle's warning: "Be careful, she's not who she seems. Indigo is—"

The transmission halted abruptly.

Colby tapped his comms unit. "Repeat that, Doyle. Over." He tried adjusting his frequency. "Doyle? Mate, what was that about Indigo?"

White noise flooded the channel. Colby switched a monitor display to Indigo's lab. Empty.

He cycled the view to the crew module's spine and there she was, toting a duffel bag. He opened a direct link. "Indigo, where you off to?"

On the monitor, Colby saw Indigo cast aside her comms band without missing a step.

Baffled, he rushed from the bridge.

Indigo listened to her comms band clatter on the floor behind her and decided there was no turning back this time.

She'd intercepted Doyle's transmission—cut it off before Colby heard too much—but it wouldn't be long before Doyle came looking for her. His speech about brutality in small groups haunted Indigo. Whatever her real intentions, ultimately it was her fault he was separated from his son, her fault that Sabin's brother had died. They'd surely blame her for everything that had gone wrong. Retribution would be swift and severe.

She dug her violet-painted fingernails into her bare wrist, trying to feel something genuine. Numb for so long, living in somebody else's skin, play-acting every swoon and sigh.

Indigo heard Colby shouting in the corridor.

She would have to hurry.

¤ ¤ ¤

Colby caught a glimpse of Indigo striding past a corridor junction up ahead. "Indigo! Slow down!"

What the hell was she doing? He bent to grab her discarded comms band and stuck it inside his vest.

Colby lost Indigo's trail. He ducked his head inside each door along the way.

A bone-rumbling tremor told him exactly where she was: the vehicle bay, and that noise was the launch door opening. Puzzling, since their only vehicle was gone.

He raced toward the bay, lost his balance, tripped over the threshold, and thrust out his hands to halt his fall.

Flat on his stomach, Colby raised his eyes to where Indigo stood at the crest of the gangplank. As snow swirled around her, she zipped up her envirosuit. Her heavy boots clanged on the metal slope until the sound of her footfalls was absorbed by the savage winds.

Colby pushed himself to his feet and cannonballed outside.

On the ice field below, the raging blizzard swallowed Indigo whole, obliterating any trace of her existence.

"Indigo!" Colby screamed louder than he ever had in his life.

He plodded a few steps into the snowstorm, his skin lashed by icy gusts. He pulled his woolen beanie down over the tips of his ears.

"Indigo!" Colby's miserable holler ended in a pathetic croak. He pictured the saliva in his mouth frozen, sealing off his throat. His imagination triggered an anxiety attack and he couldn't stop swallowing.

This wasn't going to work. He wasn't going to save the day, even if he knew what the hell was going on.

A bright circle shone down on Colby, casting a perfect, hunched silhouette on the ice. Colby spun, shielding his face from the brilliant rays.

A Manta emblazoned with APA insignias hovered above *Gaea-02*, surveying the downed spacecraft with searchlights.

"Colby, do you read me? Don't trust Indigo." Doyle's comms channel crackled.

"Did you get through?" Riana asked.

"Your guess is as good as mine." Doyle drummed his fingers on the data console. His intuition was telling him—shouting at him—that something was terribly wrong.

He hastened for the stairwell.

"Doyle?"

"Change of plans," he said over his shoulder. "Get all the prisoners ready to move."

Doyle made his way down the tower and below deck, picking up speed as he reached the launch bay. He charged to the nearest Manta airship. He jammed a fist against the launch control, then leaped into the open cockpit, ignoring the thrill he always felt when testing a plane for the first time.

The carrier deck above him parted as the launch platform ascended. Doyle strapped himself into the flight chair. His eyes glazed over at the Mandarin iconography labeling the controls.

"Okay…" If the layout used any kind of logic, he trusted his ability to wing it with a few right guesses. That was a big *if*, since half the planes he'd ever flown were seemingly designed by a million monkeys with a million screwdrivers.

"Here goes nuthin'." Doyle mashed a button sequence … which accomplished precisely nothing.

Fine. He tried the exact opposite combination. The machine responded with a growl that, to Doyle's ears, was a warm greeting. His cockpit lit up and the twin turbines throbbed a deep red.

The Manta rose sharply, gyres of heat shimmer melting snowflakes caught beneath its flight.

Doyle blasted into the storm clouds, relying solely on his innate sense of direction. His scanners were fogged beyond a few square miles, so he'd have to be on *Gaea-02*'s doorstep before he could pin down the location.

He passed over the APA manufacturing base and the ice chasm his expedition had caused to fracture; those two points of reference were enough for a rough bearing. He poured on the speed, impressed by the Manta's mobility and power.

In seconds, a fuzzy blip appeared on Doyle's radar.

Make that two blips.

Doyle dived below the cloudfront to get a visual. He found the enemy's Manta scanning the *Gaea-02* site.

A Mandarin voice invaded Doyle's cockpit. Asking for pilot identification, he presumed. When he didn't reply, the APA Manta hightailed out of there. Doyle lost all contact as it receded into the dense weather.

Hot pursuit wasn't high on Doyle's to-do list in an unfamiliar aircraft. First things first; he needed to make certain the rest of his crew was safe.

He circled above *Gaea-02*, keeping his eyes open for any more bogeys. Did Indigo contact the APA, he wondered, or had they discovered the crash landing on their own? Either way, this *Mya Lyn* had serious charges to answer.

Doyle landed beside the starship. He jogged up the gangplank to where Colby was shivering.

"We had a visitor," Colby said.

"Scout ship," Doyle confirmed. "Where's Indigo?"

"Sightseeing." Colby blew in his cupped hands and gazed into the whiteout.

CHAPTER 16
MYA LYN

She'd forgotten her gloves.

Hurrying to escape, Indigo had wriggled into a spare envirosuit but, when Colby shouted after her, she'd been distracted. Not binding the gloves on her cuff joint was a costly mistake.

Outside now, in the worst weather she'd ever experienced, Indigo could feel the heat generated by her body suit up to the wrists. Her exposed hands, however, seemed strangely foreign. Making a fist took considerable effort. Her fingers felt like rusty, metal hooks, her stylish nail polish a garish counterpoint.

Indigo turned her head to look back toward *Gaea-02*. The snowstorm blotted out the ship and swept away her footprints right up to her heel.

A little further, she goaded herself. *Keep on walking. Keep walking or they'll track you down.*

As she trudged down a glacial trough, the duffel on her shoulder felt heavier than the secret that had been crushing her for eight long years. Slowly, Indigo persuaded her frigid fingers to retrieve one item.

She let the bag tumble onto the snowclad slope. She didn't know why she'd bothered to pack a duffel. The sole item she kept in her determined grip, yes, but she should have brought only this. She'd wasted precious time bundling the three personal effects she was allowed aboard *Gaea-02*: an antique handheld computer, a Baliog beaded necklace, and the blue, plush penguin. All three were now lying underneath the rapidly mounding snow. None of them had belonged to Mya Lyn. They were Indigo's ersatz keepsakes, mementos of a youth that had never existed.

Wearing *Her* mask for so long had ingrained habits, rituals she'd trained her mind to adopt. The Indigo alter ego had gradually infiltrated Mya's sense of self. Who was she really now? Some new merged persona? All she could be sure of was the excruciating cold.

Indigo stumbled over an ankle-high ice ridge and fell to her knees. Enough. She opened her palm and there it was, the one item she'd saved. A locator beacon.

Her fingers refused to respond. She bit the three middle fingers on her right hand until each bled. Her blood flash-froze into a frosted, red jelly, but the pain was enough to restore control over her digits.

She had to work fast. Manipulating her frozen, bloody hand, Indigo laboriously tapped out a code. The beacon lit up like a supernova, almost blinding her.

The device transmitted a short-range distress signal across all known frequencies. She just hoped the APA's scout ship would find her before *Gaea-02*'s crew did.

She wouldn't give Doyle or Sabin an opportunity for vengeance. Someday, she would explain her actions to them in person.

Rising to her feet, Indigo staggered onward, wind whipping her blue-streaked hair across her face. Stinging shards of ice assailed her body. Before long, disoriented and exhausted, she collapsed in the snow.

Indigo rolled onto her back, clutching her shining beacon in one rigid, mottled claw. *Beep… beep… beep*, the device reassured her.

Growing up in the Philippines, she'd never played in snow. Like stars drifting from the sky, flakes blanketed Mya Lyn's prone body. She extended her tongue to taste a chilled, gossamer zing. It felt like something Indigo would do.

She'd forgotten her gloves.

Bohol Island was unseasonably cold lately. "The weather makes no sense anymore," her father whined daily. So Mya Lyn turned back home for her mitts and maybe a headscarf. She often didn't return from these TechRatI meetings until late, and she didn't want to catch a cold on the ferry crossing.

The TechRatI was a loose collective of hackers, misfits, and loners united by their common cause: mischief. Known among them only by her Net-handle, Indigo, such anonymity suited Mya Lyn. Normally, she was a painfully shy, awkward sixteen-year-old with straight, black hair hiding her face, but the technochatter and brazen one-upmanship of the tech rats never ceased to delight her.

She couldn't wait to tell them all about her latest exploit. Her excitement had been building all week. Tonight, she'd surely be the center of attention and her avatar would soak up the limelight. *Indigo* had reached the pinnacle of hacking. She'd breached the Shanghai Protocol, the APA's primary defense mainframe.

It took eighteen hours straight of tracers, sync-routing, and Ouroboros algorithms just to wedge her binary foot in the system's door. No one noticed her absence when she skipped school two days in a row. Mya Lyn was inconsequential and easily forgotten. The only time Mya was truly alive was as Indigo.

Jogging up the driftwood steps to her family's bungalow, Mya Lyn paid no attention to the unassuming yacht in the harbor or to the covered punt tethered on the shore. She barged in, explaining, "Forgot something. Mom, where are my..."

Her parents weren't alone. Four Chinese men in plain, gray suits glanced up at Mya Lyn's entrance. The one in charge smiled amiably and said in perfect English, "You must be Indigo."

Alarm bells rang in Mya's head. Her stomach dropped as if she were in a high-speed elevator. No one knew her identity, not even her parents. She'd kept her location heavily protected with enough false trails and shifting digital footprints to throw off even the best Net-sleuths. None had come close before. *Who were these men?*

"We have been discussing a proposition with your parents," the smiling man said. "Come sit."

This stranger's voice was overly friendly. He held out his hand, palm up. Mya noted his white deck shoes, wet sand stuck to the heels. The granules crunched on the bare floorboards when he shifted his weight. They'd traveled by sea. Asian Pacific Alliance, she decided. A traceback—somehow—from her Shanghai Protocol hack.

Seated on the sofa beside his American-born wife, Mya's father, Taroc, looked straight ahead, jaw clenched. A twelfth-generation fisherman of the ocean's dwindling stocks, he would be the last in his line. He bit his lip. Her father had plenty to be angry about in general, but Mya had rarely seen him keep his feelings bottled up like this. Only last week he'd openly menaced a UEC inspector who wanted to curtail his already miniscule catch quota. So what was happening here? Had these three told him what she did with her computers at night?

The man did not repeat his request to Mya, but his smile never wavered and his hand remained outstretched. For someone so polite and genial, he had neglected to introduce himself.

The smiling man's fingers twitched.

Kit Lyn, Mya's usually demure mother, leaped between the man and her daughter. "No, Mya, run!"

Three guns were drawn before anyone blinked.

The smiling man's open hand snapped around her mother's

wrist, effortlessly wrenching her into a tight stranglehold. His smile grew. "Be calm, my girl."

Mya Lyn's first instinct was to rush to her computer room, bar the door, and send a hard-coded Mayday to her fellow TechRatIs. Someone would pick it up and alert the authorities. The Philippines had been independent since 2017. The APA had no jurisdiction here. It would mean losing her anonymity, but that was better than losing her family. She turned on her heel.

Three strides toward her room and a loud thunk splintered the wall inches from her head, launching wood slivers like little javelins into her flushed cheek.

Not a *miss*. A demonstration.

"We hoped to settle this matter civilly," the smiling man said, "with a very generous offer to your parents."

"They want to steal your life!" her mother cried. The smiling man broke her forearm in one swift blow.

"Mom!"

A gun jammed in her father's eye kept both him and Mya Lyn at bay.

The smiling man continued over her mother's whimpers, his measured cadence almost lyrical: "You will become Indigo permanently. We have a ready-made history, a paper trail with manufactured memories. As of today, Mya Lyn must cease to exist. We will train you. You will join the United Earth Coalition but remain loyal to us. You will live this life with a smile while your parents are our guests in Shanghai."

Sobbing, her mother shook her head. Her father's rage was palpable but he dared not react.

"They will be well treated ... so long as you treat *us* well."

He wasn't giving her a choice and Mya Lyn knew it. Refusal meant death for them all. There wasn't much in the world she valued, but her parents were at the top of the short list.

"I accept."

"Of course." The smiling man dipped his head in a terse bow.

The grunt who'd fired his pistol brushed past Mya—no, from

that moment on, she was *Indigo*—to retrieve his metal slug from the wall. They would leave no sign that they had ever been there, and the APA's operatives in the Philippine National Police would hush any investigation. The Lyn family would simply vanish.

Indigo was led to the shore and onto the punt with her parents. The sea air kissed her naked fingertips, but even without her gloves, she couldn't feel the cold anymore.

She'd wanted to prove her hacking skills, and so she had, but to the wrong people. Many would pay for her mistake. Perhaps all of Earth.

Through the seasons that followed, Indigo clung steadfast to the final part of the smiling man's bargain. After a number of years—he never stated exactly how many—she would have fulfilled her glorious duty and her beloved parents would be set free.

She had to know if that day had finally arrived while she'd slept away half a lifetime.

Light shone on Indigo's face, flaring through her closed eyelids and stimulating her retinas. It wasn't her beacon, clutched tightly against her stomach, but something much brighter.

She slowly raised one frostbitten hand to shield her eyes. Beneath the painted nails, her fingertips were black, deadened flesh.

CHAPTER 17
A DRAGON WAKES

Bucking in turbulence, Doyle's Manta banked hard to follow the insistent blink on his scanner.

On, off, on, off. Whenever Doyle thought he had a fix, the blip seemed to reappear elsewhere. Frustrated, he dived below the clouds and tilted his cockpit to search the rugged ice field with his own eyes.

The Manta's advanced flight technology was a boon. Doyle's comfort with the controls had grown exponentially; its silken movement and split-second response were exhilarating. The craft handled more like a hummingbird than a jet, perfect for M38's harsh environment.

He'd seen nothing of the enemy scout, just this elusive beacon, though he was confident to whom it would ultimately lead.

Doyle hovered low, hunting with search beams. A twist of

light sparked off the ice below. *Something down there.* He swooped onto a flat plain and cut the turbines before they could melt away his ice platform.

Doyle jumped into the slush and trudged to the pulsing beacon. He swept aside the fresh snow nearby, hoping to find Indigo buried—dead or alive—but there was only ice beneath.

Colby said she'd had a duffel with her, but there was no trace of that. No bootprints either; they had been covered over by the blizzard in full swing. Doyle scooped up the emergency device and deactivated its transmission.

Shading his eyes, he scrutinized the windswept expanse.

Doyle dumped Indigo's emergency beacon on the mess hall table. "Found this, but no Indigo."

"You mean Mya Lyn," Riana corrected him.

"Whoever. She's either out there somewhere dead, or an APA scout picked her up. I honestly don't know which I'd prefer."

"I know what she deserves," Sabin scowled. He stood with the rest of the crew in a semicircle, with Riana and Doyle on the opposite side of the mess table.

"Either way, we've been forced into a tactical reassessment." Doyle activated the table display, scaling out to a map of the region. *Gaea-02* was represented by a central, yellow blot. "We've located the *Red Dragon* and she's coming our way." He tapped the red, blinking dot in the far-right corner.

"Do you still want the prisoners moved here?" Riana asked.

"I do."

"Why?"

"Insurance, but I'm hoping it won't come to that." Doyle opened an APA carrier schematic he'd downloaded from the manufacturing base. He highlighted a small section of the blueprint and asked Michi, "Recognize this?"

"Could be a portable Mass Prototype Engine. Not big enough to build large-scale items like Mantas or Walruses, but suitable for small arms, munitions batteries …"

"So they could be busy making shit for an assault on *Gaea-02*," Sabin said.

Doyle nodded. "And at their current speed, they'll be all over us in two days." He deactivated the view-table.

"Typical," Alexei snorted, his thick Kazakh accent becoming more pronounced. "You will all talk, talk, talk until we are too dead to do anything."

"Wrong. We're not waiting," Doyle said gruffly. "We're taking the initiative away from the APA. We'll use the full-scale MPE at the base to fit out the vehicles we've seized. We'll have weapon systems faster—and better—than they will. Then, I say we load up the *Green Dragon* and intercept their carrier in open waters."

Sabin practically cheered. "Now you're talking!"

The plan placated Alexei. Riana seemed uneasy but she didn't voice any objections. Doyle figured that being shot at was her wake-up call.

He continued, "Colby and I will attack from the air. Django and Sabin can take the Walruses and board the *Red Dragon* once we've disabled her."

"I can handle a Walrus too," Riana offered.

"You'll be of greater use to us here as our eyes and ears. *Gaea-02*'s scanners are superior to the *Green Dragon*'s—"

"Ours were built to peer into galaxies," Alexei said.

"—and with these storms clogging up everything, we'll need that advantage." Doyle turned to Michi. "You're responsible for our last line of defense, Ozaku. I want you and M.I.T.Z. to create autoguns, sentries, shield drones, whatever you can cobble together, in case we need to fall back and hole up in *Gaea-02* as a stronghold."

Unruffled, Michi asked, "Do you think that's likely?"

Doyle didn't answer.

"If Indigo's alive and working with them," Riana jumped in, "she could have left a back door into our system, booby traps she can remotely trigger . . ."

"We'll deal with that when the time comes." Doyle calmly shut her down before any wild speculation got out of hand. "There's plenty on everyone's plates already."

"You have not assigned me," Alexei said, pausing as he repositioned his makeshift crutch, "to my task."

"I need you to support the women here and take care of our prisoners."

"One broken ankle and I am demoted to babysitter? Feh."

"Somebody has to do it, Alexei. It's important, understood?"

"*Da.*"

"Good. You all know what you're doing?" Doyle gave them an opportunity to ask for clarification but, looking around, he was reassured by their stalwart expressions. He said softly, "We're heading into war, people. I'm . . . sorry this couldn't be avoided. Let's end it now—in victory."

The crew nodded their support.

They were a bunch of misfits, the best at what they did but way out of their league. Yet Doyle couldn't have been prouder to lead these six people. "We hit the water in thirty-six hours, so let's get ready."

After they filed out, only Alexei remained behind. Tense, he bent his neck until it cracked loudly and muttered to himself in his mother tongue.

Doyle searched Indigo's lab. Not for clues or evidence; investigating her betrayal was pointless right now. He sought his trusty flight jacket that he had left in her care. Sentimental, he knew, but since he was about to fly into battle, it might help to settle his nerves.

Doyle found his lucky garb in a storage locker. He confirmed his son's drawing was inside the breast pocket, then slung the jacket over his shoulders.

The foundry brimmed with raw energy. When Doyle's bare hand brushed against the metal railings, he was static-zapped. Ribbons of electricity ran across the ceiling arches.

Michi's appropriated Mass Prototype Engine whirred and spun like a dervish, via M.I.T.Z.'s interface.

Sabin scoured the schematic console, selecting heavy artillery he could modify to work with their vehicles: a missile launcher for his Walrus, rail guns for the UAV drones, and an ion-lancet Doyle wanted for the Mantas.

When Sabin segued into the more personal weaponry, Doyle studied him carefully. Sabin settled on a brutal-looking assault rifle: brushed scandium build, recoil dampeners, and a twelve-inch carbon-fiber barrel firing saboted subcaliber tungsten flechettes for maximum terminal effect. A smile tugging at his lips, Sabin touched the icon, sending the design to the manufacturing queue.

Doyle had put Sabin in charge of the entire range of engineering duties, but now he felt the need to intervene. "I assumed we'd stick with the ESD rifles."

"This fight could go on for a while. I don't want them waking up after half an hour to shoot me in the back, y'know?"

"You'll start a massacre with that gun."

"*Madre dias!* You and the good lady doctor can be pacifists. You grew up easy. Didn't know the pain of no water for days, fighting for your life against the smugglers and the *bandidos.* I wish I had one of these *machíns* the day *Tío* Jorge was shot."

"Then the bandits would have killed you as well."

"What do you want, man? They're gonna be armed to the teeth. I'm not facing that with a pea shooter."

"I need to know you're not out for revenge."

Sabin glanced away and quietly said, "You want to see your boy again, Doyle? 'Cos this is the only way you will."

"Don't blackmail me," Doyle hissed.

In his mind, death shouldn't—couldn't—be rationalized, nor murder justified. You did it and you bore the consequences. That was all. He'd killed his first man—that he knew for sure—a day ago. No excuses. It neither made him happy nor caused him to shed a single tear. In unguarded moments, however, Doyle could see the dead crewman burning in his mangled cockpit.

Sabin was right. Doyle's upbringing was sheltered. Even as an adult, he had spent more time among the stars than dealing with Earthly reality. The rest of the crew saw him as a soldier, but he himself knew he was a sham. A single year in glorified crowd control did not a warrior make. The only wars he'd ever waged were against gravity and wind resistance.

Riana's words came back to haunt Doyle. *He was all they had.* Better they keep faith in the facade than lose all hope in the struggle.

Sabin seemed to be waiting for an answer. If he was angling for an implicit sanction, so be it.

"Do what you have to," Doyle said. He ambled down the catwalk onto the foundry floor, where the buzz of ambient energy tingled up his spine.

Laser-arms wound down and retracted into the Mass Prototype Engine's spherical hood. The final pieces on Sabin's shopping list were complete. M.I.T.Z. followed dutifully behind as Michi unhooked the mag cart piled with finished parts and pushed it outside to the dock.

Above the base, Colby was skylarking in a Manta, getting a feel for the controls. He tested a mounted weapon, which turned the clouds fluorescent for a moment.

Michi patiently waited for Colby to notice she had another load ready for transit. From her high vantage on the clifftop, she observed the rest of the group on the *Green Dragon*'s deck. Doyle, Sabin, and Django were installing armaments on the second Manta, both Walruses, and two additional UAV drone ships. Sabin had been distant toward her since they'd slept together. Truth be told, that suited Michi fine. One fling to break the monotony, but no lingering expectations.

From this perspective, the men appeared to scurry about like the toy robots she'd made for her grandfather. Ojiisan was a talented puppeteer until his fingers curled with arthritis. That his marionettes could no longer frolic threatened to destroy him, heart and soul. So brilliant little Michi, age eight, designed and constructed her first simulacra: a delightful troupe of fluently mobile automatons that responded to her grandfather's whispered directions.

Ojiisan and his stories lived again, and Michi discovered her raison d'être.

She stroked M.I.T.Z.'s cold, plasmolded arm; here was the culmination of her life's work.

Wind blasted Michi's face as Colby deliberately swooped too low in his Manta before landing on the dock. A Japanese insult, "*Baka!*" flew from her mouth.

Colby jumped out of the cockpit, all saunter and cheek. "What's wrong, darlin'?"

Waves bashed the *Green Dragon*'s hull.

Doyle steered the vessel around the peninsula and headlong into a widespread glacier. He made rapid progress using sidescan sonar to pinpoint the easiest path through the ice, punctuated by an occasional volley from the tower-mounted plasma cannons to melt through thicker sections.

The carrier dropped anchor a mile away from the *Gaea-02* crash site. Two Walruses disembarked and sped across the floe. The pair's chunky wheels rattled up the spacecraft's gangplank, coming to rest in the vehicle bay where Alexei waited.

Doyle and Django herded two sets of chained prisoners from the Walruses. The APA men and women were demure and compliant, still in shock from the turn of events. On a vacant planet, being captured was—to say the least—unexpected.

The diminutive engineer, Fei, shuffled along at the front. He made the mistake of looking Alexei in the eye as he passed and couldn't understand the hatred in the cold stare he received. Alexei gave Fei a nudge with his crutch and pointed the way.

Doyle spotted a figure in an envirosuit hunched over a ring of lights on the ice outside. *Riana?* He told Django, "Get the prisoners settled. I'll be there in a moment," and jogged down the gangplank.

Django and Alexei led their captives to *Gaea-02*'s brig. Originally designated as the ship's asylum—mental breakdown was more likely than criminal activity—UEC psychologists had feared that label would fuel a self-fulfilling prophecy among the crew.

Django gently locked each prisoner to a wall-rail, their chains long enough to allow them to lie flat on individual sleeping mats. A toilet area was curtained off. Simple but humane.

Alexei rolled a cart of rations in. There didn't seem to be enough portions to go around. He said to Django, "I have miscalculated. Will you bring more, *tovarisch?*"

Django nodded as he clamped the final chain, then departed.

Balanced on one crutch, Alexei began doling out rations to the hungry prisoners. He wondered why he was looking after these dogs—even the pretty female officer who was trying not to catch his eye as she ate. They were the enemy.

Instead of handing the next ration to a prisoner, Alexei dumped it on the floor, hoping they would scramble for it like animals. His ire grew when a sedate young officer bent for the food-pack and humbly handed it to an older engineer.

Alexei cocked his head. He thought he heard the ominous strains of a Zauresh mourning march, and the smoke of Sobranie cigarettes gave him a coughing fit.

A mobile biochem lab, no more than an open briefcase surrounded by a ring of light-rods, had been set up on the ice. An optic-fiber core driller and javelin sample collector lay beside a wire-thin hole extending to the ocean sixty feet below. Riana knelt in the center of the rods, their bright halo lending her an angelic aura.

"Funny place for a picnic," Doyle said as he stepped into the circle of illumination.

Riana took her eye from the microscanner. "Sorry. I know I should be on the ship, but I may not get another chance to extract these samples."

"We're not leaving for an hour." Doyle crouched beside her. "Find anything?"

"Yes." She peered at the microscopic sample. "Proto-cells: self-reproducing RNA molecules. Almost exactly what I would have found on Earth some four billion years ago. But what's most puzzling is that this place is nothing like the primordial soup of nascent Earth."

"So?"

"On Earth, oxygen only came *after* life developed the ability to photosynthesize. So how was it produced here?"

"Maybe there's some kind of algae in the warmer parts of the planet?"

"Or life did evolve here, but something hit the reset button eons ago."

"Could an ice age like this do it?"

"Unlikely; life on Earth survived through several ice ages. It had to be something more… drastic. A solar flare or a radiation storm, even a cross-species virus, mutating until there was nothing left to infect."

Doyle smirked. "You trying to cheer me up?"

Riana laughed at her own morbidity. Doyle glanced at his gloved hand, imagining his bare ring finger underneath. A year ago, the very mention of a fatal virus would have plunged him headlong into deep depression. He was glad he'd healed enough to live with thoughts of Juni, even Lon, without breaking down.

"I'll help you pack up," Doyle said to Riana. "You can solve the mysteries of the universe after we get out of this mess alive."

They had her gear stowed and slung on their shoulders in minutes.

As they walked back to *Gaea-02*, Riana said, "Your honest assessment… *will* we get out of this mess?"

"The *Red Dragon*'s our ticket. If we can seize control, we'll have access to the colony ship when it arrives."

"Doyle, that's not what I asked."

He reached for Riana's gloved hand with his own. "If the rest of us don't return to *Gaea-02*, I want you to use the prisoners as collateral to negotiate your surrender. Michi's defense systems will make sure you're well protected and able to parley in peace."

"Then why don't we use that tactic now, and forget about the attack?" She studied Doyle's stoic face, then answered herself, "Because once we surrender, we'll never be free and you might never see your son again."

He nodded. "We'd probably become mine workers, slaves." Doyle sighed. "Am I being selfish? I can't tell anymore."

Riana quietly said, "The whole reason the crew agreed to Baden's plan was for a chance to continue the Gaea mission here. We can't accomplish much in chains, can we?"

Doyle was bolstered by her validation, but another, small voice nagged at his certainty. He shifted the weight of the ice drill on his shoulder. "If you ever do return to Earth, without me ... find Lon, and tell him ..."

"I know what to tell him."

Doyle squeezed Riana's hand once more before letting it go.

Snug in their APA envirosuits, they walked together toward *Gaea-02*, which stood like a monolith on the ice, welcoming them in from the storm.

Riana turned to Doyle. "Whatever the outcome, I'm glad you were here."

One ration pack remained. Alexei brandished it above the prisoners' heads, baiting and taunting them.

He lowered it to Fei, nodding for him to take the food. Fei clutched the packet but Alexei held tight.

"I was like you," Alexei said, not caring if they couldn't comprehend his words. "Chained. Hungry. Neo-Tzarists fed me like mongrel. Not so kind to my family." Fei released his grip and was perplexed when Alexei threw the food on the floor. "They drop my brother's meal, grind it with shit-stained boots."

Alexei stamped on the ration, its contents squirting over Fei's bedroll. The other prisoners huddled farther away, but Fei became limp and tried not to show any reaction.

Alexei sneered. "If he is silent . . ." He struck Fei across the face with his metal crutch. "They hit."

"And hit." A second strike glanced off Fei's jowl.

"And hit." The crutch found bone, shattering Fei's jaw and driving two broken teeth into his gum.

Whimpering, Fei shielded his face. His chains pulled taut and carved a red ring into his wrists. His fellow prisoners yelled for help in Mandarin. The more militant officers yanked at their bonds in vain.

Alexei brought his crutch down hard, breaking Fei's arm. The young engineer screamed with agony, and in Alexei's addled mind he recognized himself in Fei's place: a ten-year-old boy in Musabayev's dungeon. Raging in tears, he spat the words, "I scream for my brother, but they keep *hitting* . . ."

—each word—

"and *hitting* . . ."

—accompanied by—

"and *hitting* . . ."

—a vicious blow. Spittle flew from Alexei's mouth as he caved in Fei's skull.

Riana shucked her envirosuit and hung it on a hook. "I don't want to compound your worries, but Eckerd's condition is deteriorating. I had to place him on a respirator earlier."

"Will he improve?" Doyle asked.

"If the colony ship has more advanced facilities, there's a chance."

Leaving the vehicle bay, they heard a chorus of hysteria resounding along the ship's spine. Doyle and Riana sped to the source. They reeled back in horror as they entered the brig.

Fei was slumped like a rag doll, his broken arm still chained to the wall-rail in a macabre salute. The left side of his forehead was deformed, bone reduced to tissue paper. Clumps of matted hair hung from his torn scalp, his face a jigsaw of teeth and red.

Alexei watched impassively from the corner, his crutch wet with blood and peppered by skull fragments.

With low expectations, Riana felt for Fei's pulse. She shook her head.

"What the hell happened here?" Doyle yelled.

Terrified prisoners edged as far away as possible, wary of every muscle twitched by the *Gaea-02* crew members. Riana repeated Doyle's question in Mandarin. APA voices trembled their response, which she translated. "They say Alexei beat Fei. Unprovoked."

The Khazakhstani met Doyle's gaze firmly, without a trace of remorse, and said in stilted English, "They are bad as Neo-Tzarists."

Doyle gestured at the captives, "Look at them! They're scared kids. Most weren't even born when we left Earth. Damn it, Alexei, what's wrong with you?"

"They are all dogs. Mongrels and monsters," Alexei ranted. "Mongrels and monsters!"

Django arrived from the cargo hold with a tray of rations, which he dropped when he saw the gore. Visibly disturbed, the big man hardly heard Doyle's order, "Django, confine Alexei to his quarters." Django couldn't rip his eyes from the crimson river beneath Fei's ruined body. Doyle raised his voice. "Django? Get him out of my sight!"

Django snapped from his shock and escorted Alexei, who hopped on his bloody crutch and launched into an emphatic Kazakh tirade as they left. Doyle was glad when he was finally out of earshot.

"Insanity," he said in a hush. "He's been off-kilter since the hibernation, but I just didn't ... I never thought ..."

"The SLH procedure could have caused a chemical imbalance. Or stressed a previously undetected psychosis."

"Eckerd swore it was safe," Doyle said ruefully.

"Eckerd couldn't have prevented this," Riana said. "Don't blame him."

"I don't." Doyle pounded his fist against the wall. It was clear whom he blamed. Unable to look at the traumatized prisoners, he whispered in a strained voice, "Tell them … please, tell them I'm sorry."

CHAPTER 18
LEVIATHAN

At a fair clip, the *Green Dragon* steamed past ice-capped rock islands wrought in myriad formations: towering basalt spires; awe-inspiring plains of smooth, volcanic glass; jutting, rigid seamounts; serpentine phyllosilicates that sparkled grass-green under the carrier's navigation beams.

Sheet lightning flashed behind thick cloud blockades.

Doyle wished he could see the stars, to navigate by the patterns of a foreign sky as the earliest Earth explorers had. The localized starmap Alexei crafted before his sanity flew the coop was a gem of astral cartography. It seemed madness shared a bar stool with genius.

Colby watched his stony-faced mentor. The kid had more common sense than Doyle had credited him with; Colby nailed exactly what was weighing on his mind. "That stuff used to happen all the time in wars, right? Torture, beatings..."

"We're better than that," was all Doyle could mumble. They were making a mockery of the Gaea mission. He privately lamented the endless histories they were doomed to recycle and repeat, but he spared Colby the angst-filled rhetoric. Still, his rage bubbled just below the surface.

"Mate, don't let it get to you. It's not your fault."

"We had a chance for a fresh start and we've screwed it up already," Doyle said.

Colby flashed an inappropriate smile. "Maybe humans just aren't built for peace."

"That's supposed to be a comforting idea?"

Doyle turned up the collar on his flight jacket to block the chill blowing across his neck. He scanned the dark horizon. "Where's that damn carrier...?"

The flickery window-HUD was so imprecise that he might as well have been casting bones to divine what was out there.

The door was locked. He'd tried. It had been sealed both electronically and with a physical override that could only be unlocked manually, using the command key.

Alexei stared at the blank wall. He'd had much practice. Two weeks he'd been in this tiny box, listening to his brother's screams from the next chamber. The Neo-Tzarists feeding him muck off the floor.

No... I am confused, Alexei realized in a rare moment of lucidity. It was Doyle and that mute giant who threw him in here. They had betrayed Alexei Chechenkov. Treason most foul. *How long now until they murder me?*

His focus shifted from the wall's center to where it intersected with the ceiling. A maintenance shaft was there, too high to reach.

Or was it Musabayev's air shaft?

Yes. The word echoed in Alexei's mind. *Yes.*

Riana cycled *Gaea-02*'s long-range scanner spectrum for the best results. The *Green Dragon*'s signature appeared as clearly as M38's magnetic storms would allow, but the other carrier had dropped off the scope altogether an hour ago. Indigo's doing, Riana surmised, probably some type of radar chaff.

She tuned the frequency as low as the system permitted. A swarm of disturbance babbled a few knots from Doyle's location on the map.

Riana opened a channel to Doyle. "You should have visual of the *Red Dragon* at your five, right about…"

"Now," Doyle said, "full stop." Colby reduced the throttle.

To the starboard and slightly aft, distant lights twinkled on the enemy carrier's tower. Doyle tapped his comms band. "Sabin, Django, prepare to launch on my signal." He turned to Colby. "Send the dove."

Colby hit a sequence of keys to launch a specially prepared drone UAV, which whizzed into the sky and quickly out of sight. It would broadcast an audio message Riana had recorded in Mandarin: a parley request for the *Red Dragon*. Perhaps a token peace gesture, but Doyle was adamant it was worth trying.

Colby checked for incoming signals. "No reply."

"Give it a few minutes." Doyle caught Colby staring at the enemy carrier's hypnotic points of light. "Sure you're ready for this, kid?"

Colby snapped his fingers. "I jig better in a cockpit."

"You've never flown in combat."

"Have you?" Colby countered.

"I…"

"Doyle!" Colby pointed past the HUD to the scene outside. The *Red Dragon*'s lights had become larger much too quickly.

Doyle's heart plummeted. "That's not the carrier."

The fiery blasts came straight at them, leaving no time to dodge.

WHAM—WHAM. Two plasma cannon rounds struck the *Green Dragon*'s deck, spraying detritus like a geyser.

A wave of shrapnel lashed the tower window, with stilettos

stabbing a dozen spots simultaneously. Cracks streaked across the window until the fractures met and showered glass into the command bridge. Doyle shielded Colby with his back. A sliver nicked Doyle's bare scalp and blood ran down his collar.

The destroyed HUD componentry sparked on the floor.

Doyle shouted into his comms band, "Clear the launch bay. Get those Walruses in the water now!"

Colby saw the blood pouring over Doyle's neck. "Geez, you okay?"

"Get moving!" Doyle urged Colby down the spiral staircase.

Passing the second level, Doyle heard an airborne whistle. He herded Colby into the landing alcove to take cover. Two blasts shook the tower's foundation. A fountain of molten plasma splashed up the stairwell, turning it to slag. Doyle felt the effulgent heat on his face. A trickle of orange, superheated metal flowed toward them, changing its course on a dime before reaching Doyle's boot. The ooze drizzled over the edge.

"So much for diplomacy," Colby muttered.

"Come on." Doyle dragged him to his feet and they took off across the platform. Their primary route down the tower was cut off, but there was an emergency ladder on the port side.

Doyle heard the *Green Dragon*'s rear launch bay clang open as Sabin and Django sped their Walruses into the sea.

Colby halted at the ladder ledge. The deck was an incredibly long way down. "I'm gonna break my neck here, Doyle. I'll slip or miss a rung or some bloody thing."

"You'll do fine, kid. One step at a time." Doyle climbed onto the ladder and descended a few feet. Looking up, he waited for Colby to cautiously mount the first rung. The gangly, young pilot's nerves accentuated his clumsiness and he nearly slid off.

Doyle shouted his support, "That's good. Just concentrate. Don't let go until your footing's steady." He carefully watched Colby's steps, prepared to catch him if he fell. The kid could fly a thousand tons through the eye of a needle but he couldn't climb a damn ladder. "You're doing great, Colby. Almost there."

A thunderous blast rocked the tower. Colby hooked his elbow around a rung. His feet slipped from under him and he swung by the crook of his arm.

Doyle reached up to steady Colby until he could regain a foothold. The kid caught his breath. "Ready?" Doyle asked. Colby nodded. They shinnied down to the deck before the next plasma volley arrived.

Sabin's Walrus charged through frothy waves. Plasma seared across the blackened sky overhead.

"You with me, Django?" he asked over his comms band.

Django didn't say anything but his Walrus roared alongside Sabin's, hydrojets spewing a violent wake.

A starburst flashed in Sabin's peripheral vision. "Hard left!" he yelled to Django.

Their Walruses swerved. A stray plasma blast from the *Red Dragon*'s battery vaporized the water around them.

Steam fogged Sabin's screen; he wrenched the controls to avoid colliding with Django.

Metal scraped as their hulls met.

Below deck, Doyle and Colby sprinted across the *Green Dragon*'s launch bay. They vaulted into two waiting Manta aircraft.

Attaching the harness over his flight jacket, Doyle glimpsed the family photo he'd stuck to the cockpit window. He felt a renewed burst of confidence and punched in the launch code. "Colby, I'm sending the drones out first. Let them draw the fire away. We follow their tails in formation. Over."

"Roger."

Above their Mantas, the launch deck slid open. Red trails lit up the surrounding sky. A plasma blast exploded near the launch pad. Molten sludge splattered and dripped onto Doyle's Manta. He whirled around in the cockpit, trying to locate where the droplets splashed. He heard sizzling, but couldn't see any damage.

Doyle set the computer to run a cockpit integrity test. The results flashed green. Good enough.

Their pair of unmanned drones launched from the *Green Dragon*, buffeted by salvos from the *Red Dragon*'s plasma cannons.

The enemy's targeting systems locked onto the drones, firing leading shots on predicted flight paths. Doyle had been one step ahead, programming their pilot AI with random course variations so they couldn't be locked down. It worked like a charm; the drones led the plasma cannons on a wild goose chase.

In a shimmering haze of turbine heat, Doyle and Colby's crafts rose from the launch bay and jetted into the air a safe distance behind the drones. Once their Mantas had space to maneuver, the drones fell into formation as wingmen under each pilot's remote control.

Doyle could see Colby wave cheerfully to him from across the sky. *Weird how he lost his fear of heights a thousand feet in the air.*

Together, they dodged the *Red Dragon*'s blazing fusillade while speeding headlong at the carrier. Doyle reveled in how smoothly his Manta handled, even with the extra weight of weapon systems. He executed a pinpoint skip 'n' weave through the plasma barrage as if it were rush-hour traffic.

The UAV drones faced a tougher challenge. Their intentionally erratic programming had been effective as a diversion but was less potent for coordinated assault. With their AI dumbed down for Doyle and Colby's active command, the drones had been left a great deal more vulnerable.

A plasma burst from the *Red Dragon*'s tower hit Doyle's UAV wingman. Trailing thick smoke, it spiraled out of formation.

Doyle took full manual control of the damaged drone to guide it on a kamikaze strike. He rammed it into the bank of plasma cannons atop the tower, incinerating them in a fervid eruption.

A mangled cannon barrel was catapulted downward, deeply scoring the *Red Dragon*'s deck. The barrel came to rest beside the Manta launch bay doors as they began to slide open…

¤ ¤ ¤

Alexei had brought only two of the three personal items he was permitted aboard *Gaea-02*. The first was a platinum anklet adorned with three gem-encrusted asteroids: a gift from his father to his mother before her new observatory's dedication ceremony in the Zailiysky Alatau.

The second keepsake was his brother Viktor's stealth knife—the knife little Alexei should have used to kill Musabayev. Concealed as it was, the Commander had thought it a simple ornament. Alexei retrieved the blade from inside its snake-carved handle and reassembled the complete weapon.

He slid the honed blade beneath the computer panel and pried it from its wall mount. Wires unspooled.

How dare they presume that remanding him to his quarters would quash his computer access or bar him from the ship's system. *Fools.* By his tenth birthday, Alexei had been taught by the Kazakh resistance to outfox any security lockout. This was child's play.

Alexei yanked a clutch of cables from the panel's underside, stripped the rubber sheaths using his brother's knife, and spliced two bare wires together. The computer console beeped submissively.

Unrestricted electronic access would not open his door; the physical override saw to that. But Alexei had other plans.

He grinned madly at the maintenance shaft overhead.

This concocted gravity was a lie. The truth would set him free.

Doyle piloted his Manta in a wide circle around the *Red Dragon*'s burning tower in readiness for a strafing run. He wanted to eliminate the APA's firepower before ordering Django and Sabin to board the enemy carrier.

Riana's voice crackled on his comms band. "Doyle, three new energy sources just appeared on my scanner. They're muddled with the carrier's signal, but—wait, one's breaking off…"

Doyle turned in his cockpit to see an enemy Manta buzz away

from the *Red Dragon* and enter the fray. A second craft followed as a third ascended on its launch platform.

Doyle took evasive action as the first Manta opened fire. "Colby, crash your UAV into the launch bay. Sky's crowded enough."

Colby took control of the final drone and broke formation. Via remote, he plunged the drone into the third launch platform, destroying both the lift and the rising Manta. Chunks of metal the size of a man's head were flung at the *Red Dragon*'s tower. Windows shattered and battle-station sirens whined.

Startled APA crewmen shot their weapons through broken panes, trying to snipe Doyle and Colby. Their small arms fire was ineffectual but proved a further distraction that Doyle didn't need.

The two APA Mantas swooped behind Doyle and Colby, overwhelming them with a hail of ultra-velocity projectiles.

Shots grazed Doyle's undercarriage. He'd underestimated the sheer speed of their bullets.

Once he had their measure, Doyle focused on outmaneuvering the enemy craft. He was in his element, while the APA pilots' reactions seemed dulled by glaring inexperience. The best weapons in the world couldn't make up for a lack of skill.

Colby matched his mentor turn for turn, enthusiastically running rings around the enemy. "They're no aces," he mocked.

Doyle jinked to avoid a haphazard blast. "Probably never fired weapons before. A lucky shot'll kill you just the same, so concentrate."

"Sure, mate."

"Lead your dance partner in front of me. I'll knock out his—"

Riana's voice interrupted. "Something's strange, Doyle. Do you see anyone at your nine?"

Doyle looked to his left, but the sky below the savage tempest was empty. "Negative."

"I have a blip that keeps jumping in and out. It seems to be headed . . ."

"Got it," Doyle said as a red blush tinged the nearest cloud. A raging Manta's glowing turbines dipped below the stormfront. The Manta rolled, firing across Doyle's bow—not zippy projectiles like the others, but slower, superheated globes that dispersed at range to spray fiery death in a wider arc. Both Colby and Doyle veered sharply. The blast's edge caught them with a fine mist of particles that ate into their hulls like acid rain.

Colby yelled, "Where the bloody hell did *he* come from?"

"Safe guess that weapon's used for mining exploration. He was probably stationed at an outpost nearby."

"Sweet of him to drop by."

"Riana, widen your scans," Doyle said into his comms band. "I want plenty of warning if any more reinforcements arrive."

"I'll try." Her voice sounded weak and far away, not reassuring at all.

A hot burst speared past Doyle's cockpit, leaving a melted stripe along the plastiglass beside his face. The globule flowered in front of him. He dipped his Manta to avoid the deadly plasma shower.

The new combatant settled between the other two enemy Mantas to form the tip of an arrowhead. The flanking APA pilots corralled Doyle and Colby with a sloppy spread of bullets, narrowing their scope to avoid the middle craft's heavier firepower.

Doyle could tell this fresh pilot was a cut above the *Red Dragon*'s duo. Crisp turns, sound anticipation, and tactics that hinted at actual combat training. Doyle's own training was solely in *unarmed* flight and experimental dynamics, yet if studying the Wright Brothers had taught him anything, it was to adapt to circumstances.

"Colby, follow my lead. Air brake and vertical thrust, on my mark." He waited for the perfect moment before saying, "Go!"

Doyle and Colby's Mantas suddenly halted and jetted straight up. Beneath them, their pursuers overshot, stunned by the split-second maneuver. Doyle and Colby dove into the enemy formation from behind in a reverse leapfrog.

Rattled, the pair of flanking *Red Dragon* Mantas fled in opposite directions. Isolated, they were easy pickings. Doyle and Colby locked onto one mark each.

Doyle's finger brushed his weapon trigger.

Colby's voice was insistent in his ears. "Permission to open fire?"

Crunch time. Doyle's UEC trainers always said he was in the mold of old fighter pilots—mavericks—but he'd never put it to the test. Could he really shoot a fellow aviator out of the sky? Did he have that killer instinct? One look at Lon's photo stuck to his cockpit was all it took to decide.

"*Doyle*, permission to —"

Doyle squeezed the trigger. There was no kick, no booming sound. In contrast to the crude weapons of the enemy, Doyle had selected obscure technology as his primary offense: the ion-lancet, a short-range plasma beam. It emitted a slim cylinder of concentrated ionization, with no physical projectile at all—just pure heat energy, more than thirty thousand Kelvin. A scalpel versus a sledgehammer.

The beam dissected Doyle's prey as it turned to escape. Lopped into neat halves, the enemy Manta careened into the murky sea below.

Colby bore down, knocking a second Manta from the sky with a precision beam directed at its hydrogen fuel tank. The explosion riffled a shockwave through the clouds.

As Colby air-rolled extravagantly from his victory, the remaining APA Manta zipped in and blasted his exposed underbelly. A single shot. The white-hot slug tore through the exterior and blossomed inside to devour crucial components.

Black smoke billowed.

Warning lights flashed everywhere Colby looked. He jabbed his comms band. "Doyle, I got forty percent power and declining."

Doyle's voice was deliberately calm. "Can you still maneuver?"

"She's sluggish."

"Speed?"

"Can't dodge a dogfight, mate."

Doyle kicked his Manta into top speed. "You won't have to."

He saw Colby's Manta lose altitude for a second then suddenly lurch higher. The kid got cocky and he was paying the price. He'd need to land before the next dip took him straight into the ocean. But there was a more immediate concern.

Doyle pounced behind the Manta dogging Colby's tail.

The hotshot reinforcement hadn't launched another attack yet. Doyle suspected he was conserving ammunition; he couldn't imagine a Manta being able to cache too many of those larger blasts. And if it came directly from a mining outpost, the craft wouldn't have ancillary weaponry. *Okay, that's one less thing to worry about.* Doyle nailed down his plan, hoping to hell he was right.

"Colby, do exactly as I say. Bank left thirty degrees."

Colby jousted with his flight stick and managed to execute the movement. Barely.

"Up twenty," Doyle commanded. "Roll right and climb."

"She won't listen!"

"Climb! Pour everything into it."

Colby pushed his Manta high. The enemy rose below him but couldn't fire safely at a vertical angle. Gravity and splashback meant the APA pilot's own craft would take as much damage as Colby's—at least, that's what Doyle was counting on.

Doyle pointed his Manta into a steep climb to match them. His turbines growled worryingly. His craft should have easily handled a sustained ascent, but Doyle felt the engine skip a beat. The melting drips back on the *Green Dragon* must have done more harm than he'd realized. He dragged behind. *Damn it, Colby needs me.* Doyle forced his Manta beyond its limits to catch up with the enemy aircraft above.

Once level, he swung out to one side and shouted to Colby, "Now—dive!"

Colby's Manta plunged fast. His APA pursuer followed, unaware of Doyle's alignment in his blind spot.

Doyle arced up and around, scything his beam along the enemy Manta's side. The beast's stomach was splayed open, mechanical entrails disgorging.

Sabin and Django's Walruses would need new paint jobs, but there was no serious damage from their fender-bender.

They witnessed the final bogey topple from the sky and splash down nearby. The enemy Manta sank without a survivor.

Sabin was stultifyingly bored being a spectator. The flashing skyrockets of the battle raging high above spurred his restlessness. Django could sit there like a lump all night long awaiting orders, but he wanted in on the action *now*.

Sabin opened a comms channel to Doyle. "You forget all about us or what?"

Doyle watched Colby finally curtail his freefall. He tapped his comms band to reply to Sabin, "Hold tight, you two. Go in now and you'll be massacred."

"So tenderize 'em for us. We're catchin' a cold down here."

"I said *wait*." He muted Sabin's channel and opened one to Colby. "Status?"

Colby's cockpit was in pandemonium. Indicators flashed, sparks flew, and a haywire gimbal bobbed about. The Aussie's voice remained steady. "Power's failing. Can't get any lift, mate. I'm on a downward glide here." He rapidly surveyed the area. "*Green Dragon*'s too far to wangle. I gotta set her down on the *Red Dragon* and take my chances."

Doyle hesitated. "No. Too big a risk with those gunmen on board."

"Once I'm deckside I'll stay put until you guys clear them out. Popguns won't penetrate this shell."

"Enough of them will. Has to be another way."

Colby sounded weary. "There's no landmass close enough. Ocean'll gobble me whole if I eject."

"We could try a cockpit transfer."

"Dicey. Your Manta doesn't look too swift either." Doyle could picture Colby's cheeky grin when he said, "Relax, mate, she'll be right."

Doyle exhaled. "Okay, go in. I'll cover you."

Colby's Manta glided toward the *Red Dragon* carrier. When near enough, he engaged his VTOL jets, which jerkily lowered him closer to a clear section of the aft deck.

Every one of his instruments abruptly went blank.

His VTOL jets arrested. Colby's Manta thudded onto the carrier, crushing a crater into its surface. The Manta's frame bent in the middle, spewing the cockpit from the fuselage so that it only dangled by a crumpled strut and a jungle of wires.

Rain swirled around the smoking shell.

Doyle circled the *Red Dragon* in a descending arc. "Colby! Do you read? C'mon, kid…"

Colby's Manta exhibited no sign of life. Doyle was haunted by a vision from his nightmares: a discarded toy spaceship rocking in the breeze. Panic stabbed his chest.

Four APA gunmen charged out of the carrier's tower, firing at Colby's cockpit with semiautomatic rifles. Tungsten-carbide bullets struck and ricocheted in a chaotic glissando.

It wasn't working.

Alexei pressed the button again and received the same error code. He had bypassed the security subsystem, and entered the correct routines a dozen times over. He forced his addled brain to think logically. What could be the—*ah, of course, there must be a hardware redundancy.*

Alexei groped in the bundle of hanging wires until he found the one with two dashes and a dot repeated along its sheath. He stripped it back and jacked it into his hacked wall console, completing the circuit.

He tapped a single key.

Power all across *Gaea-02* went out in an instant.

The Candlemass ceased spinning, eliminating the artificial gravity. Spatial orientation inside the ship tilted to M38's true gravity and thus the crash site's forty-five degree angle. The effect was sudden and jolting, like a house collapsing into a sinkhole.

Flung from her bridge control chair, Riana tumbled across the slanted room in the dark.

Michi flailed in her lab until she latched onto M.I.T.Z. The robot's feet, magnetically planted to the floor, didn't budge.

Alexei clenched a penlight between his teeth. He located where his knife had fallen and tucked it in his waistband.

The wall had reoriented to become the floor, so the ceiling's height no longer posed an obstacle. He simply crawled to the maintenance shaft. There weren't even screws. A sharp tug and the grille popped.

They make it so easy, Alexei smirked. The Neo-Tzarists always were careless. Pompous and lazy in their superiority.

This time, he would not hesitate.

This time, his brother's knife would taste its mark.

Noble intentions of preserving the enemy's life were discarded. They had to be. This was war and Colby needed him.

Doyle pitched his Manta's nose down and cut a swathe across the *Red Dragon*'s deck with his plasma beam. One gunman, caught head-on, was rendered a puddle of flesh, fused with the liquefied surface of the carrier beneath.

The other three assailants ceased firing at Colby and, leaping over the shallow moat Doyle's beam had carved into the deck, they scuttled back inside the tower.

Gunfire cracked from positions along the upper levels, the onslaught divided between Doyle's Manta and Colby's crash.

Doyle hovered close to the tower and banked from side to side, striving to block enemy shots from reaching Colby. He switched his armament to secondary fire and spat a barrage of bullets. Reliable and effective. The tower's remaining glass shattered and a navigation mainframe exploded with an ear-splitting squeal. APA gunmen cowered or retreated outright. Two were caught as they ran, their heads and shoulders erupting in a cloud of red mist.

Strafing left and right along the tower's length, Doyle unleashed a metallic storm—more than two thousand rounds per second—until his barrels clicked empty. He finally eased his finger off the trigger.

All three levels of the wrecked tower smoldered; twinkling shards of glass cascaded over the derelict husk.

Doyle landed near Colby's crash site and leaped onto the tarmac. His first close range view of Colby's downed Manta shocked him. Its chitinous cockpit had been pierced a dozen times over, and the weakened shell had a distressing assortment of dings and jagged, sun-shaped tears.

From the angles of entry, Doyle inferred that some of those bull's-eyes must have transpired during the sky battle. Colby would have known his structural integrity was fubar before he'd crash-landed. Before he willingly faced a close-range torrent. *Brave, stupid kid.*

Doyle was certain his protégé was dead, but that didn't slow him from climbing onto the Manta's wing. Rainwater trickled into Colby's porous enclosure, the plastiglass too fragmented to see inside. Doyle smacked the side of his hand against the release latch. It wouldn't give. He grasped the rubber-sealed lip and pulled until his sinews felt as if they would snap. Straining in a last-ditch effort, he heaved the hatch open.

Colby lay curled in a fetal position inside. His scalp was split in two, one wrist twisted off the bone, his breathing shallow. The significance slowly dawned on Doyle. *He's alive.*

Colby's lips barely moved. "How'd I do?"

Doyle was astounded. "You did great, kid. You're a superstar."

He gently unhooked the tattered flight harness. Colby felt

light and limp as Doyle scooped him up, carrying him down from the uprooted cockpit and ducking under the smoke gushing from a turbine.

Colby groaned when Doyle laid him on the carrier deck. Then Doyle saw the bullet wounds. Two in Colby's lower abdomen, plus a third that had pulverized his hip.

He bucked off his lucky flight jacket, balled it up, and jammed it against Colby's gut to stem the blood. Doyle shouted above the howling weather into his comms band, "Riana, we need you. Jump in the spare Walrus and get here *now*."

The channel was silent.

"Riana, are you reading me? Riana!"

Riana found her way in the dark, reminding herself: *Left is down, right is up*. It felt like exploring a capsized ocean liner. She clambered over a console, her knees pressing buttons that did nothing.

She reached the bridge exit but was clueless what to do next. They had replenished *Gaea-02*'s power cells with fresh ones from the APA base, so what was the problem? Hopefully, Michi was all right and on the case. Alexei was locked away, so there was no one else to call on; they were the only people left on board except…

"Eckerd," she said with a sinking realization. His respirator was connected to the ship's grid, and with the power terminated…

Riana scrambled through the lopsided doorway.

The maintenance shaft was a tight fit for Alexei's adult frame, although in truth he hadn't grown much past age sixteen. He never minded being the shortest, the scrawniest of any crew. All men were mere dwarves to the stars above.

He tasted plastic. His teeth were grinding furrows in the penlight. He removed it from his mouth to spit out the shavings.

Did he hear something? Were they aware of his presence, hunting him along the shaft like scurrying rodents?

No. His brother Viktor was his sentry, keeping vigil outside, was he not?

Alexei sniffed the air, and the fetid odor of Sobranie cigarettes was strong enough to make him choke.

Michi vaulted a sidelong strut and clung to the corridor wall. Her thigh throbbed; she was sure she had retorn the muscle. She allowed herself a strict sixty-second rest before continuing on.

What use was setting up external defensive turrets if they had no power? She'd made herself a promise on the Wheel to be as reliable as a robot and she was not about to break that oath now.

Navigating by touch, Michi calculated she wasn't far from the main engineering hub. She almost regretted not bringing M.I.T.Z. along; he would have been slow and cumbersome, but he could at least have lit the way. Then again, light meant shadows. And she knew what tricks shadows played.

Michi slung her leg over an askew bulkhead and recognized from its ultraprotective thickness that she was in the right place. How often had she stood at this threshold watching the Jiménez brothers working on the antimatter core? Sabin and Pach, joking and razzing, pretending to be card hustlers. She wished Sabin were here now; he would have known precisely where *Gaea-02*'s problem lay. It was difficult for Michi to admit to herself that she'd become fonder of him than she intended.

Her fingers ran over the engineering control housing. Michi snapped open the underpanel, took a circuit tracer from her belt, and got to work. Sparks illuminated her face.

"Riana, come in. Please respond. Colby needs help!"

Doyle's vain pleas resonated over the open comms channel. Sabin had been listening in from his Walrus for the past two minutes as his leader's voice became increasingly desperate.

All the while, the *Red Dragon*'s sealed rear launch bay stared at Sabin, daring him. Enough was enough. Help wasn't coming; they were alone out here.

"Screw the plan," he said. Sabin flipped down his targeting computer. Thumbing the nub, he drew a square around the mark.

The system automatically adjusted the missile's payload according to the desired area of effect. *Wouldn't want the deck falling out from under Doyle and the kid, would we?*

"We're going in, Django," he said over his comms band. "Hang onto your *cajones*."

Sabin mashed the launcher. A harpoon-tipped missile soared over the waves and punctured the *Red Dragon*'s massive launch door, jutting halfway out.

Tick… tick… tick…

Sabin closed his eyes. "This one's for you, bro."

BOOM. The missile's precision warhead detonated, blowing the launch door off its bracing.

The explosion rocked Doyle on the deck. He held Colby tighter, bracing for aftershocks.

Twenty-eight tons of metal door flew between Sabin and Django's Walruses, stirring up a mini-tsunami that battered the amphibious vehicles like toy boats in a bathtub.

Sabin righted his vessel and surged forward. The *Red Dragon*'s gangplank had been blasted into the water, half torn from its fixture. Sabin's wheels gained traction on the studded surface. The precarious join held.

Django waited until Sabin was inside, then thundered into the carrier's gaping maw. The Walruses barged through displaced debris and rolled over twisted scrap metal on six giant wheels.

Sabin misjudged the launch bay's depth and had to skid before he rammed a rear wall. Django braked in time, nose nudging the side of Sabin's Walrus. Both men jumped from their vehicles brandishing assault rifles.

Klaxons howled and they heard boots clanging across the metal gridwork of the gantry above.

Sabin grinned. *About time.*

Riana had gone rock climbing regularly at the academy. It was the only part of cadet training she had actually enjoyed. No one making demands—just her and the hard, textured rockface.

After years of neglecting those muscles, she was using them now, although the slanted surfaces were smoother and freezing. Without *Gaea-02*'s temperature control, the planet's chill permeated everywhere. She couldn't see her breath in the pitch dark, but she assumed it must be clouding.

Riana mounted the wall to reach a sealed door. Running her palm over its raised motif confirmed that this was her medlab. She curled her fingertips around the seam and tugged. The door slid open without resistance.

She hurdled a cabinet to reach the table where Eckerd was strapped. Riana put two fingers to his neck. *Of course he's dead*, she chided herself. In his state, he wouldn't have survived longer than a minute or two without power to his respirator.

Deep down, she'd known since the crash that there was never really any hope of saving him. The past two weeks had only been prolonging the inevitable.

Riana removed the apparatus from Eckerd's mouth. Her first real patient and she'd lost him.

Colby's chest shuddered. His breathing grew increasingly irregular.

"C'mon, Colby, stay with me." Doyle gently shook him. "Help's on the way."

"Nah, mate," Colby whispered with flagging strength, "no Flying Doctor out here."

"Not like your dad, huh?" *Keep him talking*, Doyle told himself. "Zooming around the Aussie outback to fix people up in his, what was it, a twin-turboprop?"

"Beechcraft King Air B450." A grin lit Colby's pallid face. "He'd have a fit... knew I was shooting down planes. He saved lives, not..."

"Bull. He'd be proud of you, kid. You're the second-best pilot on this planet."

Colby's weak laugh caused a mist of blood. "Best-looking one."

He died with the grin still on his red-flecked lips.

Distraught, Doyle closed his protégé's eyes.

It struck him that he'd never once thought of Colby as a substitute for Lon, even when he missed his son the most. Their relationship was certainly less than paternal, but they were more than just workmates. Before he'd first quit the Gaea mission, Doyle had shepherded Colby from gawky, precocious adolescent into a young man who excelled despite his idiosyncrasies. Whether or not Colby's father would have been proud, Doyle *was*.

He laid Colby gently on the carrier deck.

"*No praeter solis*," Doyle intoned. The death blessing of the UEC pilot corps: *Fly beyond the sun*.

He unrolled his blood-soaked flight jacket and used it to shroud Colby's face.

A rifle barrel pressed against the back of Doyle's head.

The *Red Dragon*'s substructure was dim, grimy and, for some reason, seemed more convoluted than the *Green Dragon*'s, despite being identical in design. In short, Sabin was lost.

Seeing his companion flounder, Django took point. He knew next to nothing of naval vessels, but he knew which way was up. He heard an enemy officer on the walkway above them, moving about in a pathetic attempt at stealth.

Sabin was less aware, although he noted Django's regular pauses to listen before heading off on a new route. He swore he saw the big man's ears twitch. Django found a spiral staircase leading up to the gantry. Sabin pushed in front as if in a race.

Near the summit, Django suddenly lunged past Sabin and raised his rifle in one hand above his head. He fired a short burst across the gantry, unsighted, at knee height. A howl of pain echoed off the walls.

Sabin stood and saw an APA gunman sprawled on the gantry, clutching his shattered, bloody legs. He nodded to Django. "You're a better shot when you don't aim."

As they crossed the gantry, Django kicked the downed officer's gun over the ledge; it clanged noisily to the bottom.

Sabin and Django jogged into an engineering corridor. Here, multiple junctions led off to sensitive parts of the carrier's infrastructure. They methodically jabbed their rifles around every corner but saw no one.

Sabin grew impatient and carelessly crossed a junction without first verifying it was empty. An APA officer came out of hiding to fire her handgun dead-on at Sabin's skull.

Django lurched forward, blocking the shot with his massive shoulder. The slug burrowed into his flesh and lodged there.

Sabin returned fire, peppering the gunwoman's chest with a dozen bullets before her body hit the ground.

"Django..." Sabin started to say, but he became mesmerized by the blood oozing from Django's shoulder. "Okay, this ain't fair, man. You saved my head getting spit-roasted by a plasma punch and now you take a bullet for me? When's my turn to be the hero, huh?"

Django grinned through his grimace, sweat dotting his wide, dark brow.

Sabin examined the gunshot wound. "Don't move. I'll find their medlab, get something to patch you up."

Shaking his head, Django turned Sabin around and pushed onward instead. They had a job to finish.

Cold steel scraped Doyle's bare scalp as he rose. The gun barrel never left his skin.

He heard his captor draw a hissing breath, then speak in harsh Mandarin. Doyle didn't understand. Was he demanding a surrender or evoking last rites?

In his rush to get to Colby, Doyle had stupidly left his own weapon inside the Manta. Rain streamed into his eyes but he could only blink it away.

The Chinese man spoke again, more insistently. This time, Doyle deciphered the word for *Captain*. So, he was dealing with the boss.

Doyle tried to remember the Mandarin phrase for surrender,

but seeing Colby's corpse on the cold, wet deck stoked a fire in his belly. No capitulation. He squeezed both hands into tight fists and decided he might well die, but he'd fight to the end.

The *Red Dragon*'s Captain yelled a final command—

Blam!

A thud landed behind Doyle's feet. He whirled around. The Captain was sprawled on the deck with half his face missing. Doyle could feel the splattered gray matter dripping down the back of his own skull.

Six feet away, cradling a pistol too large for her svelte hand... stood Indigo.

Michi was vexed. There was no damage to *Gaea-02*'s power grid, nothing to indicate a hardware fault. From all indications, the system had simply shut down. Perhaps due to a software bug or on Indigo's remote command if she'd somehow breached their firewalls. And if that was the case, what else could she sabotage from afar? Michi still found it hard to accept that Indigo had been duplicitous for so long. What could drive a woman to live a double life like that?

Michi rebooted the antimatter engine. Within seconds, the ship powered up and a thrum quivered through the core.

She reinstated the artificial gravity. The shunt as *Gaea-02*'s orientation returned to normal was sharper than expected and Michi toppled onto her back.

"Dumb," she muttered from the floor.

Michi peered up as light phosphoresced from sunken orbs around the ceiling... and was startled.

Alexei loomed above her, arms folded behind his back.

"Hi," Michi said, recovering quickly from the fright. "I hard-booted the system, sorry for the flip-flop." She rose unsteadily to her feet—keeping the weight off her thigh—and reached out to balance herself against Alexei, ending up face to face with his unblinking stare.

She'd been told about his breakdown but had processed the

information without dwelling on its substance. Only now, with a queasiness in the pit of her stomach, did she connect the dots.

Alexei's face remained strangely blank. He hadn't uttered a word, but there was something threatening, even sinister, in his restraint.

The fears Michi had been masking with bravado during her time on M38 surged to the forefront. Her voice wavered. "Aren't you supposed to be locked…?"

Frowning, Michi stopped mid-sentence. She gazed down.

Alexei held his brother Viktor's blade, stabbed halfway into Michi's abdomen.

Profound shock kept her pain in momentary limbo. Her senses dulled. The metal buried within her flesh became Michi's sole point of contact with the world. She felt weightless.

Alexei gradually withdrew the blade. His eyes rolled in exquisite lunacy.

Michi's hands clutched feebly at her abdomen. Blood gushed between her fingers. Her trance broke and pain squeezed the breath from her lungs. Her legs moved by instinct alone as she hobbled out of engineering.

Alexei watched her with curious detachment, as if she were merely roadkill twitching on a stretch of dusty asphalt.

Gunshots reverberated through the narrow stairwell so quickly that Sabin lost track of their origin. He ducked as loud, sparking pings ricocheted off the railing and bounced three times before the shells lost inertia and clinked melodically down the steps like rolling coins.

He and Django had routed three APA officers, who fired wildly to cover their scrambling retreat to the tower's demolished upper floor. Sabin figured this trio must be the last defenders left standing, since he and Django had systematically cleared out the lower levels, leaving dead and injured adversaries in their wake.

Along the way, Sabin had noticed Django always aimed for leg shots, doing the bare minimum to incapacitate enemy officers. Surprising himself, Sabin began to adopt similar tactics. After he'd killed one, two, three people, his rage had subsided. It became less personal, less of a grudge match and more about winning for his friends' sakes. Duty above revenge.

Accepting *Gaea-02*'s crew as his surrogate family had crept up on Sabin; for so long, his only bond had been with his brother.

The shooting paused. After the fleeing gunmen had taken residence upstairs, they'd begun laying down suppressing fire every thirty seconds to discourage Sabin and Django from attempting a blitz. Frankly, it was getting on Sabin's nerves.

He used the lull to edge along the steps for the best view he could manage without getting his face perforated. The top level was crumbling to bits from Doyle's demolition job. That gave Sabin an idea.

He nudged Django's shoulder and pointed straight up. The big man nodded. On Sabin's mark, they both fired at the fractured ceiling directly over the APA gunmen.

They kept pumping rounds until the overhead span was Swiss-cheesed by bullet holes. Metal contorted with a hair-raising screech as remnants of the roof-mounted plasma cannons crashed through.

Indigo's hand trembled around her oversized gun. She kept it level at Doyle's head, barely reacting to the clamor from the tower behind her.

Her left hand was missing three fingers, amputated due to gangrene. She was still a sight to behold. The figure-hugging, bronze envirosuit she wore reflected light from the blazing debris. Her hair's luxurious violet streaks never looked so vivid, perhaps because her face had never been quite so pale in contrast.

Indigo glanced at Colby's body. "Is he…?"

Doyle nodded. She acted overwrought, but he doubted her friendship with Colby was ever sincere. How could it have been?

"I didn't know," Indigo said. "I swear."

"Know what?" Doyle kept on his toes, angling for an opportunity to disarm her.

"That they'd start a nuclear war. All I did was supply information. Updates of our progress, scientific reports, a few access codes. They were holding my *family*, Doyle."

"You mean Mya Lyn's family."

"*My* family. Indigo was just a name blinking on a computer screen. They were my flesh and blood."

Doyle knew firsthand how familial devotion could persuade you to sacrifice ideals and perform unconscionable acts. Maybe he could forgive her, given time, but at the moment she was unstable and holding a gun at his head. He had to play this right. "I understand," he said, feigning sympathy. "You did what you had to."

Indigo sobbed. "None of it mattered. I accessed the Captain's records when you attacked. The bastards murdered my parents the day I boarded *Gaea-02*."

A loud clap split the air as a satellite launched from the foredeck, trailing tendrils of smoke.

Sabin and Django glanced up from the APA crewmen pinned under the rubble. Past the gaping ceiling, they could see the supersonic satellite rip through the black sky, soaring ever higher.

"Not a good sign," Sabin said.

Alexei followed the trail of blood droplets as if they were breadcrumbs. Limping without a crutch, his bare feet smeared the floor red. "You try to lock me up," he shouted, his Kazakh accent thicker than ever. "You and the rest."

Michi staggered into her lab, her jumpsuit soaked in blood. Mewling like a sacrificial lamb, she stumbled across the room to lean against M.I.T.Z.

Alexei stood at the threshold. "You are all in league with the Neo-Tzarists."

Michi's hands tried to snatch back her escaping life as it hemorrhaged from her gut by the pint. She attempted to cry out but her mouth filled with gurgling blood.

"You rape my country." Alexei moved close to Michi. "You kill my family."

He raised his blade.

M.I.T.Z. snatched Alexei's wrist in one plasmolded hand. Its other hand gripped Alexei's shoulder, crunching bone.

Michi formed a single, whispered word: "Heat."

M.I.T.Z. obeyed, its indicator stripe flashing red as it bombarded Alexei's body with microwaves. The madman screamed in utter anguish while being cooked from the inside.

Michi closed her eyes for the final time, slumped against her M.I.T.Z.

The robot rotated its blue-ringed visual sensors downward. Was there concern in those electronic eyes?

As Alexei's irradiated skin bubbled and erupted, M.I.T.Z.'s attention was tuned to Michi, only Michi, its faithful keeper. Its creator.

Its mother.

Indigo watched the satellite's vapor trail fade in the drizzling rain.

"They've won," she said. "That beacon will stay in orbit and warn the APA's colony ship."

"It's yours, isn't it?" Doyle asked.

She nodded. "I programmed it before I knew about my family. I'm sorry. You have to believe me. I never wanted any of you to be hurt."

"Prove it. Put the gun down."

Indigo's aim faltered for a moment. "No. You'll kill me." She gripped her gun more firmly. "I'm a traitor."

"We need you," Doyle implored. "You could disable the beacon or jam the signal."

"And when I'm no use to you anymore? You don't care about me. All you want is to see your son again."

"If you help me, I'll—"

"I *can't* help you, Doyle. No one can."

"What are you saying?"

Indigo fumbled at her waist with her left thumb and forefinger, the only digits remaining on that hand. She removed a malleable tablet computer made from photoelectric rubber and tossed it to Doyle.

Doyle straightened the screen. Two English phrases stood out among the Chinese characters.

The name Lon Gage, and in red, capital letters stamped across a photo of Lon in his early twenties: **DECEASED**.

Spontaneous tears streaked down Doyle's granite cheeks.

Sabin and Django made sure the injured APA combatants were disarmed and bound before hurrying downstairs to investigate the launched satellite. They reached the deck landing where the aft exit was a smoldering chasm.

Beyond the vermilion haze, Sabin sighted Indigo pointing her gun at Doyle.

"*La mujer traidora*," he spat.

Sabin raised his assault rifle and rushed into the open.

Through his grief and tears, Doyle looked past Indigo. "Sabin—no!"

Too late. Sabin fired two rounds.

Indigo's chest exploded, her splintered ribs thrust outward through scraps of bronze envirosuit. She sank to the deck, eyes open and locked with Doyle's.

Rain stole the blood from under her corpse, sloshing it around Doyle's boots. He didn't feel remorse. He couldn't feel anything anymore.

Django caught up to Sabin. He knelt at Indigo's body, searching for her pulse. A formality.

Sabin asked Doyle, "You okay?"

Doyle stared, emotionless, until he could muster speech. "Round up any prisoners," he said flatly. "Bring them to the *Green Dragon*."

"The *Green*...? But we won," Sabin exclaimed. "We got the ship!"

"We won nothing."

Slogging across the rainswept carrier, Doyle let Indigo's computer tablet drop from his numb fingertips. His boot left a crease on the fold-screen, warping Lon's death record photo into a grisly caricature.

CHAPTER 19
UNDERGROWTH

A smothered dawn brightened the sky from black to muddy gray as the *Green Dragon* rocked incessantly on the ocean's convulsions. Django swayed on the foredeck. He hoped their journey to *Gaea-02* would be swift.

The bullet brooded like a malignant tumor under his skin and curtailed further writing in his leather-bound journal. Django read over the snippets he'd been able to jot down before his throbbing shoulder became unbearable. A pyrrhic victory... a war provoked... the gentle art of negotiation squandered. Django worried that Doyle might give up after learning of his son's death. The last words Django had penned were: *Doyle swings hot and cold, but he is a smart leader and a good man.*

Django contented himself by poring over past entries, since his future, like the sky above, was so gray and impenetrable.

He flipped to the first page of his journal.

11/08/2041

Today I made a choice.

Having lived every moment of my life so close to the Sahara, I can tell you if a grain of sand came from there purely by its scent. I know I am a private man, some say too quiet a man, but I am one who has seen firsthand how the silent desert landscape of my birth wields its own harsh strength.

The Sahara turns everything to sand; even people can become cruel, brittle, and dry here—if they survive. We are living through the worst drought in mankind's history. Our pillaged Earth has cried out, "No more!" She has taken enough abuse. And now, her children weep.

There is no going back for me.

Remembering his life's turning point, Django smoothed the spot where the ink had run. The spot where a lone teardrop had rippled the paper.

I have experienced my share of death in my homeland. I've seen violence and brutish acts of patriotism, but never before have I witnessed such ugliness from men wearing the United Earth Coalition uniform.

Neither the child, Kwaami, nor his family had seen fresh water for days until a group of UEC soldiers stood in the back of their truck and dangled a full bottle before the boy's eyes. He begged them, pleaded in his small, humble voice. But the truck rolled away and the soldiers decided to have some 'fun.'

When it happened, I was on Afaussata's rooftop with my rangefinder, drawing up ambitious plans for a limestone aqueduct to convey water from the deep aquifer discovered in the highlands sixty miles west. I turned my stinging eyes from the harmattan haze blowing hot across all of northern Mali to see the UEC truck speed past... and little Kwaami running behind, trying to keep up... barefooted, over scorching sand and sharp, hastate rocks, desperate to retrieve the water for his family. Such courage in one so young.

And such cowardice from those who stood in positions of authority. Testing and taunting this poor boy with their promise of liquid salvation, only to snatch it away whenever he drew close, his tiny hands left clutching dry air.

I watched from my perch as, a mile onward, they finally gave the boy what he would run until the ends of the Earth to earn. A UEC soldier threw him the water bottle, but with such deliberate force that the container burst on the ground like a grenade. The thirsty sand soaked up every drop.

Amidst a rising sirocco, I saw Kwaami collapse in dusty futility. He did not move again. Overcome by fatigue, heat, and dehydration. The Sahara had claimed another victim.

The soldiers' laughter burned hotter than any desert. They never turned back to help.

This made me FURIOUS.

Even now, Django's fist tightened with the impotent frustration of being a bystander to that tragic event. He had known the child well. Little Kwaami often played with Afaussata's children—Django's nieces and nephews.

Django vividly recalled the wrath he'd felt, and he was still surprised at the decision he made that day.

The boy's father took up arms and there was a small revolt, easily put down by local UEC troops.

I did not take part in the insurrection.

I joined the UEC instead.

This morning, I listened to Bakatu Kagea's call for calm in the village and his words, "To effect change, the individual must work from within, not as an outsider." I agree.

I am only one man, too used to working alone. I can stay here with my anger seething until I explode, or I can work to be the quiet voice of reason.

This way, I will use the UEC's resources and technology to benefit my tribe and make certain such vile acts as those that led to Kwaami's death are never repeated.

Some have already branded me a traitor, but this is how I can best make a difference. I hope whoever may find this journal understands my morality and my motives.

Would they? Django asked himself. Had his end justified his means? Completing the aqueduct had been his very first UEC-sponsored action, and he was able to arrange for Mali to be ranked high on the list of D-salt distributions. Applying his terraforming techniques to space colonization reached far beyond his original goals, but was it not all for the greater good? His sole reason for coming to M38 was to represent his people in this frightening, new universe.

He had traveled so far. He swore to never lose sight of who he was or where he came from.

The *Green Dragon* heaved as its bow barged through the brittle edge of an ice plain. Django spotted *Gaea-02*'s crash site in the distance. He overheard snatches of a radio transmission from Riana on his headset.

The news didn't bode well.

CHAPTER 20
BEYOND THE SON

Riana rolled up her sleeves and tucked in her blouse. The frightful, sobering fact was that she was the sole living creature aboard *Gaea-02.* This ship had been her home for what seemed like forever, yet never had it felt so like a mausoleum, not even when Baden died. Its frigid, dour walls and gargantuan bulkheads loomed balefully. *Will this be my crypt too?*

Waiting for *Gaea-02*'s ragtag assault force to return, Riana paced the vehicle bay. For how many hours, she lost track.

She stirred at the sound of engines. Two Walruses trundled up the gangplank, their dented shells as scratched and scraped as the occupants.

Seeing Doyle, Sabin, and Django together emphasized the potent loss for Riana. "We're . . . all that's left?"

Their thirteen-strong crew reduced to this sallow quartet. The last vestige of the Gaea mission.

Riana faced Doyle and tried to picture the boy he once was, on that Foundation Day so many years ago. Spirited, impish. She couldn't sustain the illusion long. This man was a hollowed-out husk.

Doyle didn't waste energy on a greeting. He and Sabin opened their cargo holds and led out nine bound prisoners. The injured majority were assisted by the able-bodied. Although Django tried to hide his pain, it was obvious that his shoulder would also need tending. Riana had her work cut out.

Doyle passed her a data tablet. "Something I need translated. When you have time."

He hadn't been able to leave Indigo's parting gift behind. He needed to know how and when Lon died.

Riana took the tablet. She stared at the official death record and her overwhelming sense of doom redoubled.

The brig was crowded with wall-to-wall prisoners. More captives were secured in the medlab. *Gaea-02*'s crew wouldn't need to care for them long, since whatever their mutual destiny held was bound to materialize during the next few days. Liberty ... or death.

Doyle left Sabin responsible for the captives' needs, but a jittery case of déjà vu gave him pause at the door. "Sabin?"

"Don't worry. I'm not Alexei."

Sabin had gained enough of his trust, so Doyle walked the ship's spine to reconvene with Riana as she exited from surgery.

He strode with her through *Gaea-02*'s noticeably vacant science district while she gave her report. "I removed the bullet from Django's shoulder. Hell of a patient; can't even get him to say when something hurts."

"And the APA wounded?" Doyle asked.

"Mixed results. The man missing a knee will need a full reconstruction, as long as the colony's equipped. One young woman has broken ribs—painful but not serious. There's a cranial fracture—stable—and three with flesh wounds who can be moved to the brig whenever you like."

"Okay. Keep them comfortable until then."

"There's something I think you should see." Her pace quickened.

Doyle matched her speed. "Riana, about Eckerd…"

"His respirator stopped during Alexei's blackout. There was nothing I could do."

"What I wanted to say," he hushed her, "was don't torture yourself."

Riana stopped and rubbed a crease above her left eye, a sign she was trying to ward off a migraine. Doyle's light touch on her shoulder had a calming effect. She gave a quick nod, inhaled, and with a burst of nervous energy led him past a junction where a trail of dried blood marked the way. They crossed into Michi's robotics lab.

Doyle frowned at the lights and sounds emanating from the rear module. *Why was the Mass Prototype Engine operating?* Distracted, he trod in a puddle of beige goop.

"What's this mess?"

"It's…Alexei."

Ugh. Doyle raked his shoe on the wall.

A substantial amount of blood had caked at the end of the trail. "Where's Michi's body?"

Riana pointed to the center of the lightshow, where M.I.T.Z. controlled the spinning MPE array like an unhinged conductor.

Michi's corpse was prostrate on the anvil.

Doyle couldn't believe his eyes. "What the hell is that thing doing?"

"Trying to repair her," Riana said. "The MPE can imitate Michi's superficial form, but…"

M.I.T.Z. withdrew a soft-resin Michi mannequin from the MPE's output berth. It was a perfect visual reproduction, down to the gaping stab wound in her abdomen and spiked, synthetic-fiber hair.

The dutiful robot carried Michi's replica to the far corner of the lab. *Dozens* of identical, inorganic Michis were lined up there in a row. M.I.T.Z. had clearly been at this nonstop for hours.

"The poor creature doesn't understand life," Riana said.

Unnerved, Doyle turned away. "I'll have Sabin break the programming loop." He didn't need any more reminders about the decimation of his crew.

Seeing how shaken Doyle was, Riana held his arm. "Doyle. Are *you* okay?"

"Did you read it?"

She studied his face closely when she said, "An explosion of some kind. Details were scant." After a pause, she added, "He … he was a wanted fugitive."

"Why?"

"Because he was your son."

The paternal guilt was almost too much. His legacy to Lon was a life as a hunted criminal—and even that was cut short. Doyle's hand trembled. He needed to put his pain somewhere, to direct it … but first, he had to know. "When did he die?"

"November third, 2068."

"Twenty-two," Doyle said. "He was only twenty-two."

They watched in silence as M.I.T.Z. continued its misguided task, returning to the Mass Prototype Engine in an endless cycle.

The metal slates they used as headstones froze so quickly that Doyle's skin stuck to the surface, leaving a residue of his palm print like a final goodbye wave to Colby.

Names had been laser-etched into the crude memorials, embedded in the ice beside *Gaea-02*. One for each of the crew members who'd lost their lives since crash landing on this planet. It was all symbolic, of course. The bodies were not buried here. They were kept refrigerated aboard the ship in hibernation chambers. No one had yet suggested where or how they would eventually be interred.

The central headstones belonged to Colby, Michi, and Eckerd. Two smaller faux graves, for Indigo and Alexei, were set apart from the rest due to the dishonorable nature of their deaths.

Huddled before the three larger markers, Doyle bowed his

head with Riana and Sabin. They'd been waiting for Django to arrive before commencing the quiet remembrance ceremony. He tramped over the ice with his huge arm in a sling.

"The four of us wouldn't be here, wouldn't be alive without their bravery," Riana began. "Baden would have been proud of them."

"We all are," Doyle hastily added.

Sabin knelt at Michi's headstone and recited a Shinto prayer. He noticed the others staring at him and felt a flush of embarrassment when he was done.

"That was beautiful," Riana said.

"It was, uh, for all of them. You understood it? I just copied a phonetic transcript from the databanks."

"I know a little Japanese. I think the final line means, roughly, 'Dwell no more under shadows of clouds that hang low over mountaintops; rest only in light.'"

They all glanced at the cheerless sky.

Sabin broke into their pensive thoughts, "When the colony ship sees Indigo's beacon, what do you think the APA will do? Send down troops? Blast us from orbit?"

No one was willing to speculate. Doyle continued to gaze across the lost horizon. His son was gone. His sole purpose eradicated. What did he have left to fight for?

He looked at the expectant faces of his three companions and had his answer.

The Gaea mission.

Until the last member of this crew was dead, the dream was alive. He would fight for the men and the woman beside him and for those who had already fallen. Doyle remembered his own rallying cry from a lifetime ago: *The pioneer's flame burns brightest in the darkest moments.*

He even had an inkling of what to do.

Doyle trudged to his Manta and climbed aboard. Lon and Juni smiled at him from the photo adhered to the cockpit window. He tucked it inside his flight jacket beside Lon's sketch, close to his heart. Doyle cringed at the stain on his cuff; the flash-cleaner hadn't erased all of Colby's blood.

Riana called out, "Doyle, where are you go—" but was drowned by the turbine ignition. He saluted as he took off, leaving them baffled on the ice below.

From above, the supply pod did not inspire awe.

Buried beneath a sheet of snow where they'd first discovered it on the outskirts of the APA base, its full scale was hard to visualize. Doyle flew close, angled his Manta back, and tilted both turbines to direct twin funnels of heat, melting away the snow cover.

He landed and stepped out to appraise the dripping, fully excavated pod: a white cone with a black, puppy-dog snout and rotund belly. Its hulking, metal hull glowed a dull red from the expedited thaw but was structurally intact.

Doyle smiled. "Perfect."

Hung by thick, galvanized wire rope, the pod threatened to fling Doyle's Manta from the air with every pendulum swing. The swaged cable loops attached to the aircraft's undercarriage squealed in concert with the engine's buzz-saw complaints of overload.

Doyle ignored the industrial orchestra until he had *Gaea-02* in his sights. Easing his Manta lower, he gently deposited the supply pod on an ice field. The cacophony summoned Riana, Sabin, and Django outside; they jogged down *Gaea-02*'s gangplank, meeting Doyle as his Manta landed.

Sabin pointed to the pod, its cabling splayed like unkempt hair. "What the hell's that for?"

"Our ride off this giant ice cube." Doyle jumped from his cockpit. He paced around the massive supply pod with renewed vigor. "Sabin, think you can adapt an engine stage from *Gaea-02* onto this?"

"Probably, but—"

Doyle interrupted, fast-talking. "A few spare antimatter cells, a magnetic sheath—we should get enough lift to crack the sky."

"Maybe, but—"

"We can rig some inertial dampeners, enhance the radiation screens. It's got plenty of heat shielding already, so we won't burn up inside."

"*Doyle*," Sabin said, halting his leader's ad-hoc pitch, "you've gone haywire. I know what you're thinking, but it'll never work."

Doyle stared. "Why not?"

"Well, the ... um, we'd ... There's a million reasons."

"Name one."

Doyle was aware of an alphabet of potential issues, from anti-matter leakage to zero-point navigation, but he had answers to them all if Sabin chose to challenge his concept.

Sabin flung up his arms. "Fine, you wanna ride a dinky l'il pod into orbit ..."

"No," Doyle said calmly, "I want to fire us like a rocket into the colony ship."

Sabin was suitably astonished.

Doyle continued, "The pod's docking collar is intact, and the comms platform we left in orbit can guide us straight to an airlock."

Riana caught his drift. "You want to board the ship."

Doyle's grin widened. *Yes. She understands.*

"That's suicide," Sabin renewed his objection, although Doyle suspected the engineer was secretly intrigued by the idea.

"Sabin's right," Riana said. "What you're suggesting is a huge risk on so many levels."

Doyle nodded. "I'm glad you realize that. Good."

Riana was thrown for a second. "No yelling match?"

"Extreme ideas demand damn strong justification. I would've been disappointed in you if you'd been too easily convinced."

Riana chuckled. "We're listening."

Snowflakes melted on Doyle's shoulders. His emotions welled. "The four of us have lost everything and everyone. The world we knew, the people we loved. Baden, Pach ... Lon. We have nothing left, except ..." Doyle bowed his head for a moment and drew a steadying breath. "Here's the thing. When I look at you three, I'm reminded of that dream we shared when we first boarded *Gaea-02* together. It's just a glimmer now, but it's still there—in each of us."

Riana and Django slowly nodded. Sabin scoffed, "*Mierda del toro.*"

Doyle turned Sabin's face toward the headstones. "They didn't give their lives for nothing. At least respect that."

Sabin dropped the rebel act with an apologetic nod. He motioned for Doyle to continue.

"We have one last chance to give the Gaea mission some meaning. To show the APA what we and the United Earth Coalition stand for . . . have always stood for."

Riana dredged up one of Commander Ruschen's old sound bites: "This sector's resources should be used to heal our home planet as one entity, one race." Her fire was back. "From what Fei Haisheng told me, that's not happening. Earth has split into hemispheres: the APA's oasis and a forsaken wasteland. The APA leaves only scraps for the rest of humanity."

That UEC rhetoric could always get Doyle going as a young man, and it was working its magic now. He clenched a fist. "We may not succeed, but it's worth fighting for. Otherwise, the Earth we knew dies right here on the ice."

Sabin shook his head. "We're four people against the hundreds, maybe thousands aboard that ship."

"Most will be colonists."

"Idealists," Riana said, "like us."

"They might listen. Even unite to help us colonize space the *right* way."

"For the right reasons."

Doyle nodded at Riana, pleased she was taking his words to heart. "It's the same plan we've been following all along; we'll just be engaging them by a more direct route. If we can capture the ship's bridge, that gives us a platform. These people have been lied to all their lives by General Qing-Chen. The very fact that we, the 'mythical' crew of *Gaea-02*, are still alive and kicking might be enough to open their eyes. *We can do this.* Together, I know we can."

Riana and Django, even Sabin, seemed energized by Doyle's passion. He hadn't behaved this way in years. It had been easy to forget Doyle was once the public face and speaker for the Gaea mission.

Riana's verve and buoyant spirits told Doyle she was with him—all the way.

"Django?" Doyle looked for his support and received an enthusiastic thumbs-up.

Doyle gripped Sabin's shoulder, goading the engineer. "Colony ship's due here in just over ninety hours. We've got four days to make this pod fly. You game?"

Unconvinced, Sabin circled the pod, poking his nose into every coil and cranny. He made a complete circumnavigation before stopping in front of Doyle. "Pach an' me always did love monkeying with new toys . . . Okay, count me in."

Sleep proved elusive for the next few days. The crew of four, plus rebooted M.I.T.Z., churned through the slew of work involved in adapting the supply pod for space flight.

Sabin drew up schematics while Django salvaged a rolling magnacrane from the *Green Dragon*. Doyle and Riana assisted Django's construction of sunken plinths, upon which he mag-lifted the pod. It held steady.

Django directed M.I.T.Z. via body language to do any heavy lifting he couldn't handle with his lame shoulder. The big man was an excellent physical engineer, designing wholly in his mind an intricate support structure around the site, then building it within three hours. Doyle studied his finished work closely. He was amazed by the rigidity of Django's lightweight scaffolding and the foresight of tool gullies and access culverts, all cleverly crosshatched to convey whatever they needed at hand.

For the first time, Doyle could see just how integral Django would have been to their original mission. His terraforming skills—molding the planet's surface and atmosphere—were only part of his contribution. This enigma of a man could well have built *cities*.

Doyle was both confounded and strangely amused by the way M.I.T.Z. was attuned to Django's every gesture, as if the duo shared some kind of silent lexicon. Michi would have been gratified. She had been the only one comfortable with the robot—*her* robot—but here Django was utilizing it like a prosthetic limb.

With Django and M.I.T.Z.'s help, Doyle and Sabin detached three of the dozen burn-assist radial boosters from *Gaea-02*'s engine. These were used by the crew module for minor trajectory correction, but they'd make full-blown propulsion units for the much lighter pod.

As the first night fell, Riana arranged halogen floodlights while Sabin was busy affixing the rocket array to the pod, sparks showering from his welder. Django and M.I.T.Z. fashioned additional parts the engineer needed from the MPE.

Doyle found Sabin asleep in the pod at dawn. Sabin accepted a steaming hit of java-sludge before diving straight back into his task.

"Almost got it secured," Sabin said. "Just need to get the angles right or the boosters'll rip themselves right off the frame." He nudged a loose connection, then turned to Doyle and asked, "Think you can get *Gaea-02*'s computer to run some models?"

"Sure."

Doyle soaked up the warmth inside the ship as he ran countless simulations using Sabin's specs. Once he'd found the perfect equilibrium, he transmitted the data to Sabin and began converting a guidance system for the pod. Indigo would have had it up and running in seconds, but it took Doyle considerably longer.

He typed a sequence of commands on the bridge console to reactivate the comms platform they had disengaged from *Gaea-02*'s crew module. He recalled how antsy Indigo had been when he left it dormant in orbit; now her resistance made more sense.

Doyle could picture the platform humming to life in space, its primary antimatter engine, which had carried them to this solar system, trailing, defunct, in an eternal ellipse. He established a tenuous uplink, weakened by M38's electrical atmosphere. To be safe, he would need to pilot the pod manually until they broke into orbit, after which the comms platform could take over the precarious docking procedure.

Doyle worked through the second night, scavenging four reentry seats from the crew module's landing carapace and inserting them into the pod. Scarcity of time and raw resources meant use of the Mass Prototype Engine was limited to what they couldn't find elsewhere. Sabin cut into the underside of *Gaea-02*'s hull to strip some microfilament mesh from its radiation shield. He draped it around the pod like a near-invisible veil and augmented it with a reinforced polyethylene film.

Riana aided with savvy observations and manual dexterity when not tending to her APA patients.

An afternoon siesta claimed Sabin for an hour before he laid a dense slab of sintered silica under the pod's floor as thermal insulation. A raked ceramic foundation surrounding the booster inlets sealed everything tight.

They were well ahead of schedule.

As the opaque sky dimmed on the third day, Doyle carried a bound tussock of wiring down to the pod. He heard Sabin inside swearing to himself in Spanish.

Doyle ducked when a reentry seat was flung from the pod hatch.

Poking his head out, Sabin saw Doyle and said, "We need to talk."

"Tell them." Doyle reclined in a mess chair as Sabin explained the problem to Riana and Django.

"With all the extra stuff I had to install in the pod, there's only room for three of us."

"Can't we remove some of the gear?" Riana asked.

Sabin shook his head. "Everything's necessary."

"Even the guns?"

"Especially the guns, Señora."

Riana was silent a moment, then asked, "Who stays?"

"We draw straws," proposed Sabin.

"No," Doyle said. "I'm staying."

"You're our only pilot, Doyle," Riana reminded him.

Doyle stood. "As soon as that colony ship finds the warning beacon, some military bigwig on board might have the bright idea to send down their own pod, full of enough antimatter cells to vaporize a city block. Just another of Michi's zero-sum equations for them." He waved his hand. "The safest place is in our pod."

"No offense," Riana said, glancing at Sabin, "but that pod's not what I'd call safe."

Sabin absentmindedly scratched his stubble, "I'll stay on *Gaea-02*. A good mechanic always goes down with the ship."

"You mean a good *captain*," Doyle said.

Riana pointed at Doyle. "You're retired! I'm the highest ranking officer left."

Django pounded his fist on the table, startling everyone and leaving a zigzag crack across the surface.

He tapped his own chest with one meaty finger and spoke to them for only the second time since leaving Earth. "I'm claustrophobic anyway."

End of discussion. Django was remaining there and no one was game to argue with him.

Doyle rubbed his eyes. He guessed it was around midnight. Lack of sleep was catching up with him.

He looked across the pod at Sabin, who forged ahead more driven than ever. He was no longer one half of the Jiménez brothers, and Pach wasn't an ever-present phantom over his shoulder. He was Sabin Jiménez. He was whole.

Sabin caught Doyle staring at him and said, "What?"

"You're not tired?"

"Nah."

"Those siestas really work, huh?"

"I'm just glad to be sleeping on more or less solid ground again. Brain floats around too much up there, you know?"

Doyle smiled. "You're right. Gets the better of you after a while. One day, though, us humans will evolve into a true space-faring race."

Sabin scrunched his face. "You really believe that?"

"Yeah. I do."

Sabin twisted a pair of wires on the console he was installing. "You mean, like hollow bones and thinner blood?"

Doyle peered into the pod's apex. "When you're standing on the ground and look up at the stars, what do you see?"

"Me? *Tía* Marta's *sopaipillas* dipped in honey so thick it's black and sprinkled with cinnamon."

"Most people gaze up and see the heavens; something strange, mysterious, and unknowable. Not me. I see a map of where we came from and where we need to go. So when I say evolve, I guess I mean that we'll finally start to see ourselves as children of the stars."

Sabin stared at Doyle. "Man, you really need some shuteye."

Doyle bellylaughed. He felt better than he had for days. The wrenching pain of loss uncoiled from his heart to let him be his old self for the moment. Sleep be damned.

Riana dozed in the bridge flight chair. She'd been running telemetry tests for Doyle until her eyelids bowed under the weight of fatigue.

An insistent beep roused her.

Scrabbling awake, she blinked until her eyes could focus on the screen.

She wished she hadn't.

Doyle crawled out of the pod to get some fresh air and stretch his legs after six hours in confined space.

He exhaled a foggy breath. The smoky cloud reminded him of his father—on those rare occasions when Dr. Emil Gage had spent the night in their New Mexico homestead instead of up in the mountain observatory. The astrophysicist would sneak outside to smoke a slim, hemp cigar, sending cobalt rings rising to the midnight sky.

It hadn't occurred to Doyle before but, if Lon were dead, then it was highly probable that Dad was too. "Damn, old man."

Riana came running out of *Gaea-02*. She wasn't wearing an envirosuit and must have been freezing. Doyle met her halfway across the ice slope. She spoke frantically, interrupted by deep gasps for breath. "The colony ship. Just entered this system. It's a day early, Doyle."

Sabin overheard. He threw his welder into the snow. "*Estúpido!* Why did we trust a manifest for a ship that left Earth *eight years ago*?"

Riana rubbed her arms for warmth. "Fei said the transits always arrived on time, to the hour, without exception. The APA's system is highly efficient…"

Doyle stood between Sabin and Riana. "Save the recriminations for later," he told them. "I thought the ship would be late if anything. How long until it reaches us?"

"Two hours, eighteen minutes," Riana said.

Doyle turned to Sabin. "How close are we?"

"Still a lot to do, we gotta—"

"*How long until we can take off?*"

Sabin glowered. "We'll make it. Just."

"Riana, get Django and M.I.T.Z. out here. All hands on deck." Doyle gripped Sabin's elbow and they jogged to the pod.

With all four crew members and the robot working in concert, unfinished tasks were ticked off at a rapid pace. The bulk of their time was spent on electronic routing and integrity checks. Sabin split his schedule between performing the most complex operations himself and delegating the rest. They'd formed a tight-knit team over the past three days and their collaboration was paying off.

An excess of adrenaline held exhaustion at bay. Soon enough, there were only the final touches left: a one-man job. Sabin licked his calloused thumb before crimping a wire between it and his aching index finger.

Riana rotated a holomap of planet M38. “The colony ship just entered orbit. They’ll be at the target coordinates in twenty-three minutes.”

To assist with their infiltration, she and Doyle were dressed in beige APA uniforms, the most recent style the MPE database had on record. Doyle draped his flight jacket on a chair back; it hadn’t made him feel too lucky lately anyway.

He noticed Riana was mesmerized by the planetary map. Doyle was worried about her odd stare, so he switched it off and asked, “You ready?”

Riana held her hands to stop them from shaking. “Look at me. I used to think the most exciting thing in the world was discovering a new nucleotide.” She tied her hair back. “So … this is it.”

“This is it,” Doyle echoed. He wanted to say more, about how much she had helped him along the way, but that would have sounded like last words. There’d be time for talk *after* they succeeded.

He placed his hand on *Gaea-02*’s console—a fond goodbye to the ship that had earned his esteem—and told Riana, “I’ll meet you at the launch site.”

There was something he needed to do first.

Django dispensed rations among the APA prisoners. They remained wary of the large, dark-skinned man, but the kindness evident in his features was unmissable. He took special care to treat each one with dignity. They shared a common bond; they were human.

Watching from the threshold, Doyle knew the prisoners were in good hands.

He said to Django, "If our plan works, I'll send down a ship for you." Doyle glanced at the APA men and women and added in a louder voice, "For all of you. I promise."

Most had vacant faces, but one older engineer seemed to understand Doyle's words and gave a respectful nod.

Django clasped Doyle's hand.

"Be safe," Doyle said.

Standing ready on its launch platform, the transformed supply pod was almost unrecognizable. It was a hodgepodge concoction born of tenacity and innovation, and judging strictly by appearance, one might reasonably assume it would keel over the moment its scaffold was removed.

The Wright brothers would have been impressed, Doyle thought. He silently dedicated this flight to them.

Sabin yelled from the pod, "You two got your tickets? No refunds!"

Riana and Doyle aided each other into bulky pressurized suits, which contained half-hour stores of oxygen—enough to spare, so long as nothing went too awry. They crawled into the pod's hatch. Doyle took one last look at *Gaea-02*—and Django waiting there—before sealing the exit.

Inside, the trio were cramped, with every nook of space housing one kind of improvised contraption or another. If Sabin said they were all crucial, Doyle believed him. A crooked neck was better than burning to a crisp when a system redundancy failed. Sabin ran through a checklist on the jury-rigged control board. Everything flashed green.

Doyle strapped himself in. Before he could slide his helmet on, Riana leaned across on an impulse and kissed him. Their lips held for the length of a breath—not passionate, but heartfelt.

"Thanks ... Deniece," he said.

Riana was stunned. "You knew?" Foundation Day. The day they met as carefree kids, when she'd lied about her name.

"A model of the *Gaea-01* prototype on Baden's desk jogged my memory. You haven't changed," he said, smiling as Riana, speechless, donned her headgear. "Still a brat."

Sabin winked and tapped his own helmet, ready to depart. "All systems are go."

Doyle nodded from behind his plastiglass visor. Sabin flicked a series of switches.

Panels lit up one by one.

Doyle barely heard Sabin's countdown over his beating heart. Suddenly, his stomach lurched and solar flares blazed behind his eyes.

He was crushed by the burden of a thousand burning suns.

CHAPTER 21
FINAL FLIGHT

Waves of searing heat rippled outward as the salvaged antimatter engine roared, launching the supply pod at supersonic speeds and melting a crater in the ice below.

The rocket's flash was so bright that black specks ghosted Django's corneas, even with his eyelids squeezed shut. Beside him on the gangplank, M.I.T.Z. raised its robotic head, optic receptors tracking the pod's skyward path.

The pod rattled until Doyle thought his bones would pop through his skin. His vision swam. *So tired. So very tired.*

Riana let a small moan escape. Immense *g*-forces pressured her internal organs. Her face behind her visor appeared gaunt and in a full grimace, cheeks stretched hollow like a flaccid drum.

Doyle gripped the cobbled-together flight stick. With all the shaking, his sight was too blurry to distinguish the tiny console screen. "Sabin, telemetry!"

Sabin obliged, constantly reading off updates of position, inclination, and velocity. Doyle visualized the course mapped out in his mind's eye and applied corrections accordingly.

Their pod speared through the dense atmosphere, crested by friction-flames.

Doyle's feet became blisteringly hot despite the thermal insulation. He sweated profusely; his helmet felt like a fishbowl filled with boiling water.

The hull shimmied and vibrated. Sabin steadied the control board to view the readout. "She's holding together."

Doyle wrestled with the flight stick to adjust their trajectory. If they didn't maintain escape velocity at the correct angle, they'd fall back to planet M38 as a blazing meteor.

They'd been soaring in their enclosed little bucket for nearly eight minutes, their only link to the outside a few flickering numbers on a volatile screen. Self-doubt didn't creep into Doyle's head; it kicked in the door like some rowdy salesman.

Sabin shouted, "Power cells are almost empty!"

"Just a little more…" Doyle pleaded with his makeshift craft.

Sabin's indicators redlined in a final spasm, then receded as the supply pod cleared planet M38's thermosphere and drifted into the sparser exosphere.

A sudden sense of overwhelming peace took hold: a palpable sigh throughout the pod.

As the console updated their position with a series of beeps and chimes, Sabin said with rising awe, "We're in orbit."

Riana giggled and patted the front of Doyle's helmet with her baggy glove. He blew her a kiss as weightlessness lifted him in an utterly liberating buoyancy.

Doyle's breath fogged his visor. "Jettison engine, go to retros only."

Four miniscule detonations blew the antimatter rig off the pod's foundation, to circle M38's uncongested spacelanes forever.

Before long, Doyle predicted, this virgin territory would resemble Earth's crowded ring of space debris. While the UEC once instituted a fledgling Orbital Sanitation Corps, he doubted the APA had continued it here.

If the console was correct, the pod was directly in line with the massive APA colony ship. Doyle found himself wishing he could see it with his own eyes. What a marvel of technology that vessel must be. The UEC had fabricated prototypes of large-scale settlement transports before, monstrous hulks that dwarfed anything he'd known.

He'd always dreamed of piloting one.

A radar array swiveled on the discarded tail end of *Gaea-02*'s comms platform. First it located the supply pod, then pivoted toward the colony ship. Doyle's pod was a freewheeling mote in comparison.

Three megalithic turrets sat astride the frigate's immense, horizontal trunk, capped by a bulbous command module seven stories tall. From its curved, tempered-resin windows, ghostly blue light opalesced into the void.

The goliath was rousing from a long slumber.

"The comms platform has us," Sabin said as his board indicated the takeover by remote pilot. "It's up to the computer now."

Doyle would have felt less uneasy being in direct control, his own hands dictating their fate, but he had to accept the hard fact: with their limited internal guidance system, he'd be more likely to ram them into the ship's hull.

Precise retrorockets flared intermittently from the pod in millisecond bursts. A complex geometry, a graceful arabesque. The computer positioned their pod alongside a vacant coupling on the colony ship and increased velocity until they were perfectly in sync.

Doyle licked his parched lips, watching as each coordinate was verified on the screen. A picosecond too fast or a thousandth of a degree off and the pod would be crushed like an eggshell, with them inside.

"Coming into range…" Sabin said, holding his sentence, "…now."

They felt a bump as the pod's docking collar magnetically sealed around the colony ship's coupling. It was an encouraging sign that they hadn't been annihilated on impact, but they wouldn't know if the bond was firm for a few more seconds. The delay was excruciating.

The console buzzed and Sabin threw up his arms. "Yes!"

"Seal secure. We made it." Doyle didn't hide his astonishment. *So far, so good.* Riana squeezed his shoulder in delight. He reminded them, "That's only the first step. It won't get any easier from here on in."

Doyle motioned toward the hatch, "One at a time, folks."

They undid their harnesses and floated to the exit. The pod's hatch irised open smoothly, but beyond it, the colony ship's airlock remained stubbornly shut.

"Give it a sec." Sabin evinced surprising patience. "Could be a lag in the docking interface. Protocols may've changed since they last used this pod."

The trio waited expectantly, yet nothing happened.

Sabin hit a few keys on his control board. The dead screen persisted. "Damn it, this thing isn't even sending a charge. Coupling uplink must be busted."

Doyle wedged himself against the rim to stop from drifting. "Can you fix it from here?"

"Nope." Sabin did a somersault and unlatched a compartment below his reentry chair. He hunted through a bundle of strapped-down tools, mumbling, "Know I packed it somewhere…"

With a theatrical flourish, Sabin triumphantly pulled out a plasma shear. He floated to the bulkhead and started cutting around the hatch perimeter.

Riana noticed Doyle's vacant look. "What's wrong?"

"Hmm? Oh, just…we didn't name it."

"Name what?"

"This pod." Doyle tapped the hull. "Colby would've said she was a 'fair dinkum spacecraft.' She deserves a name. So what should we call her?"

"Isn't it obvious?" Riana asked. Apparently not, from Doyle's blank stare. She elaborated: "*Gaea-03*."

Doyle smiled. "*Gaea-03* it is. Her first and final flight."

Molten fire traced a circle in the outer bulkhead of the colony ship's airlock. Wisps of smoke escaped and the donut-hole section dropped out to clang on the floor.

Air rushed into the *Gaea-03* pod as the pressure equalized.

Doyle crawled through the newly cut portal. The airlock was dark, with only a rectangle of dim light from a windowpane on the far door. Doyle made his way to it, shuffling in his pressure suit. He tried to peer out, but his unwieldy helmet scraped on the door.

Nothing indicated that the air inside the ship wasn't breathable, but—lacking a canary—taking off your helmet was always a nail-biter. Doyle slid his neck ring aside and a jet of oxygen hissed out. He gripped the helmet with both hands and pulled it over his head, the rubber collar sucking his face like a hungry squid.

Doyle inhaled the stale air and waited a moment before breathing out. No ill effects. He glanced through the pane but couldn't see anyone in the corridor outside.

"It's safe," he whispered into the pod. Doyle helped Riana exit the portal. They removed their outer suits and smoothed down their APA uniforms.

Sabin gave them each a short-brimmed military cap that shadowed their faces just enough to obscure their features. Not much of a disguise, but from a distance they could pass for APA personnel.

Sabin reached back into the pod to retrieve three ESD rifles. Doyle had insisted on nonlethal weapons. There could be no killing if they had any hope of success.

Riana took her ESD and felt the weight in her hands. She seemed uneasy, but when she noticed Doyle watching her, she hooked her elbow confidently around the rifle butt and tipped her nose along the sight to gauge her aim.

"I passed Basic," she reassured him. "Third in my class."

"Then you'll be fine."

She slung the gun over her shoulder. "Doesn't mean I have to like it."

Doyle palmed a pad to open the airlock door. The second it slid apart, a klaxon sounded and spinning red lights danced along the corridor outside.

"What the hell'd you do?" Sabin shouted.

"I don't know, it just…"

A computerized Mandarin voice wailed from speakers in the ceiling.

"They must have booby-trapped the airlocks." Sabin raced to the door. "Bastards knew we were coming, damn—"

"Shut *up*, Sabin." Riana raised her hand to stop his yammering. She concentrated on the Mandarin announcement. "It's warning of a possible hull breach. There's a loss of pressure on this level."

Realizing his mistake, Sabin rolled his eyes. "The airlock didn't repressurize fully. It'll be down a few pascals from the pod's volume. Their sensors must be super-anal."

Doyle asked Riana, "Have they isolated the breach?"

"I don't think so."

"Then it could take them a while to find our pod. Okay, we gotta hustle. Stick together and try to find a way to the bridge."

Doyle led them out of the airlock. The lighting was an irregular sequence of soft, dim pools and demented, red alarums. The trio moved swiftly along a corridor, past giant APA insignias reminding them they were in the belly of the beast.

Here, the interior walls were a ribbed, white plastic, clean and smooth unlike *Gaea-02*'s protruding, unfinished edges. Doyle tried to guess which divisions this section of the ship housed.

Airlock hatches ran along one wall, so it was probably the primary thoroughfare for arrivals and departures—and nowhere near the command module.

Riana stopped at an intersection where a signposted passage seemed to lead into the heart of the colony ship. She nodded her head. "This way."

Doyle couldn't read the Chinese symbols, but he trusted Riana and headed down the narrower passageway behind her, while Sabin brought up the rear. "Which deck are we on?"

"Third. Signs are pointing us to an elevator hub."

They reached halfway toward the next junction before the beat of rapidly approaching boots fanned the dread in their eyes.

"Here," Sabin whispered sharply. He wedged open a door they'd passed and ushered Doyle and Riana inside, securing it quietly behind himself.

The chamber was pitch black. Machinery hummed a sub-bass throb that massaged their brains and made their teeth ache.

Sabin took a deep breath and gagged. The stench in the room was unbearably foul. "Shit, what reeks?"

"You said it: waste filtration unit." Disgusted, Riana turned her face away. "Eight years of hibernating colonists—"

Doyle's hand suddenly arched over Riana's mouth, silencing her.

The bootsteps were right outside the door. The procession paused for a moment before continuing on.

After another minute of bated breath, Doyle slid the door open for Sabin and Riana to stumble out of the rank odor, sucking in the corridor's cleaner air and trying desperately not to retch.

Doyle looked in the direction the footsteps had receded. "They'll find our pod soon. Better hurry before they put this place under lockdown." He broke into a loping run, with Riana and Sabin keeping up close behind.

They took a zigzag route, turning left into another passageway, then right, then left again. Phantom footfalls haunted Doyle at each corner, but they always turned out to be confounding echoes from his companions.

They arrived at a wide crossway where two main arteries intersected. Doyle ran headlong for the junction, this time ignoring the reverberating steps.

He froze as a group of armed soldiers jogged past, mere inches from his face.

The enemy wore breather masks as a hull-breach precaution, effectively cutting down their peripheral vision. They soldiered on, unaware of Doyle's proximity.

He silently exhaled. *Close call.*

He'd noticed something worrying, however. These soldiers' uniforms—an aquamarine tunic overlaid with murky green pocket-vests—were very different from their own. Doyle's beige outfit was clearly outdated and essentially useless as an APA masquerade.

The hindmost soldier returned.

He raised his pistol between Doyle's eyes. The dual black circles of his breather mask seemed to shimmer.

Electricity sizzled past Doyle's ear as Riana's shot tagged the soldier's neck with an ESD dart. His skin fluoresced as he fell back, unconscious, into the crossway.

Doyle blinked his thanks to Riana. They'd need to hide the soldier's body before any of his cohorts returned, so Doyle and Sabin rushed into the junction, gripped the man's vest, and lifted.

Muzzle-flash sparked in the corner of Doyle's vision. A strange-looking bullet struck Sabin's chest and exploded into a thousand deadly shards, leaving his shirt in tatters and his skin a nest of bloody cuts.

Brittle bullets.

Panicked, Sabin clutched at his shredded chest.

Doyle had seen the consequences of this fiendish ammo before—but only in vids of APA invasions. Brittle bullets were composed of glass interlaced with chilled metal, resulting in a lower terminal effect but maximum pandemonium and, most important on any starship, zero structural damage. Faced with brittle bullets in close quarters, opposition forces generally surrendered quickly.

Five more shots hurtled into the crossway. One shattered against Sabin's leg, another at Doyle's feet, with three near misses bursting on the walls. A chaotic spray of sharp fragments sliced everything in their multidirectional path. Doyle felt a dozen incisions stinging his arms, stomach, and thighs.

Sabin collapsed, ragged flesh dangling from bone along his stripped-bare shin. Riana rushed into the line of fire in a near-futile attempt to stem his copious bleeding. She tore scraps off Sabin's ravaged clothing to use as compression bandages.

Doyle dropped to one knee and returned fire at three vested soldiers, whose aim seemed hindered by grogginess. Likely they'd been brought out of hibernation only a short while earlier.

Doyle's first shot sent an electrical jolt through one assailant. The other two separated, each one hugging a corridor wall to brace his aim. Doyle hit the man on his left, but the final soldier raised his pistol.

A low blast struck the soldier's leg and electricity flowed through his body. Doyle took a sidelong glance. Sabin lay prone, gripping his crackling ESD rifle in one hand. Doyle said, "Helluva shot." Sabin smiled despite his agony.

Doyle and Riana looped their arms under Sabin's shoulders and carted him into the crossway's right turn. "Gotta be near the center by now," Doyle muttered.

"We need to get Sabin medical treatment first. He's losing too much blood." Riana glanced around as they fled. "There should be an aid station on every deck. Just hold on, Sabin."

Far behind them, another squad of soldiers ran into the crossway. Confronted by the carnage, they opened fire at once. Brittle bullets took wing and fragmented, surrounding Doyle with a maelstrom of scything glass. Shrapnel snagged his stomach and tore up his torso and right arm. He shot back at the enemy, each squeeze of the trigger sending painful stabs along his raw tendons.

Held upright by Riana and Doyle, Sabin fired unsteadily, none of his shots landing on target. He clung to consciousness by a thread.

The corridor was bare and wall consoles were too slim to hide Sabin behind. A side door ahead offered refuge. Doyle and Riana upped the tempo as slashing shards cascaded around them.

Riana mashed the door's keypad but the entry hatch wouldn't open. She raised her ESD and blasted the electronic lock point blank. The high-voltage current sparked and fizzled. The door shunted ajar. Riana slipped her hand in the gap and shoved it fully open.

A hail of brittle bullets came from a new direction—more soldiers, catching them in a crossfire. Doyle spun back and forth, blazing darts into both groups of enemies. A shower of sparks erupted when his ESD barb ricocheted off a soldier's firearm. The shock singed the man's hand and knocked him out of the battle.

Doyle bled from a hundred scratches. He shook his cap and a river of glass tumbled off the brim. Even the enemy's misses were potentially lethal; their muscle-atrophied lack of accuracy was moot when a deluge of high-velocity needles accompanied every stray shot.

Sabin's ESD fell from his failing grasp. He'd held on as long as he could. His chest oozed with each sluggish breath.

Riana yelled to the soldiers in Mandarin, pleading for a ceasefire, but their only response was more shatter-bullets.

Doyle growled to Riana, "Shoot, damn it. Cover me!"

She crouched in the open doorway and made her shots count. She was a fine markswoman, taking down two onrushing soldiers in a row.

Summoning a surge of strength, Doyle hauled Sabin into the side room and laid him beside the door. "I'll get you out of this. I will."

The room was darkened but Doyle felt the sensation of a large expanse. A vague, blue glow emanated from deeper within. No time to investigate properly; Sabin would be dead in minutes if they couldn't drive back the horde of soldiers. They were facing far more armed resistance than Doyle had expected. *What have we stumbled into here?*

He reentered the fray to take some pressure off Riana. Doyle fired a single round before his ESD stopped responding, its energy absolutely sapped. He tossed aside his weapon and dived for Sabin's discarded gun.

Swiveling to fire amid a barrage of wasp-like projectiles, Doyle was hit dead-on. As the bullet's metal tip entered his shoulder, its silicon core ruptured, belching shards deep into the side of his neck.

Remnants whizzed toward Riana's face. She turned aside, the glass slicing a furrow across her left cheek.

Doyle reeled and clutched at his throat. Riana ignored her own pain to bustle him through the doorway. Gushing blood dyed her blonde hair pink. She swept him into a mad jog, neither of them knowing where they were going or where they *were*.

She sat Doyle against the side of a glowing, blue cylinder. He let his ESD tumble from his grip. Riana pulled a strip from Doyle's torn shirt and covered his neck gashes. She pressed his palm over the stopgap bandage. "Hold it tight."

Thankfully, his jugular's carotid sheath was intact. The downside was that the pieces of shrapnel were too thin and numerous for Riana to extract with her bare fingers. The larger, metal sliver embedded in his shoulder was another matter. Riana removed her belt to place it between Doyle's teeth. "Bite down."

He did, stifling his scream when her fingers dug into his flesh. She probed the jagged puncture, finally wresting the bullet-tip free.

Doyle's head lolled. He tried to keep his eyes alert to the shadows in motion outside the door.

Riana wiped her blood-slicked hands on her pants.

"Go," Doyle said weakly. "Hide. It's a big ship."

"I'm staying with you."

"Sorry… Riana… my dumb idea…"

Riana shushed him with a brief, consoling kiss and held his face against hers.

Something bucked inside the translucent, blue column behind Doyle's head. Riana reared in surprise.

She moved closer, peering into the cylinder, and saw … a foot?

Riana stood so she could see farther into the room, but this was no mere room. Countless sky-blue coronas stretched into the distance. She gravitated around to the front of the cylinder and recognized it as a hibernation chamber.

A rangy, emaciated black man floated in the luminescent liquid.

Beside him was another chamber. And another. And another; more than Riana's vision could encompass. A multitude of sleepers. Behind a short strip of recovery benches extended a second row. Past that, she could glimpse the soft, blue lights of a third row.

"It's unbelievable. There are thousands, Doyle. More people than we ever …" Her hushed voice trailed off, overawed.

An LCD blinked at the base of the nearest chamber. Riana looked closer. A timer ticked down, the occupant's hibernation set for cessation in thirty minutes. His name was displayed in block letters on a digi-panel: EAMON BOLAGO, SOUTH AFRICA.

Riana's brow furrowed. She read the adjacent chamber's label: DIMITY SIMMONS, AUSTRALIA. And the next: KASUMI RIKAKU, JAPAN.

"Doyle. These aren't APA colonists, they're …"

A unit of soldiers breached the room in fireteam formation.

Riana rushed to Doyle's side. He was grasping feebly for the ESD rifle on the floor. She kicked it out of his reach. "Enough," she whispered.

Her next words came in Mandarin and were terms of surrender. The soldiers weren't interested.

The rear guard jabbed his gun at Sabin but, seeing that he was no threat, picked up his body, slung it over his shoulder, and carried him away. The others leveled their pistols at Doyle and Riana.

Doyle was fading in and out. Whether he survived or not, this was the end of his life. They'd taken everything now. All he hoped was that they treated Riana well. He tried to say goodbye to her, but the words clotted in his throat.

One soldier pushed through his companions, signaling them to holster their weapons. Obviously of a higher rank, yet bearing no insignia that Doyle could decode, the lone man crouched. The shiny, black, oversized eyes of his breather mask regarded Doyle intently.

When the soldier reached out, Doyle vaguely noted his battle-scarred arms. He wasn't a glorified bodyguard sent to babysit the colony. This was a veteran warrior.

He removed Doyle's cap. The man's mask was disconcertingly still for a second, then his muffled voice said, "Doyle Gage?"

As the black swirls of unconsciousness claimed Doyle, his final, hazy vision was of the soldier removing his breather unit. Unmasked, he was a man in his late twenties, whose scar tissue and bleached eyes gave him the appearance of one much older.

Something about his face—in the grin that stretched leathery skin unaccustomed to smiling—reminded Doyle of his father . . . or himself as a younger man. Or was it the final photo he saw of Lon?

Another cruel dream, Doyle thought.

Another moment to be snatched away.

CR924X//8A4: *message broadcast on insurgency network, Radio Free Earth, 6/2/2072.*

"This is your General. <pause> Hope is alive."

EV207209I3//CR924X//FGI

CHAPTER 22
BEGINNINGS

Ruschen didn't try to dissuade me. He just stomped out in a huff when I handed the United Earth Coalition my notice of resignation.

The Gaea mission will be better off without a commander whose mind is somewhere else. On someone else.

At the hospital, Juni looked fatigued nursing Lon, but it was well veiled by her sensational postnatal glow.

She thanked me and said she knew it was a tough decision. I was more grateful for what she'd been through. My hand rested on the small of her back as I leaned in to kiss her.

I toyed with my son's miniature hands, staring down in ceaseless wonder at his cherubic face.

No. I had it backward.

Lon was staring down at me.

Doyle slowly gained focus on the here and now. That

battle-worn soldier's face—almost a cracked mirror image of his own—examined him closely.

"Lonnie?" Doyle's voice was hoarse. He heard the beep of monitors and clink of metal instruments. A medlab. He tried to move his neck but it was too stiff. His wounds had been cauterized and grafted with synth-skin.

"Don't strain," Lon said. "My boys really did a number on you. Sorry. You were wearing APA uniforms and your friend was speaking in Mandarin. They couldn't take any chances. Ballsy move breaching the ship like that. Grandpa always said you were a wildcard."

Doyle blinked, unsure if he was really awake. "How…?"

"Culmination of a ten-month operation. We stole this ship right out from under the APA's nose and filled it with our own people. Our own colony."

"I thought you were dead. I saw the records."

Lon shook his head. "More propaganda. The APA didn't want me made into a folk hero when I joined what was left of the UEC. They claimed you guys were dead for the same reason."

Doyle laughed—at first haltingly, then in a euphoric eruption. After all the death and heartbreak, they'd succeeded. He'd made good on his promise.

At that moment, he was above pain. Doyle rose from his cot and bear-hugged his son. Tactile reality overwhelmed his senses. He fingered the coarse threads of Lon's uniform, his son's steely frame yielding and returning his father's long-missed touch. Tears washed over Doyle's mottled cheek.

Lon closed his eyes and guffawed as though he hadn't done so in far too many years. A potent release. His disheveled hair rubbed against the side of Doyle's face as he said softly in his ear, "I knew I'd find you again. I *knew*. It's what kept me going."

"Me too, Lonnie."

After a long while, Doyle broke their embrace. "Is Dad on the ship? I owe him some Merlot."

Lon's mouth twitched involuntarily. "The APA hounded us,

wanted us for collateral in case you ever came back, but Grandpa was always one step ahead. He ... went down fighting in '68."

Doyle hadn't realistically expected to see his father again, but having his death confirmed while his emotions were so raw still hurt. Woozy, he lay down. He noticed Sabin on a nearby cot, hooked to a bank of machinery, his leg sealed in a hyperbaric accelerator. "Sabin?"

"He's stable. Doc Harpp's the best."

The impossibly young medic nodded at Doyle. He couldn't have been more than sixteen. *Maybe he's a veterinarian or a tree doctor.* Doyle raised his head suddenly. "Where's Riana?"

"She's fine. Touring the ship." Lon sat on the edge of Doyle's cot. "She told us what happened down there on M38. We were heading straight for Taurus. Wouldn't even have stopped except we picked up an emergency beacon. Thought we ought to investigate."

Doyle felt a bittersweet twang of irony. In the end, they owed Indigo their thanks for the part she'd played.

"We were half-expecting a trap," Lon continued. "Part of our plan on Earth was destroying the APA's superluminal transmitter station so they couldn't contact the colony ahead of our arrival. There was always the risk they'd rebuild in time to send a call to arms."

Doyle shook his head in admiration. "How did you pull it off? Seizing a ship this size, making it all the way here?"

"We have a fine leader," Lon said with absolute conviction.

"You're awake," Riana said as she traipsed into the medlab. Her upbeat presence added to Doyle's already heady mood. As much as he drew strength from her when she was brave and feisty, he had to admit he most liked seeing her jovial like this.

Riana's cheek had been repaired, leaving a faint scar. "How are you feeling?" she asked Doyle.

He chuckled. "I'm not. Sensory overload." He shaded his eyes from the bright overhead floodlights.

She teased, "You'll never guess who my tour guide is."

The gruff, male voice emanated from outside the circle of light, "You look exactly as I remember, Doyle. Apart from some new scratches."

The speaker stepped into view. Dirty-gray locks, aged skin like oiled parchment, a rugged self-assurance borne by wisdom and experience. Yet the familiar-looking mark slashed across his neck by an APA soldier's dagger was unmistakable.

"*Usef?*" Doyle said in bewilderment. Almost thirty years older and slimmer, but he was clearly recognizable as *Gaea-02*'s errant chemist.

"General Skouris of the United Earth Coalition at your service. Although, we're more an underground militia these days. Freedom fighters."

"Usef, you ..." Doyle's anger bubbled, threatening to erupt until he glanced at Lon and recalled what he'd said. *A great leader.* Even now, the way Lon was standing at full attention, how he subtly crossed his hands behind his back in deference when Usef entered the room. There was reverence here, a distinct devotion.

Lon confirmed his suspicions. "General Skouris is the reason we've gained a tactical foothold on Earth. And ... he saved my life."

Usef spoke before Doyle could. "As your father saved mine, Lon, when I was taken hostage. But after that, we were ... separated." He eyed Doyle, daring him to contradict his son's hero. "I never gave up hope of finding my old friends again."

Doyle contained his ire, and Riana squeezed his hand to acknowledge she shared his frustration. He wanted to tell Lon it was all lies, that Usef stole his pod, that Usef was the reason he couldn't return. But what would that achieve?

Doyle said through gritted teeth, "It's good to see you again ... General."

"Likewise," Usef replied, smirking.

"You." Sabin angrily stirred awake. "You." He sprang from his cot, paying no mind to the wires and tubes being ripped from his body in the process. Bestial, he lunged at Usef. "You got my brother killed, you bastard!"

Sabin clawed for Usef's neck: attempting to rip it open or strangle him, whatever would kill him fastest. All the progress Sabin had made in overcoming Pach's death was undone in an instant. Riana yelled for him to stop but her plea fell on deaf ears.

Lon intercepted the attack, wrenching Sabin away and locking his elbows into a clutch that tortured at every twist.

As Sabin struggled, fresh blood seeped through the bandages around his chest. Lon fought unfettered by emotion or mercy, as though he'd inflicted pain—and had it inflicted upon him—hundreds of times before.

Sabin's leg buckled and his arms nearly snapped in Lon's hold as he fell. Doyle leaped to Sabin's aid, torn between his loyalties.

"Let him go," Usef ordered.

"Sir?"

"It's okay, Lon."

Just hearing that dog speak his son's name made Doyle want to puke.

Lon released Sabin, who curled into an anguished lump.

Usef crouched close to Sabin and whispered sharply, "I've spent the last three decades atoning for my mistakes."

Dripping venom, Sabin moved his lips near Usef's ear and said, "I swear … you will die by my hand."

Usef stood, composed. He gestured to Lon and Doc Harpp. They lifted Sabin onto his cot, where the young doctor sedated him and reattached his medical apparatus.

"The ship is waking." Usef's voice was full of optimism. "If you'll excuse me." He turned on his heel and strode out.

Lon helped his father back into bed. "Rest. We'll be at Taurus soon."

"Django and our prisoners, they're—"

"Already taken care of." The corners of Lon's eyes crinkled as he reassured his father.

Doyle wondered if Lon was experiencing the same sense of disbelief. It was surreal to be together again as adults and virtual strangers. They had two lifetimes worth of events to catch up on.

Getting to know each other would have to wait a while longer, though. Lon said with a sigh, "I need to help with the thaw. Only a few dozen of us awake and several hundred needing some post-hibernation *chūn guān zhào*."

Doyle was familiar with the phrase—a bastardization of TLC—but he was surprised how easily and fluently the Mandarin had slipped into Lon's vocabulary.

"We'll talk more soon." Lon nodded to his father. "I promise." He turned to Riana. "You're a doctor, right? We could use you, if…"

"Sure," she said. "Give me a moment. I know the way."

Doyle watched Lon's upright, powerful gait as he marched out. He could only wonder what rigors his son had endured to forge him into this grim centurion.

"You got your wish," Riana said sincerely.

"Yeah." Doyle squeezed her hand in thanks. "You did, too." She tilted her head, so Doyle gestured and said, "Look around. *This* is the Gaea mission—or it could be. Baden would want you to persevere. Like you said, you're the senior Gaea officer now."

"Usef won't see it that way, Doyle."

"We'll deal with Usef." Doyle purposely lightened his tone. "But he'd better keep his distance from Sabin."

After Riana left, Doyle sank onto his cot. He was exhausted yet knew sleep would evade him. There was too much to process, to come to terms with … and most of it was extraordinarily good.

Django sat in *Gaea-02*'s vehicle bay, doing his best to ignore the cold. The robot wouldn't leave his side. At times it would make a small, unbidden movement, then cease the millisecond Django noticed. He suspected M.I.T.Z. possessed far more intelligence and capacity for autonomy than anyone else imagined. With Michi gone, who would keep it under wraps?

He thought about checking the databanks to see exactly what the robot's acronym stood for. He'd never been curious about that until now.

The others had departed hours before. Unwaveringly confident of Doyle's success, Django spent the interim projecting his own role in their future. Why did the APA give up on M38 so easily? There was little landmass to work with, true, but he believed he could make it habitable. Riana's discovery of microorganisms offered tantalizing prospects. He could use them for generating greenhouse gasses to warm the planet, the polar opposite of his ecological efforts on Earth.

Lost in his grand designs, Django didn't notice the swarm emerging from the thunderheads outside. But he did observe M.I.T.Z.'s indicator stripe flicker to green, then quickly back to blue.

Django ambled to the gangplank, picking up pace as the sky filled with aircraft.

A ring of transit drones shepherded a mammoth gravity coil between them, an artificial electromagnetic well, expanding to more than three hundred feet in diameter. They flew in formation over *Gaea-02*, toward the berthed *Green Dragon* carrier.

More pertinent to Django, a back-heavy personnel lander alighted gracefully onto the ice. There was no question in his mind that it was friendly.

He raised his fist high in welcome. And in triumph.

Being one of M41's six moons, Taurus was relatively undersized. Looking out, Doyle imagined he could cradle the orb in the palm of his hand. A perfect little world.

"Lift your arm," Riana said. She guided his hand into the sleeve of his UEC flight jacket.

"How did you . . . ?"

"Django brought it with him from *Gaea-02*." Mindful of his gauze-swathed shoulder, she fit Doyle's other arm into the jacket.

"Thanks." He chuckled. "Good as ever."

The Tauran atmosphere was so clear—in vivid contrast to M38's—that the viewpane on the colony ship's observation deck revealed every last detail below: sumptuous blue seas, stretches of lush verdure, and twinkling clusters of human settlement along each coastline.

"Now *that* is a beautiful planet," Riana said as she slid her arm around Doyle's waist from behind. Her chin nestled snugly into the worn leather on his shoulder. Their closeness felt natural, unforced—and guilt-free.

"Our new home," Doyle said.

Riana spotted Lon's shadow in the doorway.

She made her excuses. "I, uh, better see how Sabin's doing. Django's not the most talkative bedside companion." She smiled at Lon on her way out.

Neither Doyle nor Lon seemed to know how to begin their conversation. Things had been hectic the past twenty-four hours, so time together was at a premium. Yet somehow, now that they were alone, neither could break the awkward tension.

In a shaded edge of the viewpane, Doyle could see his son's reflection alongside his own. He couldn't get over how old Lon looked. They could have been twins.

"I remember that jacket," Lon finally ventured. "You wore it the day you left."

"Yeah. I, uh ..." Doyle had an age to word an apology for leaving Lon, but he never could work out how to express it adequately. *Sorry* was monumentally insufficient. He changed the topic with a nod to Lon's combat vest. "What rank are you, son?"

"Field Commander." Lon couldn't hide a trace of pride. A recent promotion, Doyle guessed.

"There's nothing on your uniform. No markings at all?"

"Keeps us anonymous in case we're captured. Full deniability. Not that it'll be an issue if we invade down there; they don't have an army as such."

"You're *invading* Taurus? Why not negotiate an accord?"

Lon grimaced. "That'll be General Skouris's call."

Doyle was heartened to hear remorse in his son's voice instead of bloodlust. "Wars never really end, do they?"

"No," Lon agreed. "They don't."

For all of Doyle's attempts to avoid conflict, he had become resigned to its inevitability. From a veteran who battles phantom enemies well past a tour of duty, to Crusades that fester and ignite ad infinitum ... to a father and son separated by time and space only to be reunited on the brink of another war. Life was circular, brutal, and precious.

Lon put his palm on the viewpane, as if he might touch the rich, living foliage on Taurus. He spoke with an unexpected weariness. "It's been a long, hard journey."

Doyle reached into his jacket's inner pocket. He pulled out a folded, crumpled sheet of paper and handed it to his son.

Tears formed in Lon's eyes as he unfolded his own childhood sketch of *Gaea-02*, showing him and his dad in the colorful cockpit. His emotions spilled over, granting Doyle a glimpse of the little boy he'd once lost.

Doyle grinned as he recalled their exchange on that final day together on Earth. "I guess they found you something to do on a spaceship, kiddo." Proud as any father could be, he slung his arm around Lon's shoulder.

Their mutual destination, Taurus, slowly spun on its axis below.

"Dad ... the APA will come after us. They'll hunt us down."

Doyle looked his son squarely in the eye. "Let 'em."

WWW.GAEAUNIVERSE.COM

www.ingramcontent.com/pod-product-compliance
Lightning Source LLC
Chambersburg PA
CBHW030423310726
48979CB00009B/1590/J

* 9 7 8 0 9 8 0 3 9 1 0 0 8 *